THE VISION

Her eyes were closed, yet they were open. The sun was shining fiercely, more fiercely than she had ever known. She moved her arm to shade her eyes and realized, with astonishment, that instead of her heavy furs, she was clad in thin woven trousers and a robe made from the summer pelts of caribou. Her hands were bare, and her skin was a strange, rich brown. She wasn't on the frozen river anymore. She was sitting amid a carpet of tall grass that rippled in a gentle breeze. Far in the distance, a herd of mammoth wandered slowly. She marveled at the beauty of this strange place. The sky was a clear, vivid blue. The grass was impossibly thick, impossibly green. And at the bottom of the slope where she sat was a huge lake, as blue as the sky.

This was the vision that Laena saw . . . the vision that she followed . . . through danger and love and struggle and the vast unknown . . . against all the odds that faced an orphan girl growing to womanhood and a woman of no tribe among alien clans . . . as she risked all to make an impossible dream come incredibly true. . . .

CHILDREN OF THE ICE

CHILDREN OF THE ICE

by

Charlotte Prentiss

AN ONYX BOOK

ONYX
Published by the Penguin Group
Penguin Books USA Inc., 375 Hudson Street,
New York, New York 10014, U.S.A.
Penguin Books Ltd, 27 Wrights Lane,
London W8 5TZ, England
Penguin Books Australia Ltd, Ringwood,
Victoria, Australia
Penguin Books Canada Ltd, 10 Alcorn Avenue,
Toronto, Ontario, Canada M4V 3B2
Penguin Books (N.Z.) Ltd, 182–190 Wairau Road,
Auckland 10, New Zealand

Penguin Books Ltd, Registered Offices:
Harmondsworth, Middlesex, England

First published by Onyx,
an imprint of New American Library,
a division of Penguin Books USA Inc.

First Printing, December, 1993
10 9 8 7 6 5 4 3 2 1

PART ONE

Chapter 1

Laena crouched beside the fire, holding her hands close to the flames, seizing their warmth. It was snug, here, in the shallow pit that had been dug beneath the roof of mammoth hide. This was her home, which she shared with her sister and her parents. Four beds of dry moss were ranged around the fire. A pile of furs lay to one side. There were a few sets of firesticks, a couple of flint knives, a leather bucket, a small store of meat, and some spare mittens—nothing more than that.

Outside, the arctic cold was waiting for her in all its cruelty. She wished she didn't have to leave this sanctuary, with its familiar smells of smoke and animal skins. But if she stayed here much longer, her little sister would come pestering her, or her father would be looking for her with chores to do.

Laena was in no mood for that. She was almost a grown woman, and she desperately needed some time that she could call her own. So she summoned her willpower, picked up her pack, turned away from the fire, and loosened the thong that secured the flap of the tent. She crawled out quickly, fastened the flap behind her, and pulled on her mittens.

She blinked in the sudden daylight. The sun hung over the hills to the south, gleaming fiercely on the slopes of snow. Laena pulled her fur hat lower over her forehead so that its fringe of dried grasses would help to filter the glare.

She glanced quickly around. The winter camp of her tribe consisted of a dozen large, low tents arranged in a circle. Each of them was like the one she dwelled in herself, fashioned from a patchwork of hide stretched across a framework of mammoth ribs, with a pit dug into the ground beneath. Wisps of smoke trailed from vent holes and wafted away in the wind.

The surrounding land was stark and bare. Clusters of stunted trees, none of them taller than a man, grew near a wide river that was deeply crusted with ice. Dry grass poked through thin, powdery snow. To the south and to the west, low hills were shrouded in white.

And yet, life endured. Laena's tribe, the Panther People, had spent their winters here for many generations. Even now, the hunters were out in search of wolves or white foxes. Winter was almost over, and the animals were returning to the land. Soon the great herds of caribou would migrate from the south, and it would be time for everyone to pack up their simple dwellings and trek east to the summer hunting grounds.

Laena paused and listened. Somewhere, a dog was barking. Down by the river, someone was chipping ice that would be melted and used as drinking water. Not far away, two children were squealing. Laena recognized them— Moru, and Lani, another little girl the same age. They'd been told to sweep snow off the tents, but they'd gotten bored with the task and were wrestling with each other, giggling as they rolled on the ground.

A man shouted to them. It was Henik, Laena's father. He was the leader of the hunters, and normally he would have been out with his men. But he'd hurt his leg while scaling a frozen slope a few days ago, and he had to rest till it healed. So here he was now, making himself useful in the camp. That meant he was interfering all the time, telling everyone what to do. Laena ducked down so that he wouldn't see her.

She peeked around the other side of the tent. Her mother, Arla, was working with two other women, setting up meat-drying racks in case the hunters brought back a kill. Laena realized that the women needed help, and she felt a twinge of guilt, because she knew she should go to them. But not today.

Henik was busy scolding Moru. Arla had her back turned. Laena decided to seize the opportunity. She jumped up and ran, heading straight for the river.

She didn't slacken her pace until she was sure she was hidden by the slope of the land. Then, with the cold air burning in her chest, she slowed to a walk and picked her way carefully among the stunted trees. Wood was so scarce here in the far north, she'd been trained from an early age to avoid damaging even the smallest sapling.

She felt good, now, out on her own. She walked with a spring in her step, and she smiled, humming to herself. She was warm inside her furs—for the time being, at least—and she felt alert and full of life.

Further on, she heard a *clink-clink* sound coming from somewhere in front of her. She paused and listened. It was Elbrau, she realized, the flintknapper, searching for stones that could be fashioned into new tools and weapons for the tribe. Elbrau was one of the elders, a quiet man who often seemed lost in his own thoughts. But he had always been friendly to Laena.

She moved ahead more slowly, placing her feet so that they made no sound. She turned her head from side to side, focusing carefully on the source of the sounds. Finally she saw Elbrau directly ahead, crouching on a broad slab of rock overlooking the river. He was intent on his work, oblivious to her.

She stood watching him. He ran his fingers over a heavy white cobble of flint, searching the limestone cortex for a crease that would have been invisible to the naked eye. The flint spoke truly to him only on certain days, revealing how it might be split into shapes of value and beauty. Perhaps this was one of those special times. She watched as he laid the flint carefully before him, then raised his hammerstone, grunted, and brought it down hard. There was a crack that echoed from the hill behind him, and a huge flake of the white cortex flew away revealing smooth, dark flint beneath.

This wasn't the right moment to interrupt him. In any case, she didn't really want to talk to him, or to listen to his stories about the hunts he had been on in summers before she was born. Today, even Elbrau's company would be a distraction from what she really needed to do.

Laena backtracked, circled around him, then continued following the river. Finally she came to a spur of land that would conceal her from the camp if anyone happened to be looking in this direction. She started following the spur, climbing up into the low hills.

The snow here had drifted deeper. She had to start placing her feet carefully, watching for drifts that could engulf her if she blundered into them. After a while, she paused and peeked over an outcropping of tumbled rock. She could see the camp far away, encircled by hills on one side and the river on the other. It looked so tiny—a frail outpost of human life in the vast, empty land covered in snow. Still, Laena was used to the emptiness of her world. She felt secure here and at peace.

Still, she had to be cautious. She carefully scanned the slopes around her, looking for any sign of life. Most carnivores were repelled from the valley by the smell of mankind, but White Bear went where he pleased, and wolves were sometimes seen trotting along the ridges. Today, though, she saw no tracks or droppings. She seemed to be totally alone.

She settled herself among the tumbled rocks, unlaced the flap of her pack, and pulled out a little catskin pouch that she had made. She slid her hands out of her mittens, opened the pouch, reached into it with elaborate care, and withdrew a length of sinew studded with beads of polished bone. This was her secret: a sacred thing that was hers alone. To an outsider, it merely looked like an ornamental belt. To Laena, it was a symbol of the end of her childhood and the beginning of her time as a woman. Soon, when she came of age, she would wear this belt under her furs. No one else would ever set eyes on it—except for the man she took as her husband, and her children, when that time came.

Laena chewed the end of the sinew to make it pliable, then painstakingly threaded it through a new bead and tied an elaborate knot.

She winced as a sudden gust of wind leeched warmth from her skin, and she thrust her hands quickly back into her mittens. She tucked them under her arms and hunched forward, waiting impatiently for the air to be still. She knew from experience how quickly frostbite could strike her unprotected skin.

The design that she was creating had been revealed to her in a dream. Dreams came often to some people and carried no special meaning. To Laena, though, it was different. Her dreams were rare, but they seemed more meaningful than life itself. They were a window into other times and places—into the future, even.

A flicker of motion distracted her. She felt a moment's irritation. Sometimes Moru made a game of following Laena at times like this, trying to track her down. Laena surveyed the landscape, trying to find what she'd seen. There: a tiny black shape against the whiteness.

It wasn't Moru. It was a man, away in the far distance, moving along a ridge that overlooked the camp.

Laena's irritation vanished as quickly as it had come. She felt puzzled. No one from her own tribe had any reason to be out there. And it was far too early for the hunters to be coming back.

She frowned as she realized that the tiny figure was moving cautiously, bending forward, following the line of the ridge, as if he was trying to stay out of sight. Then another man came into view—and still another. Laena watched, holding her breath. There were more than a dozen of them out there. A hunting party, by the look of them. But where were had they come from? And why?

Laena felt a new sensation gathering like a chill in her belly. She wound a piece of sinew around the end of her belt to prevent it from unraveling, and then, with numbing fingers, she collected the unused beads and dropped them into their pouch. She folded the belt, hid it away, stowed the catskin pouch in her pack—and hesitated. If she ran back to the camp, the intruders would see her. For some reason, this made her feel even more anxious than before. Was she being foolish, allowing herself to be unnerved for no good reason? There were stories that the elders sometimes told, of wars that had fought between tribes long before Laena was born. But in her own lifetime, there had been peace among the people who dwelled up and down the Great River. Maybe, she decided, she should find Elbrau and ask his advice.

She ran down the hill toward the river. Her moccasins kicked up snow that sparkled in the sun. Her furs flapped around her. Frigid air rasped in and out of her lungs.

She was almost out of breath when she finally heard him working up ahead. "Elbrau!" she shouted.

He was still sitting on the rock where she had seen him earlier. He heard her voice and looked up sharply, like a sleeper who had woken suddenly from a dream. The wind caught the end of one thick braid, flapping it across his chin. He brushed it away with an impatient gesture, then recognized her, and his stern expression softened. "Laena," he said, "what brings you here?" He noticed how out of breath she was, and he frowned. "Is something wrong?"

She paused and bent forward, resting with the palms of her hands on her knees. Finally, she had enough breath to speak. "People coming," she gasped.

Elbrau looked puzzled. "What people?"

"I don't know. They were following the ridge. They were hiding."

Elbrau tossed the cobble into his flint bag and got to his feet. "Are you sure, child?"

She felt a moment's anger at being called a child. He knew quite well that she was almost a woman. It had been him, after all, who had given her the bone beads that she needed for her belt.

"Of course I'm sure," she said. "They were hiding themselves behind the ridge. I don't understand why, but that's what they were doing."

Elbrau swung down from the rock and landed lightly beside her. "Perhaps they're strangers who want to see that we're peaceful before they greet us and continue on their way."

For a moment, Laena found his explanation convincing. But then she realized that it couldn't be true. "It's early in the year for a tribe to be roaming so far from its home."

Elbrau nodded slowly. "That's true. All right, come. Quickly now."

She followed him, keeping close to the river, so that the slope of its bank concealed them. They'd gone less than a hundred paces when Elbrau suddenly held up his hand and stopped.

Laena listened. She heard footsteps coming toward them, crunching on the gravelly soil that lay just beneath the thin skin of snow. Laena felt a wave of fear—then saw who it was. "Moru!" she exclaimed.

The little girl came running toward her. She shouted with pleasure and threw herself forward with her arms spread wide.

"Shhh!" Laena scooped up the child. "Quiet!"

"Why? Why quiet?" Moru was still grinning.

"Do as I say." Laena's voice was pitched low, but the tone was commanding. "What are you doing here, anyway? You should be back at the camp."

Moru looked hurt. "I was searching for you. I was following your tracks in the snow."

"Shhh." Elbrau held up his hand again.

Faintly, there was a sound from the direction of the camp. It sounded like a shout of surprise—or alarm.

"Wait here," Elbrau told them. "Hide yourselves, do you understand?"

Laena nodded, feeling worried by the sharpness in his voice.

Elbrau turned and ran. Within moments, he had disappeared among the rocks and saplings.

"What's happening?" Moru said. Her eyes were wide as she stared up at Laena. She almost looked as if she might cry.

Laena shook her head. "I don't know. I saw strangers approaching the camp. Maybe—maybe they are bad people." She circled her arm around Moru and hugged her protectively.

"What do they want?" Moru asked.

"I don't know!" Laena hissed at her.

The light faded for a moment as clouds crossed the sun. A few scattered flakes of snow whirled by. The trees writhed in a gust of wind, and water gurgled faintly beneath the ice of the river. Laena scraped snow away from a patch of rock and crouched there with Moru, huddling with her against the wind.

It was nerve-wracking, not knowing what was going on. Laena understood that Elbrau was trying to protect her, but she felt too old to be treated like that. If the people of her tribe were faced with a real threat, shouldn't she be with them?

More shouts came from the direction of the camp. Dogs started barking.

Laena tried to think of an excuse to free herself from her promise to stay here. What if her people were driven out of their homes? They might be forced to leave her behind. That sounded unlikely, but it would have to do. "Come," she said, grabbing Moru's hand and starting along the path that Elbrau had taken. "Let's find out what's happening."

She moved as silently as she could, constantly checking her surroundings. She kept telling herself that there was nothing to be worried about, but she still felt dread in the pit of her stomach. At a break in the trees, she got down and crawled across the snow, gesturing for Moru to do the same.

Together, they crawled till they were just a hundred paces from the camp, hidden only by the sloping land. They raised their heads cautiously, and peered ahead.

A crowd of people had gathered among the tents. All the women were there, with Elbrau, her father, Henik, and Gorag, the chieftain of the Panther Tribe. The women were holding their babies. Children were standing close by their parents. The dogs had stopped barking, and the scene was strangely, frighteningly silent.

The strangers had come down out of the hills. They were standing in a group, just a dozen paces outside the circle of the tents, and now that Laena saw their faces, she realized that they weren't strangers at all. They were hunters from the White Bear Tribe, whose territory lay to the west. All of them were holding spears.

"I warned you." The words were shrill, shouted by a tall, gaunt man draped in a huge bear pelt. His eyes were wide and his lips pulled back from his teeth, making his face look like a skull. His name was Jalenau, and he was the leader of the White Bear people. "Last autumn, at the meeting of the tribes, I warned you." He was holding two spears in his left hand, and one in his right. He raised his right arm and shook the spear threateningly.

Gorag, the chieftain of the Panther People, was facing the intruder. He was broad-shouldered, heavily built, a grizzled beast of a man. Scars crisscrossed his weather-worn face, so that it looked as much of a patchwork as the furs he wore. Gorag could be a wild fighter, but Laena realized he was in no position to defend his tribe. He was holding only one spear to Jalenau's three, and his menfolk were all out of the camp, apart from Henik, who was injured, and Elbrau, who was too old to hunt and fight.

"You have no right," Gorag shouted, "coming here like this. You know that, Jalenau."

Jalenau lifted his spear higher. His eyes gleamed. "You tell me I don't have the right to speak for my people?"

Gorag paused, as if he wasn't sure how to respond to Jalenau's shrill tone. He lowered his voice. "You know, Jalenau, your father was a friend of mine." He spoke the words calmly, slowly. Laena strained her ears, wanting to understand what was happening, even while the spectacle in front of her made her sick with fear. "He was a great hunter, Jalenau. His spirit could be looking down on us, now. Do you think he'd approve, seeing you threatening our women and children?'' Gorag paused for a second. ''If you're an honorable man, the way your father was, you'll settle this peacefully. Either that, or you'll settle it just with me, man-to-man.'' Gorag thumped his chest with his fist.

For a moment, Jalenau seemed to waver. Laena saw the muscles move in his face. But then, suddenly, he swung his arm, as if he wanted to slice Gorag's throat with the spear. ''You've got no right to speak of my father! You Panther people must return the food you've stolen. Either that, or you'll pay with your blood.'' He glanced at his men on either side of him, and they moved closer till their shoulders were almost touching.

Gorag nodded to himself. He turned and beckoned to Henik. ''Come, my friend.'' He clapped his hand on Henik's shoulder. ''Speak truly. Is there any truth in Jalenau's complaints?''

Laena felt an awful mixture of pride and fear as she watched her father moving closer to Jalenau and the other White Bear hunters. He frowned at Gorag. ''You know it's not true,'' he said. ''No Panther would steal White Bear food.''

''Liar!'' Jalenau shouted.

''Henik, see if you can convince Jalenau,'' said Gorag, stepping aside. ''He knows you are an honorable man.''

Henik turned to face the invaders. ''There are more people in your tribe than there used to be,'' he said. ''But there are fewer animals to hunt. The summers have been drier and warmer, and the sea rises higher each year, so there's less grass for the animals to feed on. We talked about this at the Gathering of the Tribes, Jalenau. You know it's true.''

Jalenau made a short, angry sound, as if the reasonable tone of Henik's voice enraged him even more than Gorag's challenge. ''There are fewer animals, Henik, because you people killed them. You invaded our land, while our people are hungry—''

''No!'' Normally, Laena's father was stern but kind, slow to anger. She had hardly ever heard him raise his voice. ''Only a fool blames other people for his misfortune,'' Henik went on. ''Only a coward comes here threatening us like this, when our hunters are away from the camp. Go back to your own people before you shame yourself further.'' And Henik turned away in disgust.

Jalenau's eyes were wide and staring. He uttered a sudden piercing scream that rang around the valley, and he hurled his spear with all his strength.

The flint-tipped shaft buried itself deep in Henik's right shoulder. Beside Laena, Moru shrieked. She started scrambling up onto her feet. Laena instinctively grabbed her, wrapped her arms around her, and pulled her back to the ground. Meanwhile, she stared at the terrible spectacle before her.

Henik grunted in surprise and pain. He clasped both hands around the shaft of the spear and started tugging at it, with the muscles of his cheeks quivering. Blood welled up and ran down the spear shaft. Finally, with a cry of fury, Henik pulled the spear free and flung it aside. He took a shaky step backward, clasping his left hand over the wound as blood continued pulsing out between his fingers.

Suddenly Elbrau bellowed in rage. He raised his own spear and cast it at Jalenau with all his strength.

Jalenau threw himself to one side, and the weapon buried itself in the man who had been standing behind him. The tension was broken. The White Bears shouted a war cry, drew their arms back, and threw their spears into the Panther tribe. Then they charged forward.

Several women were struck by the volley. They slumped down, screaming. The other women seized their children, turned, and ran. The White Bear hunters went running after them, fanning out, trying to encircle them.

Elbrau snatched up a spear, turned, and thrust it deep into the stomach of a White Bear warrior who was bearing down upon him. Gorag had been standing to one side. He snarled and raised his own weapon as Jalenau charged toward him. But Gorag didn't throw his weapon; he ducked aside at the last moment, then backed away, glancing around quickly.

One of the enemy hunters lost his balance and fell onto a tent. The bones under the hide cracked and collapsed, leaving the man floundering as the tent collapsed under him. Gorag danced forward and jabbed the man through the base of his throat, pulled his spear back, then turned quickly, ready to defend himself.

A young boy ran past, seized the fallen White Bear's spear, and joined the fighting. But before he could take another step he was skewered by a shaft thrown by one of the attackers.

Laena felt as if she were gripped by a huge fist, unable to breathe, unable to move. She could only watch dumbly as violence engulfed the camp. She stared in horror at her father, blood running from his shoulder and down his arm, as he stumbled backward, vainly trying to deflect an onslaught from two more of the White Bear hunters. She saw Elbrau seizing Jalenau with his bare hands, whirling him around, and butting him in the face. Jalenau swung his last remaining spear, trying to fend off the flintknapper. The shaft smacked against Elbrau's temple, making him stagger backward.

The brush near Laena and Moru crackled as several women and children came leaping through. Then they were gone, with hunters chasing after them.

Laena saw her own mother running for safety. Should she go after her? She was still immobilized by the horror of what she saw. All around, the White Bear hunters were cutting down the Panther People. The frozen earth steamed with hot blood.

"Laena!" Moru grabbed her arm and shook it.

Laena saw Gorag retreating toward the hills, parrying spear thrusts from a pair of Jalenau's warriors, glancing behind him for a way to escape. A woman lunged out from behind one of the tents, brandishing a length of bone that she had taken from the drying racks. She swung it at a White Bear, who ducked beneath it and tackled her. The two of them fell to the ground, grappling with each other.

"Laena! Laena!" Moru shook her violently. "Run!"

A sharp pain suddenly stung Laena's face and she pulled back, blinking. Moru had scratched her. The little girl's hands were bare, her fingers curled into claws. "Get up!"

Laena jumped up, seized Moru's hand, turned away from the massacre, and plunged into the low trees lining the river. She was like a terrified animal now, no longer able to think, only knowing she must flee. Now that she had regained her ability to move, all she could do was run as fast and as far as possible. She dragged her sister after her, and together they ran, first along the river, then up into the hills where Laena had been earlier. But still she saw in her mind the horror of the bloodshed, and she imagined White Bear hunters chasing after her. She kept her grip tight on Moru's wrist and dragged her over the ridge, into the next valley, and onward.

She didn't know how far they had gone when she finally collapsed. She saw a dark shadow in the snow—a cave that had been scooped out by the wind. She dove into it and lay there gasping, clutching Moru, trembling with fear. Her vision was wavering, there was a hissing sound in her ears, and she heard her own pulse tap-tapping impossibly fast. She closed her eyes for a moment, gasping for breath.

Slowly, she managed to calm herself. Then she saw in her imagination the image of her father, bleeding, and her mother running in fear. Laena moaned and opened her eyes, afraid that she would find White Bear hunters scrambling toward her through the snow, poised to attack her.

But the land here was peaceful. The wind blew, raising white dust from the snowy ridges. Nothing else moved in the stillness.

Laena finally managed to slow her breathing and her heartbeats. She felt Moru clinging to her, and when she looked down, she found the little girl staring up at her with wide, fearful eyes.

"Don't worry." Laena's voice sounded strained. It was an effort to speak. She hugged Moru, trying to comfort her. "We're safe now, little one."

And yet, she knew it might not be true. If her father, and her mother, and Elbrau, and Gorag, and all the other people of her tribe were dead—how could she hope to survive here in the wilderness?

Chapter 2

"I'm cold." Moru's voice sounded small and scared. She clutched Laena's furs and pressed herself close, and Laena felt the little girl trembling. Their panic-stricken run across the slopes had warmed them at first, but that warmth was fading fast.

Laena still felt stunned by what she had seen. More than that, though, she felt scared, as she started to think about the situation they were in. She had perspired heavily while she ran, and her undergarments, fashioned from caribou hide, now felt clammy against her skin. That made them useless as a barrier against the subfreezing temperatures. If she didn't have a fire to warm herself, and shelter from the weather, she might not live through the night. Nor was nighttime far away: the land still lay in winter's grip, and the days were short.

But what could she do? Jalenau had driven the Panther people out of their camp. She felt sure that he and his hunters would still be there, guarding it, while the Panther people who had survived—if there were any fled for their lives. How could she hope to find them?

Moru's hands clenched on Laena's arm. "Laena, I'm cold!"

Laena sat up. If her mother or her father were still alive, they'd be looking for her. But where?

Laena made up her mind. "We must follow our tracks back the way we came."

"No!" Moru screamed. Her fingers clenched tighter. "They'll kill us!"

"Not if we hide from them," she said, with more confidence than she felt. "Listen, we can't stay here. I don't have any flints to start a fire, and we don't have any weapons, and even if we did, neither of us would know how to use it.

Come on!'' And she dragged the little girl out of the snow cave.

Reluctantly, Moru followed Laena back toward the summit of the nearest hill, retracing their tracks in the snow. Laena moved cautiously, watching for the slightest sign of life. She still felt deeply scared. How strange it was that not so long ago, she'd wanted to hide from her family. Suddenly, everything had been turned upside down. She felt the lack of her people and her home like a terrible aching void inside her.

''Where are we?'' Moru's voice sounded plaintive.

Laena scanned the landscape. ''We came further than I thought,'' she said. ''But the river lies that way.'' She pointed beyond the next ridge.

Moru started forward, but this time Laena held her back. She strained her ears, listening for the faintest sound. She looked all around, watching for the smallest movement. ''All right. Slowly now.''

Together they trekked across the white wilderness. The snow here was deep, which made walking very difficult. The exercise warmed Laena a little, but she knew it was a false warmth. She was using more of her precious reserves of energy, and when she stopped again, the cold would seem even fiercer than it had before.

Finally they saw the river at the bottom of the next valley. Laena stopped and listened. She held her breath as she heard faint rustling sounds in the far distance.

There was something moving along the opposite bank of the river. Something far larger than a man. It was a mammoth, a young bull, ambling along, ripping up clumps of dry grass. It swung the clumps with its trunk and beat them against its legs to knock off clods of frozen earth before it crammed the grass into its mouth.

Laena waited respectfully for the mammoth to pass. As she watched it, she felt some faint hope. Maybe its calm strength was a sign—an omen telling her that she, too, should be strong.

With Moru at her side, she picked her way slowly down the slope. Finally she reached the river and started toward the Panther camp. She passed the rock where Elbrau had sat, and she found herself wishing she could somehow turn time backward. Everything had seemed so easy and so reassuring, earlier in the day. But in retrospect, she saw that the safety she had felt had been an illusion.

She crept among the saplings and the tall grass, picking her way back toward the camp. It was hard, very hard, to go near the place where she had seen such terrible things. She had to pause for a moment and try to calm herself, try to drive out of her mind the visions of blood and death.

Maybe she could pretend that the massacre had been just a figment of her imagination. She imagined returning, finding her mother roasting fresh meat, her father sharpening his spear, children playing around the fire—

No; if she was going to survive, she would have to face the truth of what had happened. She would have to—

"Kaelie!"

The word was a whisper, but it made Laena jump. With her heart racing, she dropped into a defensive crouch and turned quickly, searching for any sign of life among the saplings.

"Kaelie!" The voice came again.

"Who's there?" she hissed.

"Jobia. By the river."

She saw him then, hiding behind a snow-topped boulder. He was a young hunter from her tribe, only a year older than herself. She usually made a point of avoiding him, because he was boastful and he was a bully, always picking on her and teasing her when the adults weren't looking. At this moment, though, his presence made her feel a great wave of relief.

She hurried toward him, pulling Moru after her. As she came closer, she saw that his face and furs were smeared with dirt. One of his mittens had been sliced open, and it was crusted with blood. Otherwise, though, he seemed unharmed.

"What are you doing here?" he whispered.

"I was sent to keep watch. You realize the White Bears are in our camp? You'd have been killed if you'd gone back there."

Laena's feeling of relief was swept away as quickly as it had come, giving way to irritation. "Of course I realize. Where are my father and mother? Where are all our people?"

Jobia held up his hand. "Not so loud!"

Her voice had been no louder than his. She tried to hold back her anger. "My father and mother," she persisted. "Are they alive?"

Jobia gave a curt nod. "I saw your mother with the rest of them. They're hiding that way." He jerked his head downriver. "Beside the little creek. You know, Jalenau speared your father. He's badly wounded."

"Yes," said Laena. "I saw it happen." And she felt tears in the corners of the eyes as she remembered her father's shout of pain. She shook her head quickly, determined that Jobia shouldn't see her showing any sign of weakness.

But he wasn't paying attention. "I fought to the last," he told her. "My spear tasted Bear blood today. Two dead, and two wounded." He held up his mitten. "One of them sliced my hand, but it didn't stop me."

She glared at him. "So you're a man now, is that it?"

He stiffened, not liking her tone of voice. "Yes, why not? I fought like a man."

"And now you're hiding like a rabbit."

Jobia scowled at her. His hand tightened on his spear. "You listen to me," he began.

"Take us to the creek," Moru interrupted him. "Take us there!" She grabbed Jobia's arm and shook it from side to side. "I want my mother!"

Jobia gave a grunt of irritation. He jerked his arm out of Moru's grip, and glared at Laena. "First, you apologize."

Laena felt her anger rise up again—then realized it was foolish and pointless to squabble with this boy. She wasn't angry with him; she was angry with Jalenau and his tribe, for what they had done. So why take it out on Jobia?

With difficulty, she suppressed her emotions. "I'm sorry," she muttered. After all, it wasn't his fault.

"All right," he said. "I'll take you. Come on."

She took Moru's hand and they followed Jobia back along the river, pausing often to look and listen. They reached the creek finally, and branched up it, wending their way between hillsides that closed in either side, till the creek became just a narrow brook between steep walls of rock.

It was a long, slow walk. The light began to fade, and Laena started feeling cold again. Her stomach was empty—but she knew there would be no food for her tonight.

The valley opened out ahead, and Jobia held up his hand. They paused, hearing faint noises ahead. Jobia made the sound of a mountain cat, and an answering call came from some bushes ahead. There was the figure of a man there, hiding among the vegetation. As they advanced toward him, Laena realized it was Gorag, their chieftain.

The sight of him made her feel a little better. He had been a strong leader, over the years. Surely, he would know what to do.

But when she looked at him, she saw that his face was smeared with blood and there was a strange blankness in his eyes. Suddenly she remembered seeing him backing away, then running from the battle.

"So you're alive, after all," he said. He eyed her without any emotion that she could see—no pleasure, no warmth. "Go on," he said. "Go to your parents." And he looked away.

"His wife was killed in the fighting," Jobia whispered to Laena as they moved on by. "His sister, too."

"He should have defended them," Laena said.

"He did! He fought fiercely!"

She looked at Jobia's face. He was glaring at her, full of righteousness. Was it possible that he'd seen more than she had? Laena felt confused. She didn't know what to think. "I'm sure you're right," she said diplomatically.

Jobia led them ahead to a place where the river was broad and shallow, and tall reeds stood amid pools of ice and frozen mud. A small fire was burning. Here, at last, were the remnants of the Panther People. Laena stopped, not wanting to believe what she saw. She counted eight adults and four children, here in this frozen marsh, hunched in their furs, trying to warm themselves around the pitiful fire.

Laena had known her share of hardship, especially when the tribe made its annual pilgrimage to and from the summer hunting grounds. Life in the arctic wilderness was often uncomfortable. But she had never known a catastrophe like this. In the space of an afternoon, everything that she trusted had been proved false; everything she relied on had been snatched away.

Moru, meanwhile, was running forward. Laena watched

as the little girl seized hold of one of the huddled women, who turned to her with a startled cry.

Slowly, as if she was awakening from a dream, Laena realized she was looking at her own mother.

Chapter 3

Laena felt suddenly weak. She almost collapsed as her mother turned to her and seized her with one arm while she hugged Moru with the other. Moru was sobbing with relief. Laena felt like crying herself as her mother crooned to her, smiling down at her, wrapping her furs around her.

Then Laena saw Henik looming over her, weak and pale from loss of blood. He laid his heavy arm around Laena's shoulders, and she saw gladness soften the grim lines in his face.

For a moment, she felt all her anxiety and her grief drain away. But then she remembered where she was, and she looked around at the rest of the Panther people. Elbrau was coming toward her, limping from a wound in his thigh. Two of the women were so badly injured that they were barely able to move. The children were unhurt, but they stared at Laena with dull eyes, and none of them said a word.

Everyone, she saw, was stricken with despair. Nor were they grieving just for the people who had died; they were scared for themselves. Only three men were left alive, and of them, Gorag was the only one who still had most of his strength. He couldn't possibly kill enough game to feed seven adults and four children. Nor could they survive for long without proper protection from the weather.

"Is there any news of our hunters?" she asked, looking hopefully from Henik to Elbrau.

"No sign," Henik said. He nodded toward Jobia. "Arla sent the young one here to watch our camp in case they, or you, or anyone else tried to return."

A muscle twitched in Jobia's face. He obviously didn't enjoy being reminded of his youth. "I did my duty," he said. His voice rose defiantly. "I brought you your daughters, and I protected them along the way."

Henik smiled faintly. "Indeed that's so. I'm grateful to you, young Jobia."

Jobia stared at Henik as if he couldn't decide whether he was making fun of him. But Arla stepped between them. "We have work to do before darkness sets in," she said. "Moru, stay here with your father, see that he's warm, and bring him water if he needs it. He's more badly hurt than he admits. Laena, come with me."

Her mother's tone was so stern, Laena felt stung by it. "Why are you angry?" she said as she followed Arla away. "Aren't you happy to see me?"

Arla turned abruptly. She laid her hand on Laena's shoulder. "Of course I'm happy to see you. It has taken a weight from my heart, Laena. But we have to be practical now. We can't let ourselves feel too much. We have to survive. You understand?"

Laena nodded slowly.

"Come." Arla's hand was firm on Laena's shoulder. "Sela died earlier. She's over by the creek. She won't be needing her furs now, so we'll use them to wrap the people who are wounded. They'll be feeling the cold, tonight."

Numbly, Laena followed her mother toward the creek. Sela was lying on her back beside the ice. Laena approached her and paused, staring down at her face. Sela had been her aunt; her mother's sister. And now, in an instant, Sela was like a beast felled by a hunter's spear.

Arla's face was enigmatic as she pressed a flint knife into Laena's hand. "Slit her furs with this. Bring the rest to me."

"Wait!" Laena clutched at her.

Arla paused. She waited.

"What—" Laena tried to steady her voice. "What's going to happen to us?"

Arla said nothing. Her expression didn't change.

"We don't have any food," Laena went on. "We don't have any tents. How can we—"

"Tonight, we'll huddle together for warmth. Tomorrow, we'll decide whether to stay here and hope the White Bears don't find us, or trek to our summer camp."

Laena tried to imagine either of the possibilities. She shook her head. "But we can't—"

Arla seized her suddenly and gave her a little shake.

"We'll do whatever we can, for as long as we can. Do you want us to lie down and die?"

Laena looked up into her mother's fierce eyes. Arla was right; they had to fight, no matter how hopeless it seemed. "I'll try," Laena said.

Arla gave her a quick hug. "Good. I'm proud of you, Laena." She turned and strode away among the tall reeds.

Grimly, Laena crouched down beside Sela's body. She took a firm grip on the flint knife, then sawed through the stitches of sinew at the shoulder seams. In the fading light, it was hard to see what she was doing. But she had skinned game often enough, and her fingers guided her with practiced skill as she moved the blade.

The outer robes fell loose as she sliced apart the seam along Sela's left side. Laena peeled the furs away, rolled them up, and set them on the ground.

Under her furs, Sela wore the summer pelts of caribou. The sinew stitches were newer here, and they resisted Laena's knife. She at back on her heels and nibbled the flint blade, snapping off tiny flakes between her teeth. Then she continued her grim work, trying not to think about the awfulness of what she was doing.

Finally she lifted the caribou skins. She didn't want to look, but she couldn't stop herself. Sela's body was a pale shape in the deepening twilight, and Laena saw the woman's belt around her waist. The twined, knotted thongs were shiny from years of rubbing and polishing against her skin. The mellow richness of mammoth ivory beads trailed across the belt in a complex pattern—meaningless to anyone save Sela—and here and there a piece of quartz gleamed dully.

Laena felt awed by the care and craft that had gone into the belt. At the same time, she felt ashamed. She shouldn't be staring at something so private. Quickly, she cut the belt loose. Normally it would have been laid to rest with Sela, returning her spirit to the earth, from where it had come. But there was no time for that, and no way to dig a hole in the frozen earth. Laena hesitated, then coiled the belt and thrust it under some loose stones close by. That would have to do.

Laena turned back to the furs, gathered them in her arms, and stood up. Before she could move, she heard footsteps approaching. Her mother came up in the semidarkness, with Jobia at her side.

"Leave the furs here for now," Arla said. "We have another chore to do."

Laena slowly set the furs back on the ground. She wasn't sure she could face another job like this.

"The night beasts—the jackals and the wolves—they'll be lured by the smell of our blood," Arla went on. There was a new tension in her voice that hadn't been there before. "We must find something that will distract them. You take hold of Sela's legs. Jobia and I will take her arms."

Gradually, Laena made sense of what her mother was saying. "You want to feed Sela to the animals?"

"Her soul has no use for her body now. She must serve those of us who still live. Come on, Laena."

Arla's voice was as stern as ever. Dumbly, Laena stooped and lifted her aunt's ankles. Together, the three of them dragged Sela up the slope, into the wilderness.

Laena found herself staring down at Sela, wondering how it was that life could be stolen away so suddenly. Did the spirit really live on, as her people believed? As she stared at Sela, she suddenly found herself doubting the truth of it. Sela was dead; it was as simple as that.

"Leave her here," Jobia said. "A few paces upwind from that rock."

Arla paused. "Why here?"

Jobia surveyed the hillside. The snow gleamed eerily in the last light from the darkening sky. "That rock can hide me tonight. I'll wait beside it, and any beast that comes close will taste the point of my spear."

Arla grunted in disapproval. "What if it's a fanged cat? Or a bear? One spear won't discourage them. It'll just make them eager for your blood."

Jobia shook his head. "I'll hunt tonight. You'll see."

Arla didn't argue further. Laena wasn't surprised; it was the way of things for a woman to obey the word of a man. Jobia hadn't gone through the coming-of-age ceremony, but as he'd said himself, he deserved to be treated as a man now that he'd fought beside other men.

Laena felt herself wondering why it should be this way. Now that her life was in turmoil, she was asking questions that she had never thought of before. Why should Arla defer to Jobia? She was a wise woman, and she was more than twice his age. Why was a woman's place by the hearth, while only men were fit to become hunters? The tribe would be safer if women knew how to use spears. They could all hunt game, and they could have defended themselves against the White Bears.

She looked at Jobia. He was bigger than she was, and stronger. But she didn't see any reason why she shouldn't learn to use a spear as well as he did—if she was ever given the chance.

She was deep in thought as she followed Jobia and her mother back to the rest of the tribe. But her thoughtfulness didn't last long. There was more work to do, making beds of reeds and laying furs across them for the wounded to lie on.

One of the wounded women was Jobia's mother, a woman named Heese. She complained about the pain from deep gashes in her abdomen. Jobia had lost his father two years ago in a hunting accident, and his mother was the last of his kin. Perhaps, Laena thought, it was only natural that he wanted to feel strong and impress people as a man.

The other wounded woman, Hirgar, was unconscious. Her skin was hot to the touch, despite the cold air, and Laena didn't think she would last through the night. She was a cousin of Gorag, and the chieftain came over and sat beside her for a while. But he still seemed distracted. In the light from the moon, Laena saw him staring across the frozen marsh, back toward the land he had lost.

"Gorag seems strange," Laena whispered to her father as they lay down together with the rest of the tribe, huddling beside the fire, trying to conserve their warmth.

"He's grieving for his kin," Henik murmured to her.

But was that really the reason? If he had truly cared for his wife and his sister, wouldn't he have tried harder to defend them?

Then she remembered Gorag stepping away from Henik, leaving him unprotected in front of Jalenau. "Father—"

"Quiet, child. Let's sleep while we can."

For a moment, her spirit of rebellion rose up inside her. She wasn't a child. She shouldn't have to obey his orders.

But he was wounded, she reminded herself. He needed to rest.

"Be thankful, Laena," her mother murmured. "Our family is still whole. Thank fate for that."

"Yes, Mother," she whispered. And yet—why should she be thankful? Her whole world had been destroyed. Her stomach was empty, and she might die with the last remnants of her people in this frozen swamp.

She struggled to quieten her thoughts. No one else seemed to be having any trouble going to sleep. The people of the tribe were lying quietly, and all she could hear was their slow, heavy breathing. That was a peaceful sound, reminding her of all the nights she had spent in her tent with her parents. And so, finally, Laena managed to slip into a fretful sleep.

Sometime later she woke to find the black sky flickering with colored curtains of light. Her father was standing, silhouetted against the radiance. She cried out and reached for him, afraid that he was leaving her.

He stooped and touched her face. "Shh. It's my turn to stand guard. Sleep, Laena. Things will be better tomorrow."

She wanted to trust the truth of his words. She wanted to be comforted by him as she always had been. But her faith had been damaged. She was no longer a child, and she no longer trusted fate. Even her father's words now sounded empty to her ears.

Chapter 4

Laena woke to find her mother shaking her shoulder. "Up, child." Arla's voice was as stern as it had been the day before. "There's a lot to be done."

Laena struggled onto her feet—and found that she could barely stand. Her legs were stiff and her feet were numb from the cold. She felt light-headed and her belly ached with hunger. She blinked, looking around. A heavy gray mist lay over the frozen creek, and the sky was thick with clouds.

"Fetch fuel for a fire," her mother was saying. "Make sure you get dry tinder. If there's too much smoke, the White Bears will have no trouble finding us."

Laena nodded blearily. "Yes, Mother." She looked around. "Can Moru—"

"No, Moru can't help you. She has to help skin the beast."

"The beast?" Laena's eyes widened.

"Jobia did as he promised, last night. We have fresh game. A lion, would you believe? Get busy, child, if you want breakfast!"

Laena saw several women crouching on the ground nearby, working with their knives. She moved closer. The lion was thin and old, and one of its feet seemed to have been crushed in an accident from years ago. But it was truly a lion, nonetheless.

"I told you," said a voice.

Laena turned and found Jobia behind her. He looked pale, exhausted from his night vigil. But he stood proud, and he eyed her in a knowing way that made her want to hide herself from him.

It made her angry that he could have such an effect, just

by the way he stared at her. "How much help did you need to kill that cat?" she snapped at him.

"I needed no help!" He stepped forward and his hand flew out, too quickly for Laena to dodge. He flipped her hood back, grabbed her by her hair, and hauled her toward him. "It seems to me, you need a lesson in respect."

Laena found her face close to his. She groped in her pouch, pulled out her knife, and brought it up with its point toward his face. It was an impulsive gesture, not at all the kind of thing she would normally have done. She had changed, she realized, in the short time since the White Bears had attacked.

"Laena!" It was Arla's voice. "Laena, the fire needs fuel."

"Let me go," Laena hissed.

Jobia stared at the blade. He didn't seem scared by it, but he was certainly surprised. Slowly, he released his grip. "You'd better put that knife away." He drew himself up. "What do you know about using a blade?"

Laena realized she was trembling. Never before had she threatened one of her tribe. Feeling confused, she turned away. She thrust her knife back in her bag, pulled her hood tight around her face, and trudged out to look for the dry tinder that they needed.

A little later, the fire was burning brightly. When its heat had softened the frozen ground, its ashes were swept aside and the women used their hands to scoop out a shallow pit in the marshy soil. Children brought chunks of ice to fill the pit, and a fresh fire was built nearby. This was used to heat stones brought from beside the creek, and the hot stones were dropped in the pit full of ice water. Soon it had turned to water; and soon after that, the water was simmering. The people of the tribe gathered around.

Strips of meat were spitted on spears and toasted over the flames. As was his right, Jobia called names and handed out the sizzling meat as it became ready. He stinted no one—but he used his privilege to see that Laena was the last to get a share.

For a time everyone was silent, greedily tearing at the food and satisfying their grinding hunger. Then they drank from the hot water; then they ate some more; and then they used what was left of the water to wash themselves and clean their wounds.

Finally, Gorag addressed them. He no longer had the lost look that Laena had seen the previous night. He stood tall, and he spoke with conviction.

"People," he said, standing before them. "First let us pay tribute to the young man who has brought us this feast." He gestured to Jobia, who stood up looking solemn, with his head held high. "He listened to the lessons I taught him as a hunter, and he learned them well. There's no doubt now that he has become a man entitled to our respect. This I have said, and it is so."

The people of the tribe nodded and murmured assent. The big cat had been old and crippled, but killing it had been a real challenge for just one man, nonetheless. At the same time, Laena found herself wondering when Gorag had ever bothered to give Jobia any lessons in hunting. It had been Yorenah, one of the missing hunters, who had trained Jobia after the boy's father had died.

"Now," said Gorag, slowly rubbing his palms together. "We have a difficult choice. I've thought hard on this, and I've spoken with Elbrau and Henik. I've looked at the signs. If we stay here, the White Bears will probably find us after a few days. If we return to our camp, they'll kill us; there's no doubt of that. So we really have no choice. We must go to our summer camp, foraging as we can along the way." He paused to let that sink in. "If anyone wishes to speak, now is the time."

Henik stood up. "What about the people who are too weak to travel?" He gestured to his own wounded shoulder. "I can make it myself, but your own cousin is still in a coma. And Jobia's mother, Heese, is too weak to walk."

Gorag gazed at Henik calmly. "My cousin Hirgar has passed on."

There was a surprised murmur from the people gathered around.

"But I fed her just a short while ago," Arla protested.

"She has passed on," Gorag repeated. His tone was harsh, and there was a hardness in his eyes. "I did what had to be done."

There was a sudden silence. Everyone stared at him.

Gorag nodded slowly. "It wasn't easy, but there was no

other way. We aren't strong enough to care for people who can't fend for themselves.'' He bared his teeth, and Laena flinched as she saw the fierceness in his scarred, bruised face. ''Does anyone question that? Do any of you doubt my wisdom?'' And he turned slowly, staring at each in turn.

No one spoke. Henik and Elbrau were the only other full-grown men, and they were both weakened by their wounds. No one else would challenge the chieftain.

But Jobia spoke up. ''What of my mother?'' he said. His voice sounded higher pitched than normal, and Laena saw the way he nervously gripped his spear. ''Would you have me kill her, as you killed Hirgar?''

Once again, silence descended over the tribe. The only sound was the crackling and hissing of the fire.

Gorag stared steadily at Jobia. Laena expected him to discipline the boy for speaking so insolently, but when the chieftain spoke, his voice was calm. ''Clearly,'' said Gorag, ''your mother cannot travel with us.''

Jobia slammed the butt of his spear down into the dirt. ''No!'' he shouted.

Henik stepped forward, quickly putting himself between the two of them. ''There's another way,'' he said. ''We can rest here until Heese regains her strength—''

Gorag gestured dismissively. ''That will take days. The White Bears don't have far to come. They'll find us, and they'll kill us.'' He folded his arms. ''We must move on. This I have said, and it is so.''

''I will not leave my mother!'' Jobia shouted.

''We could build a travois for Heese—a simple sled, to take her with us,'' said Henik.

There was a murmuring of agreement at this. Gorag stared slowly around the group, weighing their mood. He scowled. ''All right, build the travois. But it'll slow us down. To save one person's life, we may all end up dying.''

''We'll manage,'' said Jobia. ''I'll drag the travois myself if I have to.''

Henik stepped closer to Gorag. He nodded respectfully. ''It's a wise chieftain,'' he said quietly, ''who bends to the will of his people.''

Gorag stared at Henik for a moment, then turned away. He raised his spear and stabbed it into the ground, then bent and used his knife to carve a line in the earth. ''When the shadow of my spear touches this line, we'll set off on our journey. We'll cross the river and make camp beyond the Eastern Hills before night. This I have said, and it is so.''

After the meeting had broken up, Laena went to Hirgar. The woman was lying in furs that Laena had wrapped around her the previous night—the same furs she had cut from Sela's body. And now Hirgar herself was dead. There was a deep slash at either side of her neck where Gorag had opened the skin with his knife. Already, her blood was freezing on the ground.

"He had no right. A leader doesn't murder his own people. His own kin, even!''

Laena turned and saw Jobia standing over her. She felt such a confused mixture of emotions, she didn't know what to say.

"Help me, Kaelie, to build a travois to carry my mother.''

Laena felt a twist of resentment. "My name is Laena, not Kaelie. And building things is man's work.'' She got up and walked away, heading toward the creek.

Behind her, she heard him make a noise of disgust. But she was not in a mood to do him any favors, or ally herself with him against Gorag. And she needed time to think.

She sat awhile beside the frozen creek, fingering the beads of the unfinished belt in her catskin pouch. The belt was like a link with her past, when everything had seemed simple and she had always known what to expect. There had been rituals to mark the passing of the seasons, and ceremonies to signify the transitions in a person's life.

That was over now. Those times were gone. Moved by a sudden impulse, Laena gathered up the unfinished belt and the ivory beads. She drew her arm back, then hurled them out across the creek. For a moment she felt a stab of regret, as the beads scattered across the ice and the belt itself whirled away, disappearing into a fissure between two floes. But then Laena felt a weight lifting off her. She was free to live from day to day now, in whatever way seemed best.

Behind her, she heard activity in the marshy hollow. Jobia had persuaded Henik and Elbrau to help him, and they were fashioning a travois by lashing the boughs of some thin saplings between a pair of spears.

Laena walked back and watched as Sela's furs were spread

across the saplings and Heese was lifted onto the rough bed. Her eyes were closed, and a rasping sound came from her throat as she took slow, weak breaths.

Two of the women hacked the last of the lion's meat from its bones, wrapped the meat in the beast's own skin, and fastened it to the travois. Finally, Gorag called them all around him.

"It is time," he said, pointing to the shadow on the ground. Once again, he stared at them each in turn. "This is our greatest test. We must be brave, and strong, and determined. If anyone doubts that we should make this journey, he should stay here. There will be no room for doubt when we're on our way."

The people of the tribe stood in silence. No one moved.

"Elbrau," Gorag called, "are you pledged to our people?"

The flintknapper gave a curt nod. "I am."

"Henik?"

Henik sighed. There was a deep weariness in his face. "You know it is so."

"Jobia?"

Jobia stared directly back at Gorag. "I am pledged," he said. His expression was unreadable.

"Good," said Gorag. Unexpectedly, he smiled, and Laena saw the strength and cunning in his old face. It occurred to her that he must have known that Jobia wouldn't leave his own mother to die. The way Gorag had arranged it, it was Jobia's responsibility now that Hirgar was coming with them, and Jobia would be to blame if the burden was too heavy. On the other hand, if the trek was successful, Gorag would take the credit for leading it.

"The journey will be hard," Gorag was saying. "But we are the Panther people. We are strong. We will prevail."

Everyone raised their arms and gave a cheer—a subdued cheer, for even now they were conscious that their enemies might be close enough to hear them. But Laena saw new hope in the faces of the people as they got ready to leave. She wished she could share it herself. She knew how arduous the trek would be, and she wondered how many of the people smiling around her would still be alive when they reached their destination.

* * *

They walked down the creek in single file, moving cautiously, pausing often to scan the land on either side. Soon they reached the Great River; and here they paused to assess the obstacle blocking their path.

The river was wide, and it was burdened with treacherous, jumbled ice. Normally, no one would attempt to cross it till the ice broke up in the spring thaw. But now, they had no choice.

Gorag lowered himself cautiously and started picking his way over the ice, testing it with the point of his spear. Elbrau followed him, and then Jobia, dragging Heese on the travois. They placed their feet with elaborate care; but even so, Jobia twice lost his balance and fell. The travois fell with him, jostling Heese, who groaned faintly.

Laena herself started across, holding her mother's arm with one hand and Moru with the other. They had gone just five paces when a sudden cracking sound made them stop motionless.

Moru let out a terrified wail. Laena turned to her and hugged her close, trying to quieten her. "The ice speaks loudly in this season," she said. "Don't you remember, from last spring?"

As the days grew a little warmer, the ice started shifting and grinding against itself. Sometimes, when the pressure was too great, weaker sections were crushed. The noise was explosive, resounding across the entire width of the river. In a month from now, when the spring melt came, the booming, cracking sounds would go on for days at a time.

Cautiously, they continued on across the river. It seemed to take an eternity. Once Laena stepped on a section of ice that seemed solid, only to find that it was a thin shell. Her foot plunged through and a whole section gave way, sending her falling into a cavity beneath. She would have been swallowed whole if her mother hadn't been holding her. As it was, she felt as if her arm had been wrenched out of its socket.

It was an immense relief when they climbed the bank on the opposite side. One by one they reached safety and gathered around Gorag, who stood grinning, slapping the shoulders of each one who reached him.

"The omens are good," he said when the last of the stragglers had arrived.

People were laughing with relief. It truly seemed as if the spirits were smiling on them. No one had been injured on the ice, and the river lay between as a barrier, keeping them safe from their enemies.

But Laena still felt fearful. She wondered why she experienced such a strange, dark foreboding. Was it merely her imagination—or did she sense a fate that the others were too blind to see?

Chapter 5

Laena bit a mouthful from the chunk of meat she had warmed over the fire and chewed it slowly, tormented by the unbearable temptation to swallow the precious food. She felt the women of the tribe staring at her, some of them with suspicion, some of them with revulsion. She ignored them as best she could and bent down over Heese where the woman lay in the travois, her breath coming in shallow gasps.

Repressing her squeamishness, Laena pressed her mouth to the injured woman and forced the chewed food between her lips. Heese swallowed feebly but greedily, and Laena felt her cheeks burn with embarrassment. She was treating the woman as if she were a child who was being weaned. But no one else was willing to make the effort, and Laena could not bear to see Heese die for lack of human kindness.

The meat was the last from the lion that Jobia had killed. Laena had to think for a moment to remember how long ago that had been. Three days? The time was blurring together in an unchanging vista of gray, gravelly soil streaked with snow. They were trekking across a featureless plain that seemed as if it stretched without a break to the horizon, and beyond.

There were hardly any animals in this wilderness. The reason was simple: without hills there were no banks of drifted snow, without snow there was little water, without water there were no plants, and if there were no plants, there was no food for animals to graze on.

Gorag had told them to hoard the meat for as long as possible. But now the last of it was gone, and Laena felt hopeless as she looked down at Heese and saw her trying to ask for more. She stroked her forehead and tucked the furs tighter around her. "Courage," she whispered, as much

to herself as to the wounded woman. "The men are trying
to decide what to do. We'll find a way."

Heese was shivering in her furs in the cold morning air,
and Laena was shivering too. She closed her eyes a moment, searching for the strength she needed.

She felt a tug on her arm and found Moru beside her,
staring up at her with sisterly concern. Moru was so young,
she didn't seem to believe the extent of the danger that faced
them all. So long as her mother and father were alive and
well, the child had the idea that everything would come out
all right.

She held out to Laena a piece of catskin crudely shaped
as a shallow bowl. In it was a small puddle of melted snow.
"For you, Laena."

Laena smiled, touched by the kindness. "Thank you, little one." She raised the skin to her lips and drank—then
felt a stab of guilt and turned to Heese. Reluctantly, she let
Heese swallow the rest of the water.

Everyone was suffering from thirst. The snow was thin,
and many cups of it had to be gathered and melted to pro-
duce a single cup of water. Moru and the other young children made themselves useful collecting it, but there was
never enough.

"At least we won't starve to death," said a voice close by.
Laena looked around and saw Laerni, the oldest of all the
women. She was a cousin of Elbrau, stooped but strong, her
face deeply lined, perpetually grim. She seldom spoke, and
when she did, she seldom had anything pleasant to say.

Laena looked at her questioningly. "We won't starve?"

Laerni gave her a crooked smile, and something malev-
olent flashed in her eyes. "You'll freeze first, girl, in this
weather."

Laena felt angry with herself for being so easily tricked.
She was so desperate, she could no longer think calmly and
clearly. And Laerni had taken advantage of that.

She felt herself trembling with anger. It was against all
her training to rebuke an elder, but Laena decided she didn't
care. She opened her mouth—then heard someone calling
her name.

It was her mother's voice. "Laena! The men are asking
for you!"

Laena turned, feeling disconcerted. Gorag, Henik, Elbrau, and Jobia were thirty paces away, hunkered down beside a miserable little fire that had been scraped together from some sparse animal droppings. Arla was close by, beckoning to her. Laena started over to them, puzzled that she should have been summoned.

Gorag wasted no time on preliminaries. "We have decided," he said staring at Laena, "what must be done."

She kneeled down beside her father, feeling grateful for the fire's meager warmth. She looked around at the men. In the past, she had always trusted their wisdom. Even now, she felt herself automatically assuming that they knew best. And yet—was it so?

She looked at Gorag's battle-scarred face. He could be ruthless and he could be cunning, there was no doubt of that. But was he truly a wise man? She shook her head in confusion. Her father was more cautious than Gorag, and caution was a part of wisdom. But in that case, why should Gorag be the chieftain? Was it just because he had always been fiercer than the other man?

Unaware of Laena's thoughts, Gorag was scratching lines in the stony earth. "We are partway between the Great River," he pointed to one line, "and the East River. Your father here believes we have two more days before we reach the East River. I have decided that this is so."

Laena nodded dumbly. Why was Gorag telling her this?

Henik coughed, a ritual signal that he wished to speak. "There will be game near the East River," he said. "It's too early for the migration, but there will be wolves and foxes, just the same as there were wolves and foxes near the Great River. If we can get there, we can eat again."

Laena felt herself salivate at the mere thought of food. Still she said nothing, deferring to the men around her.

"The trouble is, we may not get there," said Gorag. He bared his teeth and gestured in the direction of Heese. "Jobia's mother has held us back, as I knew she would. Now, our food is gone."

Laena glanced quickly at Jobia. His face looked grim, but he said nothing.

Elbrau spoke up. "Because Gorag blames Jobia, he has decided to send Jobia ahead to find game and bring it back to us." He paused thoughtfully. "There's some justice in that, and some sense. Jobia is the youngest and the strongest, so he'll travel fastest. He's a good hunter.''

Jobia still said nothing.

"I don't understand," Laena began, "why I—"

"You are to travel with him," said Henik.

Laena felt she must have misheard her father. She stared at him.

"You will leave at once," Henik went on. "There is very little time. If you start now and travel fast, you may just reach the river by tonight."

Elbrau fumbled in his pouch. "Here," he said. He opened his fingers in front of Laena. "Jobia has a spear that is his by right, because he used it to kill the lion. If you find trees by the river, tall enough so that their trunks can serve as shafts, these spearheads may be of use to you."

Dumbly, Laena took them. "I still don't understand—"

Henik stood up. His hand fell on her shoulder. "Come," he said.

Laena didn't try to protest any further. She walked with him till they were out of earshot of the others.

"This is a very dangerous time," he said to her softly. "You understand that, I am sure."

Laena sensed somehow that he was confiding in her in a way that he never had before. She nodded, afraid to speak.

"At this dangerous time, we have to speak more plainly than usual. Otherwise, we won't survive. But this plain talk is to be kept between you and me only. You understand?"

She nodded again. He had never addressed her quite like this before, and it felt like a privilege. At the same time, though, it scared her.

Henik nodded. "All right, I will tell you plainly that Jobia is headstrong. He's a danger to himself, and that means he's a danger to all of us. I don't trust him alone. I'd go with him myself, but I'm still weak from my wound. Elbrau, likewise, isn't strong enough."

"What about Gorag?" Laena broke in. "He's strong, and he's our chieftain—"

Henik's hand tightened painfully on her shoulder. "Gorag must stay with us." His eyes moved restlessly. "If he and Jobia left the tribe—" He paused. "That's not a good idea."

"You mean, they'd abandon us?" She stared at him in confusion.

Henik looked angry. "Never talk like that, about our chieftain. Do you understand?"

The words were like a slap. She blinked, feeling hurt and confused. "But, I thought—"

"I've said too much already. Listen, Laena. You are young, and you're almost as strong as Jobia. You can keep pace with him, and you can help him if necessary. The other children aren't old enough." He sighed. "If I had a male child, I would send him. But I only have you."

Her head was reeling as she tried to make sense of it all. He was honoring her with a task of extreme importance—yet at the same time, he was telling her she was second-best to a boy-child. He was confiding in her—but he was telling her that there were things she wasn't fit to know.

There wasn't time to resolve her confusion. Already he was pushing her back toward the others. "Go with Jobia." He paused, giving her a stern look. "Remember, we are depending on you." He squeezed her shoulders, then patted her cheek.

She studied his face and saw, to her surprise, a deep sadness. Suddenly it was clear to her: he didn't expect to see her again.

She drew herself up. "I won't disappoint you, Father," she said. To herself, she vowed: *I'll prove myself, the same as Jobia did when he killed the lion. I'll make you proud of me. I swear I will.*

Arla came over to her. She pressed something into Laena's hand—some scraps of cat meat, Laena realized. "I kept a little of my share," she said. "You'll need it more than I will."

Laena opened her mouth to object.

"No arguments." Arla's voice was as stern as always, but there was a softness in her eyes. "Say good-bye to Moru."

Laena turned and went to her sister. Numbly, she hugged the little girl.

Then Jobia was walking over to her. "So you're going to be my traveling companion," he said. He sounded as confused as she felt. It must be a blow to his pride, she realized, to have her escorting him.

"Believe me," Laena said, "it doesn't please me to travel with you, any more than it pleases you to travel with me."

Jobia scowled at her. He made quick feinting motions with his spear, and she saw the anger in his eyes. She stood her ground, though, and stared steadily back at him.

He grunted with irritation and stabbed the tip of his spear into the gravelly soil. He tossed his head impatiently. "So let's be on our way," he said.

Chapter 6

For an hour, the two of them strode fast across the snow-streaked plateau. Laena's chest ached from the cold, her leg muscles were cramping, there was a terrible emptiness inside her, and she was starting to feel dizzy. But she kept on in stoic silence, refusing to acknowledge her discomfort.

Finally they reached a dip in the land where snow had gathered more deeply and there was some tall grass among a scattering of scrawny bushes.

"We will rest here," said Jobia. He squatted down on a nearby rock, breathing hard, and Laena realized that the pace had been as hard on him as it had been on her. The knowledge renewed her own strength; and the strength fueled her defiance. She yearned to rest herself, but she decided not to allow herself that luxury. She noticed that there were dead branches on some of the little bushes, which were far too precious to ignore. She stumbled over to them, gathered as many as possible, and piled them on a dry, flat rock. Then she slumped down, still gasping for breath, and took a set of firesticks from her pouch.

She was so dizzy, she dropped the sticks. She had to pause and wait for her head to clear. Then she picked the sticks up, carefully piled some fragments of tinder in a hollow in one of them, and fitted the other into it. She pressed her palms on either side of the vertical stick and started rubbing her hands to and fro, spinning it. Soon the tinder was turning black and smoldering. She blew on it. A spark flared; and another. She piled on more fragments of tinder, and tiny pieces of bark. Within a short time, a fire was burning.

Jobia watched her as she worked. "You are strong," he said with a mixture of resentment and respect.

She glanced at him, trying not to show the satisfaction

that she felt. Then she turned back to the fire and crouched over it, trapping as much of its heat as she could.

Jobia moved over and positioned himself so that the fire lay between them. "I see now," he went on, "that it's true, what Gorag said."

She looked at his face. He had dark eyes, a wide, slightly sullen mouth, and a square jaw. She might have found him good-looking, if he hadn't been so unpleasant to her in the past. She wondered why he was showing her some respect now. Something had changed in him, and she didn't think it was just because she had managed to keep pace with him. "What did Gorag say?" she asked.

He narrowed his eyes. "That you are almost a woman now. Your time is near."

She made a noise of irritation. "You and Gorag have no right—"

"When men are together, they have a right to discuss anything they choose." He looked down at her body. "You'll make a fine woman, I'm thinking."

"Quiet!" She raised her hand as if to strike him.

Quickly, he seized her wrist.

For a moment, the two of them matched their strength, and the only sound was their harsh breathing. Jobia was stronger than she was; it angered her to admit it, but it was true. Inexorably, he started forcing her arm backward.

She gave a little cry of frustration and tried to wrench her arm free.

He kept his grip. She smelled his musky body scent as he levered himself up onto his feet and pushed forward with all his weight, forcing her backward.

"Stop!" she shouted at him. Her anger now was turning to fear.

His face was flushed and his breath was coming faster. "Perhaps your time has come already, and you've been concealing it," he said. "Why else would your father send you out here alone with me?"

"No!" she shouted. "That's not so!"

He forced her down till she found herself lying on her back beneath him. The ground was hard and cold under her shoulders. She tried to seize him by his hair, but he held her wrists down and pressed the shaft of his spear across them, so that he could keep her pinned with one hand. She writhed and tried to kick him, but his body was so heavy she couldn't drag her knee up. She felt him fumbling in her furs.

"I'll tell everyone," she screamed at him. "You'll be punished for this. They'll cast you out."

He stared down at her. His face was less than a hand's breadth from hers. She saw a vein pulsing at his temple, and saw the angry desire in his eyes. "The laws of our tribe mean nothing here," he said. She heard just a hint of uncertainty in his voice, though. He knew how serious it was for a man to take a woman before she had come of age.

Laena shook her head violently from side to side. "I'll scream so loudly, they'll hear me across the plain. My father will come and kill you!"

"Be quiet." He moved his hand to cover her mouth.

She bit him, hard. He should have expected it, but he didn't. He swore and pulled back, and Laena seized her opportunity. She hurled him off her, scrambled up—and froze. Something had moved behind Jobia. A shadow.

She didn't have to speak. He saw the change in her eyes. Quickly, he turned.

As he did so, the shadow shifted and a gray shape emerged from behind a snowdrift. It came toward them, moving fast. There was a scrabbling of feet on loose stone, and a guttural roar.

The attacker was almost as large as a man, but clearly, it was a beast. A fanged cat, Laena realized. She scrambled backward in panic. She rolled over, jumped up, and ran.

Jobia was trying to bring up his spear to defend himself. Laena looked over her shoulder and saw the cat leaping at him. He had no time to aim his weapon; instead, he had to throw himself aside. The beast came so close that its claws grazed his arm. He shouted in fear and pain and swung his spear, hitting the cat's head as the momentum of its attack took it past him.

Laena felt torn with indecision. If she stopped, she'd risk being killed. But she couldn't abandon Jobia, even after the way he'd treated her.

She turned and waved her arms, trying to draw the cat's attention. "Hai! Hai!" she shouted. It paused, lashing its tail. It looked briefly in her direction, then back at Jobia, who was trying to edge away from it.

The cat was half starved, she saw, and a half-starved beast was always the most dangerous. Suddenly she realized how much she needed Jobia out here. She couldn't survive without his hunting skills. Grimly, she kicked at a ridge of frozen earth, loosened a clod, and hurled it. The missile struck the cat on its hindquarters, and it turned back toward her, snarling.

Jobia seized the moment. He scrambled up, lunged forward, and thrust hard with his spear. His timing was good, and the cat screamed with outrage as the flint tip struck its shoulder. It whirled around, hissing and spitting, and Jobia jumped back, still holding his spear, keeping the point of it aimed at the cat's eyes.

Laena threw another clod, this time hitting the beast on its sensitive nose. It looked at her again and seemed to reach a decision. It ignored Jobia and came bounding toward her. With a jolt of fear, she glimpsed jaws gaping wide, great curving teeth gleaming yellow.

Laena felt herself running, but her legs seemed to move with awful slowness. There was a ringing in her ears. She was so terrified her breath seemed trapped in her throat. She glanced back and saw the cat gathering itself to spring at her. She cried out despairingly.

Jobia threw his spear. It flew through the air and sank its tip in the rear haunches of the cat.

The beast howled in pain. For a moment it forgot about Laena as it stopped and tried to grab the spear in its jaws. But the spear was buried deep, just outside the cat's reach, and it stuck fast.

In fear now, the cat started backing away from Laena and Jobia. Its eyes were wide and its breath was coming in gasps. With a wail, it retreated the way it had come, moving in an awkward, limping run.

Laena was closest to it, and she saw it taking their only weapon, their only chance to defend themselves and kill game. Without really understanding what she was doing, she ran after it.

"No!" Jobia shouted. "Stop!"

But she couldn't stop. She ran wildly, desperately, her feet slipping on the icy ground.

The cat was crippled by the spear, so it couldn't move fast. Within a hundred paces, she caught up with it. She threw herself toward it with disregard for her own safety and seized the spear where it still dangled from the cat's haunches. She felt the rough wood of the shaft under her palms, seized it, and jerked at it savagely.

The weapon came free and she found herself losing her balance, slamming down on her side on the ground. The impact winded her, and for a moment she lay gasping. Somewhere behind her, she heard Jobia cursing, coming to her aid. But the cat was right in front of her. Seeing her stretched out defenselessly, its hunger overcame its fear. She saw it gathering itself to leap at her.

Laena had never used a spear. Women were not trained as hunters; they were not deemed fit. Still, she had seen the men practicing with their weapons often enough. As the cat sprang at her, she brought the spear up.

In that brief moment, she couldn't tell whether her aim was true or whether it was a matter of chance. But the point of the spear caught the cat in its mouth as it leaped at her, and the spear slid deep.

The shaft was wrenched out of her hands as the cat screamed and fell down with blood gushing from its throat. It writhed on the ground. Its claws raked her arm. She scrambled clear, her pulse thudding fast, her whole body trembling.

Jobia came up beside her, gave her a brief, furious look, then circled around the wounded cat. Quickly, he darted forward, seized the spear, and jerked it out of the beast's mouth.

"Careful!" Laena shouted. "It's dying, can't you see?"

"Yes. And it'll die faster now," Jobia said.

He was right: more blood was spurting since the spear had been pulled free. The cat made terrible coughing, screeching sounds. Laena watched in silence, not enjoying the spectacle, but proud of what she had done. She wished her father had been there to see. Her father, and Elbrau, and Gorag.

"You were lucky," Jobia was saying. "Very lucky."

"And brave besides," she said, giving him a challenging look.

He glowered at her. "I saved your life back there." He tossed his head.

"And maybe I saved your life, too," she said. "Not just

your life, either. The lives of all our people. They won't starve now.''

Jobia's face twisted as if he wanted to say something more. Finally he threw his spear down, turned, and strode away.

He stood staring out over the plain with his fists clenched at his sides, ignoring her. Laena felt a strange, secret satisfaction as she stooped, picked up the spear, then turned back toward the fanged cat and waited for it to die.

Chapter 7

While Jobia sat a few hundred paces away, Laena methodically gathered more fuel for the fire and set about skinning the beast that she had killed. Her instincts told her that they should drag it back to their people as quickly as possible, to satisfy the tribe's desperate need for food. But as Jobia had pointed out, the people were already heading this way and would arrive soon enough. It made better sense to wait for them.

She wanted to have food ready for them when they reached this little dip in the land. And sure enough, a while later, she had just started cooking the first strips of meat over the fire when the little group of tiny human figures came into view in the distance.

Jobia came marching down the slope toward her. "I'll take my spear now," he said. His tone was commanding. He paused a couple of paces from her and held out his hand.

Laena picked up the spear, but she kept it by her side. "I don't think so, Jobia."

He stepped closer. His anger was returning, worse than before. "I said give it to me!"

She felt scared defying him, but she shook her head. "I don't trust you. I'll keep this spear till my people are here to protect me."

He gave her a murderous look. "If you tell them—"

"I won't tell them what you tried to do to me." She picked up the spear and stood facing him. "But I won't give you your spear till they get here."

It gave her a tense, churning feeling in her stomach, facing him this way. It was almost unthinkable for a woman to do what she was doing. But she told herself that if she had had the courage to kill a wild beast, she should certainly have the courage to go against Jobia.

He edged even closer. "If you don't give it to me, I'll have to take it from you."

She sprang to her feet and angled the spear toward his throat. "No!" she shouted.

He hesitated, looking surprised as he saw the determination in her eyes. She noticed a jaw muscle clench at the side of his face. He lowered his head like a young bull. "I'll tell Gorag about this. I'll tell him you defied me."

"You do that," she shouted back at him, "and I'll tell everyone that you tried to force yourself on me before it's even my time to become a woman."

He balled his fists, and she saw him measuring the distance between them. Her grip tightened on the spear, and she felt her body start to tremble again, the same as when she had faced the cat. At the same time, though, she marveled at the power that the weapon gave her. So long as it was in her hands, Jobia's authority as a man was stolen away as if it had never been.

He spat on the ground. "All right," he muttered, "keep the spear. It makes no difference. The people are almost here anyway." He turned his back and strode away.

Laena felt her face grow warm as a feeling first of surprise, then of exultation flowed through her. He had given in to her. She had achieved something that had never been hers before. Was this the reason why men were so possessive of their weapons and their right to use them? So they could feel superior not only to animals, but to women as well?

She watched Jobia march away, trying to hold on to the remnants of his pride. When he'd retreated to a safe distance, Laena squatted back down beside the cooking fire. At the same time, though, she took care to keep an eye on the young hunter, and she kept the spear close at hand.

There was much excitement in the tribe when they finally arrived. Everyone fell upon the meat, more concerned with satisfying their hunger than with learning how the beast had been found and killed.

Henik and Arla greeted Laena with tears in their eyes, and she felt a great wave of relief as they hugged her. All the vitality suddenly seemed to ebb from her muscles, leaving her feeling weak and helpless. The tension and panic of the past hour seemed to catch up with her in a rush, and she had to sit and rest.

Bit by bit she told Henik what had happened, only leaving out the part where Jobia had tried to molest her. She saw pride in Henik's face, but a look of concern besides. He ruffled her thick black hair in a gesture of affection she had known since her early childhood. But there was a new manner about him as he did it. He seemed troubled. She wanted to ask him—hadn't she pleased him? Hadn't she done what he wanted?

Later, as the people gathered around the campfire, Gorag called on her to tell them what she had told Henik about the killing of the fanged cat. She still saw the uncertainty in his eyes, though, and she kept her story brief, taking care to mention that Jobia had been the one who had wounded the animal and stopped it from attacking her.

Still, her story made an impression on the tribe. Everyone stared at her, except for Jobia, who wouldn't look at her at all. At first she thought that the people must be grateful to her for giving them meat. And maybe they were; but there was something else in their eyes, as well. They looked worried. She had done something that no woman should have done, which meant that they didn't know how to deal with her anymore.

Gorag stood up when she finished speaking. "Thanks to you, Laena, and you, Jobia, we have enough food to take us to the East River." Gorag's eyes flickered, noting the quick look that passed between the two of them. He turned to Henik, and his scarred lips pulled back in a savage grin. "You have a formidable daughter, my old friend. And look, she's still holding the spear." He moved forward and plucked it out of her hands. He turned and gave it to Jobia. "There," he said. "I feel safer now."

There was a shout of laughter from the tribe, and the tension that Laena had sensed was erased. Gorag had reassured them, she realized. He was telling them that Laena was still a young girl, and nothing had changed.

She felt her cheeks burning. One day, she vowed to herself, she would make them realize that something *had* changed. She was no longer the same young girl that she had been before. And one day, they would have to face that fact.

* * *

That evening, as the men and women of the tribe lay down together, Laena huddled close to her mother. "Why is it," she whispered as the people settled in to sleep, "that men hunt while women sew, and men lead while women follow? Who decided it should be this way?"

Laena felt her mother shift beside her, trying to find comfort on the hard ground. "There are no answers to questions like those," she murmured. "Each of us has a place that we take, just as each animal has a way to run and sleep and hunt its prey. Would you ask me who decided that a caribou should flee from a lion? That's just the way things are, and how they have to be."

Laena lay staring at the stars for a moment, listening to the breathing of the men and women around her as they sank into slumber. "Mother," she persisted, "a caribou could never hunt a lion, because it hasn't got any claws or ripping teeth. But—I'm not so different from a man. I have hands to throw a spear. I killed a fanged cat. Why can't I have the same respect that a man has, if I can do the same things that he does?"

Her mother grunted, in irritation or weariness. "Killing the cat was brave and good, daughter. But you'll be a woman soon, and you must take on the duties of a woman, or you'll find yourself rejected by the tribe. Your willfulness is already attracting attention. There'll be more trouble with men like Gorag and Jobia if you continue as you are. You should learn your place. Otherwise, they'll try to put you in it anyway, and the lessons will be painful."

Laena felt a pang of anxiety—and of anguish. She wanted to shout out that it wasn't her fault, and it wasn't fair. "I still don't understand why it has to be this way," she said.

Her mother turned, and Laena saw the woman's wise face looming beside her in the faint moonlight. "There are forces in the world, Laena. Forces of nature. You must bend with them as a reed bends with the wind. Otherwise, they may break you."

Sometime in the middle of the night—when the fire had burned low and the moon had set, and the darkness was almost total—Laena woke with a start. She felt her pulse beating fast, and she wondered what had roused her so suddenly. She was still surrounded by the slumbering forms of the tribespeople, and her mother's body lay comfortingly close beside her.

But everything felt subtly different. People tended to shift in their sleep, as those on the edge of the group grew cold and burrowed back into the mass of bodies at the center, while those at the center sometimes moved in the opposite direction, seeking fresh air.

A hand fell upon Laena's forehead, and she realized with a shock that the person beside her was no longer her mother. "You told her," a voice whispered, while the mittened hand groped downward and pressed over Laena's mouth. "You told Arla what I did."

Laena reached up and quickly knocked the hand aside. "Jobia?" she hissed. "Is that you?"

His hand crept back, nudging her shoulder, then her chest, poking at her in the blackness. "I heard you whispering to her," he murmured, his lips close to Laena's ear. "You told her!"

"I did not. I kept my word." Laena wondered if she should cry for help; but if she did, what could she accuse Jobia of doing? She didn't want to draw any more attention to herself than she had already.

He was silent for a moment. "Maybe you're telling the truth," he muttered. "But I don't trust any girl who did what you did to me today. And I warn you, I haven't finished with you. One day I'll have my chance, and I'll make you give me whatever I want." He rolled on top of her, pinning her with his weight, and she felt his breath on her face. "You'll learn how a woman should act with a man. And after I've finished with you, you may even thank me for it."

Before she could protest or cry out, he lifted himself off her. She felt him crawling swiftly away, till she could no longer tell where he lay among all the others around her.

Laena felt tears itching at the corners of her eyes. For a few brief hours, she'd imagined that she'd proved herself somehow. Yet now it seemed that she'd merely made herself unpopular. No one respected her; no one thanked her for what she had done.

Maybe Arla was right, and she should bend to the ways of her people. But would that mean surrendering herself to

Jobia, if he decided someday to take her as his mate? It was inconceivable. She would rather be cast out.

It seemed a cruel choice indeed, between one kind of misery and another. Surely, there had to be another way.

Chapter 8

During the next day, and the day after that, she tried to be quiet and uncomplaining and helpful to her elders. When she found Jobia staring at her, she merely looked away. If her father gave her a task, she obeyed unquestioningly.

It cost her some of her pride, but she felt she had no choice—for the time being. The trek across the plateau was still long and hard, even with the meat of the fanged cat to sustain them. It was no time to be stirring up dissent.

She spent as much time as she could with Moru, playing with her little sister when the tribe paused to rest, and concocting make-believe stories while they marched side by side.

"Once upon a time," Laena said, building a fable as she went along, "there was a fearless warrior who hunted a white panther for two days and two nights. Finally he trapped the panther in a steep fissure in the rocks. The panther begged the hunter not to kill it, for it was an enchanted creature that could speak, and if the hunter spared its life, it promised to grant him one wish. So the hunter said he wished for a woman who was as wise and as strong as himself, so that they could share their lives together. And the panther turned into a beautiful woman, and the hunter put down his spear, and they lived happily ever after."

And Moru said, "Is that a True Thing, Laena?"

And Laena answered, "No, little one. But wouldn't it be nice if it was?"

As the journey wore on, Moru's young legs became tired, and Laena had to carry her some of the way.

"I wish I were like you, Laena," the little girl said in a voice that sounded small and sad.

"In what way?" Laena asked.

"You know so many things. And you're strong. When

I'm older, I want to be strong like you. I want to learn to throw a spear, just like you, when you killed the fanged cat.''

Laena shook her head sadly. "I think you should not try to be like me," she said. "It's not such a fine thing. My strength makes men jealous and angry. It turns them against me.''

Moru frowned. Her eyes looked dark and stern. "Who's turned against you, Laena?''

Laena sighed, wishing she hadn't been drawn into this conversation. "It doesn't matter, little one. They will not harm me.''

"They mustn't!" Moru said, her voice even grimmer than before. "If anyone hurts you, Laena, I swear I'll kill them.''

Laena laughed. "Thank you. But I hope I won't need your protection.''

"I mean it, Laena!" Moru scowled with childlike conviction.

Laena put her arm around the little girl's shoulders. "I'm sorry. I wasn't making fun of you. I'm glad you'll be watching out for me.''

Moru nodded to herself. She seemed placated by Laena's apology, but her face was as serious as ever.

On the next day, Jobia's mother died.

Heese had never really recovered her strength after losing so much blood from the wounds that had been inflicted by the White Bear hunters. The constant bumping and jostling of her travois had also taken its toll, and for the past day, she had been in a coma.

Under a bleak sky of ragged gray clouds, the tribe gathered around her lifeless form. Laena looked at Henik, Arla, and the other people she had known since her earliest years, and she saw that life was as fragile and brief as a flame: it must be fed constantly with fuel, or it would flicker out in a moment.

She looked away from the people who still lived. She turned her attention to the one who had died. Tentatively, she touched Heese's face, remembering the times she had fed the woman and tried to care for her. The skin was hard and cold, already freezing in the bitter wind.

Elbrau began reciting the ritual prayer for the dead, but

Laena hardly heard the familiar words. She looked again from one face to another, as the people stood huddled in their furs with their eyes downcast. One day, sooner or later, they, too, would be cold and pale and lifeless. The thought made Laena shiver. Again she found herself asking that seemingly unanswerable question: Why did it have to be this way?

Elbrau made the ceremony as brief as possible. Laena saw in the faces of the tribespeople that they had little time or sympathy for Heese's fate, so long as their own was in question. They were eager to reach the East River, and they didn't want any more painful reminders of their own mortality.

Even Jobia seemed unmoved as Elbrau finished speaking. The flintknapper stooped and rolled Heese off the travois and onto the ground, then started methodically stripping her furs from her lifeless form. It made sense, of course: nothing should be abandoned or wasted so long as they were stranded on this barren plain. But it seemed heartless, nonetheless, and Laena had to turn away from the sight.

There was no way to dig a grave in the frozen soil, and there were no large stones to build a cairn. So they simply abandoned Heese's lifeless form under the gray sky. Laena looked back a few times as the trek continued, and each time Heese's body was a smaller shape in the wilderness; until finally it disappeared from view altogether.

That evening, when the only light in the sky was a thin red line to the southwest, they finally reached their goal.

"Ho!" A shout came from far ahead, where Henik was scouting the land. "The river! I see its ice!"

A thin cheer erupted from the band. Gorag's back stiffened and he grinned, taking the news as a personal triumph. "Good fortune is with us now," he proclaimed loudly. "This journey tested our strength as it was never tested before, and we have passed that test. I sense the spirits smiling on us. The time of suffering is over at last."

"We still have to cross the river," Elbrau said quietly. "It'll be night by the time we actually reach its banks, and our food is almost gone."

Gorag shook his head dismissively. "I fancy there will

be game by the river. We'll eat well, soon enough.'' He clapped his hands. "We'll camp tonight on that ridge. No need to ration our meat. We'll have all we can eat, tomorrow. Think of that, people!''

"Maybe so," said Elbrau.

Laena looked at his face, and she saw doubt etched into it. Why was he so doubtful, while Gorag was so confident? It made her uneasy, because she trusted Elbrau more.

But there wasn't time for her to wonder and worry about it. She was soon searching for tinder and droppings to build a fire, as the Panther People settled down for the night and the glow of sunset faded in the sky. By the time they were huddled around the flames, the landscape was lost in darkness. In the distance, though, Laena could see the river as an expanse of ghostly white ice, a sprawling swath that lay at the foot of the long slope where they had made their camp.

Gorag, meanwhile, was infecting the others with his good spirits, and there was talking and laughter—the first laughter that Laena had heard in many days. He told some hunting stories, weaving fables of outrageous courage. Then Elbrau was persuaded to tell some legends of the Times Before, when there had been no men or women on this world and the animals had played together in a great green garden where there was such abundance, such plenty, no creature ever needed to prey upon another.

As the food warmed her belly and the fire warmed her face, Laena found her attention wandering. The magic of the old stories didn't seduce her tonight. She stared away from the fire, out across the valley. The Great River, beside their old winter campground, had been a formidable obstacle. But the East River ahead of them was many times wider, sheathed in ice that looked far more treacherous. Laena stared at it, remembering how it had looked the last time they had come on their annual spring migration. The ice had melted, the water had been shallow, and they had found a stretch where they could simply wade across.

But spring was still several moons distant, and the ice was still heaped high. How did Gorag imagine they could cross it? How could he seem so casually confident?

* * *

That night, she dreamed. It was an intense vision such as she had not experienced in many moons. She saw a human figure wandering through a white wasteland with his arms outstretched as if he were blind. She wanted to cry out a warning to him, for she knew something terrible was about to happen. But even though she strained to speak, her throat refused to utter a sound. And when she tried to move, her limbs refused to obey.

Then the figure in the whiteness turned to face her, and she saw with a shock that it was Jobia. "Laena!" he shouted. His face was hideous with anger and frustration as he blundered sightlessly toward her. "Laena, I swear, when I find you—"

She felt fear not just for his fate but for her own. The landscape darkened as if a cloud had passed over the sun. She saw a giant black bird swooping down, spiraling around Jobia, spreading a terrible stench of decay. The bird screamed and lashed out with one of its huge legs. Its claws gleamed like ice and were wickedly sharp. One of them sliced into the back of Jobia's neck.

His head spun away from his body, and blood gushed into the whiteness. His body fell over, thrashing and bleeding, and there was a booming sound, like thunder, as if the heavens themselves were marking the terrible spectacle.

Laena woke suddenly. Her muscles were straining, her pulse was pounding, and her mouth was dry. The booming sound hadn't been her imagination, she realized. The ice on the East River was groaning and cracking, just like the ice on the Great River. Even now, the echoes were dying away across the valley.

But the white wasteland of her vision was nowhere to be seen. There was nothing but darkness. It was still night, and the people of her tribe slumbered peacefully around her.

Laena shuddered. She tried to calm herself. Her dream reminded her that Jobia had vowed to seize her and force her to obey him. Even now, she found herself peering into the darkness, afraid that he might be sidling up beside her.

But that was not her only concern. Her dreams were sometimes windows into the future. Several times, she had experienced intense visions that had come true, in some fashion, days or months later.

She saw again the giant claw slicing Jobia's head from his body, and she moaned softly. She couldn't imagine how such a thing could happen in the real world. And even though she had come to hate Jobia, she prayed that her dream would be a false prophecy.

Chapter 9

As dawn streaked the sky pink and gray and the first rays of sunlight warmed the frozen river, the ice cracked and boomed more loudly and more often. The noise roused the sleeping tribespeople and they struggled up, stamping their feet and slapping themselves to drive the chill from their bones.

Some people were grumbling about being woken up, and about the lack of food. But one by one the people fell silent as they looked down at the frozen expanse at the bottom of the valley—and saw the prize that waited for them on the opposite bank, if they could only reach it.

The low hills were dotted with moving shapes. Caribou, scores of them—one of the great migratory herds, grazing on what was left of the grass and brush, gathering for the move north to their mating grounds.

"See?" Gorag turned, grinning as he had the night before. "We'll be eating well, soon enough." He slapped his hands against the furs on his chest and laughed out loud.

"The ice is treacherous at this time," said a quiet voice. "It won't be easy to find a path across it."

Laena turned, realizing it was her father who had spoken.

Gorag spat on the ground. "How would you know about that, eh, my old friend?" He studied Henik through narrowed eyes. "None of us has ever been here this early in the year. The ice could still be solid."

Henik returned Gorag's stare. "The days are warming. The ice will be soft, laced with water. I think you know this for a fact—old friend."

Gorag sighed and shook his head, as if it tested his goodwill to have to deal with such irritating pessimism. "You think I can't find a way across? Is that it?"

Henik paused. Laena saw him studying Gorag as if trying

to see into the man. "I've led your hunting parties for ten years," he said quietly. "I've taken your hunters across river ice more times than I can count. I've done it more times than you have, Gorag. And even I would think twice before taking our people onto that ice."

Gorag ambled slowly over to Henik. All the people were watching, as the day slowly brightened. Laena saw looks of hope in their faces. Clearly, they wanted to believe in Gorag. Their survival depended on it.

Gorag clapped Henik on his good shoulder. The chieftain was no longer grinning; his face had become deeply serious. "I think I understand you, my friend," he said. "You were badly wounded by Jalenau's spear. You aren't as strong as you once were. You're telling me that it's too big a task for you to take us across that river." He nodded sympathetically. "I understand."

Henik shook the man's hand away. "No," he said sharply. "I'm saying it's too big a task for any of us, wounded or not."

Gorag paused thoughtfully for a moment. "What about the boy?" he said.

"Jobia? You want him to lead the way?" Henik laughed scornfully. "He has no experience. It's impossible."

Gorag held up his hand. "Think about it, my friend. He's quick and clever, he's strong, and he weighs less than you or me. We can tie a catgut line around his waist, so if he falls through—"

Henik angrily shook his head. "It would be much more sensible to explore the side of the river that we're on. There could be game to the south, for all we know."

"I'll hear none of that!" Gorag's voice was suddenly loud and angry. "You know yourself, the herds always follow the eastern shore." He turned to Elbrau. "Am I right?"

Elbrau nodded reluctantly. "Yes, but—"

"We would starve to death, searching up and down. Have you forgotten there's no food left?" Gorag grimaced. "No, we have to find a way across, and Jobia is our best chance." He turned quickly. "What do you say, boy?"

Jobia was standing close by. As Laena watched him, his face reddened. "You had said I was to be a man, after I killed the cat by the creek." He sounded embarrassed, and he couldn't bring himself to look Gorag in the face.

Gorag laughed. "Why, so I did." He slapped Jobia's arm. "And so you are, a man. Of course you are. Does anyone doubt that?" He glanced around at the rest of the tribe, then turned back to Jobia. "So, brave one, how does it strike you, this task I'm talking about now? You think you're strong enough to do it?"

"Of course." Jobia drew himself up. "Of course I can do it!"

Laena had a sudden vision of him feeling his way across the white ice—like a blind man, with his arms outstretched. She was gripped by a moment of pure horror. "No!" she shouted.

Everyone fell silent. They turned and stared at her.

Gorag scowled at her. She saw the anger in his eyes. "How dare you speak that way, when men are conferring together. Henik, I swear, you should teach this daughter of yours some better manners."

"But it's too dangerous!" Laena blurted out. She hesitated, feeling the silence of the tribe like a blow against her. "Jobia will be—will be hurt."

"Enough!" Gorag shouted. "Be silent!"

It was hopeless, Laena realized. They couldn't see what she had seen. Even if she told them about her dream, they would dismiss it.

She looked from Gorag to Henik. He was looking at her with an expression of weary regret. She turned to Jobia—and found him smiling at her. To him, of course, it sounded as if she was concerned about his welfare. He must think that she secretly desired him, after all.

She gave him a look of disgust, then turned her back.

"All right," she heard Gorag saying behind her. "We'll tie the gut around Jobia's chest, under his arms. Henik, you'll follow right behind him and tell him where to tread. Elbrau, you and I will follow right behind, and we'll both keep hold of the line. Come on, everyone! To the river!"

"Why did you say he shouldn't go on the ice?" Moru asked as the people moved down the slope, talking excitedly among themselves.

"I dreamed, last night," said Laena. She clenched her fists in frustration. "I dreamed that he'll die."

Moru frowned. She was silent for a long moment. "This dream," she said finally, "it was a True Thing?"

"Yes," said Laena. "I'm afraid so."

"Then it will be true," Moru said with a shrug. "It will be true, and it makes no different what you say to anyone."

Laena sighed. She hugged Moru. "I'm afraid you're right," she said quietly. "All the same, I had to try to stop them. But I'm no match for Gorag. No one is. He planned this whole thing."

Moru stared up at her. "Planned what, Laena?"

"He told us to eat all the food, so we'd be hungry this morning, and desperate. He knew we'd see game across the river. He knows it's dangerous—and knew how to get Jobia to take the risk." She shook her head, as surprised by her own insight as she was by Gorag's schemes. In the past, she had never thought twice about decisions that were made by the elders of the tribe. But since the massacre, everything was different. She had become responsible for her own survival as she never had been before, and it had made her question everything around her.

Moru stared up at Laena, not quite understanding. "Gorag is our leader. He takes care of us."

"Gorag takes care of Gorag," said Laena, speaking more to herself. She realized that it was no accident that he had picked Jobia for this dangerous task. Jobia had the least experience, so he was the least valuable. And he was more ambitious than the two other men. He could become a threat one day to Gorag's own authority.

Laena turned suddenly to Moru. She seized her by the shoulders and stared intently into her eyes. "Gorag is not a good man," she said. "You understand? Be careful of him. Do not trust him. Remember this!"

Moru stared at her, too shocked to speak. Laena could see in the little girl's eyes that she understood, and she would remember.

By the time the sun had crept above the far range of hills, Jobia was poised on the riverbank with the catgut knotted around him. Henik tied the free end of the cord around the wrist of his good arm. The man's face was full of doubt, but he said nothing.

"Ready?" said Gorag.

Before either of them could answer, there was a violent cracking, crashing sound, even louder than those that had come before. Laena felt the ground shudder under her feet, and she saw ice and water flying into the air, gleaming in the sun. Less than forty paces away, two blocks of tough, greenish ice had crushed a weaker area between them, reducing it to fragments. The force was frightening in its explosive power, and for the first time, Jobia looked unsure of himself.

But still he nodded. "I'm ready," he said.

Laena watched helplessly as he started out into the ice, feeling his way, just like the figure in her dream, a black silhouette against the white. Henik followed, calling out warnings and advice. Painfully slowly, they started picking a safe path.

One by one, the rest of the people followed. Elbrau went first, then Gorag, then the women and children.

"You see, Laena," said her mother, holding her hand tightly as they stepped onto the ice themselves, "it will be all right."

"But Laena had a dream," said Moru, holding Laena's other hand. "She dreamed—"

Arla shook her head impatiently. "This is no time for foolishness. Watch where you put your feet, child. Careful!"

For a little while, there was no sound but the grunts and gasps of the people as they struggled across the slick, fragile surface. Every footstep was an adventure; time and again, Laena found a thin frozen shell giving way under her weight, plunging her hands or feet into pockets of frigid water.

But they reached the midpoint of the river; and she dared to think that perhaps she had been wrong, or had misinterpreted the vision that had come to her.

A deep, shuddering, groaning sound came from beneath them. Henik dropped quickly to his hands and knees. "All of you, get down!" he shouted. "All of you!"

Laena, her mother, and the rest of the people hurried to obey. Henik turned back to Jobia. "You, too! Do what I say!"

Jobia glared at Henik. He looked resentful. He never liked taking orders. He'd been chosen to lead the party across the ice, and all the way Henik had been telling him what to do.

Why should he drop down on his hands and knees like an animal? There was no danger—

The ice rose up under him, screeching, crashing, destroying itself.

Jobia's look of resentment became a look of panic.

The ice boomed and broke. Huge shards of it flew with terrible momentum. Jobia screamed as a spinning segment smashed into the side of his neck. Its wicked edge sliced deep, and Jobia flailed his arms. He fell backward, spraying blood in a wide arc.

The roar of the ice faded away to echoes, and the shrieks and oaths of the people could be heard. Laena struggled back up onto her feet, staring in horror. Never had she found a vision so accurately, horrifyingly confirmed.

"Jobia!" Henik shouted. He was still on his hands and knees. He scrambled forward, cursing. "Help me here, Elbrau. Gorag! Help me!"

But there could be no help. Jobia's blood was making a terrible rushing sound as it spurted rhythmically from the wound in his neck and spattered across the ice, steaming in the morning sunlight. Henik tried to contain it by pressing with the palm of his hand but the flow was so powerful it forced its way out.

Several of the women started wailing, but Laena found herself staring in silence. Jobia was lying on his back with his mouth open, his eyes closed, his limbs trembling with shock. The blood had formed a pool bigger than Jobia himself.

The flow from his neck gradually diminished. Jobia's face turned pale. His limbs ceased their trembling. He made a guttural, choking sound, and then he lay still—as lifeless as his mother had been the previous day.

Henik got up onto his feet. He was saturated with blood. He pointed at Gorag, and red droplets fell on the ice below. "You're to blame for this!" he shouted. "I warned you. Everyone here heard me warn you."

"No." Gorag faced Henik squarely. "You said it was dangerous, but you never said that the boy would die." He paused, waiting for the words to sink in. And then, without warning, he turned. His lips pulled back from his teeth, and he pointed at her. "You, *you* were the one who said this would happen. She jinxed us, do you see?" Gorag glanced quickly around at the rest of the tribe, then nodded, confirming his own judgment. "She jinxed us with her talk about Jobia dying. *She's* the one to blame."

Laena was too startled, too dismayed to speak. But Henik was already moving toward Gorag, grabbing him, spinning him around. "My daughter meant no harm. She cared for Jobia's life." His eyes narrowed. "Perhaps she even cared for it more than you."

Gorag knocked Henik's hand aside. He lowered his head. "You're forgetting yourself, Henik." His voice was low, but there was a nasty edge to it, and the sound chilled Laena.

"I tell you the girl is blameless!" Henik shouted, although Laena could see he was intimidated by the chieftain.

"Blameless, is she? You trust her, eh?"

"Of course I trust her! She saved our lives, man, when she killed the fanged cat. You dined on its meat yourself. Have you forgotten that?"

Gorag nodded slowly. "Very well. If you trust her, then you should let her lead the way now."

Laena felt dizzy. A numbness spread through her. Was she now to be sacrificed?

"Gorag," said a voice from behind Laena—her mother's voice, she suddenly realized. "You killed Jobia. You will not kill my daughter, too."

There was a confused murmuring among the Panther People. Arla had never spoken out like this against the chieftain. No woman had ever done such a thing.

Gorag glared at her. Then his eyes moved, assessing the mood of the rest of the tribe. When he spoke, he wasn't angry, as Laena had expected. His voice was calm and reasonable. "You know that I'm just trying to save our lives," he said. "You know that. Your daughter is fast on her feet, and she's lighter than Jobia. She's the best scout we have. You can see the sense in that."

"She is a girl-child!" Arla shouted. Her voice was shrill with anger.

Gorag smiled. "She is no ordinary girl-child. She hunts, she kills—"

Arla's grip tightened around Laena's shoulders. "You shall not take her."

Gorag sighed. "Then what would you have us do? Turn around and go back, so we can starve?"

"You are our leader!" Arla screamed at him. "Lead us!"

Before Gorag could reply, Henik held up his hand. "Enough of this," he said. His voice was quiet, but the sternness of it acted like an antidote. Everyone turned to look at him.

"I will find the way forward," said Henik.

There was a moment's silence.

"No," Arla said. Her voice was no longer shrill, but still there was an edge of anger—and fear. "Your wound hasn't had a chance to heal properly. It isn't safe."

"I know the ice better than anyone." There was an implacable finality in his tone.

Laena shut her eyes for a moment. She tried to see forward, tried to imagine Henik's fate, tried to see it in her mind. But all she saw was the redness of her own eyelids.

Well, it made no difference. She knew that if Henik fell, she would blame herself. She couldn't bear the thought that she had allowed her mother to protect her, and her father might die as a result.

Carefully, she disengaged herself from her mother's arm. "Stop," she called out.

Henik paused. He turned and looked.

"I will lead the way." She started forward.

"No!" Arla wailed.

"Gorag is right," said Laena. "I am no ordinary girl-child."

Chapter 10

Her parents protested, and even Moru clung to her and begged her not to do it. In the end, though, there was no one who could stop Laena; because what she said was true. She was fast and light, and she had the best chance of leading the tribe to safety.

Grimly, Henik bound the catgut around her waist. She tried not to look at the blood on it; tried not to think about Jobia's body still lying nearby. She kept telling herself that anything was better than seeing her father fall to his death and feeling that she had caused it.

"Do exactly as I say," he told her quietly. "If Jobia had done as I said, he'd still be alive now."

"I'm not as headstrong as he was," she said.

A faint, weary smile appeared on Henik's face. "Not quite," he said. He ruffled his hand through her hair. "Anyway, take this spear. Use the tip to test the ice before you step on it. If you're moving forward and you don't trust the surface, hold the shaft level between your hands—yes, like that—so it'll support you if you fall into a hole. Understand?"

She nodded wordlessly. Now that she was actually going through with her plan, she felt consumed with fear. She didn't trust herself to speak.

"I have this end of the cord secure around my wrist," Henik went on. He turned to Elbrau. "Follow close behind me."

The flintknapper nodded. "If Laena falls, I'll be here to help pull her back."

Part of Laena wanted to shout out that she had changed her mind—that she was too young and scared to do this. But then she glanced at Gorag, and she saw that his expression had shifted. There was a look of satisfaction in his eyes, as if he took pleasure in her plight.

Anger filled her, and suddenly she wasn't afraid anymore. She imagined how it would feel to defy Gorag's expectations. If she could guide his people to safety, displaying the courage he lacked himself, maybe it wouldn't be so easy for him to manipulate them in future.

"Are you ready?" Henik asked her.

"Yes," she said. Her voice was strong and clear.

He patted her shoulder. "Fortune go with you."

Cautiously, she stepped forward.

She placed her feet with exquisite care, moving onto a level sheet of ice that seemed heavy and solid. Yet as soon as it took her weight, it made a fracturing sound like flint struck with a hammerstone. The sheet collapsed into fragments in front of her and she found herself teetering, staring down into a deep cavity with fast-running river water at the bottom. The water was probably shallow—hardly enough to drown her. But that, she knew, was not the real danger. The water could drag her under the ice, or its temperature alone could kill her. Her sodden furs would offer no protection from the chill, so that even if she was dragged back to safety, she would still be likely to die from the cold.

Henik tugged gently on the cord, helping her back from the brink. "One step toward me," he called to her, calm and reassuring. "Good. Now try to the left, there."

Carefully, probing with the spear, she did as he said. The ice, she realized, was even more treacherous in the center of the river than it had been near the banks. Fresh water had been seeping down the hillsides as the snow began to melt, and this water had fed the river, which undermined the ice sheet. Meanwhile, the warmth of the sun had smoothed the upper surface, blurring the edges of the plates, making it hard for Laena to tell which areas were still solid and which were eggshell-thin.

She jabbed the ice ahead of her and found a path that seemed safe. Quickly she made a mark with the point of the spear to guide the people who would be following after her.

She moved onward. Again and again, she struck with the spear and found the ice collapsing, revealing a dark cavity below. Soon she found her arms aching from the work she was doing. She glanced behind her—and realized that with all her effort, the winding path had taken her only twenty paces toward the opposite bank.

"Be patient," Henik called to her, sensing her thoughts. "You're doing well. Don't hurry."

She nodded, then turned back to the ice before her. It resisted her spear-thrust, and it took her weight as she moved onto it. But other people in the tribe were twice as heavy. She stamped her foot to make sure the surface would support them.

It gave way without warning. She screamed in sudden terror as she fell. The world spun around her—and then the spear-shaft slammed up against her stomach, and she found herself clinging to it, wrapped around it, her legs kicking in empty space.

The spear had been just long enough to span the hole that had opened under her, and even though the wooden shaft flexed frighteningly under her weight, it was supporting her above black, icy water rushing under the ice.

The rope around her waist tightened painfully. "Don't try to move!" Henik shouted. "Just hold tight."

She nodded wordlessly. The impact of the spear against her stomach had winded her, and she could barely speak. She felt tears in her eyes as the thought came to her that if this had happened to her father, the shaft would have broken under his weight.

She heard footsteps crunching on the ice. She looked up and saw Henik on one side of her, Elbrau on the other, their bulk blotting out the bright sky. "Can you hold her?" Elbrau called to Henik. "Your shoulder—"

"I can manage."

She felt her father reaching for her, sliding his hand under her armpit. "Careful!" she gasped, afraid for him.

Elbrau moved around behind Henik. "She's right. Take care."

"I have her." Grunting with the effort, Henik hoisted her up. "She's heavier than I remember," he said.

Laena glimpsed his face as he turned, dragging her to safety. Gently, he set her down. He was smiling at her.

That was when he fell.

The ice suddenly seemed to shift underfoot. At first she imagined another small section giving way; but this was different. There was a long, eerie crackling noise, like the sound that came when the rib cage of an animal was spread apart by a butchering party. There was a flurry of tiny ice shards and water droplets, and the hole that had almost claimed Laena suddenly opened wider, much wider, splitting into a crevasse.

"The whole sheet is breaking up!" Elbrau shouted.

Henik was already slipping, losing his balance, falling on his side, sliding down.

"No!" Laena screamed. She flung herself backward and tried to seize something—anything—for support. Elbrau immediately understood and threw himself beside her, grabbing her shoulders, as Henik disappeared into the crevasse and the catgut cord jerked tight around Laena's waist.

"Hold on!" Elbrau shouted at her.

She struggled to obey, but her mittens slipped over the slick surface and she felt herself being dragged inexorably toward the hole where her father had disappeared.

Elbrau swore. He seized the cord, took a turn of it around his wrists, and braced himself, digging his heels into a patch of rough ice at the edge of the chasm. "I have you, Henik!" he shouted.

Laena heard an answering cry, barely audible above the rushing of river water and crackling noises as more of the ice fractured apart.

Elbrau pulled on the cord and Laena saw his face twist in pain as the catgut cut into his mittens. He grunted, bearing down on his good leg. His boot started shredding, leaving a trail of brown specks of animal hide on the white ice. "Gorag!" he shouted. "Get over here! help me!"

The crackling sounds gradually diminished, and Laena heard the anxious babble of the people behind her. She tried to add her own weight to Elbrau's efforts, and she felt the catgut cord thrumming with tension. Then Gorag was behind her, his ugly face unreadable. He reached for the cord and hauled on it, and she cried out with relief as she saw their efforts bearing fruit.

Bit by bit they edged back from the gulf that had opened. They dragged Henik up, gasping with the effort, and he was able to reach up to the rim of the hole. They saw the top of his head, his mittens reaching out, his sleeves gleaming with river water.

"He's safe," Gorag muttered.

"Not yet," Elbrau said.

The wet cord was frayed from rubbing across the sharp edges of the ice. In front of Laena's eyes, the catgut suddenly snapped.

She sprawled backward, along with Elbrau and Gorag. At the same time, she heard a despairing cry from her father. A moment later she heard a muffled splash; and after that, there was nothing.

Laena stared at the spot where he had been. She scrambled up onto her hands and threw herself to the edge.

Dark water ran swiftly at the bottom of the crevasse. Her father was nowhere to be seen.

"It's dragged him under," said a quiet voice beside her. Elbrau laid his hand on Laena's shoulder.

She turned, blinking. "What do you mean?"

"He's under the ice sheet now." He gestured to the vast white expanse that cloaked the river all around them.

She shook her head violently. "No, no, he was just here. Find him, Elbrau!"

Elbrau pulled her back. "He's gone, Laena."

She struggled in his grip. "No!" she shouted. "He can't be gone!"

But then she looked into Elbrau's face and saw his sadness, and she could no longer deny the terrible thing that had happened.

She started screaming her grief and rage. She struggled with him as he held her, waiting patiently for the fit to pass. "Calm now," he kept saying. "Calm, Laena. We have to save ourselves."

But how could she be calm? And what did it matter, saving themselves, if her father was dead?

Finally she felt herself being seized by someone else. It was her mother holding her, comforting her. "But I killed him," Laena heard herself saying. "I didn't pull hard enough. It's my fault."

"It was not your fault," Arla told her. "Fate took him, as fate took Jobia. No one could have done anything. No one could have foreseen this."

I could have foreseen it, Laena thought with sudden clarity. She had seen Jobia die, in her dream; why hadn't she seen her father? She felt a flash of fury. What use was her special talent if it didn't obey her? For that matter, even when it did reveal the future to her, there was still nothing she could do. She was helpless, totally helpless.

A grumbling, grinding sound distracted her from her grief, and once again the ice trembled beneath them.

"Over here!" she heard someone shout. It was Gorag's voice. "It's safe over here!"

Finally, Laena thought to herself, he shows some courage—when his own life is in danger.

"On your feet, Laena." Arla's voice was suddenly harsh. "Take Moru's hand. Hear me, Daughter!"

Instinctively, Laena obeyed. She barely knew what she was doing; but when her mother spoke that way, she did as she was told.

All the Panther People were moving as fast as they could, scrambling across the ice, their eyes wide with fear as they felt it rumbling and shaking under them. Gorag was standing on a small plateau that stood higher and seemed more solid than the rest.

The people slipped and fell, picked themselves up again and threw themselves forward as segments of the ice gave way and opened up beneath them. Laena ran the last few steps, dragged Moru after her, and hauled herself up to safety.

Everyone gathered together, huddling close to one another for mutual reassurance. Laena found herself breathing in sobs, overcome by the horror of everything that had happened. She realized that something was encumbering her—the cord still knotted around her waist. Angrily, she reached into her pouch, found her flint knife, and cut through the catgut. She flung it aside and sat back down, hugging her knees up against her chest and burying her face in her arms.

When she felt a little calmer, she raised her head and opened her eyes. She blinked. The riverbanks seemed to be moving. Was she hallucinating? No; the ice that had choked the river was starting to flow with it, breaking into fragments as it did so.

"This isn't safe at all," she said, feeling the slab tilting beneath her, then resettling itself, jostling with the smaller floes that scraped against its edges. "We're adrift!"

Chapter 11

All around them the ice floes were grinding, jostling, turning as they floated downriver. It was a giant white mosaic ripping itself slowly to pieces, and the Panther People were stranded near the center. Laena clung to her mother and Moru, and they clung to others on either side of them. The ice table that they sat on shook under them as it scraped against its neighbors. It tilted, then righted itself, then drifted a short way in clear water. There was no way to escape from it. For the time being, they could only sit and wait.

Beside Laena, Moru had curled into a ball. The little girl was shivering—with fear, or from the cold, it was impossible to tell.

"Courage," Laena whispered. "If we drift closer to the shore, we'll be safe again."

Moru's face peeked out from her fur hood. "Truly, Laena? Is it a True Thing?"

Laena hesitated. It would be easy to give reassurance, but it would be wrong. "I don't know," she admitted. "No one can say."

"Can't you dream it?" said Moru.

She knew it wouldn't work, just as it hadn't worked when she had tried to foresee her father's fate. Still, she closed her eyes anyway. How did the pictures come into her head? She didn't even know. She imagined the ice that they clung to, and she conjured in her mind a view of the people on it. Where were they now, and where would they be by the day's end?

It was like trying to see in the dark. She felt angry and frustrated. She pressed her hands to her eyes as if she could force a vision into them. But all she saw were faint luminous patterns flowering and dying behind her lids.

She sighed. "I'm sorry," she said, feeling defeated. "I see nothing."

For a moment, Moru didn't answer. Then she said, "This is Gorag's fault."

Before Laena could answer, the ice tilted under them again—even more this time. Everyone cried out, and Laena felt herself sliding. She spread herself flat, scrabbling with her hands, trying to hold on.

Gradually, the ice leveled itself again. But she could see that as it floated clear of other chunks around it, it was liable to move more freely.

"Here," said a voice. A strong hand put something into her palm. "Hold this."

She looked up and saw Elbrau. From his pouch he had taken a dozen thongs, which he had tied together. He was tethering them to short, sharp lengths of bone which he was hammering into the slab of ice.

"So long as we keep firm hold," said the flintknapper, "we will live."

But how long could that be? The sun was already high in the sky, their bellies were empty, and their fragile refuge was stranded in a deadly shifting pattern of floes, far from either shore.

Laena picked up an ice fragment and looked at it longingly, knowing how it could help to alleviate her growing thirst. Unfortunately, it would also steal heat out of her body; and she had none to spare.

She tossed the ice aside, huddled down again with Moru and her mother, and closed her eyes. If she could do nothing to save herself, she could at least conserve her strength.

Also, she realized, she was exhausted. Her fear and her physical efforts had both taken their toll on her.

She coiled Elbrau's thong around her mittened hand, then thrust her hands inside her furs, hugging herself. She drew up her knees. For a moment she felt dizzy, as the ice turned under her. Then she found herself thinking about her father, remembering his last despairing cry. She groaned, trying to drive it out of her mind.

Bit by bit, she managed to get her thoughts back under control, and she felt fatigue creeping over her.

Sometime later—she could not say how long—she tried to open her eyes. Strangely, her eyelids seemed as if they were sealed shut. She felt a pang of concern, and she tried to cry out. But no sound escaped her throat. Her body seemed lifeless, refusing to obey her.

Then her eyes were open, as if they'd been open all the time. She stared around in confusion. The light seemed impossibly bright. The sun was shining fiercely, more fiercely than she had ever known; and it was directly above, at the zenith. Never had she seen such a thing. How could it be?

She moved her arm to shade her eyes and realized, with astonishment, that instead of her heavy furs, she was clad in thin woven trousers and a robe made from the summer pelts of caribou. Her hands were bare, and her skin was a strange, rich brown.

She wasn't on the river anymore. She was sitting amid a carpet of tall grass that rippled in a gentle breeze. Far in the distance, a herd of browsing mammoth wandered slowly.

She turned, marveling at the beauty of this strange place. The sky was a clear, vivid blue. The grass was impossibly thick, impossibly green. And at the bottom of the slope where she sat was a huge lake, as blue as the sky.

A figure was standing on the shore, tall and strong, his skin a dark brown like her own. He was holding a spear, leaning on it, looking toward her. She tried to make out his face, but the sunlight glared on the water behind him, making it hard for her to see.

"Laena!" he called to her. And he waved.

It was her father's voice. She drew in her breath and felt her pulse pounding. Could it really be him?

She started up onto her feet—but the ground seemed to tilt under her, and suddenly the bright vision was gone, and the grinding of the ice crashed back into her senses.

Leana opened her eyes in darkness. The sun had set, and all around her were the people of her tribe, still huddling together, barely visible in dim moonlight. Her limbs were stiff and painful with cold. She moaned, slumping back beside her mother and Moru. Where was the strange, wonderful landscape that she had seen? Why had it been sent to torment her?

The picture that had come into her head was surely a land beyond this; a higher realm, where the dead returned to life. Did that mean that she, too, was about to die, so she would join her father there?

She shuddered. The vision had been more powerful, more disturbing, than anything she had ever seen before. Even as she blinked in the darkness, it haunted her still.

But there was no more time to think about it. The slab of ice shuddered violently under her as it smashed into something heavy and solid directly ahead.

The ice had run aground, she realized. It wasn't rocking and turning in the river current anymore.

Laena's mind had been dulled by the cold, and she was still haunted by her vision. Her thoughts were sluggish and confused. Why did it seem so important that they were no longer moving?

Something moved. A large figure, looming up. Instinctively, she gave a little cry.

"Laena?" The voice was Elbrau's. "Is that you, girl?"

She tried to speak. For a moment, as in her dream, she found that her voice would not obey her. Her tongue seemed swollen in her throat. "It's me," she managed to croak.

"We've run aground."

She nodded dumbly.

He turned quickly, peering into the darkness. He swore. "I was sleeping. When did this happen?"

"Just now."

"Get up, girl!" He bent and used his knife to slash the thong anchoring her to the ice. "See there?"

She tried to focus her eyes. She saw only blackness.

"The ice here is packed tight," Elbrau told her. We're at a bend in the river. The land's just a dozen paces away." He turned and cut the thongs anchoring the other people around him. "Get up, all of you!" he shouted.

A few of them moved, but they were as slow as Laena's own thoughts.

Gorag moved in front of Laena. She recognized his craggy profile, outlined by the moonlight. He stared at the shore, then gave a guttural yell and lurched forward. She saw him leap clumsily onto a neaby floe. He fell onto his hands and knees, then struggled up again and stumbled toward the shore without glancing back.

Laena realized she was clutching Moru in her arms. She couldn't leave the little girl. She had to carry her. But it was a terrible burden, and she was so very, very tired. She got up onto her knees, then paused, swaying.

A strong hand gripped the fur that she wore. She felt herself being lifted and turned. Elbrau loomed over her as he had before. "Jump!" he shouted at her.

Laena moaned. Every muscle seemed frozen, cramped, and bruised. But with his help, she half stepped, half fell from the slab of ice to a neighboring sheet. "Hurry!" Elbrau urged her.

Laena hesitated. One clear thought spoke loudly in her head. "My mother!"

"You first." Elbrau stepped down, seized her again, and dragged her forward relentlessly. Her feet slipped. She took a pace, then another, and suddenly she found something hard and gritty under her moccasins. She heard her feet crunch on loose stones. Tall grass brushed her legs.

She sank to her knees, overwhelmed with relief. Moru struggled and made a little whimpering sound. "We are safe," Laena crooned to her. "Safe."

The ice howled behind her. Laena turned, still hugging the bundle of fur that was Moru. She saw the frozen river, ghostly white in the night.

Upstream, more floes had gathered and were being driven by the current. They were bearing down on the accumulation at the bend. There was a familiar booming sound as the ice fractured. It sprang up explosively, and Laena drew in her breath as she saw a stiff human body tossed into the air.

The floes jostled each other with a hideous scraping sound. The slab that the Panther People had taken as their refuge was ripped free from the mass around it. Laena heard screams and saw figures rolling and tumbling. There was a splash as someone tried to leap to safety and was taken by the river. Another splash; another cry.

Laena drew in her breath. She didn't want to believe that what she saw could be really happening.

She felt her knees giving way under her. The world tilted, as if she were still on the ice floe herself. There was a hissing sound in her ears, and her thoughts were drifting, taking her with them. She pitched forward, but she never felt herself hit the ground.

Chapter 12

Laena felt flame running in her veins, searing her from within. She cried out in pain.

She thrashed and struggled, but the pain just got worse. Feeling desperate and tormented, she opened her eyes. Orange light was flickering in front of her, dazzling her. She recoiled from it with a cry.

"You're awake. Good."

The voice that spoke to her was strained and husky, each syllable spoken with great weariness. She turned her head, flinching from the agony that the movement caused her, and saw Elbrau squatting a couple of paces away. The flintknapper's face gleamed with sweat. He looked drained, and his eyes were haunted as he warmed himself by the roaring fire.

Between Elbrau and Laena lay Moru. The little girl's eyes were closed, but she wriggled in her furs as Laena watched, and she whimpered softly.

"I'm alive," Laena said, her voice a whisper. "You are alive, and so is Moru."

Elbrau leaned forward and threw chunks of animal fat onto the fire. "Alive, yes." He did not smile. "We are safe and warm and we have food, too, when you're ready."

Laena grunted, steeling herself to fight the pain that flowed again across her body. She had had frostbite before, but nothing like this, afflicting every part of her. She clenched her jaw and waited, trying to be patient, as the burning waves slowly, gradually receded.

"My mother," she gasped. "Where's my mother?"

"Not yet," said Elbrau. "Be patient."

"But is she alive?"

Elbrau looked at her, and she saw the answer on his face. Laena let out a moan of anguish. She felt tears on her face. She rolled onto her side, clutching herself, feeling more alone than she had ever in her life. She lay there for a while, trying not to think and not to feel, while the warmth of the fire seeped into her body, driving away the coldness that had almost claimed her.

As she grew warmer, she felt stronger. She couldn't think about her mother; not yet. She had to think of herself, and her sister.

She sat up, looked around, and realized she was sitting in a wide, shallow pit that had been dug in the snow. Its walls flickered orange in the firelight, while overhead the sky was still black.

Moru was still beside her, lying with her eyes closed, whimpering to herself. Laena reached out to her.

"Leave her," said Elbrau. "She'll be all right. Right now, it'll hurt her if you touch her."

Laena drew her hand back. She looked up at Elbrau's face. "How," she said, "did you manage—"

"I worked with Gorag," Elbrau said. "We foraged and built the fire. That was almost the end of me. I could hardly even hold the firesticks. My hands were like this"—the flintknapper curled his fingers—"and when the fire warmed them, it felt as though they were being crushed. I may never be able to work the flint again."

Laena nodded slowly. Suddenly she realized how hungry she was. She reached for some meat and gorged herself on it, relishing the juices that assaulted her mouth with their pungent flavor. "This meat," she said. "Where did it come from?"

"Gorag was still strong. He happened on some caribou in the darkness, he killed one, and he brought it here. He feasted awhile, and now he's gone to hunt more." Elbrau paused. "He took care of himself better than the rest of us, on the ice. He kept himself warm in furs from people who had passed on."

There was something in Elbrau's voice, and something in his eyes: a warning.

Laena imagined Gorag rummaging among the bodies of the newly dead, cutting their furs off them. She shuddered. "How many died?" she asked in a small voice. She was afraid she already knew the answer.

"There's just the four of us now, Laena. You, your sister, and Gorag, and me."

She had expected it; and yet, still, it stunned her. "You're sure that my mother—"

"I saw her fall." He drew a slow, deep breath. "I was too late to save her."

Laena blinked. Once again, she pushed the knowledge away. She couldn't begin to think about it.

"I saved you and your sister." Elbrau's voice had a plaintive edge. "First save the young, then the old; isn't that the way?"

"Yes, that is the way." Laena got to her feet, ignoring the tingling pain that ran up her legs. She moved around the fire to Elbrau, squatted beside him, and laid her hand on his shoulder. "Thank you, Elbrau. You saved me and Moru. Thank you."

He tried to smile at her, but his eyes still looked haunted.

Laena heard a sound from behind her. Moru was sitting up, opening her eyes.

Laena reached out to the little girl and gently massaged her limbs. Then she took some caribou grease and rubbed it into Moru's face where the skin had turned a blotchy red-and-white and was starting to peel.

Moru stared at Laena without seeming to comprehend what she saw. "Mama," she whispered.

Laena picked the child up in her arms. "I'm sorry, Moru. Mama's gone." Laena heard herself speaking the words, and the truth of them was like a wave of blackness spreading out inside her. She hugged Moru, trying to draw comfort from the life that still endured in her. "I will have to be your mother now."

Gorag returned a little later, dragging the eviscerated carcass of another caribou. He dumped it at the edge of the pit, then jumped down beside the fire. He slapped his mittened hands together, knocked frozen snow off them, and stared slowly around. In the orange light, his scarred face wore a wicked grin. "So, here we are. The survivors."

Elbrau nodded slowly. He said nothing.

Gorag shook off his mittens, grabbed a hunk of sizzling meat, and ripped into it. "We're the lucky ones, eh?"

"Perhaps we are. But we should show a little respect for the ones who were not so lucky," said Elbrau.

Gorag grunted. "This is no time for mourning. Be thankful you're alive. There's more game here than you've seen in a year. Eat!''

''But this is a place of death,'' said Laena.

Gorag grunted dismissively. ''Tell me a place that isn't. Anyhow, the dead won't grudge us our appetite, eh, girl?'' His eyes dwelled on her as he gnawed the meat in his hands.

Laena felt a movement beside her and found Moru edging closer. The little girl was staring at Gorag with wide eyes, but she seemed not so much fearful as fierce.

''Here.'' Laena took a small piece of meat and touched it to Moru's mouth, trying to distract her. ''Gorag is right that we must feed ourselves.''

Gorag spat out a piece of gristle. ''Of course I'm right. We'd still be starving on the other side of the river if it wasn't for me. Remember that.''

Laena felt anger stir inside her. ''My mother and father would still be alive, if it wasn't for you,'' she blurted out.

Gorag shook his head. Moving methodically, he set down the meat and wiped his hands. Then he stood up. He moved toward Laena till he stood over her. ''It's time,'' he said, ''for you to learn some respect.''

He reached down, seized Laena by her furs, and hauled her up. He smacked her face with the palm of his hand, first her left cheek and then her right, so swiftly that she had no time to defend herself. His own face was just a palm's breadth away, and his heavy odor assaulted her senses.

''Let her go!'' The voice was shrill.

Laena managed to twist in Gorag's grip. She looked down and saw Moru throwing herself forward. The little girl hammered the chieftain with her tiny fists, her face contorted with rage.

Gorag laughed. He dumped Laena back on the ground, turned, raised his knee, and kicked Moru away from him.

''Gorag,'' said Elbrau, rising to his feet. ''Stop this.''

''They both need to learn,'' said Gorag. He took a step toward Moru.

Moru scrambled up, but she didn't run from him. She seized a stick from the fire and whirled it. The burning end hit Gorag's forehead and he stumbled back with a cry of disbelief, beating sparks off his furs.

''Stop this!'' Elbrau strode behind Gorag and grabbed him by his upper arms, pinning him.

"Brat!" Gorag shouted. He struggled to free himself.

"Laena, hold your sister." Elbrau's voice was sharp.

Laena reached for Moru, restraining her just as she started toward Gorag again.

"There will be no more of this," Elbrau said. "Do you all understand? There are only four of us. If we fight each other we will not survive."

There was a short silence. Laena heard Gorag breathing heavily, and the fire sizzling, and her own pulse loud in her ears.

"Don't ever hurt my sister!" Moru shouted in her shrill young voice.

"I'm not hurt," Laena told her, trying to will herself to be calm. "And Elbrau is right. We mustn't fight each other."

Slowly, Moru relaxed. "Just don't hurt her," she said again.

"All right," Gorag growled. "Let me go."

Slowly, Elbrau released his grip.

Gorag flexed his arms and his shoulders. He circled around the fire, glowering first at Elbrau, then at Laena and Moru. "I'm still your chieftain," he shouted, hammering his chest with his fist. "I killed this meat. I brought you here. Remember that. And pay me the respect I'm due."

Laena looked up at him. Her body was trembling with a mixture of emotion—fear, anger, and the vicious need to strike out, to avenge the deaths of her parents. But she said nothing.

"Gorag speaks some truth," said Elbrau. Once again, he gave Laena a look of warning. "He's our chieftain and deserves our respect. You should apologize to him, Laena."

Her anger rose higher, but still, somehow, she held it back. Be calm, she told herself. Do what is necessary. Justice must wait till later.

"I apologize," she said—though the words made her feel sick as she spoke them. "You are our chieftain, Gorag, and I pledge my loyalty to you."

He grinned slowly. "That's better," he said. He sat back down and seized another lump of meat. As he raised it to his mouth and bit into it, he stared at Laena, and his eyes gleamed in the firelight.

Chapter 13

The next day was a day to rest and eat; to lie beside the fire and be thankful for its warmth; to find new strength, and try to think about the days that lay ahead. The sky brightened and Laena found herself looking toward the river, wondering where the ice floe had run aground. To her surprise, she found that the river was no longer choked with ice. It had broken into small chunks that flowed freely, with clear water between them. And there was no sign of the disaster that had afflicted the people of her tribe.

Laena still felt terribly weary, so she stayed beside the fire, dozing on and off, with Moru lying beside her. Gorag left them soon after dawn, but Elbrau stayed with them, and his quiet presence was a source of comfort and strength.

"Do you truly believe," Laena asked him as the day grew warmer, "that there is really a spirit realm for people who die in this world?"

He studied her for a moment. "Many times," he said, "you've heard me speak the eulogy for the dead. You've heard me bid them good fortune in the land beyond. Isn't that so?"

"But the things you say, and the things you believe yourself, might not be the same," she persisted.

He smiled slowly and reached out to pat her cheek. She felt the broken skin of his frostbitten fingers, the warmth of his hand, and something else besides. It was not quite the affection her father had shown toward her; nor was it Jobia's crude lust. It stirred an odd yearning in her that made her uneasy, wanting to pull back from him.

"You know a lot for your age, Laena," he said. "But knowledge doesn't always help us. Why question the old ways, the words that bring comfort when a loved one dies? Where's the sense in that?"

Laena glanced at Moru. The little girl was sitting silently, but her eyes were alert as she listened.

Laena turned back to Elbrau and spread her hands. "I just want to know the truth," she said. And she told him her vision of the warm, green world where her father waited for her. "Have you ever seen a place like that, Elbrau? Even in your dreams?"

He stared into the fire. This time, when he spoke, he didn't sound as if he was trying to reassure her. He sounded as if he spoke from the heart. "I don't know what you saw, Laena. And only you can know what it means, if it means anything at all."

"But—"

He held up his hand. "Be patient. You're still young. In time, maybe, the meaning will come clear. But I'm afraid it isn't clear to me."

Gorag returned to them then. He didn't say where he'd been, or why he'd left them by the fire. He just eyed each of them in turn as he picked up a chunk of meat and started devouring it.

Laena wanted to press Elbrau further, to dig down to his deepest beliefs. But she sensed that this wasn't the time to talk about it.

That night, once again she dreamed of the warm green landscape. The sun beat down upon her, warming her like the gaze of a friend. Brightly colored birds called to one another, and she glimpsed one of them flitting from tree to tree, its plumage shimmering like a rainbow.

Then she turned toward the vast blue water. This time, there wasn't a single figure standing there, calling to her. There were two people: a man and a woman.

She leaped to her feet and shaded her eyes, trying to make out their faces. She heard them shouting something. They waved and beckoned, and she felt a craving so deep and powerful, it threatened to devour her body and spirit.

"Mother!" she cried out. "Father!"

She started running down the grassy slope toward them. But as she did so, the warm, green place dissolved into cold grayness, and she found herself back in the world of snow and ice as the first pale light of dawn touched the sky.

For a moment she lay immobile, feeling stricken by her

loss. This time, she felt sure, the land she had seen was not merely a spirit land. It had seemed completely, utterly real. But where could it exist? How could her mother and father be there? How could she ever find them?

She became aware of voices and realized that Gorag and Elbrau were sitting together on the opposite side of the fire, which had sunk down to a heap of red embers. Gorag was methodically rewinding the bindings of his spear—the only spear that was left—while he spoke in a grim monotone. "We will stay here," he was saying. "I searched all around. There's no tracks, no sign of men. We'll kill more caribou and store the meat in ice pits. The girl and her sister can cure the skins and we'll make tents and new clothing." He stared steadily at Elbrau. "I have decided, and it is so."

"But this isn't our land," said Elbrau. "We drifted a long way before we came ashore."

Gorag set down his spear. "It's our land if we choose to make it ours. The Panther People will thrive here. We'll start anew."

Elbrau flexed his fingers. He winced at the familiar pain from the broken skin. "But the land of the Wolf Tribe can't be far away. You know their reputation; they don't show any kindness to strangers. If they come upon us, they'll kill us, or worse."

Gorag shrugged. "We can always hide, if necessary. With just four of us, it would be easy enough to stay out of sight."

Elbrau brooded a moment. He shifted uncomfortably, glancing at Gorag, then away, afraid to challenge him but unable to go along with the chieftain's plan. "Maybe we should go to them in friendship."

Gorag gave a bark of anger and disgust. He kicked out, and his moccasin hit Elbrau's leg. "What are you, an old woman?" He stood up and pressed his fist to his chest. "We are Panther People!" His voice was deep and strong. "We'll never go groveling like some wounded dog, throwing away our pride."

Elbrau grimaced, and Laena saw how the pain and fear of the past few days had eaten away his courage. "Too much pride will kill us all," he muttered.

Gorag spat on the ground. "What will it take to show you we're safe here? Do you want to scout the land with me so you can see with your own eyes?'' He nudged Elbrau again with his toe.

Elbrau sighed. "All right."

Gorag nodded. "Stoke the fire, and we'll be on our way."

Elbrau started up onto his feet.

Gorag reached out and held him back. "On second thought, let's get the girl to stoke it." He started toward Laena, then paused, seeing her looking up at him. "Oh, you're awake, eh?" He bent down suddenly, knocked her hood back, and grabbed her by her ear, twisting it painfully. "You were listening, weren't you?" He twisted harder, till she let out a little cry and tears started from her eyes. "I've warned you before. You better learn your place, woman."

"I'm not a woman! I'm still a child!"

He let go of her and appraised her face and body. "Near enough, I'm thinking." He gestured to the fire. "Build that up while we're gone." Then he turned away. "Come on, Elbrau. Let's get this done."

"First let me tell her where our meat is stored," said the flintknapper.

Gorag shrugged. He swung himself up out of the pit. Faintly, Laena heard him urinating in half-melted snow.

Elbrau squatted beside her. "Look after yourself, Laena. Be careful."

Laena searched his face and saw the worry in his eyes. She placed her hand over his. "Take us away from him, Elbrau," she whispered. "The three of us can run to the Wolf Tribe one night while he's asleep."

The flintknapper blinked. He looked down at her small hand as if something pained him. "I've thought about it," he whispered. "It might be possible. If I could find the Wolves and speak to them —" He trailed off. He shook his head. "But if Gorag heard us leave, and came after us—I'm not a warrior. He's stronger and younger than I am. He'd kill me and take you from me. Moru, too."

Laena curled her fingers, clutching Elbrau's sleeve. "Then please be careful," she whispered. "I don't trust him."

"I won't show him my back. And I have my knife." He showed her a slim, finely fashioned flint blade, then thrust it back into the sleeve of his furs.

"Elbrau!" Gorag sounded impatient. "Come on, man!"

Elbrau touched Laena's cheek, lightly, tenderly. "I'll return soon enough."

Then he turned and was gone.

Laena rebuilt the fire. A little later, she woke Moru. They both ate from the store of meat, and then, after she'd told Moru the conversation that she'd overheard between Elbrau and Gorag, there was nothing to do but wait.

Gorag returned soon enough. Laena heard his familiar tread, his moccasins marching through the mud and slush. She peered out from their hiding place by the fire, feeling a sense of puzzlement that there was only one pair of footsteps instead of two. Then, as she saw that Gorag was alone, the puzzlement turned to dread.

"Where is he?" she demanded, rising up to face him. She couldn't believe it—couldn't let herself believe it. Elbrau was the last person she felt close to in the whole world, other than her sister. It wasn't possible that he could have disappeared. *"Where's Elbrau?"*

Gorag paused. He looked down at her. His face was unreadable behind his beard, which was rimmed in frost. "He'll be along later," he said. He pushed past her and squatted by the fire.

"But *where is he?*" Laena screamed. She hurled herself at Gorag and grabbed his furs, tugging on them.

"What's wrong with you?" he snapped at her. He cuffed her head, knocking her aside. "Elbrau's gone scouting, looking for the Wolves. He said he'd be back tonight, maybe tomorrow."

Laena looked at Gorag's face. For a moment, she wavered, wanting desperately to believe. But there was something evasive in his eyes; something that told her she would never be seeing Elbrau again.

Something welled up inside her—a tense, hurting pressure in her chest. Suddenly she gave vent to it, and the sound was piercingly loud. She clenched her fists and threw herself at Gorag, pounding him blindly.

At first her attack seemed to surprise him. He scrambled up and stepped back, raising his arms to protect himself from her. Then he bared his teeth and growled and seized her by the throat. He threw her down so that she fell on her face in the mud. She tried to breathe but found snow in her mouth, snow in her eyes. She tried to get up, but Gorag planted his foot on the back of her neck, holding her there.

"I'm going to say this once," he shouted at her. "Once only. You cross me again, and you'll regret it for the rest of your life. You'll hurt, and you'll go on hurting. Understand?" And he bore down with his foot, forcing her face deeper into the snow. She felt the sheer strength of the man, and it sent a wave of fear through her. He could kill her easily, or do anything else—anything at all. Clearly, with Elbrau gone, there would be nothing to stop him.

"Let her go!" came a thin, plaintive cry.

For a moment the pressure of Gorag's foot was released. Laena squirmed around in time to see Moru running forward, raising her little arms as if she could somehow reach all the way up to Gorag's throat and strangle him.

He grabbed her wrists in his huge hands, spun her, and dumped her down beside Laena. He loomed over the two of them. "Listen to me!" he shouted.

Laena reached for Moru and restrained her. "Stop!" she shouted. "There's nothing you can do, Moru. Nothing."

Gorag stood over them with his hands on his hips. He nodded to himself. "Good," he said. "All right, it's just the three of us now. Till Elbrau gets back." His lips pulled back from his teeth, and his eyes narrowed. "You, Moru. You give me any more trouble, I'll cast you out. You, Laena, you learn to do exactly what I say, or I'll tie you hand and foot and teach you the lessons the hard way. Understand?"

"No!" Moru shrieked. "No!"

"Keep her quiet," Gorag said to Laena. He turned his back, went to the fire, and sat down, ignoring them.

"Hush," said Laena. She seized Moru and hugged her, so tightly that the little girl could hardly breathe. "Hush now."

"Take me away from here," Moru whimpered, turning and pressing her face against Laena's cheek. "Let's go somewhere else, Laena."

Laena tried to imagine setting out across the land, alone with her sister, with no way to hunt or defend themselves. It was impossible; they wouldn't last more than a couple of days.

"I'm sorry," she whispered. "I'm sorry, Moru. There's nowhere else for us to go."

"Will Elbrau really come back?" Moru asked Laena late that night, when Gorag had eaten his dinner and was lying beside the fire, snoring peacefully under the stars.

"I don't think so." It hurt Laena to say the words, but she had never lied to her sister, and she wasn't about to start.

"Why not, Laena? Doesn't he like us anymore?"

Laena wondered which would be more cruel: to hold out some hope, or to say what she feared had happened. She was too young to be a mother to Moru; she didn't know how to do it. She wished there was someone else who could share the burden with her.

"I think something has happened to Elbrau," she said carefully. "But I can't be sure. I know he'll come back to us if he can."

Moru nodded to herself. Apparently, the explanation had satisfied her. She turned and stared at Gorag lying beside the fire. "We could kill him now," she said.

Laena seized her arm and squeezed it warningly. "Don't be foolish."

"We could! I could hit him with a rock!"

"Hush." She watched Gorag nervously, but he slept on, oblivious. "We need him, if we are going to live. The trouble is, he knows that. That's why he sleeps so soundly. Maybe one day, when we're older and stronger, we can leave him. Or maybe we'll find some other people who can help us. But so long as he's the only man with us, he's our only hope. Remember that, Moru."

The little girl looked up at Laena. She made a little sound of distress. "I don't like him! I hate him!"

Laena sighed. "Yes," she said, feeling despair overwhelming her. "I know."

Chapter 14

The next day was not as bad as she'd feared. Now that El-brau had gone, Gorag seemed more confident of his power over her and Moru. He gave orders, but they were no different from the kinds of things that Laena's father used to tell her to do. Gorag didn't threaten her, he didn't shout at her, and he wasn't cruel.

Naturally, she distrusted his kindness. She knew that he wouldn't hesitate to act on the threats he'd made, if she provoked him again. And so, she bided her time and kept her thoughts and feelings to herself. If he had decided to put on a friendly face toward her, she could do the same—for now.

In the morning he took Laena and Moru to the river. Herds of caribou had started arriving along the west bank, and they were splashing across to the east bank where the water was shallow. Gorag dug a little hiding place in a bank of snow, then lay in wait as the animals started streaming past. They were almost close enough to touch, and he could easily pick off the ones he wanted.

He speared five of them altogether, then got Laena and Moru to help him drag their carcasses back to the camp. He dug fresh storage pits while they went to work reducing the animals to meat and hides and useful bone. It was a long, backbreaking chore, but it was something that Laena was familiar with, and it occupied her mind.

When she had the time, she made a needle and awl from the scapula of one animal and labored to repair her garments, which had been badly ripped while she was on the river ice. She even worked after dark, squinting by the fire to sew new boots from the freshly cured skins.

"You've done well," Gorag told her when they finally stopped for the night. "Your father would have been proud."

Mention of her father gave her a terrible pang—of anger, and of loss. She remembered how he had fallen and disappeared under the ice, and she glared at Gorag, wondering if there was any way she could ever avenge herself against him. Still, she forced herself to conceal her feelings. Not now, she told herself; it would do no good. "I'm glad you appreciate my work," she said.

Gorag reached out and patted the side of her face. "You're a strong girl, Laena."

Laena flinched back and Moru jumped to her feet, clenching her fists.

Gorag waved her away. "No more of that." He squatted back on his haunches and grabbed another hunk of meat. "We three have got to learn to get along. That's the only way, isn't it?" He grinned at Laena. "We're the last of the Panther People. We need each other now."

Laena glanced at Moru. Neither of them said anything.

"Friends," Gorag said. "We're going to be friends." Still grinning, he lay back and pulled his furs around himself, getting ready for sleep.

The next day he worked with Laena, rubbing brains and fat into several hides to make them pliable and waterproof. After that, they stitched the hides together to make two tents—one for Gorag, one for the two girls. They lashed together long bones with sinew to make supports for the tents, and they anchored them using pegs that they fashioned from the tips of antlers.

Another day passed, and still Gorag seemed easygoing, chatting with them, smiling a lot, never raising his voice in anger. Did he honestly expect Laena to forget how he had betrayed her people? Did he really think she could ever enjoy his company? Well, time was on his side now. She had nowhere to go, and no one else to turn to. Still, she vowed, she would never forgive him; never allow herself to trust him.

The weather started getting noticeably warmer, and the ground became soft underfoot. The migration of caribou reached a new peak as the animals streamed north in their thousands. They shied away from the camp and its scent of people, but day and night the air was filled with the clicking of their antlers and the rumble of their hooves. Where the animals had passed, the ground was churned into a sea of mud.

It was no longer even necessary to spear them. The bodies of caribou that had drowned in the river were washed ashore, and the icy water preserved their meat, so it was still fresh when Laena and Gorag hauled it out. There was so much meat, Gorag had to dig more pits to contain it all.

As the store of food grew larger, Laena began wondering how much she really needed him to feed and protect her. She imagined herself and Moru sneaking away into the night, carrying enough food to last them a month or more.

But when the food finally ran out, what then? Laena knew that the migration of caribou would soon be over, and after that, game would be relatively scarce. She didn't have the skills of a hunter, and Gorag certainly wasn't going to teach her. Even if she and Moru could get away from him—how would they survive?

She wondered if there was a tribe that would accept them. But then she remembered hearing Elbrau say that the Wolf People were close by, and they were hostile to strangers. It was hopeless, Laena realized. She was free to come and go as she pleased, and yet she was trapped here.

Within a few more days, as she'd expected, the herds of caribou dwindled to just a scattering of animals. Now came the herd followers—wolves and foxes and cats that lived by pulling down the stragglers. Gorag stayed close to camp with his spear at the ready during this dangerous time, and he ordered the girls to keep fires burning in a wide circle around their tents and food caches. Moru and Laena piled fat on the flames, working in shifts all through each night, and as a result of their precautions, the predators left them alone.

When the migration finally ended, there was less work for her to do. Days passed, and spring started edging into summer. All the snow was gone, and the prairie was green with moss and ferns. It wasn't the lush green that Laena had seen in her vision, but it was pleasant, nonetheless.

One day a small herd of mammoths ambled along the river, trumpeting to one another. Gorag looked at them with longing. "If only I had some hunters!" he exclaimed. "We could winter here with all that meat."

His mention of the winter made Laena feel nervous. Gorag was still easygoing, and he hadn't said anything about wanting her as his mate. Surely, though, that couldn't be far away. She wondered how many days she had left, before she finally became a woman. That was something she tried not to think about, for the implications were too frightening.

Two days later, Gorag came upon her as she drew water in a hide bucket by the river. He squatted down beside her, watching her carefully. He was sleek and well-fed these days, but he still had the hard, devious way of looking at her that she had come to know so well. "I've come here so we can talk alone," he said.

Laena quickly dumped the leather bucket between them. She waited, feeling her skin prickling.

"I've done well for us the past month," he told her, studying her in a way that made her want to cover herself with her winter furs. "You've got to agree that I've taken care of you, and your sister, too."

Laena didn't quite trust herself to speak. Her hands clenched on the handle of the bucket.

"I think you know what I want, Laena," he went on. "You're nearly a woman, and I'm a man without a wife. When your change comes, which will be soon—I want you to share my tent with me."

Laena flinched as if the words had slapped her. Still she said nothing, though her emotions surged inside her.

"Don't push me away," Gorag said, and there was an edge of warning in his voice. He hesitated, then drew back. "I'll take good care of you," he went on, more quietly. "You've seen that. There were some bad times, but they're in the past. We can start our tribe again, you and me. Think of the honor, Laena. You'll be the mother of the Panther People."

She imagined lying close to him. She imagined him touching her. It filled her with dread, and she thought that she might actually prefer to kill herself, drown herself in the river rather than submit to him.

He placed his hand on her shoulder. "Why not pledge yourself, Laena."

She jerked away from him. "No!" she cried. Her voice was so shrill, it surprised her.

"Why not?" The edge was back in his voice, and he jumped up onto his feet. "Is it Elbrau? I saw the way he used to look at you. Are you still waiting for him to come back?"

"No." She shook her head, trying not to cry. "No, Elbrau was a friend, a good friend, nothing more. And he's never coming back. I know that."

"You do, eh?" He was still watching her closely.

Suddenly the tension between them was too much to bear. She turned to face him. "He's not coming back, because you killed him!"

"Ah," said Gorag, speaking softly. "You think I killed one of my own."

"Yes. I know you did."

He shook his head slowly. "I don't have to answer to you." He turned and started striding away. But after he took a few paces, he stopped and pointed at her. "You'll be my mate," he shouted. "When the time is right. You have no choice, and you know it."

That night, Laena feared he might come for her. She lay close beside Moru in their tent, and she jumped at the slightest noise from the wind or from small creatures in the tall grass that now grew along the riverbank.

But Gorag stayed in his own tent, and she heard his heavy breathing as he slept. *Why is he waiting,* she wondered. Why didn't he seize her and take her, as he had threatened to do before? The waiting was almost worse than if he forced himself on her. Was that why he was doing it, just to wear her down? Did he think that if he waited long enough, she would simply give in?

For a moment she wondered if she could actually do that. In a way, it would be a relief. If she gave him what he wanted, he would be decent to her, and she wouldn't have to fear him.

But then she realized what she was thinking, and it horrified her. There had to be something better than this. There had to be! She remembered her vision of the green, sunny place. Hadn't she once vowed to find it, so she could be reunited with her mother and father? How could she let herself turn away from her real destiny, and surrender to the man who had brought about the death of her parents?

Fiercely, she warned herself to hold on to her self-respect, no matter how much it caused her to suffer. She had lost almost everything else; if she ever lost her self-respect, truly she would have lost everything.

More days passed, and Gorag went back to biding his time, always polite to her, never releasing the rage that seemed locked below the surface.

Summer came nearer, and lemmings started breeding amid the ferns and moss. Laena had to make sure that the food caches were tightly sealed against them. In the afternoons she hunted them, throwing a large skin over them and then smacking them with a bone club. Their fat little bodies were a welcome change from caribou meat, and with a few roots from the riverbank they made a succulent stew.

But the change of diet seemed to upset her stomach. For the whole of one day she felt queasy; and then, the next morning, she woke with sharp cramps that made her double over.

Moru looked at her with concern. "Are you all right?" she asked. "What's wrong?"

"The food," said Laena. It was hard to talk, and even harder to move, but she didn't want to alarm the little girl. "Perhaps I'll feel better after I go and empty myself."

She struggled out of the tent, wincing as another cramping pain seized her stomach. Gorag was already up, feeding the fire, and he paused and looked at her. "Are you sick, girl?"

"No." She said it as firmly as she could. "I'll be back in just a moment."

She hurried to an erosion channel not far from their camp. It was filled with slush and silty water, and it served them as a latrine.

Laena paused by it, trying to straighten up and catch her breath. She fumbled with the thong that secured her leather trousers, then let them slide down her legs. She started to squat—then stopped in sudden fear.

The inside of the seat of her trousers was red with blood. She stared at the fresh stains, unable to make sense of what she saw. Had she cut herself in her sleep? Had the food made her bleed inside?

And then, with sudden certainty, she knew. Her mother had told her that it was normal for a grown woman to bleed; it happened every month.

So she was a grown woman now.

She felt a spasm of fear. She had to keep this news from Gorag.

There were footsteps behind her. Hastily, Laena started pulling up her trousers. But the clammy leather resisted her, bunching around her knees.

It was Gorag; she recognized his tread. She heard him coming closer. Then she heard him draw in his breath. Laena finally managed to haul her trousers up—but as she turned to face him, she knew with an awful sinking certainty that he had seen her secret.

"Well," said Gorag in a voice that was slow and quiet, and all the more frightening for that. "Well now, Laena."

"No!" Laena shouted as he started toward her. She turned to run—but the channel blocked her path, and it was too wide for her to leap across.

He was on her before she had a chance to get away, and she felt his calloused hands gripping her arms, his warm breath on her face. She brought up her hands, but he was far too strong, and she knew there was no way she could fight him off. He threw her backward, and she landed hard on the ground, crying out in pain. He fell down onto her and fumbled with her clothes, and she kicked out at him, but he managed to haul her trousers off one of her legs, and then he was pressing himself on her, crushing her with his weight.

Laena screamed. His scarred face loomed over her, and she raked his cheeks with her fingernails. He grunted with anger, raised his hand, and slapped her face.

She felt stunned, not just by the blow but by the awfulness of what was going to happen to her. She gave a despairing cry as she admitted to herself that there was nothing she could do. His bare skin pressed against hers and she realized that he had opened his own clothes. He was forcing her legs apart, and his breathing seemed so loud, it filled her whole awareness. Laena closed her eyes. Please, she thought, let it be quick—

There was a sudden thumping sound. Gorag grunted and gasped, and his fingers lost their grip.

For a moment Laena lay motionless, still with her eyes closed, trembling, not knowing what to think.

Again, the heavy thumping sound.

Gorag's hands fell away from her completely.

Laena squirmed and managed to struggle out from under him. She opened her eyes and saw him lying with his face in the dirt. Standing over him was Moru, still holding the rock that she had used twice to strike Gorag on the back of his head.

Laena scrambled up. "What have you done!" she cried.

The little girl dropped the rock and ran to Laena. Wordlessly, they hugged. Both of them were trembling—Laena with relief, Moru with fear.

"I told you I'd kill him," Moru said in a quavery voice. She looked at Laena as if she wanted to cry. "I told you! Did I do a bad thing?"

Laena stroked her hair, soothing her as well as she could. "It's all right, little one," she said. She took slow, deep breaths, trying to ease her panic. "It's all right now. Everything's all right now. You did a good thing."

But as she looked at Gorag stretched out on the ground with blood oozing from the back of his head, she knew that their real problems were only just beginning.

Chapter 15

They rolled Gorag's body toward the erosion channel. Blood was still seeping out of the deep wound in his head, his eyes were tightly shut, and his body showed no sign of life. They pushed him over the edge and he splashed down into the water at the bottom of the channel, lying there on his back, moving with the current that was flowing sluggishly toward the river beyond.

Laena stood staring at him for a long moment, trembling with emotions that she could hardly name—relief, shock, dismay. She realized that she was crying. But the tears were not for Gorag; they were for herself and her little sister, freed from the man who had tormented them, but alone now as they had never been before.

She watched Gorag's body drifting slowly around a curve in the channel. Gradually he disappeared from view, leaving only a thin red trail on the surface of the water to mark his passing.

Laena turned away. She took Moru's hand, and together they walked back to the camp.

Laena reassured herself that at least they wouldn't starve. The food caches that they had dug in the permafrost were still full of meat, which would easily last them until the winter. Also, they had tools and skins. They could take care of their basic needs.

And yet—one day the meat would all be eaten, and the skins would be in tatters. One day the tools would break or wear out. Predators might come, or people of other tribes. What then?

Laena sat beside the campfire and closed her eyes, hugging her arms around herself, trying to imagine what the future might have in store. Where was her talent when she needed it? No matter how hard she tried to make pictures blossom inside her head, all she saw was blackness.

The blackness frightened her, so she opened her eyes again and tried to calm herself by thinking slowly and clearly about the months that lay ahead. In the fall, the caribou would migrate back the way they had come, and she should be able to feed herself on the bodies of the ones that drowned in the river. There might even be enough meat to sustain her and her sister till the following spring. Meanwhile, with practice, she might teach herself some of the skill that Elbrau had possessed, to make some crude tools. She might even learn how to throw a spear.

But the world seemed so big, and the tasks seemed so daunting, and her fear kept creeping back into her, no matter how hard she tried to calm herself. She was afraid of the stillness of their camp. She was afraid of the awful weight of responsibility that was settling upon her. She feared the things she would have to do, and she feared the things she would not know how to do. She feared the nights that would come, when she would lie awake or sit by the fire, waiting for . . . what?

There had to be something to sustain her—some reserve of inner strength. She searched her soul; but the only thing she found that could comfort her was her vision of her parents in a green and sunny world. She had vowed to find them in that land, hadn't she? In which case—could this be the time?

The thought was exciting and disturbing. She stared across the valley. It, too, was green at this time of the year. Moss and dwarf willow and waving grass were glowing in the strong, mellow sunlight. Still, it was barren compared with the place she had seen in her dream. And anyway, this place would be thickly covered in snow again, soon enough, when winter reimposed its grip.

Was there really a land where it never snowed, and summer lasted all year round? It seemed impossible; but from her vision, she sensed that it was so. And if all her other visions had come true, why should this one be any different?

She stood up slowly feeling a new determination, tentative at first, but growing stronger. A long journey might be even more difficult and taxing than staying here in the valley. But if it gave her something to hope for and believe in, that would give her the strength to carry on. Really, it was clear: there was only one thing to do.

At first, Laena didn't tell Moru about her dream. She didn't want the little girl to start hoping for something that might not exist. All she said was that they should try to find a place where it would be easier for them to live.

"But it seems easy here," Moru protested.

Laena took hold of her hands. "The snow will come again," she said quietly. "We will run out of food. Life here will not always be pleasant."

"But I like it here. Laena, I don't want to leave." She sounded as if she was about to cry.

Laena remembered the sternness of her mother, when the Panther People had been huddling together in the frozen swamp and everything had seemed so hopeless. She tried to harden herself, to display that same kind of strength. "We *have* to move on," she said, squeezing Moru's hands so tightly, the little girl flinched. "You must trust me."

Moru bowed her head. She was silent for a long moment. "Will we find new people to look after us?"

Laena nodded. "I think we will." As she spoke the words, she felt her courage waver. But then she reminded herself of her vision, and once again she forced her doubts aside. "There is a better place for us, Sister. I know that for a fact." She hesitated, and lowered her voice. "I have dreamed it."

Moru stared at Laena's face. "You did?"

Laena nodded. "I did. So, we must prepare ourselves. There's a lot to be done." And she started to name all the tasks that were necessary.

The preparations lasted through the rest of the day, and all through the next. Laena repaired their clothing and sleeping bags, while Moru dried and smoked as much of the caribou meat as they could carry. The venison was sliced and draped over racks made from bone, while a fire burned slowly beneath. Moru spent most of her time sitting among the racks, turning the meat occasionally, and whisking flies with a brush made of grass stalks.

Laena tried to decide how much clothing to bring. Moru was still a young child, and she couldn't carry a heavy load.

Neither of them would last long if they overburdened themselves. On the other hand, they had to be well prepared. In the end, Laena packed only their sleeping bags and a change of outergarments—nothing else. Their tent was far too heavy, and there was no way they could carry it. When winter came, they would need protection—but she would deal with that when the time came. She told herself to have faith; really, that was the only way.

On the morning of the third day, Laena looked at everything they had done and decided that they were as ready as they would ever be. Along with her clothing and the smoked meat, she had packed four sets of firesticks and dry tinder, some sinews and bone needles that Gorag had crudely fashioned during the past weeks, a leather cup that she had made herself, and a spare pair of leggings.

She paused a moment, wishing that Elbrau were still with her. His wise company had always been reassuring, and his skills as a toolmaker were indispensable. She wondered how and where Gorag had killed the flintknapper—for there was no doubt in her mind that that was what had happened. For a moment she felt overwhelmed with emotions: grief at the loss of her friend, rage at Gorag, and loneliness, pure and simple.

Then she reminded herself of her mother, and she told herself once again to be strong. She truly believed there was a destiny for her beyond this lonely wilderness. Very well then: she would follow it.

She summoned Moru, and together they gathered stones to build cairns on top of their remaining food caches, so that predators would be unable to get into them. If they ever needed to pass this way again, the food should still be waiting for them. In any case, she couldn't allow the food to go to waste; it would be disrespectful to the spirits of the animals which had provided it.

Then she folded their tent, hid it inside one of the empty food caches, and built one last cairn to mark it. She threw earth over their campfire, turned to Moru, and helped the little girl to don her backpack. "Are you certain that it's comfortable?" she asked, giving her a searching look.

Moru gave a curt nod. "I can manage."

She wants me to respect her, Laena thought to herself. *She wants to be an adult like me.* And yet, Laena knew, neither of them was an adult. This was like a game they were playing. A foolish, dangerous game.

She shook her head quickly. She'd made up her mind. There were no other options open to her.

She gave Moru's shoulder a squeeze, then donned her own pack. She picked up Gorag's spear, and then, before she could allow herself any second thoughts, she led the way out of the camp.

Laena told Moru to walk ahead of her, so she could keep an eye on her at all times. They kept close to the river, following it upstream, toward the south. The sun was hottest when it shone from the south; everyone knew that. So, if there truly was a warm, green land where snow never came, the south was surely the place where it should be.

In the far distance, Laena saw mountain peaks standing like a wall at the end of this wide, fertile valley. Would she need to travel beyond the mountains? She couldn't imagine it. Even her father, with all his climbing skills, had never tackled the steepest, snowiest slopes.

Well, she would follow the river, and travel as far as she could, and see what happened.

They walked through the morning, and as the day brightened, Laena started singing some of the old songs to Moru—the songs that the tribe used to sing when they were making the long trek between their winter camp and the summer hunting grounds. Moru joined in, and she even smiled sometimes, when she looked over her shoulder at Laena. The sky was clear, the wind was gentle, and Laena started to feel a new lightness in her spirit. *Think how much worse it would have been,* she reminded herself, *if Gorag had lived.* It was frightening to be on her own, but at least she was free.

When they grew tired under the heavy load of their packs, they sat on a little hill of soft grass and ate a sparse meal of dried meat with some fat that had been pounded with berries. Insects hummed and flashed in the sunlight, and a gentle breeze cast patterns across the surface of the river. Laena paused often, listening; but the rustling she heard was just the wind in the trees, and it seemed as if she and her sister were completely alone in the valley.

Moru lay down for a nap while Laena sat beside her,

trying to remain alert for any sign of danger. It was strange, she thought, that they had seen no sign of game. This was the time of year when musk oxen, steppe bison, and mammoth normally fattened themselves on the lush grasses of the river bottoms.

She remembered what her father had said—that the warmer weather was changing the world as ice melted and water rose higher, claiming the land, forcing the animals to move elsewhere. Was that why the country was so empty?

The idea disturbed her. If game was only going to be plentiful during the migrations, people would no longer be able to live. The world that she had grown up in would no longer exist.

Then Moru woke, and it was time to think of their immediate future. They drank from the river, taking turns to kneel and dip the leather cup. Then they walked on through the long afternoon.

The sun was still shining when Laena decided to make camp for the night. In these northern latitudes, during the summer months, the sun barely set at all. She was grateful for that: it would make it easier for her to get through the night, without darkness exacerbating her fears.

Laena found a knoll overlooking the river. There were a few stunted trees here, which made her feel a little more secure. She searched for some tinder, then unpacked her best set of firesticks. There was something reassuring about the ritual of fitting one stick into the other, spinning it between her palms, sprinkling the tiny wood fragments, spinning the stick again, and watching the embers start to glow. When little flames finally flickered into life, Laena smiled, feeling them warm her spirit as well as her flesh.

She turned and found Moru sitting on the mossy ground close by, leaning against one of the trees. The little girl was still wearing her pack, but her eyes were closed, and she was breathing deeply, fast asleep.

Laena felt tempted to leave the little girl where she sat. But she knew that wouldn't be wise. Moru was still growing; she needed regular meals.

Laena unpacked some of their meat, warmed it over the fire, then shook her sister's shoulder. Moru's eyes opened, but only halfway.

"Eat," Laena said gently.

Moru made a sleepy sound. She didn't move.

When Moru had been a baby, Laena had pushed scraps of food into her mouth. So she could do the same now. Piece by piece, she started feeding her sister. Moru chewed it sleepily, and swallowed, with her eyes half open. And then, without a word, she slipped back into sleep.

Laena gently laid the little girl down and dragged her sleeping bag over her. Then, when Moru was taken care of, Laena fed herself and lay beside her sister. One person should really stand watch, she thought to herself—but she didn't know how to force herself to stay awake. They were hidden here among the trees, she told herself. She had seen no sign of predators, or of hostile tribes. They would simply have to hope for the best, this first night out on their own.

And so, with the sun still glowing in the west, Laena fell asleep.

Twice during the night, she woke with a start. Once, she thought she heard someone scream—then realized she had been woken by an owl. The second time, she heard faint rustlings and realized that there was a mole or a mouse close by, going about its business. She felt glad that there was some life out here, after all. It made her a little less lonely.

Then, suddenly, it was morning. The fire was nothing but a little heap of gray ash. Where Laena's hair had spilled out of her sleeping bag, it was wet with dew. She felt cold, her muscles ached, and she was hungry.

She made another fire, roused Moru, gave her the leather cup, and sent her to the river to get water. Soon they were both eating breakfast. Already, Laena realized, they were exceeding the rations that she had planned. But their hunger was fierce; it demanded satisfaction.

When they had filled themselves, Moru sat quietly, staring at the landscape, while Laena stowed their bedding in their packs.

"Laena?"

She paused and turned. "Yes, little one?"

"The land here looks the same."

"You mean, the same as where we camped before, with Gorag?"

"Yes." Moru nodded. "The same."

Laena shrugged. "We haven't come very far."

Moru turned and stared at her. "We walked for a *whole day*!"

Gradually, Laena realized what was in her sister's head. "It will probably take many days," she said gently, "many months, even, before we reach the place we're searching for."

"Months?" Moru looked at her in disbelief.

Laena gave a curt nod. "Now, help me tie the packs."

Moru stared at her for a long moment. Then, with a grim face, she reluctantly obeyed.

They continued on their way, and once again Laena sang the old songs of her tribe. This time, though, Moru didn't join in. The little girl's grim expression never changed, and Laena had to keep urging her to walk faster.

Inwardly, Laena began feeling worried. If Moru was already resenting the journey, how would they get through the time ahead? Laena realized how much she depended on her sister for company. They had always been especially close; they had hardly ever squabbled. She didn't know how she could cope if Moru retreated from her, or turned against her.

But then, around midday, they found something that made Moru forget her sullenness—temporarily, at least.

At the crest of a low hill overlooking a bend in the river, strange shapes were silhouetted against the sky. At first, Laena dropped down into the long grass beside the river and pulled Moru beside her. Together, they watched and waited for long moments, sniffing the air and trying to see or hear any sign of movement. But the day was as still and calm as before.

Cautiously, Laena moved forward. The shapes were bones, she realized—mammoth ribs, which had once supported tents of animal hide. There was a camp at the top of the hill; or the remains of one.

She debated whether to circle around it and continue on their way. No; they needed to know if it was inhabited. Cautiously, pausing often, Laena led Moru up the hillside, crawling up gullies so as to remain unseen. But the closer she came to the camp, the more confident she became. The place had long since been abandoned.

A pyramid of rocks stood at the edge of the camp, taller than a man—a huge cairn, whose purpose Laena couldn't begin to guess. All the tribal tents had gone, leaving only the ribs of bone behind. Laena finally summoned the courage to walk openly among them, till she came to a blackened circle of earth that lay at the center. The ground around it had been trodden by many feet, and she could imagine the people who had once gathered here around their fire, talking together, singing together, eating together.

Laena shivered. The place reminded her of her own winter camp, abandoned by her tribe. What had happened here? Where had everyone gone?

Moru didn't seem to share Laena's concerns. She let out a whoop of excitement and started running in and out among the frames of bone. Then she went to the cairn and started pulling some of its stones away.

She stopped suddenly. "Laena!" she cried. "Laena, come and look!"

Laena had been searching some of the hollows in the ground where the tents had stood, hoping she might find something useful that the people had left behind—a flint knife, perhaps, or even a spearhead. She turned quickly when she heard Moru's shout. "What is it?"

"Come quick! Come look!"

Laena grunted with irritation. She went and joined her sister, who was peering into the cairn. It was hollow inside, and there was something white in there—something made of bone. Laena reached in and dragged it out, and found that it was a wolf's skull. A strange pattern had been daubed on it with crushed ocher, and the jaws were lashed together with sinew.

"What does it mean?" Moru asked. She took the skull out of Laena's hands and shook it. "What's it for?"

Laena felt a strange prickling sensation across the back of her neck and shoulders. "Put it back," she said. She heard her own voice, and there was a sharpness to it. "It's not for us to play with."

"But what's it *for*?" Moru obstinately held on to the skull, sniffing at it.

"I don't know what it's for. Just put it back. Here, I'll help you to rebuild the cairn." Laena quickly stacked the stones in place. "We must move on. There's nothing here for us. The people who lived here took everything valuable with them."

"But I want to stay here!" Moru wailed.

"No. It's not a good place for us to be." She didn't know why she said that; but it was true, she realized. She felt unsafe in this place, for the first time since they had set out on their journey.

So they left the camp behind. When Laena looked back at it, though, she still felt the same twinge of fear that had gripped her when they had unearthed the skull. There was something ominous about the relics silhouetted against the sky.

They stopped early that evening, and Laena insisted they take turns keeping watch. It was harder than she'd expected, though, to sit in silence while Moru slept. And when it was Moru's turn, the little girl simply couldn't stay awake. Laena lay in her sleeping bag, watching Moru sitting propped up against a tree. Within moments the little girl's head nodded forward, and her eyes fell shut.

Laena herself was so tired she could hardly think. She knew she should go and wake Moru and scold her. But at the same time, she knew it would be futile. She couldn't force her to stay awake. And she couldn't keep checking on her through the night. She needed her own rest.

She felt a wave of sadness. She had tried to do the right thing, she had tried to rise above her fears and be bold and brave, but this was much more tiring and difficult and lonely than she had ever imagined. How could she contemplate more days and weeks of this trek south, with no one to talk to, no one to turn to, but her little sister? The thought filled her with despair.

But even that was a weak force compared with her exhaustion. Her body felt so heavy, so weary, and her thoughts were sluggish in her head. One moment she was caught up in her own loneliness, wishing desperately for something that would give her hope. The next moment, she was asleep.

And then, without warning, it was morning. Laena opened her eyes—and found that her wish had been granted.

Chapter 16

There was someone sitting less than a dozen paces away, watching them. Laena squinted against the bright morning light. And then the figure moved.

Laena cried out in sudden fear. She sat up, clutching at her sleeping bag. Then she grabbed her spear.

The figure slowly got to its feet and started coming closer. Laena heard her pulse fluttering inside her ears. She scrambled onto her feet—and at the same time, she realized that the person coming toward her was a woman. An old woman, with long gray hair. She was wearing an ankle-length coat fashioned from musk-ox hides. It shimmered brown, making her look like the animal itself. Her face, meanwhile, was lined by age, darkened by the sun.

The woman paused as she saw Laena holding the spear, and she said something. Laena couldn't understand any of the words, but the woman's tone was gentle, as if she was trying to be reassuring.

"What's happening?" It was Moru's voice. She had been woken by Laena's startled cry. She looked up, blinking.

Laena's throat felt so tight she couldn't speak. She kept her grip on her spear. The tip of it trembled as she pointed it toward the stranger's face.

"Are you from the west?" the stranger said. This time, the words were clear, although the accent was harsh and strange. "Where is your tribe, girl? Is this your daughter?"

Moru was staring at the stranger. "I'm not her daughter, I'm her sister!" she blurted out.

The old woman grunted. "So, the little one speaks." She looked back at Laena and spread her hands, showing that they were empty. "Put down your spear. You have nothing to fear from me."

Slowly, Laena lowered the point of her spear, though she

kept her grip on the shaft. She glanced quickly around, suddenly wondering if the old woman had been sent to distract her while hunters gathered behind her. But the land was as empty as it had been the previous day, and the only sound was the lapping of the river at the grassy bank, fifty paces distant.

The old woman sat back down on the ground just ten paces away, moving deliberately, taking her time. "Tell me your name," she said.

Laena swallowed, forcing herself to be calm. "I'm Laena," she said. And then, boldly, she added: "Who are you?"

The old woman gave a dry, rasping laugh. "Maybe I'll tell you, but not with you standing there like that, holding your spear, and me sitting here on the ground."

Cautiously, Laena squatted down. She hesitated, then laid the spear in the grass where she could still grab it if she had to.

The woman nodded. She wasn't quite as old as Laena had first thought. She seemed very dignified, though, even as she sat on the ground. "That's better," she said. "Now, in answer to your question, my name is Nan. I am a wanderer." She watched Laena with eyes that were a strange pale brown.

Laena's fear was ebbing, but still she told herself to be cautious. "Why did you creep up on us like that?"

Nan calmly shook her head. If she had been afraid of Laena's spear, she showed no sign of it. "I didn't creep up on you, girl. In fact, I made some noise. That's what woke you."

"Oh," said Laena. She felt embarrassed at having left herself so vulnerable that even an old woman could come upon her in her sleep.

"How old are you?" Nan asked. "Thirteen summers?"

"Twelve," Laena said.

"I'm eight," Moru put in.

Nan smiled. There was kindness in her face, among all the deep, stern wrinkles. There was wisdom, too. Suddenly Laena found herself wanting, very much, to trust this woman. Had she really been sent by fate somehow, to answer Laena's wish for someone to turn to? Laena couldn't let herself believe that, but she found herself hoping for it, all the same.

"Where's the rest of your tribe?" Nan asked.

"We're on our own," Laena said. "Our people were all—were all killed." That was probably the best way to explain it. "Another tribe came—"

"We crossed the river," Moru interrupted. "It was full of ice, and my mother—my father died, and my mother—"

Nan was looking at them with an air of concern. "But what are you doing, wandering around out here? Where are you going?"

Laena glanced at Moru. The little girl looked up at her, waiting for her to speak. "We were traveling south," said Laena. "Upriver."

"South, yes, but where?"

Laena considered trying to explain their goal—but then, immediately, she thought better of it. "We don't know exactly where."

The old woman was silent for a moment. Her eyes studied Laena, unblinking. "Hoping to find somewhere safe, I suppose."

Laena nodded. "Yes."

"Well." Nan laid the palms of her hands on her knees. "Well, this isn't the place." She sighed. "Now that I've found you, I suppose I have to decide what to do with you. But first, we should eat together. Do you have food?"

"Yes," said Laena. "A little," she added, realizing that they were in no position to give it away to strangers.

"All right, you start a fire, and I'll fetch some water." Nan stood up without waiting for Laena to answer, and went to a bag that she had left lying on the ground behind her. With her back turned, she started rummaging through it. She pulled out a leather cup, slightly larger than the one that Laena owned, and she started down toward the river, still without bothering to look back.

"Who is she?" Moru whispered, giving Laena a searching look.

"Her name's Nan," said Laena. "She said so."

"But she's telling us what to do," said Moru.

Laena turned and opened her pack. She pulled out her firesticks. "She's an elder. She has the right."

"Is she going to eat our food?"

Laena felt a wave of irritation. "She may be able to help us," she said sharply. "Be polite to her, Moru. Please?"

Nan started back toward them, carrying the cup full of water. Laena bowed her head and set to work with the fire-sticks.

A little later, they sat around a small fire eating some of the caribou meat. The flames crackled, and the tang of wood smoke mingled with the pungent flavor of the meat. Laena felt herself being warmed by the fire, and she felt some of the courage returning. "Where is your tribe?" she asked Nan. "Did something bad happen to them?"

Nan was silent for a moment, chewing slowly. "They were taken by a storm when I was as young as you are now," she said. "Many years ago. So I went wandering. Another tribe took me in—" She broke off. "It's a long story, girl. Let's just say that some people settle down, and others do better on their own."

"You mean you travel alone, and fend for yourself? How is that possible?"

Nan shrugged. "I go from tribe to tribe, and they feed me. You see, I'm a healer."

Suddenly, Laena understood. There had been an old man who visited the Panther People each year, bringing herbal medicines and offering his skills. She looked at Nan with new respect.

"I get by," Nan went on. "Although it's not an easy life. Especially now, with things changing so much." She looked thoughtfully at Laena and Moru. "You aren't the only ones who've been made homeless in the west, you know. And it's even worse to the north. Not enough food, and the sea rising up and claiming the land. People are turning against each other."

"But it seems pleasant enough here," said Laena, looking around at the green valley.

"Well so it is," Nan agreed. She took another piece of meat and nibbled on it. "Can you guess why?"

Laena said nothing. She didn't enjoy admitting her own ignorance.

"This land belongs to the Wolf People," Nan said, as if it should have been obvious. "They show no kindness to strangers. That's why you don't see refugees coming here. No one has the courage to do so.''

Laena felt a tense, cold sensation in her stomach. Could she really believe what Nan was saying?

"We saw a camp," Moru said. "Yesterday. Back there. Is that where the Wolf People used to live?''

Nan nodded. "Some of them. There was a sickness there, which killed a lot of them. The Wolves are superstitious, so they abandoned that site.''

"There was a thing in a pile of stones," Moru said. "A wolf skull. I found it.''

Nan gave her a sharp look. "You mean you opened the cairn?'' Her warmth had gone. The lines in her face deepened, and her eyes were fierce.

Moru edged backward. She glanced uneasily at Laena.

"I put the skull back inside,'' said Laena.

"I hope you did, girl. I hope you left it exactly the way you found it. That skull is to warn away the evil spirits that brought the plague. The Wolf People kill anyone who disturbs their totems.''

"But we didn't do anything wrong!'' Moru protested.

"To the Wolves, you did.'' Nan slapped the ground. "It's not as green and pleasant here as it seems. There's death in this land.'' She paused for a moment, and her eyes became reflective. "I found the skeleton of a man just last week. There was a flint blade among his bones, stained with his own blood.'' She shook her head. "Most tribes put food in the belly of a traveler and honor him for the tales he brings. But not the Wolf Tribe. The only thing they put in a stranger's belly is a knife.''

Moru stared accusingly at Laena. "You didn't tell me,'' she complained. "You said we were safe here.''

"I didn't know!'' Laena snapped at her. She felt a surge of emotions. "How was I supposed to know? I was doing my best. I told you we should take turns sleeping, didn't I?''

"Hush, hush.'' Nan held up her hands. "You're right, there was no way for you to have known.''

Laena realized, with confusion, that she was on the verge of tears. "What are you doing here,'' she asked the old woman, "if it's such a terrible place?''

Nan smiled. "I've met the Wolf People, and I've treated their sick and divined their dreams. I know their language.

That was what I spoke to you, when you first noticed me. They know that I'm useful to them.''

There was a short silence. A gust of wind came up the wide valley, chilling Laena under her furs. She glanced around again, and the land no longer seemed as pleasant as it had before. There were so many places where enemies might be hiding; so many dangers that she couldn't have foreseen. ''Nan—'' she began. She wasn't sure how to say what she wanted to say. ''Nan, I don't know that I'm really old enough to be—to be doing what I'm doing, out here. You seem to know so much, and you've been here before—''

''You want to come with me?'' Nan nodded. ''Of course.''

Laena stared at her. Could it really be so simple?

''I'm an old woman,'' Nan said. ''I could use some help. Besides, people helped me when I was young myself and I had nowhere to go. It's the way of the world to pass a favor on. Yes, you can both come with me. Till you find a place where you're welcome, and you're happy to settle down again.''

Laena felt the tension suddenly ebb out of her. Tension that she hadn't known was there. ''Thank you!'' she blurted out.

The old woman inclined her head. She didn't smile. ''Just understand, both of you, you have to do what I say. I don't want any arguments, and I'll expect you to do your fair share of the chores.''

Laena blinked. She realized slowly that she wasn't being offered a gift after all; there would be some conditions attached to it. She wouldn't be in control of her own destiny anymore. Her freedom would be gone. And she would be turning away from the decision she had made, just two days ago, to follow her vision.

''Can I ask you,'' she said cautiously, ''which way you're traveling?''

''I'll follow the river a little further, then turn to the east.'' Nan nodded inland.

Laena was silent for a long moment. ''You wouldn't want to continue moving south?''

Nan laughed, but there was no humor in the sound ''See the mountains there, child? In two days, three at the most, you'd find yourself facing snow and ice in the middle of summer, with cliffs so steep there's no way anyone could ever climb them. There's nothing for us there. Take my word for that.''

Laena hesitated. Nan had spent her whole life wandering these lands. And yet—Laena's vision spoke with a higher truth. "Maybe there's something beyond the mountains," she said.

Nan gestured dismissively. "No one knows."

In that case, Laena thought to herself, her vision could still be true. Evidently, though, this was not the time when she was going to fulfill it. At least not yet. She needed Nan, or someone like her, while she was still young, without the means to feed herself or defend herself. She had taken a terrible risk just by walking here in this valley.

One day, Laena promised herself, she would be strong enough to go where no one had gone before. One day, when she was truly a grown woman.

She turned away from the mountains and looked again at Nan. "It will be an honor to travel with you," she said. "And I promise you, we'll follow your guidance."

After they packed their possessions, Nan stood for a moment, surveying the place where Laena and Moru had spent the night. "We should cover our tracks," she said, half to herself. She pointed to the flattened grass where the sleeping bags had been. "Ruffle that up. I'll see what I can do to hide the patch where the fire was. It won't stand a close inspection, but it'll be better than nothing." She groped under her coat, pulled out a flint knife, and cut a few branches out of some bushes.

Moru started scuffing the grass with her feet, but Laena stood motionless, staring at the knife in Nan's hand.

Nan stopped and frowned at her. "Something wrong, girl?"

Laena reached out. "May I?" She saw that her hand was trembling. She was being foolish, she knew. But still, she had to be sure. "May I see that knife?"

Nan held it out to her.

Laena closed her fingers around it. She felt a numb sensation in her chest. "Where did you get it?"

"As it happens, I found it," Nan said.

The numbness seemed to spread, till Laena felt as if the

world were receding around her. "Where?" she demanded. "I have to know where."

"I found it in the bones of a dead man. The one I told you about. He was lying in a gully six days from here, downriver."

Laena sat down hard on the ground. "Elbrau," she said.

"Ah." Nan's eyes softened with understanding. "He was one of your tribe."

"Yes," Laena said. She rubbed her thumb along the flint blade, then around the thongs that bound its leather handle. "I recognized the workmanship of the blade," she said, remembering when Elbrau had shown her the knife and tucked it in the sleeve of his furs. "It's the same as my spear. He made that, too."

Nan nodded. "I could see it wasn't the work of a Wolf craftsman." She laid her hand on Laena's shoulder. "Do you know how your friend died?"

"No." Laena gestured helplessly. She tried to imagine how Gorag might have tricked Elbrau into surrendering his weapon, or how he might have stolen it when Elbrau had been off guard. She shook her head; it didn't matter. Elbrau was dead, and there was no longer any doubt about it.

"Take comfort from this," said Nan. "I laid your friend's bones in the earth. He will rest. His spirit will not wander."

"Take it," Laena said. She couldn't face the thought of owning the weapon that had killed Elbrau. "Keep it, Nan. He would have been pleased that you have use for it."

She scrambled up and walked away, down toward the river where she could be alone. The surface of the water lay flat, moving sluggishly, gleaming in the bright sunlight. She stared at it for a long while, without really thinking.

Behind her, she heard Nan getting back to work, planting the pieces of the bushes to conceal the ashes left by fire. Moru murmured a question, and Nan answered, but it all seemed far away.

Laena stared at the water. Downstream from here, Gorag's body had slipped into the river, following the people he had already led to their deaths. By now, his body would have floated beyond the crossings, past the sad ruin that the Panthers had called home.

Laena gathered the hate she felt for Gorag and savored it for a long moment, holding it in her chest, her stomach, her soul. Then, reluctantly, she let it go. To kill with hate was bad enough; to live with it was much worse.

The water chuckled against the riverbank. She turned away from it, feeling lighter, stronger, and better able to face the world. With new energy, she started back to where Nan and Moru were waiting for her.

Chapter 17

Four days later, they camped beside a narrow tributary that tumbled down a steep hillside crowded with trees. The air smelled fragrant here, up in the hills. Still, Laena had little time to admire the scenery.

"Again," Nan commanded.

Laena pushed her hair back from her forehead. Her arms felt impossibly heavy, and her muscles ached fiercely. "What was wrong this time?"

"Your knot was loose. Remember, blood is like water that bubbles up from a spring. It always tries to find ways to escape. If your knot isn't tight enough, the blood of a wounded person will escape and the person will die." Nan squatted beside Laena and took the thong from her hands. "Watch me. Like this." Her fingers expertly twisted the thong, looped it around the upthrust stone that stood in front of them, and tied a knot in one smooth motion. "You have to pull harder. Then the thong will grip." Nan sat back. She nodded. "Try again."

Laena pried with her fingernails at the knot that Nan had made. She undid it, shook out the thong, then whipped it around the stone.

"Much better!" Nan said.

Laena looked at her. The old woman sounded pleased. Laena could hardly believe it.

"Now tell me," Nan went on, "what you do next."

Laena blinked. It was taking her a moment to realize that she had finally satisfied her teacher. It took her another moment to find an answer to the new question she had been asked. "I must pack the wound, Nan."

"Correct. How can you do that?"

"I bind a piece of soft hide tightly over it. Or I use dry

moss, crumbled to a fine powder, to make the blood thicken.''

"And after that?''

Laena closed her eyes, struggling to remember. The tasks and questions were endless. "After that, I remove the thong. Otherwise, the limb will die.''

"Good, Laena!''

Laena opened her eyes and found Nan smiling at her. During the past four days, she had learned to hope for that smile, to wait for it and seek it out. When Nan smiled, the ordeal was over—for the time being, at least.

Laena pressed her palms on either side of her waist and leaned backward, stretching. When she had set out with Nan on this journey, she had shyly asked the old woman to teach her some of her healing skills. Laena had imagined a few quiet conversations like the ones she used to have with Elbrau, when he would talk to her about his craft. She'd never dreamed that Nan would take the request so seriously—or that being a healer could entail so much learning and so much work.

They had trekked across rugged terrain, moving steadily higher, following a small river through hillsides strewn with tumbled rock. And every evening, Nan gave lessons—how to identify herbs, how to tie knots, how to treat fevers, to cauterize wounds, to dig for roots—it went on and on.

This evening, Moru had already finished eating and was curled up inside her sleeping bag beside the campfire. Laena, meanwhile, had not been allowed to eat dinner. "I feel very tired," she said.

Nan brushed the complaint aside with a wave of her hand. "The tiredness will pass. The harder you work, the stronger you grow. And the more you learn, the easier it is to learn more.''

Laena had heard this before from the old woman. The worst part was, Nan genuinely seemed to believe it. Laena had never imagined it was possible for one person to know so much, or be so strong.

Nan reached out and patted her shoulder. "It's hard, at first," she said, in a slightly kinder tone. "But if you have the willpower to stick with it, you'll find it's all worthwhile. Remember, when you become a healer, you become more than a woman. A healer is welcome at any hearth.''

Laena looked at her doubtfully. "Even the hearths of the Wolf Tribe?"

"Even there." Nan paused for a moment. She surveyed the terrain around them. They had moved up into a high-walled valley where the river ran fast, throwing itself from one rock to the next in a flurry of white spray. Pine trees grew all around—more than Laena had ever seen in her life. The sky was still bright, but the sun had long since crept below the tops of the pines.

Nan sighed. "I suppose there's not enough light for more lessons tonight," she said. She picked up a roasting stick laden with meat and placed it over the flames.

Laena felt a great wave of relief. But at the same time, she couldn't relax completely. "I'm still scared of meeting the Wolves," she said. "What if they see me, and Moru, and—"

Nan gestured impatiently, cutting her off. "They will accept you."

"How can you be so sure?"

Nan eyed her calmly. "Their scouts are already out there. They've seen us. They know we're here."

Laena stiffened. She looked quickly around—and saw only the trees, and the rocks, and the river.

"They followed us today," Nan went on. She lifted the stick off the fire. "Eat. You're young, you need food."

Laena looked at Nan's face. Its deep lines seemed so severe, and so wise. She couldn't imagine being so calm in the face of an enemy.

"Worry only about the things you can do," Nan said. "Think now: is there anything we can do about the Wolf People? No. Not at present." She shrugged. "So, we eat."

Grudgingly, Laena took a piece of meat. Despite her fear, she found she was ravenously hungry. Her mouth watered uncontrollably as soon as the food touched her lips. "But they could come up on us while we're asleep, the same way you did, when Moru and I were beside the river."

Nan shrugged again. "They don't need to wait till we're sleeping. They could just as easily kill us while we're awake. An old woman and two young girls, with one spear between the three of us—" She grunted.

Well, that was probably true. But the truth didn't make Laena feel any less nervous.

A little later, when they had eaten their fill, she and Nan wrapped themselves against the cold and lay down on beds that they had fashioned from grass and moss. Tired as she was, Laena found herself listening for any tiny sound that would betray the presence of someone close by. But all she heard was the steady rushing of water and hissing of spray.

Even without the Wolf People to worry her, she would have found it hard to rest. The things that she was learning cried out to be examined and mulled over. The land itself was new to her, and even with her eyes closed she still saw its strange shapes and contours. Where she had grown up, the Flat Hills had been the highest ground she had known. Here, she found herself faced with slopes that seemed to lead forever upward. She had to smile when she remembered thinking that she and Moru could have scaled the mountains that lay to the south. These hills here were daunting enough, mottled with patches of snow and shale and slippery moss, littered with boulders that looked as if some giant had thrown them down from the sky.

And the trees were so thick here. They stood so close together, there was hardly enough room to walk among them. They were taller than a man—and that, too, made Laena shake her head in wonder. The trees of her childhood had been no more than chest-high, and often less than that. Dwarf willows that grew near the camp of the Panther People had rarely been taller than a person's knees.

She understood now why fantastic stories were told about the lands to the east. She was amazed by everything she saw. With so much to think about, and with the new threat of Wolf hunters watching her as she lay beneath the open sky—how could she hope to sleep?

Suddenly the sun had shifted. She blinked, feeling confused. The whole night had passed as quickly as the beating of a bird's wing. A fire was crackling and Nan was squatting beside it, feeding dry twigs to the flames. The sky was a pale blue, and the air was cold and clear.

Nan eyed Laena. "Are you rested, girl?"

Laena sat up. She winced as her muscles protested. Walking uphill during the past few days had stretched and flexed her body in ways she had never known before, and the pack on her back had chafed her skin. Slowly, she struggled onto her feet.

"Fetch some more wood," said Nan. "We have none left."

Laena nodded. Her job was the same every morning: search the ground for dead branches, gather them in her arms, and bring them back to feed the fire for breakfast. This, too, seemed strange to her. Where she was from, a man might spend years searching for a stick that would serve well enough as a spear shaft. People might use some tiny scraps of wood to start a fire, but after that, they burned animal droppings or (if there were carcasses to spare) animal fat. To burn a whole pile of wood seemed shockingly wasteful.

Still, there could never be a shortage of timber around here. She turned toward the trees—and froze.

Someone was sitting on a mossy boulder no more than a dozen paces away. He was a young hunter, Laena realized. There was a spear across his knees. She gave a sudden cry of fear. Instinctively, she stepped back.

"There's nothing to worry about," said Nan, still going about her business, blowing on the flames, coaxing them higher. "It's a good sign that he's decided to show himself."

Laena stared at the man. His clothes seemed strange to her. He wasn't wearing moccasins. His feet were clad in shoes that came up so high, they wrapped his ankles and his calves. The leather gleamed as if it was wet, and it was crisscrossed with thongs that were knotted at the top. His coat had seams that were turned outward instead of inward, and instead of a fur-lined hood, he wore a cap made out of the head of a wolf. Laena shivered; the cap made it look as if he had two heads, one on top of the other.

The hunter nodded solemnly to her. A gust of wind rolled up the valley, and his black hair blew around his face. She saw that the strands were long and unkempt, not braided in the custom of her tribe.

"You have to understand how the Wolves think," Nan said, studying Laena with her pale brown eyes. "Our visitor could have watched us and never let us see him. But he's here now, which means he accepts us as his equals. Not his friends, necessarily; but not his enemies, either."

Laena felt torn with indecision, not sure whether to look at the man or look away from him. "What should I do?" she whispered.

"We'll give him some meat. If he accepts, he won't think of us as strangers any longer. But the meat should be hot, and I've run out of wood. So go and gather some sticks, Laena, to feed the fire."

Laena nodded dumbly. She walked in a wide circle around the Wolf tribesman, then ran as fast as she could to the nearest trees. A few moments later, when she had two armfuls of deadwood, she ran back to Nan.

"Very good, girl." Nan was already heating some of their diminishing supply of meat over the delicate flames. She speared a choice piece and held it out to Laena. "Take it to him."

Laena looked into Nan's face. Nan looked back, implacably.

"You're sure," Laena said, "that it's safe?"

Nan made a little impatient sound. "I'm not sure of anything. But it has to be done. Go on now."

Laena drew a deep breath. She took the meat on the skewer, turned, and picked her way toward the hunter. Moru, she saw, was still sleeping in blissful ignorance of what was happening around her.

"Try to smile," Nan called after her. "Show him you're friendly."

Laena's face felt stiff with fear, but she made her mouth widen in an awkward imitation of a smile. The man nodded to her again, and he set his spear down with its point in the earth. That seemed a good sign, at least.

Slowly, Laena held out the offering of food. The man took it from her. He eyed her a moment, while he sniffed the meat. Then he smacked his lips loudly and grinned. As Laena watched, he started eating.

"Now come back here," Nan called to Laena. "And wake Moru. We have to eat, too. And then we must get ready to move on."

Laena went and shook her sister's shoulder. She sat Moru up, showed her the Wolf hunter, and hugged the little girl to calm her. "Nan says it's all right," she whispered. "We have to eat breakfast. Try to ignore him."

Moru still looked startled as Laena dragged her to the

fire. But she was young enough to trust her elders more instinctively than Laena, and when Nan told her to eat, she started forcing down the food as fast as possible.

When the meal was over, Nan threw the roasting sticks onto the flames. "Make sure your packs are ready," she said.

"But where are we going?" Laena asked.

"Wherever the Wolf People take us."

Laena felt angry and frustrated. Thinking back to when she had asked to travel with Nan, she'd realized she would give up her freedom, but she hadn't imagined it would be quite like this. Nan hadn't seemed so tough or demanding at first. Well—she still was friendly, in her way. But she seldom said a word more than she had to, and she still treated Laena like a child.

Laena turned to protest—and noticed that the Wolf hunter was no longer alone.

She gave a little gasp as she saw a dozen men emerging from the trees, all of them holding spears, all of them moving with swift, muscled grace. The tallest of the newcomers exchanged a few words with the man to whom Laena had given some meat. Then both of them turned and looked at Nan, and the tall one took a few steps toward her. He held his spear pointdown, but he shook it and shouted something that sounded like a challenge.

Nan slowly stood up, taking her time, brushing scraps of dead grass off her coat, and moving with dignity. She straightened her back and calmly eyed the man who stood before her. She cleared her throat and called out a few words in the man's own tongue.

He looked surprised. He spoke again and pointed down-river, as if he was warning them to leave.

The grim lines in Nan's face seemed to grow deeper. She held out her right hand with its palm toward the ground, and made a fierce, downward motion. She shouted something. And then, unexpectedly, she turned her back on him.

The hunter looked even more surprised than before. Laena watched, feeling astonished. Clearly, Nan had angered the man. He took another step forward. He bared his teeth, and for a horrible moment Laena remembered the way that Jalenau of the White Bear Tribe had looked, just before he had speared Henik and started the massacre of the Panther People.

But the Wolf hunter didn't throw his spear. He glared at Nan, still standing with her back to him, and his face reddened. He yelled something. His voice sounded shrill.

Nan turned her head just far enough to give him a brief, disdainful look. She started talking, and it was a long tumble of words, flowing as fast as the river that splashed beside them. There was no mistaking her tone. She sounded the way she did when she was giving Laena one of her strictest lessons.

Laena found herself clutching Moru, while Moru clutched her in return. But as they watched, they realized that Nan had somehow seized the upper hand. The Wolf hunter was starting to back away, not as angry as before, as if Nan's words were beating his resistance out of him. Finally he held up his left hand and made a gesture of contrition.

Nan finally stopped talking. She turned so that she faced the man fully. There was a long moment of silence, as they stared at each other, with Nan looking fierce and proud, and the hunter looking confused. Finally, with dignity, she inclined her head to him.

He thrust his spear into the soft moss and spread his hands to show they were empty. Then he bowed to her.

When he straightened up, Nan was smiling. She turned and beckoned to Laena and Moru. "Pick up your packs," she said. "Follow me. We'll be traveling with the Wolf Tribe from now on."

The hunters led them along a tiny trail up a steep hillside, away from the river. The path snaked between the trees, and it was strewn with stones and gravel that shifted unexpectedly underfoot. One of the men carried Moru on his back, but Laena had to fend for herself, and the pace was grueling.

"What did you say back there?" she whispered to Nan when they emerged from the trees onto a ridge that wasn't quite so steep and she had a chance to walk beside the old woman. "And what did you do with your hand?" She imitated the pushing-down motion.

"Never do that!" Nan warned her. "Among the Wolf Tribe, it's the way an old person tells a young person that he's acting like a child. See, I wanted him to treat me with respect.''

Laena stared at her. "You weren't afraid of insulting his pride as a hunter?''

Nan shook her head. "It had to be done.''

"But—wasn't it a dangerous thing to do?''

Unexpectedly, Nan put her arm around Laena's shoulders. "Listen to me, Laena.'' She bent her head close to Laena's ear. "If I had knuckled under to him, he would have lost his respect for us, and we would have ended up doing whatever he wanted. Would you have liked that?'' She glanced briefly at Laena's face and body. "You're not a girl anymore; you've gone through the change, I do believe. I think you know what the Wolf men would have wanted from a pretty young woman like you.''

Laena felt her cheeks redden. She didn't know what to say.

"I have my own status to think about, too,'' Nan went on. "So I pretended he was a brash little boy. It was the only way.''

Laena looked up at Nan's face, searching for any sign of self-doubt. "Didn't you feel at all afraid?''

Nan paused, looking thoughtful. "Perhaps. Perhaps I did. But it doesn't make any difference, do you see? Even if you feel afraid, you must never, ever show it.''

Laena realized that if she could ever learn how that was done, it might be the most valuable lesson that Nan could ever teach her. She opened her mouth to ask how the old woman had learned to mask her feelings so well; but before she could speak, there was a shout from the hunter at the head of the procession.

"Ah,'' said Nan. "We've reached the guard. This is what I've been waiting for, Laena. The camp of the Wolf Tribe.''

Chapter 18

The camp was on a hilltop, but the forest around it was so thick, everything was hidden completely from the outside world. The Wolf hunters led Laena, Nan, and Moru past three lookouts—men perched in the high branches of the tallest trees, their skin painted with stripes of black dye to make them almost invisible in the shadows under the canopy of foliage. The only part of their impassive faces that seemed truly alive was their eyes, gleaming in the dim light, watching Laena with feral intensity as she passed by.

The camp itself had been built in a clearing littered with tree stumps. Evidently, the Wolf People had torn down scores of the tall pines, although Laena found it hard to imagine an ax that would have been big enough to do the job. Where the trees had been, she saw tents that awed her with their size—so large, they could hold a dozen people or more, with enough room to allow the tallest hunter to stand upright inside. For a moment Laena imagined the size of the bones that must support the tents. What kind of creature had the Wolf People managed to kill that would be so enormous? Then she realized that the tents were not supported by a framework of bones at all. With so many trees all around, wooden poles would have been plentiful.

There was a small group of hunters sitting in a clearing, talking together while they shaped new spears with their flint knives. Another group was practicing with their weapons, throwing them into targets that they had made from vines tightly wrapped around leaves and moss. At first, the men paid little attention to the hunting party as it made its way into the camp. Then one of the Wolf People noticed her. He let out a short, sharp shout, and his companions turned away from their target practice. Gradually, the whole camp fell silent, and Laena's face burned red as she felt every man staring at her with obvious interest.

She ducked her head, trying to avoid the eyes that were watching her. At the same time, she realized that there were no old men or young boys in this place. No women, either—she didn't see a single female. Were they inside the big tents? Did the men not allow their women outside at all?

But she didn't have a chance to voice her questions. With Nan ahead of her and Moru still riding on the shoulders of one of their guides, Laena was led among the big tents, into a small space right at the center of the camp.

Here, she found the chieftain of the Wolves. He was a large man—even larger than Gorag had been—and his powerful body was draped with wolf skins stitched together to form a tent-sized cape. His black hair hung like a shiny black mane, dangling well below his shoulders.

What captured her attention most of all, though, was the thing he was sitting in. It was made of stout branches lashed together with leather thongs. The bark had been stripped from the branches, and they had been polished to a rich brown luster, forming a framework that supported the chieftain well above the ground. He was like a big, strong cat, Laena thought to herself, perched up in a tree, surveying his territory below him.

The man who had been carrying Moru set her down on the ground and gave her a little push toward Laena. Laena took the little girl's hand and squeezed it, trying to give her little sister the reassurance that she wanted to feel herself. Meanwhile, the hunting party was gathering around the chieftain in a semicircle, and their leader was stepping forward, bowing, with Nan standing close beside him. He coughed politely and started making an elaborate speech which Laena guessed was the story of how he had found his captives.

The chieftain made an impatient gesture. He climbed down from his wooden throne, moving with surprising grace for a man of his size. He strode directly toward Nan, grinned at her, spread his great arms, and wrapped them around her.

When he released her a moment later, Nan was looking oddly pleased with herself. She turned to Laena and beckoned her to come forward. "This is Rorgar, chieftain of the Wolves," she said. "Bow to him, then stand and hold out your hands with the palms facing upward. And don't look him in the eye till he speaks to you."

Laena bowed low, remembering the way that the tall leader of the hunting party had bowed to Nan after she scolded him. Beside her, Moru did her best to imitate her. Then Laena held out her hands.

Rorgar said something that she didn't understand. He gave her a curt nod, and he grinned. He wasn't so much like a big cat, Laena realized. He was more like a bear. She had expected to feel intimidated by him, but now, as he smiled at her, she felt welcomed, and she found herself smiling back. He wasn't like the rest of the men in his tribe. He was as strong as Gorag had been, maybe stronger, but his strength wasn't menacing. She looked up at his face, and she found herself wanting to trust him.

He turned and said something to a boy who had been sitting beside the throne. He scrambled up quickly and stepped forward, and Laena realized he was the youngest male she had seen here—although, she judged, he had come of age and could just about be considered a man. He looked at Laena with frank curiosity, then gave a quick, perfunctory bow, while the chieftain said something more in his deep voice.

"He says this is his son, Sordir, aged fourteen years," Nan translated. She turned to Rorgar, and the two of them exchanged a few more words in the Wolf tongue. Then Nan turned back to Laena. "Rorgar remembers me from the last time I traveled among the Wolf People, and since you are my apprentice, and Moru is your sister, you are welcome here as respected guests of the tribe. Sordir will take you and Moru to the tent where you'll be sleeping tonight." Nan laid her hand reassuringly on Laena's shoulder. "You see," she went on in a softer tone, "I told you there was nothing to worry about."

Laena nodded. She hesitated, wanting to ask a dozen different questions, but she felt self-conscious surrounded by the hunting party, with Rorgar still staring down at her.

"Go with Sordir," Nan said.

Laena held back. "What about you?"

The odd little smile crept back to Nan's face. "Rorgar

wasn't the chieftain the last time I was here. He took charge after the old chieftain died.'' She glanced at the big man. "I'll join you later, Laena. He and I have a few things to talk about.''

Sordir led the way along a path between the large tents. The open area where the men had been working with their weapons was on the other side of the village. Here among the tents, Laena realized she was out of sight and out of earshot of just about everyone. There was only Moru, beside her, and Sordir, leading the way.

Sordir stopped outside the last tent. Beyond it, the forest was a wall of dense, dark green. The young hunter loosened two thongs that secured the entrance flap of the tent, then swung it open and gestured for them to go inside. Well, Laena thought to herself, Nan had said this was safe, and Nan seemed to know the Wolf People well enough. Trying not to show the nervousness she felt, she ducked her head and walked in.

The walls of the tent were of oiled mammoth hide, scraped completely free of hair, and so neatly stitched together that barely a pinpoint of light penetrated the seams. There were some ventilation slits, though, and a faint gray radiance filtered in through them.

As Laena's eyes adjusted to the dimness, she admired the massive wooden framework that supported the panels of hide. Up above her head, nets had been slung below the pole that ran along the ridge of the tent. The nets were woven from some kind of vine, and they were packed full of dried meat, bowls fashioned from tree bark, wooden utensils, flint tools, and fur clothing.

Sordir touched Laena's arm, then gestured at her pack and beckoned with both hands. Cautiously, she took off the pack and held it out to him. He opened it, pulled out her sleeping bag, and threw it across a wooden framework that stood near one of the walls of the tent. There were six of these wooden frames, with long, flat leather sacks in them, and she couldn't imagine what they were for.

She looked at Sordir, wishing she could speak his language. He grinned at her, flopped down on her sleeping bag, rolled on his side, and pretended to sleep. Then he stood up and gestured for Laena to try it.

Cautiously, she lowered her weight. The wooden framework creaked, and she half expected it to collapse under her. But it took her weight easily. She realized that the leather sack was stuffed full of dry grass, and she was lying on the most comfortable bed she had ever known.

"Me, too!" said Moru. "Laena, my turn!"

Laena stood up and moved aside. She and Sordir watched as the little girl tested the bed with her toe, then kneeled on it, then bounced up and down on it. She squealed with delight.

Meanwhile, Sordir was quietly studying Laena. She turned and found him staring at her, and she forced herself to meet his eyes. He was a little taller than she was, and his skin was slightly darker. He had a strong, square jaw, like his father, and his smile was just as friendly. His teeth gleamed in the dim light. He brushed his hair back from his face, then pointed to his chest. "Sordir," he said.

She nodded to show that she already knew that. She pointed to herself, and then her sister. "Laena. Moru."

Sordir nodded slowly. With a few quick motions, he shrugged off the fur jacket that he was wearing. He pulled back his shoulders, flexed his muscles, and ran his fingers over his chest, while Laena watched. Then he dropped suddenly to one knee, picked up a spear that was standing in the corner of the tent, and pantomimed throwing it. He pointed to a caribou hide draped across one of the sleeping frames, thumped his chest with his fist, and nodded solemnly.

"You're strong. And you killed that caribou," said Laena.

Sordir smiled again. He stood up, clenched his fists, and bowed his head to her.

Laena clapped her hands. It was the only way she could think of making a response that he might understand. Even though he was bragging a little, it didn't annoy her as it had when Jobia had made his boasts. Jobia was always trying to prove he was more than he really was. Sordir was simply telling her what he could do and what he had done.

He really did seem strong, and he was very sure of himself. She could smell the musky scent of his young, powerful body. Slowly, he reached out and touched her face with just the tips of his fingers. Tentatively at first, then more boldly, he traced the contours of her features in the same way that he had followed the shape of his own chest.

Laena wanted him to stop, because he was making her nervous. At the same time, she felt her pulse running fast, and a strange tension started growing, radiating through her from her belly. It was a heavy, warm feeling, and she realized with a sudden jolt of surprise that she was starting to feel strangely excited.

Sordir moved a little closer. He touched Laena's shoulder, then her arm. Finally, he took her hand.

Laena felt a thickness in her throat. So much had happened, and it had all happened so quickly. She was starting to feel dizzy, here in this dark tent in the heart of a forest that was so dense, she doubted she could find her way out of it without anyone to guide her. She gathered her willpower, pulled back from Sordir, and raised both her hands with the palms toward him. Quickly, she shook her head.

Sordir paused. He watched her for a moment, and smiled again. Then he put his hands on his hips. He threw his head back and laughed.

She felt a rush of embarrassment. Was he laughing at her? Should she have responded differently? What should she have done? And what would *he* have done, if she hadn't called a halt?

Sordir took a step backward. He pointed to Laena, then pointed to the bed with her sleeping bag on it, and he nodded to her. Then he turned to Moru, who was sitting silently, staring up at him with wide eyes. He bent down, picked her up, and tossed her onto another of the beds with casual ease. Without another glance, he opened the flap of the tent and strode out.

Suddenly all the strength seemed to leave Laena's muscles. She sat down hard.

"Laena?" Moru called to her. "Laena, what's going on?"

She realized that her mouth was very dry. She tried to moisten her lips. "I think he wants us to stay here and rest awhile, little one."

The little girl blinked in the dimness. "But what was he doing? Why was he touching you like that?"

Laena felt suddenly irritated by the presence of her sister.

"I don't know!" she snapped. "And anyway, it's nothing you need to think about. Just lie down over there, Moru. Take a nap."

Moru heard the edge in Laena's voice. She looked resentful. "All right," she said. She reclined on the leather mattress, and she was silent for a moment. "I think I like him," she added, half to herself.

And so do I, Laena thought to herself. She found herself blushing, remembering how he had touched her face. He was a complete stranger, and yet he had acted as if he had a perfect right to do—to do anything at all. It was shocking, and yet it didn't shock her at all.

She had lied to Moru, when she'd said she hadn't known what Sordir was doing. She had known exactly what he wanted. And to her amazement, for the first time in her life, she realized that a part of her had wanted it, too.

"Laena!"

The voice came from outside the tent. She sat up quickly, feeling startled. "Who's there?" she called. And then she remembered where she was, and she realized there could only be one person calling her name.

The tent flap opened and Nan poked her head inside. "Rorgar needs to speak to you," she said. "And to Moru. Come quickly."

Laena wondered what was wrong—if, in fact, anything was wrong. She felt confused. How long had she been asleep?

She got up quickly, went to Moru, took her hand, and followed Nan outside. The sky was still bright over the camp, but she couldn't tell where the sun was. "What's the matter?" she asked.

"Nothing. Nothing at all. But it's bad manners to keep the chieftain waiting. Come along."

She and Moru followed Nan back to the center of the camp. Rorgar was sitting in his big chair once again, and several of his hunters were standing on either side of him. Laena looked at their faces, trying to decide if they had been in the hunting party that had brought her here.

"Sit on the ground in front of him," said Nan.

Obediently, Laena seated herself. The earth was warm from the fire, and the cool air was heavy with the smell of pine trees. Birds sang in the forest at the edge of the camp, and from one of the tents Laena heard the clink of stone on stone, and someone singing. It sounded like a work song, and she imagined a man making tools—a flintknapper like Elbrau.

"You Panther," said Rorgar.

Laena blinked, surprised to hear the chieftain speak her language. Maybe Nan had taught him those two words.

"Yes," Laena said. She put her arm around Moru. "We are of the Panther Tribe."

Rorgar shook his head slowly. "No Panther here."

"He means that you can't remain a Panther if you stay in the Wolf country," said Nan. She turned back to Rorgar and said the same thing in his dialect. He nodded his agreement.

"But," Laena protested, "in that case—"

"You must renounce your tribe," said Nan.

Laena blinked. She felt a strangeness, as if she were in a dream. How could she stop being who she was?

"All of your people have died," Nan continued patiently. "There are no more Panthers. It is time to break your ties with the past, Laena."

The idea shocked her. She thought of her parents, and the pride they had always felt in their tribal heritage. "I can't—" she began.

Rorgar said something sharply in his own language. Nan listened, then turned again to Laena. "He says the people of the plains—the Panthers, the White Bears—have come to the Wolves from time to time, and used their land. The Wolves refuse to allow it. Usually, they kill intruders. Either you must renounce the Panthers, or you must leave immediately."

Laena felt a deep pang. Everything kept changing, too fast for her to adjust. How could she cope with this? She needed days to think about it. She couldn't change herself and renounce her tribe here and now, within just a few moments. She thought of her parents again, and of all the other people she had known. Surely, their spirits would be offended if she turned away from them.

"Laena, listen to me," Nan said. "The Wolves aren't asking you to change your beliefs. They don't want you to be one of them. You must simply say that you are not a

Panther anymore. Then Rorgar can tell the others that you're Laena of No People. If you have no people—and you don't, anymore—you will be allowed to stay in the lands of the Wolves. Which, incidentally, is an unusual privilege.''

Laena stared at Nan. She knew she could not defy her, for there would be nowhere else to go. "I . . ." She swallowed and tried again. "I have no people?"

"That's right. You're like me, Laena. I'm Nan of No People; didn't you realize that? I answer to no one but myself."

And when Nan put it like that, it didn't sound quite so bad. Laena had always felt something different between herself and the people around her. She had always tended to be solitary. "Laena of No People," she said to herself.

"Good." Nan nodded encouragingly. "Now tell Rorgar."

"I have no people." She turned to the chieftain, and felt something fall away from her as she said it—another of the bonds with her past. It was scary, yet it was not as bad as she had expected. "I am Laena of No People." Her voice was louder now, and proud.

"Good!" said Nan. She clapped her hands. "Now Moru."

"Say the same as I did," Laena coaxed her.

Moru looked doubtful. "No people?"

"Very good. Louder."

"No people!"

Rorgar grinned. He wasn't fierce and grim anymore, he was a big, friendly bear again. He grabbed Laena and Moru by their shoulders and gave them a little shake. He rattled off some words in his own language and nodded emphatically.

"Tomorrow we will journey to their East Camp, on a plain that lies the other side of the range of hills that we've been climbing," Nan translated. "This camp is for the menfolk only. Hunters practice their skills here, without the distraction of women."

Laena looked around with sudden understanding. She realized, too, why many of the hunters had been staring at her with such interest. How strange, to deprive themselves of women this way!

"There will be a feast now," said Nan. "You'll tell the tribe your story, Laena, and I will tell mine." Unexpectedly, she pulled Laena close and hugged her. "How do you feel?"

"I—I feel all right," said Laena. In truth, she felt dazed.

"This is an important day for you," Nan said. She stared in Laena's eyes with an odd expression. Then, brusquely, she patted Laena's cheek and turned away.

A little later, Rorgar led Nan, Laena, and Moru to the clearing where the hunters had been practicing with their weapons. A big fire had been built there, fresh meat was roasting over it, and everyone was sitting around it in a circle. With surprise, Laena saw that the men had painted their skins. Their bare arms were red with berry juice, and they had used charcoal to draw black circles around their mouths and eyes.

Everyone bent forward and bowed their heads as Rorgar seated himself on a tall rock in front of the fire. Then the hunters pushed their fists into the air, tilted their heads back, and gave an eerie, piercing howl. It was a wolf howl, Laena realized. The sound was so loud, it echoed from the surrounding hills.

Laena sat between Nan and Moru, close beside Rorgar, and several of the men stood up. They came over to her carrying offerings of food—and the first of the men, she realized, was Sordir. The strangeness of him disconcerted her at first. His hair had been tied back, his face was decorated with patterns of red and black, and he was wearing a long cape of wolf pelts, like his father's.

He was holding a piece of birch bark in both hands, which he placed in front of her on the ground. Laena glanced at the other men gathered around the fire, and all of them seemed to be watching her. She turned to Nan. "What am I supposed to do?"

"He's brought you a gift, girl." She nodded to the square of birchbark, where a small morsel of meat lay in the center of it. "Do you know what that is? It's a thrush. It takes a lot of skill to catch a songbird. And if he's offering it to you, it means he admires you. Taste it, and show him you appreciate it."

Feeling self-conscious, Laena tried the meat. It was soft and fragrant, quite different from the venison she was familiar with. She smiled at Sordir and nodded to him. "Thank you," she said in her language.

He said something in reply, pitching his voice deep, looking straight into her eyes.

"He says you are as beautiful as the bird itself," Nan translated. "He says he wants to guard your tent tonight."

Laena felt the thickness in her throat again. She was embarrassed—and yet, at the same time, she was pleased. She groped for words, and found herself unable to think of any.

Nan solved the problem for her. She leaned forward and said something in the Wolf tongue, while Sordir listened respectfully. When she finished, Sordir wasn't smiling anymore. He gave Laena a slow, searching look, and then, silently, he moved away.

"Whatever did you say to him?" Laena asked.

"I told him you'd be honored to have him protect you," Nan said. "I also told him that if he touches you, I'll see that his father hears about it." She patted Laena on the shoulder. "You won't have any trouble from him now."

Laena blinked. Contradictory emotions chased each other around inside her—relief, anger, disappointment. It seemed unlike Nan to intrude like that, without even asking what Laena wanted.

But there was no time to talk about it. Another man was standing in front of her, and there were others waiting behind him, all of them carrying choice offerings of meat that they had killed and prepared themselves. They presented the food to Laena—and to Moru, and to Nan.

Nan exclaimed with delight over each little mouthful, and Laena did her best to imitate her. Privately, she thought it was strange that in a camp where the men practiced hunting and killing, they also did what she thought of as women's work, building the fire, preparing the meat, cooking it, and now serving it. Yet the men showed no shame, and clearly, they were excellent hunters. Laena suddenly wondered—if they could do the work of a woman, did that mean a woman should be able to do the work of a man?

The feast lasted a long time, for there were many hunters, and each of them had to make his offering. By the end of the meal, Laena's stomach felt swollen and her mouth was dry. She couldn't remember when she had ever eaten so much.

Still, the event had only just begun. Rorgar stood up and made a welcoming speech, which Nan translated for Laena and Moru. He praised her for her wisdom and her healing skills, and he explained that Laena was her apprentice. He went on to say that Laena and Moru had renounced their old tribe, and at this, all the men gave their wolf-howl again.

It was time, then, for the visitors to tell their stories. Nan took the lead, and since she spoke entirely in the Wolf language, Laena could understand none of it. Then her own turn came, and she stood up, feeling very small and defenseless surrounded by the hunters, with their skin gleaming gold in the light from the fire and their faces painted like masks, turned expectantly toward her.

"Tell them where you are from, and what happened to your tribe," Nan whispered.

So Laena described the camp where she had once lived, and she described the terrible massacre. She had to pause frequently for Nan to rephrase everything in the Wolf tongue, which was just as well, because it gave her a chance to calm herself. For the past days and weeks, she had tried not to think about everything she had lived through. Now that she was delving back into her past, she felt herself tremble with emotion. She had lost so much, and it had hurt so much. And here she was now, a wanderer, still without a home.

Then she spoke about her parents, and she found herself remembering her vision of the warm, green land. She didn't say anything about that—she hadn't even told Nan about it— but it comforted her, for it made her remember that there really was a purpose to her life beyond the difficulties of the present time.

At the end of her story, the men around the fire were silent. She had expected them to start howling again, but they just stared at her as she sat back down between Nan and Moru.

Slowly, Rorgar got to his feet. The silence dragged on as the chieftain rubbed his jaw thoughtfully. He looked at Laena, and his face seemed troubled. "Did I say something to offend everyone?" Laena whispered nervously.

Nan quickly shook her head. She held up her hand as Rorgar started speaking.

"He says the Wolf People are sad to hear of your suffering,'' Nan translated. ''They are glad that you have come here, where you can enjoy their hospitality. They hope it will help you to forget your misfortune.''

Now the howling started again, and smiles broke out on the faces of the hunters gathered around the fire.

''But I don't understand,'' Laena complained. ''You said that these people are fierce warriors who kill anyone who enters their land. So why should they care what happened to me?''

''Because now you're not an outsider anymore,'' Nan said. ''They're vicious to anyone who isn't one of them. But if they accept you, they're the most generous people you can hope to find.'' Nan spread her hands. ''Some men are like that, Laena. They can be brutal and full of hate to their enemies. But if you're a friend, they're warmhearted and kind.''

Meanwhile, Rorgar had started making another speech—a long one this time. Laena sat and listened, even though the words made no sense. She felt drained by the emotions that she had relived, and she was sated with all the food. She didn't know anymore what she thought of the Wolf Tribe. They were so strange to her, she couldn't begin to understand them.

The hunters started singing songs after Rorgar's speech was over. Moru fell asleep against Laena, and Laena felt herself getting drowsy as she rested against Nan.

Sometime later—Laena couldn't tell how long—the feast was finally over. The sky was a deep, dark blue, and the fire had burned low. The air felt cold on Laena's flushed cheeks. She blinked as she saw hunters getting up, moving away from the fire.

''Laena!'' Nan's voice was sharp enough to cut through the drowsiness that cloaked Laena's mind. ''Laena, listen to me.''

''What is it?'' Laena asked sleepily.

Nan bent her head to Laena's ear. ''You have come of age, yes? But you have not coupled with a man.''

Laena felt disconcerted. In her tribe, it would have been unthinkable for anyone other than her mother to ask her something like that. But, she reminded herself, she no longer had a tribe. And Nan must have a reason for speaking this way. ''What you say is true,'' she said cautiously.

Nan nodded. "I don't think you'll have any trouble from Sordir, after what I told him earlier. But I saw how he kept looking at you while the men were singing their hunting songs. When he comes to your tent tonight, keep the flap tied shut. Understand?"

Laena didn't know what to say. She wanted to tell Nan to mind her own business; and yet, in a way, she also wanted her advice.

"And when he sits outside," Nan went on, "which he will, since he asked for the privilege of guarding you—you'll let him sit there."

Laena shook her head. "Nan, I don't see why—"

"Are you ready to bear a child, girl? That's what happens when a man couples with a woman. You know that, don't you?" Nan gave her a little shake. "Don't you?"

"Yes," Laena muttered. It was hard to put the two things together in her head—the warm, stirring sensations that she had felt when Sordir had touched her, and the idea that he might make her pregnant. It didn't even seem possible. She just wanted to enjoy those feelings again—to have him close to her, smiling at her, stirring sensations that she'd never had a chance to explore before. Would that be so terrible? Why did Nan have to make it seem so unpleasant?

"Promise me you will do as I say," Nan said.

Laena looked up and found the old woman glaring at her. She realized there was no escape from those eyes. Nan wouldn't let her go of her until she promised, and if Laena broke her word, she somehow sensed that Nan would know.

"Promise!" Nan demanded again.

"All right, I promise."

"One day soon, I'll tell you how to take care of yourself," Nan went on in a slightly kinder tone. "You can have your pleasure, Laena, if you're careful. But tonight is not the night." She stood up suddenly and jerked Laena up onto her feet. Laena turned around—and found Sordir standing in front of her, smiling at her, waiting to take her back to her tent.

"Remember what I said," Nan said, giving Laena a last warning look.

Laena shook Moru awake, and the two of them followed Sordir among the tents. Laena watched the young hunter as he walked ahead of them, moving lightly, swiftly, silently through the twilight. She remembered again how it had felt to be touched by him, and she found herself wanting it again, with a deep, fierce yearning.

But she had given her word to Nan. She depended on Nan for her survival, here in this strange land, so she would be foolish to anger the old lady. And yet, Nan surely wouldn't cast Laena out just for breaking a promise, would she?

Laena didn't know what to think. They reached the tent where she would be spending the night, and Sordir stepped to one side, holding the flap open and gesturing for Laena to take Moru inside.

She did so, feeling grateful for the extra moment to try to gather her thoughts. She tucked Moru into her sleeping bag, and kissed the little girl on the forehead. Then she turned back to the entrance of the tent, where Sordir was waiting. She felt her stomach clench tight, and she was so nervous, it was hard to breathe. What should she do?

He saw her standing there staring at him, and he seemed to take it as an invitation. Quickly, he came into the tent. He was like a lithe black shadow in the dimness. She could smell the musky odor of his body, and she could feel the warmth of his flesh. He reached out and took hold of her wrist. His touch was gentle, but it was very strong. Laena gave a little cry as she looked up at him.

Quickly, he pulled her to him. His arms seemed to envelop her completely. His body was so hard and strong, and it was telling her to yield, to lie down under him, to open herself.

His teeth nipped her neck, and she felt the most amazing tingling sensations coursing through her. An ache started growing inside her, and her body no longer seemed as if it would obey her. His hands moved lower, cupping her buttocks and drawing her hips up against his.

The muscles in his body clenched tight, and his arms crushed her breath out of her. Then, with one hand, he fumbled with her furs. She felt his fingers brushing the soft skin of her waist. His hand slid lower across her abdomen—and Laena felt as if she were suddenly waking from a dream. "No!" she said, so loudly that she surprised herself. She brought up both arms and wedged them against Sordir's chest. Using all her strength, she levered herself away from him.

He grunted with surprise. She heard him breathing heavily. For a moment, they stared at each other in the dimness. She found herself gasping for breath, and not just from the exertion of breaking free.

"I'm sorry," she said, knowing he couldn't understand, but hoping he would hear the kindness in her voice. "Not now. I'm sorry." With a trembling hand, she reached out and pushed him firmly toward the open flap of the tent.

He retreated, taking small, slow steps. He said something in his language, which she couldn't understand. It sounded resentful, and for a moment she felt herself weaken. But no; she wasn't ready for him. She knew that now. "You have to go," she said. And this time, he seemed to realize that she meant it, and she could not be swayed.

Once he was outside, she quickly tied the tent flap shut, as Nan had told her. She retreated to her bed and tried to make herself comfortable on it. But her pulse was still thudding, and her skin was tingling, and there was a wetness between her thighs that she had never known before. For a moment she thought she was bleeding again—but this, she discovered, was different. She touched herself there, and her whole body started throbbing in rhythm with her heartbeats.

She took her hand away and tried to think of something else. But she was much too confused and excited to sleep. Eventually, after a long while, she crept to the tent flap and peeped out through a small gap. He was still out there, sitting cross-legged on the ground, waiting patiently. She had no doubt that he'd stay there all night if she didn't allow him in.

Laena shivered. It was strange to have a man act this way toward her. Sordir was so strong, so powerful—and yet when she had said no she had forced him to do what *she* wanted. Did that mean that in this special way she was more powerful than he was? The thought gave her a thrill of a new kind. She imagined having him come to her the next night. If she refused him then, would he wait patiently outside her tent a second time? What else would he do for her, if she told him to?

Laena went back to her bed. She felt a little calmer now, although she was still confused. She realized she had a lot to learn about the affairs between women and men, and she wished her mother were still alive to teach her.

Still, she had Nan, and Nan had promised to advise her. The last thing that Laena thought before she finally fell asleep was that she had a lot of questions to ask Nan, about the business of being a woman.

Chapter 19

"Wake up!"

Laena heard a high-pitched voice, opened her eyes, and found Moru shaking her. "It's late," the little girl was complaining. "And it's raining. Listen."

Laena heard raindrops drumming on the tent. She rolled over, feeling confused. There had been so many dreams crowding her mind through the night, tugging at her emotions. Sordir had been in most of them. She wondered, apprehensively, if he was still waiting outside the tent even now, sitting in the rain.

"Look through the flap," she whispered to Moru. "Tell me if you see anyone."

Obediently, the little girl went and peeked out. "No one there," she said.

Laena felt a wave of relief. At the same time, she realized that she felt disappointed. Just thinking about Sordir gave her a little taste of the longing she had felt for him the previous night.

Moru was still looking out. "I see Nan coming," she said.

A moment later, the old lady was unlacing the tent flap. She came inside, shaking water off her furs. "Ready for breakfast?" she said, looking down at Moru.

"Yes!" Moru shouted.

Nan patted the young one's head. "Good, go to the campfire. There's still some food left."

Moru ran out, and Nan watched her go. Then she turned to Laena. "I hope you took my advice last night."

Laena wondered whether she should simply refuse to answer the question. She looked up into Nan's face, wondering how she might react. The old lady was waiting implacably, and Laena realized that she would wait just as implacably as Sordir had waited outside the tent. And if Laena still refused to answer, Nan would be unhelpful, to say the least.

So, there was no way around it. If Laena wanted Nan as a teacher and a friend, she would have to do what Nan wanted. "I let him hug me," she said in a low, tense voice. "And then I pushed him outside."

Nan gave a curt nod. "Thank you, Laena. I know you think it's none of my business, but it has to be my business, because if you get pregnant, I'll be the one who has to cope with it." She sat on the end of Laena's bed and clasped her hands in her lap. "Now, do you know how babies are made?"

Laena felt her cheeks growing red. It was awful, feeling forced into this conversation, with no way to resist. She drew a deep breath. "A man and woman lie together, and—"

Nan made an irritable gesture. "I mean how they are *really* made. A man puts himself inside you, here." She clutched herself between the legs, while she watched Laena carefully. "You know that?"

Laena nodded reluctantly.

"He moves, and he puts white juice inside you. And that's what a baby grows from. Did you know that?"

Laena hesitated. She hadn't known, and she realized that she was actually interested, despite herself. "Is it like water, fertilizing the soil?" she said.

"No. It's like planting a seed, which grows in your belly. Sometimes the seed fails to sprout, and nothing happens. But as often as not, it does grow, and suddenly you're a mother whether you want it or not."

"Oh," said Laena.

"Now, there're ways to keep a man happy, and to have him keep you happy, without him putting it there," Nan went on, patting her belly. "I'll describe them to you, if you want to know." She paused. "Do you want to know?"

Laena hesitated. She couldn't deny it. "All right," she said.

"Good. I'll tell you while we're on our way to the East Camp. It's a two-day hike." She paused. "By the way, Sordir will be coming along. He asked Rorgar if he could be our guide. You must have got him excited, with that hug of yours."

Laena felt something leap inside her. She tried to imagine what it would be like to spend two more days with Sordir, walking with him across the hills, watching him move, and knowing that he was watching her. She shivered. The emotions were so powerful they astonished her. Part of her mind seemed to have freed itself from her control. She couldn't predict how her emotions might stir her from one moment to the next.

Nan had turned away and was squinting out of the tent flap. "This rain should stop soon," she said. "We'll leave then. Meanwhile, you'd best get a good breakfast. It's a hard trail, across the ridge."

The camp seemed virtually empty. Most of the men were out hunting, and the only sound was the pattering of raindrops on the tents and the grass.

Sordir was waiting with Rorgar and Moru by the fire. As soon as he saw Laena, he strode forward, holding out a wooden plate with another offering of meat on it.

"Thank you," she said shyly. She half expected him to be angry with her for shutting him out of her tent, but he smiled warmly and sat down opposite her, watching intently while she ate.

By the time she finished, the rain had stopped. Nan came and told her and Moru to get ready to leave. Sordir gave them a supply of dried meat which they stowed in their packs. They gathered their things from the tent, then went back to the center of the camp, where Nan was waiting.

Rorgar was there. The big man put his arms around Nan and hugged her. It was a tight, close hug, and Laena realized that it wasn't just a sign of friendship. With sudden certainly, Laena knew that Nan hadn't shut Rorgar out of *her* tent, the previous night.

The thought was unexpected and confusing. Nan was so much older than Rorgar, she could have been his mother. And yet, here she was embracing him—doing what she had told Laena not to do.

Rorgar let go of her and turned away. While he stood with his back to her, Nan said something to Sordir, and he nodded. He picked up a spear and then led Nan, Laena, and Moru out of the camp.

Rorgar didn't watch them go. He kept his back turned.

As Laena reached the trees, she took a last look, and he was still standing in the center of the camp, still staring in the opposite direction.

"The Wolves believe it's bad luck to watch a guest leave," Nan explained. "If they didn't like you, or didn't want you to come back, *then* they'd stare at you as you left."

Sordir led them onward, picking their way among the tall pines. Laena quickly became confused and lost her sense of direction, for there was no path to follow here, and the sky was overcast where it showed between the branches. But Sordir moved with quick assurance, and a little later they emerged from the trees onto a steep hillside where the soil was so thin, only moss could grow.

Sordir led them to a faint trail that started zigzagging up the hill. The ground was still wet from the rain, so it was slippery underfoot. No one said anything as they toiled slowly upward. There was nothing but the sound of their breathing in the damp morning air. Laena had to smile as she remembered thinking how exciting it would be watching Sordir leading them. In fact, she had to spend all her time looking for footholds and reaching for rocks to keep her balance.

They reached the top of the slope and paused for a minute, resting. The gray clouds were so thick and low they engulfed the tops of the hills nearby. Sordir squinted at them and exchanged a few quick words with Nan.

"He says we may have to walk up into the clouds," Nan translated. "But he's walked this path many times, and if we follow him closely, everything will be all right."

Laena stared at Nan. "Into the clouds?" she said. It sounded like a fantasy.

"We'll be climbing higher," said Nan. "Clouds are just mist, nothing more. Still, it's dangerous if you don't know what you're doing, because you can't see very far, and there's no way to tell which way you're going. I hope Sordir is as experienced as he claims he is."

Laena looked at him. He had been watching her, she realized. It must be just as frustrating for him, not being able to understand her language, as it was for her, not being able to understand his. She gave him a shy smile, and straight away he grinned back at her. He pointed to her left, at a mountain whose rocky slopes were almost entirely lost in cloud. He said something, then turned to Nan and waited for her to translate.

"He says that he and some other hunters have climbed that peak," Nan said. She waited while Sordir added a few more words in his tongue. "He said they used ropes made from mammoth gut."

Laena's eyes widened. "Do you think that could be so?"

Nan grunted noncommittally. "I've heard tales of it. I've never seen it done. Still, the Wolf People are tough. If anyone would do something like that, it would be them."

Sordir was grinning. He could tell from her tone of voice that she was impressed by his story.

He turned then and continued up the ridge where they stood.

A short time later, the clouds were all around them. The rocks were damp under Laena's hands, and she could only see a few paces in each direction. Moru called out to her, sounding lost and scared, so she got the little girl to walk ahead of her, directly between her and Nan. Even so, Moru kept glancing nervously over her shoulder to make sure that Laena was still there.

Laena herself felt anxious now, because she couldn't imagine that Sordir really knew where he was going. She could barely even see him; he was a faint gray shape, nothing more. Yet he strode ahead as briskly as ever, his feet crunching over the loose rock, leading the way upward.

The mist settled on her furs, making them glisten as if they were coated with spiderweb. It was cold on her cheeks, and it turned her breath into white plumes.

But then, just as she was beginning to feel deeply afraid, the grayness began to grow brighter overhead. They climbed one last section of the trail, steeper than anything that had gone before. And suddenly the sky was blue above and the sun was shining down.

Laena blinked in the sudden radiance. She found herself on a small rocky plateau. When she turned and looked behind her, the clouds were below her, stretching out like a field of mounded snow. They looked almost solid enough to walk on.

Moru was tugging at her arm. "Look here, Laena," she called.

Laena turned. She took a few steps and saw a gentle slope

to the east, descending to a wide, flat plain that stretched away into the far, far distance. There were no clouds here at all; they had all been trapped behind the slope that she had climbed.

Nan was sitting with Sordir, resting on a boulder. He opened his pack, pulled out some meat, and offered it to Laena.

She took a piece, but she found herself looking again at the land which lay ahead. It was different from anything she had seen before. The plain seemed to be completely covered in brown grass. A river snaked lazily across it, and she saw tiny specks that must be animals grazing. It was much richer, much lusher than the plains she had known. There, the grass only grew in hollows and slopes that collected water from melting snow. The ground was rough and stony, showing itself atop every little ridge.

Sordir was saying something. Nan listened, then turned to Laena. "He says the main camp of the Wolves is over there," she said, and pointed to a range of hills at the far end of the plain. "We should reach it by tomorrow night."

Laena nodded. "Were you here before, Nan?"

The old lady laughed. "I was, but I've forgotten when. I've traveled so much, it all starts to jumble together in my mind."

"Are there nice people there?" asked Moru. She was looking at Nan with large eyes, while she reached up and held on to Laena's hand.

"Some of them are nice," Nan said, choosing her words carefully.

"Can we stay with them?"

Nan glanced at Laena, then back at Moru. "We'll have to see if they invite us."

"It's hard for her, not having a home," Laena said.

Nan gave a curt nod. "Well, there's nothing we can do about that."

Descending to the plain was easy enough, and then they were down among the tall grass, with soft earth underfoot. It was pleasant here, with the sun warming them. Even so, Laena thought to herself, it still wasn't the land that she had seen in her vision. The grass wasn't thick enough or green enough; and the sky wasn't blue enough.

She walked beside Sordir some of the way, while Nan dropped back a few paces with Moru. Laena tried to teach Sordir some words from her language—for the sun, the clouds, the river, and the earth. In return, he taught a little of his tongue. But it was hard for her to concentrate walking beside him, feeling him close to her, and catching glimpses of his strong body out of the corner of her eye. She found herself brushing against him, as if by accident. She stepped on a stone and stumbled, and he quickly reached for her, even though she didn't really need his help. He caught her with his hands on either side of her waist, and held her for just a moment. She blinked at him shyly, and found herself looking up into his dark brown eyes. Something surged inside her, making her feel the same way as the night before, as if she couldn't breathe. She took his hand and moved it away from her, but as she did so, she let her fingers slide over the soft skin on the inside of his arm, under the sleeve of his jacket. She saw his nostrils flare as he took a quick breath, and she realized for the first time that he might be just as confused by his emotions as she was by hers.

Maybe, she thought, there would be a chance to steal some time with him alone, when Nan and Moru were asleep and the sun finally sank below the mountains behind them. She would be careful, remembering what Nan had told her. She wouldn't let Sordir place his seed inside her. She just wanted to feel his hands on her body, his mouth on the side of her neck—

She cut off the train of thought. It was distracting her so much, she couldn't concentrate on where she was walking.

When Sordir finally called a halt, they had journeyed halfway across the plain. They climbed a low rise in the land overlooking a bend in the wide, meandering river, and found an area of blackened earth where travelers had built fires before them.

Sordir gave instructions, which Nan translated. Laena and Moru were told to fetch wood while Nan laid out the bedding.

Soon, flames were hissing and crackling. Sordir carefully placed some large stones in the fire, then sat down, cross-legged, with a bundle of the tall grasses beside him. While Laena watched, he quickly wove the grasses into a wide, shallow bowl. He lined it with thick, dark clay, then used a couple of strong sticks to pull some of the hot stones out of the fire. He placed them inside the bowl and rolled them around it to harden the lining. Then he took the bowl down to the river, filled it with water, and carried it back to the fire. He pulled the rest of the hot stones out of the flames and dumped them in the water. Finally, he soaked their supply of dried meat in the simmering water, to soften it till it was tender.

They were all hungry after the long march, and the food tasted good. They ate together in silence at first, and then, as the sky darkened, Sordir tried to talk to Laena.

She understood a few words of his language now, but the rest of it was still impossible for her to understand. Nan translated for her, and Sordir described his hunting skills, his strength, and his intention one day to take over from Rorgar as the chieftain of the Wolf Tribe.

Laena tried to concentrate, but she found her mind wandering. She watched Sordir as he leaned forward, speaking so seriously, staring at her so intensely. His face and body seemed much more interesting than the things he was saying. But where could she go with him to be alone? The plain stretched away all around them. The grass was tall, but it wasn't tall enough to conceal them if they sat down in it. And even though the light was fading, at this time of year it never grew totally dark.

Laena looked again at Sordir, not knowing what to do. Then she realized he had stopped talking, and Nan had stopped translating. He was frowning, as if something troubled him.

He stood up suddenly, and pressed his hands to his stomach. He grimaced and muttered something.

"He says the food isn't agreeing with him," Nan said.

Sordir turned to the bowl he had made, cupped his hands in it, and raised some water to his mouth. He drank, and drank again.

"Is he all right?" asked Moru. She had been sitting beside Laena, saying nothing, but taking everything in.

Nan gently took Sordir's arm and turned him to face her. She peered into his face, then touched her fingers to his forehead. "There doesn't seem to be anything wrong," she said, half to herself. "Perhaps a piece of the meat was bad."

Sordir said something more. He turned away, then lay down near the fire.

"He apologizes," Nan said. "He has cramps in his stomach, and he needs to rest."

There was an uncomfortable silence. Laena blinked. She wondered if it was really true. Could Sordir be pretending for some reason? He had seemed perfectly strong and healthy, striding across the plain. Maybe, she thought, he wanted some time to himself. She had thought he wanted to be with her; but now, clearly, that wasn't on his mind at all. She felt confused and disappointed. If only she could speak his language!

"We should all get some rest," Nan said. She threw some more wood on the fire, then started laying out the sleeping bags. "Look at Moru here. She's half asleep already."

"No, I'm not," said Moru. But even as she spoke, she was yawning, lying beside the fire with her eyes half closed.

Laena stood up uncertainly. "You're sure Sordir is all right?"

Nan shrugged. "So far as I can tell." She urged Moru into her sleeping bag, then turned back to Laena. "What's on your mind?"

Laena slowly shook her head. "Nothing," she said.

Laena lay awake for a while, staring at the sky, listening to the world around her. Moru was muttering something in her sleep. She stirred briefly, then lay still again, and her breathing quietened. Sordir was on the opposite side of the fire, and he wasn't making a sound. Maybe he really was sick, though Laena still couldn't believe it.

Somewhere, an owl shrieked. Nan grunted to herself and turned over in her sleeping bag, making a rustling sound.

"Nan?" Laena whispered. "Are you still awake?"

The old lady turned to face Laena. "Yes, I'm awake. I don't sleep as easily as I used to, especially on summer nights."

Laena was silent for a moment. There was so much that she wanted to know. "Can I ask you something?" she whispered.

The old woman nodded. "Anything. You can always ask me anything."

"Did you, and Rorgar—"

"We coupled together last night, yes." She said it without hesitation.

Laena stared at her. In her tribe, such things had been taboo. When a woman coupled with a man who wasn't her husband, she would be ashamed to admit it.

"Each of us has a code to live by," Nan said, seeing the look on Laena's face. "I'm Nan of No People, so I live by my own code." She paused for a moment. "You understand," she went on, "I was paired with a man, a long time ago. I cooked for him, I made clothes for him, and I even bore his child."

Laena's eyes widened.

"But my son was killed by wolves," Nan said. "And it was just as well. The life I was living was not what I wanted. I needed to be my own master. So I left my tribe. I resolved to take my pleasure where I found it: walking alone under the moon, or sitting and watching the ocean, or feeling the sun on my face. I would never tie myself to one man or one place or one group of people. That was my choice, Laena, and I have never regretted it."

"I see," said Laena. The idea frightened her; but there was something big and exciting about it, besides.

"When the men of the Wolves are in their Men's Camp, they grow hungry for women. I've coupled with Rorgar before. He's younger than I am, and he's strong and virile, and that pleases me. I take care, though, that his seed doesn't flow into me. I'm not too old to get pregnant again, but I'm old enough and wise enough to make sure it doesn't happen. Is that what you wanted to know?"

Laena slowly considered the things Nan had told her. "Should I have a code of my own to live by?"

Nan shrugged. "In time, I expect you'll decide what makes you happy, and what doesn't. Till then, you'll just have to put up with me giving you advice."

Laena couldn't help smiling. And in the dim light, she saw Nan smiling back. "Thank you," she said.

When she opened her eyes, the land had changed. Trees loomed all around, dark and forbidding. Where the sky showed between their webbed branches, it was a dim gray. She wondered where she was. She stood up. The ground felt soft under her feet and she swayed, almost losing her balance. "Nan?" she called. "Moru?"

There were scrabbling noises in the undergrowth, among the trees. Laena's skin prickled.

She started forward, forcing her way between bushes and brambles. She heard a moaning sound directly ahead of her.

Suddenly she found herself in a clearing in the forest. In the center of the clearing was something lumpy and gray. She blinked in the dim light and took another cautious step forward.

The gray mass moved. It was not a single thing, she realized. It was a mass of living creatures. Wolves, lying close together on the ground. They were panting as if there wasn't enough air for them to breathe. Again, one of them moaned.

"I don't understand," Laena said to herself. And then: "Am I dreaming?"

"Yes, you're dreaming," said a voice.

She turned quickly—and found Sordir sitting on a boulder at the edge of the clearing.

She started toward him. "You speak my language!"

"Either that, or you speak mine," he said.

His face was hidden in shadow. She stopped directly in front of him. Then she reached out to touch him. She knew she wasn't supposed to, although she couldn't remember why not. "Sordir—"

"Yes?" He raised his face to look at her.

Laena screamed. His skin was black and oily. His hair hung across his forehead in a matted mess. He raised his hands and they were skeletal, as if the flesh had rotted on the bones.

"No!" Laena screamed.

"Come and lie with me, Laena." He lurched to his feet and started toward her.

The ground was soft under her feet again. In the clearing behind her, one of the wolves moaned.

"Don't touch me!" Laena screamed.

"It's all right," Sordir told her. His breath smelled of wet earth. "It's only a dream, Laena."

"No!" she screamed again.

And then she felt herself being roughly shaken. She opened her eyes and found she was sprawling on the ground, half out of her sleeping bag. Her mouth was dry, her pulse was pounding. The sky was dim gray. Nan was bending over her.

Laena groaned with relief. She swallowed painfully.

"Are you all right?" Nan said.

"Yes," Laena gasped. "Just a dream."

"A dream?"

Laena nodded. "I'm sorry. Sorry I woke you."

"I'm a light sleeper. I've learned to be." Nan glanced quickly around. "Sordir didn't disturb you?"

"No. No, Nan, he didn't."

She grunted to herself, then straightened up and walked around the glowing embers of the fire. She reached the place where Sordir had bedded down, and bent over him.

Only a dream, Laena told herself.

"Laena!" Nan called. There was a new edge to her voice.

Laena felt a quick, sudden chill. "What is it?" she called, wanting to know, and at the same time knowing already what she was going to hear.

"Come here, girl. Sordir's not well. I may need your help."

Chapter 20

Sordir's eyes were open, but he seemed to be having trouble focusing on Nan and Laena as they bent over him. He turned his head from side to side and muttered something that Laena couldn't understand.

"He says he's thirsty," said Nan. "Get him some water."

"But what's wrong with him?"

"I don't know yet. Quickly, bring some water!"

There was hardly any light to see by, but Laena managed to find the bowl that Sordir had made the previous night. She ran to the river, filled the bowl, and ran back.

"He's feverish," Nan said. She held Sordir's head up, raised the bowl to his lips, and he gulped from it. He was trembling, Laena noticed. She stared at him, feeling numb, not wanting to believe that this was happening.

Sordir slumped back onto the ground, taking quick, shallow breaths. Then he rolled onto his side and groaned. He clutched his stomach and vomited.

Laena gave a little cry of distress.

"Why are you looking at him like that?" Nan asked sharply.

Laena bit her lip. She didn't answer.

Nan took Laena's arm. "What is it? Are *you* sick, too?"

"No! No, there's nothing wrong with me." She shook her head. Nan was too observant. It was impossible to keep things from her. "It was in my dream," Laena said.

Nan's eyes narrowed. "What was in your dream?"

She gestured helplessly. "He was dying. Or dead. But alive. His skin was all black."

Nan made a tut-tutting noise. "You're telling me you had some sort of vision?"

Reluctantly, Laena nodded.

Nan frowned at her. "And was this the first time you ever had a dream like that?"

Laena shook her head. "I dreamed the death of my father, before it happened. And of a boy in my tribe. There'll be weeks or months when I don't dream at all. But then, something like this happens." It was too much for her to bear. She pressed her hands over her face and started sobbing. "It's so awful," she said. "It feels as if it's my fault."

Nan grabbed her arm and shook it roughly. "It's not your fault, and your tears aren't going to do any good to anyone. Listen to me!"

Her voice was so sharp, Laena flinched. She stared at Nan.

"We have to help him," Nan said, staring fiercely at her. "Understand?"

Laena nodded dumbly.

"Get my pack and bring it here. Is Moru awake?"

"I don't think so."

"Let her sleep for now. Get my pack, girl!"

Laena scrambled around the embers of the fire, grabbed Nan's backpack, and brought it to her. Nan started rummaging through it, peering in the faint gray light. She took out several little pouches, sniffed one of them, put it aside, sniffed another, and grunted with satisfaction.

Next she took out a little cup made of birchbark. She poured into it some of the water that still remained in the wicker basket, then opened the pouch and shook dried herbs from it into the cup.

She took two branches and held the cup between them over the embers of the fire. "This will calm his stomach," she said. "We'll deal with his fever later, if it persists."

After a couple of minutes, she took the cup from the fire. She dipped her finger into it, nodded to herself, then turned to Sordir. "Lift his head up."

Laena moved around him and cradled his head in her arms. He was heavier than she expected. She looked down at him and remembered again the way he had been in her dream. *Please, get better,* she thought. *Please.*

Nan held the cup to his lips, said something to him sharply, and he tried to drink from it. After a couple of attempts, he managed to swallow most of the herbal mixture, and this time he didn't vomit anything back up. He slumped back onto the ground and grunted in pain, hugging himself.

"What do we do now?" Laena asked.

"We keep him warm, and we wait." Nan looked up at Laena. "We should also hope that he gets better before any of his people come here and hold us responsible for what's happened to him."

They built up the fire, woke Moru, and ate some of their dried meat. Sordir started shivering, so they wrapped him in all their furs. "He's strong," Nan said. "Strong enough to stand the fever for a while. A fever can do good, if the person's strong enough."

The sun climbed, the sky brightened, and insects came to life in the tall grass all around. In the far, far distance, Laena saw some animals that could have been mammoth, but nothing else moved on the wide expanse of the plain, and the only sound was an occasional bird call, or a faint wet noise when a fish jumped in the river.

Soon after noon, Sordir started coughing. The spasm seized his whole body, making him flop around on the ground. His face turned pink, then red. Each time he drew a breath, there was a bubbling sound in his throat. Finally he started coughing up thick yellow mucus.

"Spitting sickness," said Nan.

Laena stared at her. "Are you sure?"

"Yes." Nan eyed her. "Have you ever seen it before?"

Laena nodded. "In my tribe, five years ago. I had it myself, and so did Moru. It killed several people."

"Young ones or old ones?"

"Young."

Nan grunted to herself, and her face turned grimmer. "We need fresh herbs. Pay attention." She took a stick and scratched a picture in the bare earth near the campfire. "Both of you, go down by the river and search near the shallow water for plants with leaves that look like this. Understand?"

Laena inspected the drawing doubtfully. "What if we get the wrong ones?"

"Bring back anything you can find. I'll know what's right and what isn't. Quickly now, both of you."

Together, they ran down to the river bank. Laena started along it in one direction, Moru the other.

Inside herself, Laena no longer felt any hope. None of her other visions had never been proven wrong, so why should this one be any different? Sordir would die, just like everybody else she had ever truly cared for. She would search for the herbs, and she would do anything else that Nan told her to do, but she knew it was pointless.

But then she reminded herself that Sordir hadn't actually died in her dream. And Nan was very wise; maybe her wisdom would make a difference. Laena so much wanted to believe that Sordir would live. She remembered his touch, the smell of his body, and the desire that had leaped up inside her. Surely, fate couldn't be so cruel as to deprive her so soon after she had discovered these magical feelings.

She came to a tiny stream that fed the river. The ground here was wet and marshy, and dozens of little plants grew close together. Laena crouched down and sorted through them. A whole bunch looked as if they might be right. She grabbed them and ran back the way she'd come.

When she gave them to Nan, the old woman sorted through them and nodded with satisfaction. Then Moru came running up with fistfuls of grass, dandelions, and anything else she had been able to seize hold of. Among the mass of weeds, there were a couple of delicate fronds that met with Nan's approval.

She laid them on a flat stone, used another stone to crush them, then heated them in another cup of water. ''Sit him up,'' she told Laena and Moru.

They struggled with Sordir. He kept coughing, and the spasms made him jerk out of their grasp. He no longer seemed properly aware of anything around him. His skin was furiously hot, and the phlegm that he spat out was streaked with blood.

Nan held the steaming herbal mixture close to his face. ''Breathe!'' she shouted to him. Then, realizing she had spoken in plains language, she repeated herself in the Wolf tongue.

Sordir took some shuddering breaths, inhaling from the cup. He groaned and coughed some more.

Nan reheated the cup, and they held it in front of his face

again. "I've never seen the sickness work so quickly," she muttered.

"But the herbs seem to be helping," said Laena.

"Maybe. I don't know. All right, tip his head back a little. He's breathed enough; he should drink the rest now."

Laena and Moru managed to hold Sordir while Nan pried his lips apart. Carefully, she trickled the mixture into his mouth. Laena watched his throat move as he swallowed it reflexively.

They set him down again. "We have to wait some more," said Nan.

The afternoon wore on, and Sordir seemed to fall asleep. His breathing quietened, and he relaxed.

Moru moved closer to him. She watched his face, then looked at Nan. "Is he all right now?" she asked.

"Maybe," said Nan. "I don't know for sure."

"But you know everything," said Moru.

Nan ruffled Moru's hair with the palm of her hand. "I wish I did, child. I wish I did."

"You did say you'd seen the spitting sickness before," said Laena.

"Yes, I've seen it. Although this looks a little different from the way I remember it."

Laena frowned. "Isn't a sickness always the same?"

Nan settled herself back by the fire. If Sordir's condition was worrying her, she didn't show it. Laena wondered if there was anything that would make Nan show a hint of weakness, or of dismay.

"So far as I can tell," Nan said, "some illnesses never change. But others do seem to, over the years, as they pass from one person to the next, and from one tribe to the next. Suppose you have a tribe that doesn't get many visitors, and a stranger comes to see them. The stranger can bring the new kind of sickness with him, even if he seems healthy himself. And if the new kind is different enough from the old kind, people will catch it. Young people, especially, because they never had it the first time around."

Laena thought back. "I remember, when I caught the spitting sickness myself, it was just after someone had visited our tribe," she said. Then she grew quiet, as she realized the implications. "You think—you think I was the one who brought this new kind of spitting sickness to the Wolf Tribe?''

"You, or Moru," said Nan. She said it casually, as if she were discussing the weather.

"But that's terrible!" Laena hugged her arms around herself. She felt tears starting down her cheeks. "I couldn't bear it, if I was the one who made Sordir sick!"

Nan made a little impatient sound. "You didn't do it, the sickness did it. That's what a sickness does. It takes advantage of people. There's nothing any of us can do about that."

Laena slumped down beside the fire. She was cursed, she thought to herself. It truly was her fault that everyone around her kept dying. There was something deeply, terribly wrong with her.

She looked up at Nan. "What about you?" she said, still sniffing back tears. "Are you going to get the sickness, too?"

Nan shook her head. "If it was going to happen, it would have happened by now. In any case, I've met so many people and I've had so many illnesses over the years, I doubt there's much left that can hurt me now."

Behind her, Sordir groaned and started making choking noises. Nan went quickly to him, and Laena joined her, while Moru sat and watched with wide, anxious eyes.

Laena saw his face, and she gave a cry of horror. His eyes were open, but they had rolled up so that the pupils were hidden and only the whites were visible. He was making awful gasping, throttled noises. His face had turned purple. He was shaking all over.

"Quickly!" said Nan. She lay behind him, locked her arms around his waist from behind, and squeezed hard. "He's choking. Press your mouth against his, girl. You have to suck out the stuff in his throat."

Laena stared at his darkening face. She felt faint. The whole world was getting misty around her. He looked just the way he had in her dream.

Nan hugged Sordir tighter, trying to squeeze the blockage out of him. "Do what I said, girl!" she shouted.

Dumbly, Laena obeyed. It seemed exciting and forbidden to be close to Sordir like this, and to have his mouth against hers. At the same time, it repulsed her. Fate had taken her fantasies and made them into a travesty. The warm feelings were gone. Everything was ruined.

She repressed a shudder as she sucked hard, and thick, foul-tasting stuff came up. She felt a spasm of loathing, drew back quickly, and spat it out.

"Again!" Nan shouted to her.

Laena did it again. And again. Dimly, she realized that Sordir had started thrashing around. When she glimpsed his face, she saw it was now so dark, it was almost black.

Then his body went rigid. He arched his back, trembled one last time, and grew still.

Laena felt Nan's hands on her shoulders, pulling her away, turning her, cradling her. "All right," Nan was saying, quietly, gently. "All right now. You did your best, Laena. You did everything that you could do. Calm now. Hush."

Laena was sobbing uncontrollably. The spasm came from deep down in her abdomen. She clung to Nan, moaning, pressing her face against the woman's breast, and she felt a tide of grief sweeping over her, sucking her down. All the pain of the past months seemed to merge together like a black ocean, till she couldn't think anymore. She just cried and cried.

It took a long time for her sadness to exhaust itself. Finally, she managed to stop crying. She saw Moru watching her, solemn and sad. She looked up and saw Nan still watching over her, with more kindness than Laena had ever seen before. "I'm sorry," Laena said, rubbing her sleeve across her face. "I'm really sorry."

Nan patted her on the shoulder. "You have no reason to be sorry for anything."

Laena managed to sit up. "Thank you," she said. "Thank you for being kind to me."

Nan sighed. "You deserved some kindness, after all you've been through."

Laena glanced apprehensively at Sordir. Then she forced herself to move closer and look at him squarely. There was no point in trying to pretend; she had to face what had happened.

His eyes were still open, eerily white in his darkened face. His mouth was gaping. His body seemed as if it were still straining to breathe. Clearly, though, he was dead.

Laena touched his forehead lightly. She turned then and

saw Moru watching her, looking scared. "Here, little one."
She went to her sister, and reached out to her. "It's over.
There's nothing to be afraid of now."

Cautiously, Moru allowed herself to be hugged. "Are
you all right, Laena?"

Laena nodded. "I'm all right." She felt empty inside,
and sick with grief. But there was nothing she could do
about that. She hugged Moru to her and sat with her for a
while, just staring into the flickering fire.

"Should we bury him?" Laena asked.

Nan was stowing her herbs back in her pack. She shook
her head. "We don't have the tools to dig a grave, we don't
have any stones to cover him, and we don't have the time.
We'll just leave him here. There's nothing else we can do."

Laena nodded wordlessly.

"Gather your things," Nan told her.

Laena nodded toward the east. "Are we still going to the
other Wolves' camp?"

"Certainly not. Do you want to make them sick, too?"

Laena blinked. "I—didn't think. Of course not." She
hesitated. "Do you think all the other men, back in the
forest, have caught the same sickness from me?"

"I don't know. They cut themselves off from the outside
world; it's a possibility."

"This is so terrible." Laena's voice was a whisper.

"It will be terrible for us, girl, if it's true. Remember
what I told you about the Wolf tribe? They're the most generous people you can hope to meet, if they accept you as a
friend. But if they have a reason to turn against you—" Nan
shook her head. "Suppose there's a lot of hunters sickening
and dying in the men's camp. Rorgar won't be happy about
that. He'll blame us for it. He'll most likely send out a party
to kill us all."

"But Nan, that's not right! You were his friend!"

Nan sighed in exasperation. "I was his friend, yes. But
if I brought someone to the tribe who carried a sickness that
killed some of his best hunters, I'm not his friend any longer. The Wolf people don't give their trust easily, and the
world's a hard place, Laena, and you'd better get used to it,
else you won't survive for very long."

Laena shook her head. *Why* did the world have to be this way? And why did Nan have to be so harsh?

But then, bit by bit, she realized that the old woman was right. She simply had to accept the way things were, if she wanted to go on living.

"Let's move on," she said quietly.

Nan patted her cheek. "Good girl." She turned to Moru. "How about you? Are you ready to come with us, now?"

Moru moved close to Laena. She gave Nan a wary look, and nodded slowly.

"Good. Gather your things, and let's not waste any more time."

Chapter 21

"We can't go very far south," said Nan as they walked beside the river, following it upstream. "There's still no way across the mountains there." She gestured at the white peaks looming above the haze. "As for the land to the north, that's where I had been when I found you. There were tribes warring with each other, and not enough land or food to go around. So it seems to me we should keep on east for a while, following the river here."

Laena looked at her face, surprised as always that she could sound so sure of herself. "If the Wolves see us—"

"We'll stay by the river, in the dip in the land. The river goes south of their East Camp, and they have no reason to come this way."

Laena wasn't much reassured. "All right," she said, "but even if we pass by the East Camp—then what? Our food will run out—"

"It won't run out for a couple of days. Anyway, we still have Sordir's spear. I've used one in the past, when I've had to." Nan squinted into the distance. "I seem to recall another tribe farther upriver. Fish-eating people. Maybe we can stay with them for a while." She picked up a flat stone that she saw lying in the tall grass and threw it expertly with a flick of her wrist. It skipped across the river, bouncing once, twice, and a third time before finally sliding beneath the surface.

"Fish-eating people?"

"Yes. They catch the fish with spears."

Laena had never heard of such a thing. It didn't seem possible.

"If we stay with the fish-eating people," Moru said, "will they get sick from us like Sordir did?"

Nan made a tut-tutting sound. "You're as bad as your

sister, always full of questions, always afraid the worst is going to happen.''

Moru was silent a moment. "But will they?" she persisted.

Nan sighed. Clearly, she wasn't going to be able to escape answering the question. "I don't know. What happened with Sordir isn't very common, you know. Especially if a tribe trades with other tribes, which I believe the Fish People do. Personally, I doubt we have anything to worry about.''

Moru stared at her, looking doubtful. "So it's going to be all right?''

"Yes, girl!" She patted Moru on the cheek, a little harder than necessary. "It'll be all right. Now, no more questions.''

They walked through the long summer evening, keeping close by the river. Twice Nan heard a faint sound and made them stop and hide. They dropped down into the tall grass, grateful for the cover it provided. But the first time, the noise turned out to be just a rabbit. And the second time, it was a caribou that had somehow become separated from its herd.

When Nan realized it was a caribou she jumped up and hurled Sordir's spear. It was a long throw which any hunter would have had trouble making. Even so, the shaft came within a couple of paces of its target. The caribou leaped away, looking startled with its ears pricked up and its white tail twitching, as it bounded up the slope and out of sight.

"Who taught you to do that?" Laena asked as they continued on beside the river.

"Taught myself," said Nan.

"A man didn't teach you?''

Nan gave a short, humorless laugh. "Don't be foolish, girl. What man would ever do that?''

Laena sighed. "I suppose you're right." She scuffed her moccasin through the grass. "But I don't see why it has to be that way.''

Nan paused and faced Laena squarely. "Think about it. If women hunted, there'd be no real use for men. The men understand that, so naturally, they make sure it doesn't happen.''

Laena was silent for a moment. "Women need men for more than just hunting," she said.

"What are you talking about, families? Sex?" Nan gestured dismissively. "Not as much as you might think. You'll see, as you get older."

Laena shook her head. It bothered her when Nan made herself sound so tough and so cold. "I wasn't just talking about families and sex," she said. "A man could be a companion. Isn't that what your mate is supposed to be?"

Nan gave a humorless laugh. "I've heard that said. I wouldn't know, myself."

Laena suddenly felt sorry for her, for being so bitter. *One day*, Laena told herself, *I will meet a man who will be good to me, just as loyal and kind as my father was to my mother.*

But the words sounded hollow in her head. How could she think of finding a lifetime companion, when she didn't even know where she was going to spend her life? And how could she dream of a man who would be good to her, when she had caused poor Sordir to sicken and die?

Later, they stopped and rested in a little hollow in the land. Nan shared out some of the dried meat, but they didn't build a fire. The Wolves' East Camp was not far away, and there was no point in attracting their attention.

"I'm tired," Moru complained. "And I'm cold."

Nan gave her one of the furs that she had taken off Sordir after he died. "Wrap yourself in that."

Moru took it from her, curled up in it, and quickly went to sleep.

"She's still young for this kind of trek," Nan said. "But there's no alternative. In fact, it would be best if we don't sleep too long. I'd like to get past the Wolves' camp as quickly as possible. Rorgar may have sent one of his men to tell them about us."

Laena nodded without speaking. She drew her knees up to her chin, and wrapped her arms around them.

"Are you all right?" Nan asked.

"I was just thinking," she said in a small voice. "Hoping I wouldn't have any more dreams tonight."

"Visions, you mean?" Nan lay down in her sleeping bag. "You should tell me more about the one you had last night." She tucked the furs up around her chin, then reached for her pack and put it behind her head. The spear, Laena noticed, was close behind her, where she could seize hold of it in a moment.

Laena lay down an arm's length away. The grass rippled around her in a momentary breeze, and with her head resting on the ground, it looked to her as if the tall stems reached up to the sky. Haltingly, she started to describe the dream that she had had. "I don't know if I'd really call it a vision," she finished up. "Because I was asleep, and it did seem just like an ordinary dream."

"Call it what you like, it told the future, didn't it?"

"Yes." Laena sighed. "But what's the use of that? It didn't help me to do anything, or change anything."

"A true vision never does," said Nan. "If it showed you something, and you could stop it from happening, then the vision wouldn't be true, would it?"

Laena shook her head sadly. "I just don't understand."

"Well, you can't expect to. Not yet, anyway. You're young, you have a talent, and you have to learn to use it. You have to notice if you dream these special dreams at a particular time of the month, or if you eat particular food, or if you sleep a particular way. You have to study it, Laena."

Nan made it sound like just another part of a healer's work—simple and practical, like all her other skills. "I just wish it would go away," Laena said grimly.

"No!" Nan propped herself up on one elbow. Her tone was sharp, and she gave Laena a severe look. "Never say that! If you could run fast, would you want your joints to go stiff and your muscles to go limp? Of course not. You'd be thankful for your ability, and you'd use it."

Laena closed her eyes. She didn't like it when Nan scolded her. She was exhausted, and she still felt haunted by Sordir's blackened face. She wished she could just forget about everything that was difficult, or dangerous, or painful to her.

"You'll feel a lot better," Nan went on, "if you get to grips with these dreams of yours, instead of hiding from them. Maybe some of them can give you hope."

Yes, Laena thought to herself: one of them had. At least, so far. She wondered, suddenly, if there was a hidden meaning in her warm, green vision, which she hadn't thought of before. That was a terrible idea.

She squirmed around. "Nan? How is it you know so much about dreams that tell the future?"

Nan sighed. "Some other time, Laena. I'll tell you some other time."

Laena studied the old woman's face. "Did you ever have a dream like that yourself?"

Nan gave Laena a short, sharp look. "Maybe I did," she said. And then, without another word, she rolled over and turned her back, leaving Laena alone with all her thoughts and questions.

Chapter 22

Late the next day, as they continued heading upstream, Laena realized that the hillsides on each side of the river were gradually rising higher and steeper. The valley was turning into a deep gash in the land.

The river became a torrent that tumbled across a bed of boulders, throwing up spray that drifted like mist in the cold air. The hissing and roaring of the water seemed to build up inside Laena's head, and she started imagining that the river was talking to her, speaking of its need to escape the mountains and find its way to the lowlands, where it could wind lazily between flat, grassy banks.

The way ahead grew steeper still, and they came to places where the narrow path beside the river had crumbled away. Often they had to pick their way across slopes where loose shale slipped underfoot and there were no large rocks or bushes to hold on to. The going became so difficult Laena began to wonder what lay ahead. Certainly it seemed unlikely that there would be any animals here to hunt. And their food was almost all gone.

"Is this where the Fish People are?" Moru asked Nan.

"We're getting close. Be patient, little one."

"But what about the Wolf People? Do they ever come this way?"

"Questions, questions." Nan reached solid ground and paused, leaning against a boulder and resting for a moment. "As it happens, there was a time when the Wolf Tribe came here often, because they claimed this land was theirs. They told the Fishers to leave, but the Fishers refused. Back then, their chief was a man named Orwael."

"Did you know him?" Moru interrupted. She sat down on a rock and squinted up at Nan, shading her eyes from the sun.

"Child, I'm not that old. This happened long ago."

"How long, Nan?"

Nan made an exasperated sound; but she was smiling, despite herself. "How can I tell you the story, if you keep interrupting?" She patted the girl on the side of her head. "Think of a year. That's a long time. Think of ten years—that's even longer than you've been alive." She held up one finger. "That's ten years. Now think of another ten years." She held up another finger. "And another, and another, and another." She held up all the fingers and thumbs of both her hands. "That's how long ago it was."

Moru nodded slowly, still staring at Nan.

"Anyway," Nan went on, "Orwael was not a warrior. He never even hunted; never threw a spear. He was slow and quiet, but when he decided something was wrong, he would never allow anyone to force him to do it."

"Was that what happened with the Wolf People?" Moru asked.

Nan folded her arms. "Child, shall I tell the story?"

Moru looked down at the ground. "Sorry, Nan."

"You're forgiven. Anyway: Orwael warned the Wolf People that if they attacked the Fishers, a catastrophe would strike them down. But the Wolf People didn't take it seriously. They sent a party of warriors to drive the Fishers out of this valley. Old Orwael went out to meet them, alone and unarmed."

"Up there?" Moru pointed to the deep cleft at the top of the valley, where the river came spilling down in a cascade of foam.

"It might have been there, yes. Orwael confronted them, and warned them to turn back, but they refused. They thrust a spear into him, and killed him. And then they went on toward the homes of the Fishers, feeling confident that they would kill everyone else just as easily."

"But?" said Laena with a quiet smile.

"But," said Nan, "there was a sudden rock slide. The Wolf warriors were buried in the avalanche, and all of them were killed, except for one man who ran back to his home in the Wolf Tribe. He told everyone what had happened after they'd ignored old Orwael's warning, and ever since that day, people say that Orwael's spirit guards the valley, and the Fishers live in peace, protected by him."

There was a pause in which the only sound was the rushing of the river. Laena squinted at the ridge up ahead, and the vivid wedge of blue sky above. Then she looked carefully at Nan. "Do you believe that legend yourself?"

"Why, I'm not entirely sure." The old woman gave her a sly smile. "Maybe there are forces in the world that are more powerful than men with spears. Maybe old Orwael was a great shaman, and he saw that if he died, he would be able to protect his people far better from the spirit world. Or maybe he was just an old fool, and the avalanche killed everyone by accident." Her eyes narrowed as she watched Laena. "Now, what do you think?"

"I don't know, Nan."

"Well," said Nan, "it doesn't matter, does it? So long as the Wolf People *think* it's true, they let the Fishers live in peace." She stood up and shouldered her pack. "Now, it's getting late, and we haven't much food left, and I want to get to the Fishers before nighttime. Come on, there's still a way to go." She paused to stretch her shoulders and her back, and then carefully she picked her way along the narrow strip of land beside the river.

Laena followed. She looked up at the steep hillsides where delicate pale green ferns and grasses clung in tiny crevices among the loose rock. She tried to imagine the Wolf warriors marching this way, heading for the defenseless Fishers. The thought gave her a tight, hollow feeling in her belly. She was sure she would never have had the courage to go out, as Orwael had done, and sacrifice her life for her tribe.

Then she reminded herself that she had no tribe. Moru was the only kinfolk she had. She looked back at the little girl as she carefully placed her feet where Laena had stepped on the treacherous slope. Laena would risk her life to save Moru, there was no question about that. She only hoped it would never be necessary.

They climbed up to the top of the rise in the land, and the next part of the valley came into view. The river was more tranquil here. Its surface was smooth as it snaked between the slopes. It seemed shadowy and mysterious, walled in by hillsides so steep that they looked impossible for any man to climb. This place was deep in shadow; it seemed as if sunlight could never penetrate such a deep cleft in the land. But up at the top, where the slopes were topped with craggy outcroppings, the rocks glowed yellow in the sun.

As Laena paused and surveyed this hidden canyon among the mountains, she felt a strange sense of security erasing the fears that had been lingering at the back of her mind ever since Sordir had died. She wondered suddenly if the legend of Orwael might really be true, and she had entered into a realm where his spirit spread calmness over the land.

But her peace of mind was short-lived. As she looked ahead, she suddenly realized that a man was standing on the path ahead.

She opened her mouth to speak, but Nan held up her hand. She, too, had seen the stranger. "He hasn't noticed us," Nan whispered. "See, he's looking at the river."

Laena paused. Nan was right. The man was heavily muscled, like a hunter, and he was holding a spear. But it was the strangest weapon that Laena had ever seen. Its shaft was forked near the end, terminating in two separate stone points. And he was aiming it down toward the surface of the water.

Nan grunted to herself. She started boldly forward.

He heard her footsteps after a moment, and he looked up quickly. She called out to him, and after a moment he shouted something back.

Nan didn't pause till she was less than twenty paces from the stranger. She had been carrying Laena's spear; but now she thrust it into the soil beside her. Slowly, without taking her eyes off the hunter, she bowed to him.

The man smiled. He said something which Laena couldn't understand—some words in yet another language, different from anything she had heard before. And then, formally, he returned her bow.

Nan spoke some more—slowly, stumbling over the words. The hunter replied briefly and gestured further along the valley.

Nan nodded to herself. She turned back toward Laena and Moru. "He says he remembers me. He says I healed his mother, five years ago. He says we'll be welcome here, for a while at least."

Laena felt a wave of relief. She had been trying not to hope for anything, because she couldn't stand any more disappointments. But now, for the first time, she dared to imagine that these people would be as friendly as Nan had said. Maybe here, at last, she and Moru could find a place to rest and feel at home.

Laena took Moru's hand and walked forward.

"Bow to him," Nan told her. "Both of you. Point to yourselves and speak your names."

Laena did as she was told. The man inclined his head toward her, pressed his fist against his chest, and solemnly said something that sounded like *Horill*. He smiled, and his face looked simple and friendly. He was strong, but there was nothing threatening about his strength.

Horill took hold of his spear, said something to Nan, then turned and led the way further upstream.

"He's taking us to the Fisher village," Nan said.

"Is that the spear he uses to catch fish?" Moru asked.

"Yes, it is."

Moru stared at the river. "Do you think I could ever do that?"

"Probably not. The menfolk of the Fishers do the hunting, the same as in any tribe. But I'm sure they'd teach you how to prepare the fish that they catch."

They walked on till they came to a place where the river had scoured a wider path through the land. A curving shelf of red rock had been left high and dry, overlooking the water, just wide enough for the Fishers to build on. They had piled boulders on the outside edge of the shelf, directly above the river. Wooden beams bridged the gap between these boulders and the steep wall of the valley. Earth had been strewn across the beams, and grass and small bushes now grew there. People were living in this strange shelter, Laena realized. It was their home.

She looked up. Holes had been carved in the soft, sandy cliffs, and these man-made caves provided additional shelter. Grooves had been scored in the rock to serve as footholds and handholds so that the Fishers could climb to their caves from the valley floor.

Laena had only seen two kinds of dwellings before: the low, entrenched tents of her own people, and the bigger, free-standing tents of the Wolf Tribe. She had never even imagined a home that wasn't made of animal skin. The huts built by the Fishers looked as if they grew out of the land itself, strong and permanent. One of them could last for an entire lifetime.

Horill glanced over his shoulder as they approached the village, and he said something to Nan.

"He's taking us to the chieftain," Nan translated. "A man named Faltor. His father was the chief before him, and his grandfather, too. As for his great-great-grandfather—you can probably guess who he was."

"Orwael?" said Moru.

"Quite right."

"Do you know Faltor from the last time you were here?" Laena asked.

"Yes, I remember him. I just hope he'll remember me."

As they walked among the buildings, faces appeared in some of the cave mouths and people called excitedly to each other. The voices echoed eerily in the narrow valley. But no one came climbing out of the caves or running out of the huts. Evidently, visitors weren't such a novelty here.

Horill said something and gestured toward a house that looked no different from the others perched on the shelf of rock. A woman was sitting on a boulder beside it, slitting a fish with a flint knife. She expertly removed the bones and hung the gray meat on a rack over a smoldering fire. Then she looked up and saw Nan, and she shouted something.

A figure emerged from the house. For some reason, Laena had expected a wise old man with a bent back and white hair. Instead she saw someone not very different from Horill. He stood straight and tall, with calm assurance. His long black hair was parted in the middle, hanging down either side of his face. He blinked in the daylight, saw Nan, and stood staring at her. Then he gave a shout of greeting, walked forward, and seized her shoulders between his hands.

Then it was time for Laena and Moru to be introduced; and then Faltor invited them into his house. It took Laena a minute for her eyes to get accustomed to the dimness. The entrance had a heavy skin flap draped over it, and the smoke hole in the roof let in only a small amount of light.

Thick logs ran from one side of the hut to the other at knee height. She almost tripped over one of them before she realized that she was supposed to sit on it. The wood had been polished smooth by all the people who had been there before her.

Faltor sat opposite. She listened while he and Nan talked in the Fisher language, and she felt frustrated at being unable to understand, especially when Nan gestured at her and Faltor gave her a slow, thoughtful look.

Finally, Nan turned to Laena and started talking in her tongue. "We've arrived at a good time," she said. "When I was last here, the Fishers had a healer who was a secretive old man, very difficult to get along with. He died a month ago. He had an apprentice—a woman named Worin—but he kept a lot of his methods to himself, so Worin never really learned the healing arts. Anyway, they have a need for my services, which is why Faltor was so pleased to see me. I've told them that since you're my apprentice, and Moru is your sister, the two of you have to stay here with me."

Laena took it all in. "That's—good," she said.

"They don't normally accept guests for more than a couple of nights," said Nan. "They're friendly, but they don't have a lot of room. Still, as I say, they need a healer." She smiled at Laena and patted her cheek. "Come, girl, don't look so worried! This is good fortune."

Laena looked uneasily at Faltor, then back at Nan. "You're sure?"

"Yes, girl, I'm sure!" She turned to Faltor, talked to him for a moment, then looked again at Laena. "I explained that you've lost your parents. He says he sympathizes. He had a wife when I was last here. She died two years ago. She was young, and it was a terrible misfortune. He misses her still."

Faltor said something more.

"But he believes we should not dwell on the past," Nan said. "He says you are truly welcome, and you will find good fortune here. You, and Moru."

Laena stared at Faltor. The man was older than she had first realized, but his round face had hardly been touched by time, and his eyes were sharp and clear. She felt the same sense of peace about him that she had felt when she first entered the valley. His tranquility was like a deep, still pool which nothing could easily disturb.

He inclined his head toward her, and he gave her a gentle, understanding smile.

"Thank you," she said in her language. And before she really knew what was happening, she found herself smiling back at him.

Chapter 23

Laena woke to the sounds of the village. Women were chanting as they worked by the river, sewing clothes and gutting fish. Somewhere a fire was crackling, and there was a faint scraping sound of flint against wood as one of the men honed the shaft of a new spear.

She rolled over and winced as her muscles protested. She had been living among the Fisher People for ten days, and she still wasn't used to sleeping in a cave. The floor was lumpy, hard, and cold, and it was always covered in fine grit. Really, she thought, a cave might be suitable for an animal, but it was no place for a person to live.

But still, she was glad to be here. She sat up, looked out, and realized she had overslept. The valley was so narrow, sunlight only shone directly into it for a brief spell around noon each day. The rest of the time, the village was cloaked in shadow. That was hard to get used to, for someone who had grown up in the flatlands to the west.

She turned and found that Moru was already awake, crouching in the back of the cave, eating a simple breakfast of dried fish. The little girl was obviously happy that they had found a place to stay at last. She had already made friends among children of the Fisher Tribe, and she had even started learning their language.

"Did you sleep well?" Laena said, crawling across the matt of grasses that served as their bed. The cave was barely big enough for the two of them, but it was the only spare living space that the Fishers had to offer.

"Yes, thanks." Moru set aside the bowl of fish and picked up her coat. She had been mending a ripped seam, Laena realized.

"Here," said Laena, "let me help." She found a new thong in her bag of possessions, and a bone needle. She seated herself beside her sister and started chewing the end of the thong to soften it.

Moru looked at her. She shook her head. "We shouldn't do that anymore."

Laena stopped. "What?"

Moru pointed at the chewed thong.

"But—I have to thread the needle."

"I know. But you can do it like this." She took the thong from Laena, dipped it in the leather bowl of water that they kept in the cave, then took two stones and pounded the thong between them. "This is the best way."

Laena suddenly understood what she really meant. "You mean, it's the way the Fishers do it."

Moru shook her head with the earnest wisdom of an eight-year-old. "It's the way you're *supposed* to do it." She threaded the needle without looking at Laena.

Just in the space of the last ten days, a difference had grown between her and Moru which had never been there before. It was a difference of attitude, of loyalty. As yet, it only showed in tiny things. But now Laena saw with sudden clarity that it could become a real rift, if she allowed it to do so.

Did that mean she should change her ways, to fit in with these pleasant, friendly people? Laena could stay among them as long as she wanted; that now seemed clear enough. But what *did* she want?

That was a big question; too big to think about so early in the morning. She moved around and started braiding Moru's hair.

Moru jerked her head away. "Please don't," she said.

"Why not?" Laena asked, though she already knew the answer.

"I don't like it that way anymore."

"Did the Fisher children tell you it looked funny?"

Moru didn't answer. She finished repairing her coat, then used a flint knife to cut the remainder of the thong.

"They did, didn't they?" Laena persisted.

Moru pulled away from her. "I have to go down by the river now. Horill is teaching me to gut salmon."

Laena sighed. "All right. I expect I'll see you later."

"Yes, see you later." Moru scrambled to the mouth of the cave with a couple of quick, agile movements. She reached out to the hand-hold in the rock and swung away, out of sight.

Laena sat alone, looking at her small bag of possessions beside the mat where she had slept. She felt a twist of sadness. There was no real point in clinging to the traditions of the Panther People. After all, she had renounced her old tribe. And yet, when she imagined changing her ways, it felt wrong.

She eyed the dried fish that Moru had been eating. It wasn't the only food in the Fisher diet, because they also ate animals that they hunted in the land that lay above the valley. But fish found its way into at least one meal every day, and Laena was getting sick of it.

She looked up as she heard a sudden piping sound from outside. It sounded like birdsong, but she had already learned that it was not. In a cave further along the cliff, a young man named Joq had mastered the art of cutting holes in reeds and blowing through them to make sounds. She often heard him playing his strange, haunting little tunes.

She peered out and saw him sitting in the mouth of his cave with his legs dangling out, almost close enough for her to touch. He had untidy hair, he usually went barefoot, and his clothes always looked ragged and worn. His face was gentle and childlike, and the features were so delicate they seemed more like a woman's than a man's. He didn't excite her the way Sordir had. But he was so different from any boy that Laena had known, she felt fascinated by him.

She watched him sitting there, playing his flute. He must have seen her out of the corner of his eye, but he acted as if she didn't exist. He was a loner; no one in the tribe seemed to like him very much. But he didn't seem to care.

"Joq!" It was Joq's father, Orleh, shouting from inside their cave. "Joq, stop it!" He spoke in the Fisher tongue, but Laena had learned enough to understand a simple sentence like that.

The boy paid no attention. He played his tune till he reached the end. Then he continued to sit there, staring down at the river.

"Joq!" Orleh's voice was loud and harsh, and he always seemed to be angry with the boy. "Come here and help your mother."

Joq cast the flute aside, and the short length of reed drifted away on the breeze, landing amid the grass and weeds that grew in the dirt on the roofs of the huts below. Joq yawned and squinted up at the sky. Then, lazily, he glanced at Laena. He gave her a sleepy smile before he disappeared into his cave.

Laena wondered if that was his way of being friendly. Well, it didn't matter either way. She turned and looked once more at her own little home. The floor was so gritty, she really should sweep it out. The sleeping mats needed to be turned and refreshed with new grasses. Her own hair needed braiding. But she couldn't face doing the chores. Nan was probably waiting for her; and Nan would be as bad-tempered as Orleh if Laena kept her waiting too long.

She reached for the handholds in the rock, then carefully lowered herself out of her cave. She didn't have Moru's casual confidence when it came to climbing.

Down among the huts, she smiled shyly as people in the tribe greeted her. She didn't know quite what to say, because she hadn't learned enough of their language, and she still couldn't remember many of their names. But they were always friendly; they always called "hello."

So why did she still feel like an outsider? Why didn't she feel as if she belonged here?

Well, maybe in time she would—if she chose to stay. She picked her way along a narrow path between the huts and the river. She felt herself growing anxious as she neared the house where Faltor lived. It wasn't Faltor himself who made her so apprehensive; it was his son, Mertan, who worried her.

She came to the small space outside the doorway of Faltor's dwelling, and her worst fear was fulfilled as she found Mertan sitting cross-legged on the ground with a dozen spears laid out beside him. She realized that he was the one she had heard earlier, working on his spear shafts, meticulously paring the wood till it was perfectly balanced.

He looked up and saw her, and he quickly laid his tools aside. "Laena!" he called out. He scrambled onto his feet.

She bowed her head in the formal greeting that the Fishers used. 'Good morning, Mertan.''

She noticed then that a girl was with him. Her name was Turi, and she was sitting to one side, reclining on a chair built from logs. She was long-limbed and graceful, with large, soft brown eyes, so that she almost looked like a woodland creature—a fawn, or an antelope. Her hair was long, hanging to her waist, and she had woven some wildflowers into it.

Turi was always showing herself off, whenever Laena saw her. She was older than Laena, and could have taken a mate a year ago, but it seemed clear that she was waiting for Mertan, as if no one other than the chief's son would be good enough for her.

Mertan was as handsome as Turi was beautiful. He had inherited his father's strong features and flawless skin, and he moved with easy, muscled grace. He was a fine hunter—probably the finest in the tribe, despite his youth. And one day, without a doubt, he would become chief of the Fishers.

He looked at Laena, and Laena felt herself clenching up inside. She was dowdy and plain by comparison with Mertan or Turi, and she could barely speak their language. "I go," she said in the Fisher tongue. "To Nan."

"Wait." Mertan moved in front of her, blocking her path.

Laena hesitated. She looked at Turi, and found Turi staring at her watchfully. "Hello," Laena said to her. Then she realized she had spoken in the old language of the Panther People. She felt her face turning red as she repeated herself in the Fisher tongue.

Turi didn't smile at her. "Good morning," she said coolly.

"I go," Laena said again.

"I'll come with you," said Mertan.

This was what she had been dreading. Every day, for the past four days, he had insisted on walking with her. She couldn't understand why he wanted her company. She was unattractive compared with Turi, and she lacked skills that were considered important in the Fisher Tribe. She could barely communicate with him, and she didn't know what she was supposed to do in all the different social situations. She felt incompetent and helpless.

But here was Mertan, falling into step beside her, his bronze skin gleaming in the morning light. The path was so narrow, it was impossible to avoid touching him as they walked together. She was vividly aware of his strength and the warmth of his body, and it distracted her so much she found it hard to think.

Just for a moment she allowed herself to imagine how it would feel to be held by him, the same way Sordir had held her. The thought made her feel dizzy. She tried to push it out of her mind.

Something brushed against her hair. She turned quickly, and found that it was his hand. Instinctively, she took a step back.

He smiled to reassure her. "Your hair is—" He used a word that she didn't understand.

He'd noticed that she hadn't bothered to braid her hair that morning. Well, if Moru was right and the Fishers thought it looked foolish, why should she bother?

"Let me," he said. He moved behind her, divided her hair into three strands, and started braiding them. Laena felt a tormenting mixture of emotions. Why was he doing this? Was he showing her that she could never be like a Fisher, like Turi, or like him? Was he mocking the way she looked? And what would people think if they saw him standing so close to her? Turi was already hostile; that was clear enough. Laena wished with all her heart that Mertan would leave her alone. And yet she knew that if he did, she would feel terribly hurt.

"There," he said when he had finished. "Good now."

"Good?" she looked at him doubtfully.

He nodded. "Very good." He touched her cheek and smiled at her.

Laena blinked with embarrassment. "Is not Fisher," she said, pointing to her hair.

"More-good than Fisher," he said. He saw the doubt in her eyes, and his smile broadened. He said something more, using words that she hadn't heard before.

She shook her head. "I don't understand."

"Ask Nan." And then, slowly, he repeated what he had said.

She echoed him, to make sure she had it right.

"Yes," he said. "Ask Nan. Nan understands." He stroked her braided hair with the flat of his hand, then drew back from her. He smiled and bowed, then turned and walked back along the path to his father's hut.

Laena told herself not to watch him as he strode away, but she couldn't stop herself. There was something about the way he moved; like a panther, she realized. Was that the foolish reason why his presence seemed so compelling?

Abruptly, Laena realized she was standing outside the hut where Nan lived. It had belonged to the old healer who had died. Nan shared it now with Worin, the woman who had been the old healer's apprentice.

Laena closed her eyes for a moment, trying to calm herself. Then she opened the flap that covered the doorway to Nan's home, and she stepped inside.

It was spacious, but it was cluttered with furniture and bric-a-brac. There were four beds, so that anyone who needed constant care could stay close to the healer day and night. A fire smoldered in the center of the stone floor, its smoke drifting lazily through a hole in the roof. A bark dish hung above the embers, containing some simmering broth. The place smelled of herbs and roots, powders and salves.

Nan was sitting with Worin, and Laena realized with a pang of nostalgia that the old lady was teaching the Fisher how to prevent bleeding by using a tourniquet. It seemed so long ago that Laena herself had learned that lesson.

Worin wrestled with the thong, looping it around her own leg for practice. She was clumsy, and she obviously disliked being told what to do. Until Nan had arrived, Worin had been the only person in the village with any healing skills at all; consequently, she had thought of herself as the healer, even though she wasn't really qualified.

Laena told herself that she should feel sorry for Worin. And yet, she didn't. There was something dark and dour about the woman, which made it hard to like her and impossible to get close to her. A reddish birthmark covered the entire left side of her face. She had a long, prominent nose, wide, thin lips, and a receding chin. She was terribly ugly, and she knew it—and she resented that, too.

"Good morning," said Laena from the doorway.

Worin dropped the thong. She stared for a moment at Laena, then stood up, turned her back, and started stirring the big dish of broth.

"Good morning, Laena," said Nan. "I was wondering where you were."

"I'm sorry, the morning light is so dim, I don't wake up—"

Nan waved aside Laena's excuses. "It doesn't matter. There's nothing urgent for us today."

Laena tried to decide how to say what she wanted to say. "Nan, can I talk to you? I have a question."

"Of course." She nodded toward Worin. "She still doesn't understand the Panther language. Say whatever you want."

Laena sat down on a tree stump that had been stripped of its bark and painstakingly polished. The idea of permanent furnishings in a permanent home still surprised her after her childhood in a tribe that trekked between its summer home and its winter home each year. In her childhood, furnishings had had to be light enough and simple enough to carry.

She moved close to Nan. "It's about Mertan," she said.

"What about Mertan?" Nan watched Laena placidly.

Laena drew a slow breath and tried to relax the tightness of her abdomen. "This morning he said something, and he told me you would explain it to me." She murmured the words to Nan, trying to keep her voice low so that Worin wouldn't overhear.

After Laena finished speaking, Nan was silent for a long moment, looking very thoughtful. "Well," she said finally.

Laena took hold of Nan's hand. "Is it something bad? An insult?"

The old woman plucked her fingers free from Laena's anxious grip. "No, no." She glanced at Worin, who still had her back turned while she stirred the dish. "It means," said Nan, "you are a beautiful woman, he admires you, and he will hunt for you next month."

At first Laena thought that Nan must be lying to her for some reason. Then she saw that the old woman's face was serious, and she felt overwhelmed with confusion. "But it can't be so!"

"It is." Nan shrugged. "You're fortunate, Laena."

It was Laena's turn to be silent for a while. "I—don't understand why he feels that way," she said.

"You're a pretty young woman," said Nan. "And sometimes, you know, an outsider, with different ways, seems to have an air of magic about her. It excites people." She looked away, and Laena wondered if she was remembering things from her own past. "Men like to capture things,"

Nan went on. "They prove their strength by capturing a woman who is free to roam, like a cat—like a panther?"

Laena realized the implications, and they made sense, in a way. And yet, at the same time, she still found it hard to believe. There was nothing magical about her; she was just a person like other people, and Mertan hardly even knew her. Meanwhile, from her point of view, Mertan roused a fierce yearning in her; but that didn't seem real, either, because *she* hardly knew *him*.

"What did he mean," Laena said, "about hunting game for me next month?"

"He means the Fall Hunt," said Nan. "It's an important time for the Fisher Tribe. They kill as much as they can, to see them through the winter. It's a time for young people to choose one another, too. The single men offer their finest prey to the women, and each woman chooses the man she wants."

"Oh," Laena said softly.

Nan gave her a long, brooding look. "Laena, fate is being kind to you for a change. Can't you see that? Don't you realize what an honor it is, for Mertan to choose you? Why, that girl Turi has been waiting for him for a whole year." Nan laughed. "She'll be furious when she finds out that he wants you."

Laena felt tears pricking the corners of her eyes. "But I don't want her to be furious! I want the people here to like me!"

Nan grunted with irritation. "If you end up with Mertan, you'll get respect—you see that, don't you? And when people respect you, they have to like you, whether they want to or not."

Laena could see that there was some truth in that. And yet, somehow, it still wasn't what she wanted.

She looked up, sensing someone was watching her. Worin had sidled around the cooking fire and was barely visible behind the hazy purple smoke, silently staring at Laena. Laena gave a little start, and she cried out.

"Now what?" said Nan. She turned quickly, but Worin was even quicker. By the time Nan looked at her, she had turned away and was stirring the broth as if nothing had happened.

* * *

That evening Laena made her way back to the cave that she tried to think of as her home. It had been an easy day, since none of the villagers currently needed a healer's skills. Nan had spent several hours teaching Laena more of the Fishers' language, and then Laena had been put to work pounding plants, making potions to replenish the stock that Nan liked to keep on hand.

Twice more, Worin had eyed Laena strangely, when Nan hadn't been looking. Laena had tried to talk to the woman, but she answered in words that Laena didn't understand. In the end, Laena just decided to ignore her.

She heard the Fishers in their huts as she walked through the village, and they sounded cheerful, chatting and laughing with one another. Most of them were easygoing people, quick to smile, and with good reason: their life here was comfortable all the year round. They had no enemies, the river always brought them a fresh supply of food, and they never had to uproot themselves and move from one place to another. Why shouldn't they be happy?

She started climbing the cliff to her cave, then paused as she heard Orleh shouting at Joq again. Laena couldn't understand all of the words, but she knew enough to make sense of it. Orleh was telling Joq that he was an embarrassment to his family. He was wasting all his days, sitting around playing his flute and carving wood.

Suddenly Laena heard a smacking sound.

"Don't hit him!" That was Joq's mother, a timid woman named Weeps. She was easily intimidated by her husband, yet at this moment she sounded fierce.

Orleh shouted something in reply. He seemed to be saying he should have hit Joq more often in the past.

There was a brief lull, and then Orleh started shouting again. Something about a girl. Worin? Yes, he said Worin's name, and something about the hunt, and he sounded angrier than ever.

"Worin likes him." It was Weeps speaking again. "She's not such a bad girl. He could do worse."

"Get out." Orleh's voice interrupted. "Go to her hut, Joq, if that's what you want. Take this—this thing with you."

A moment later, before Laena could get up into her own cave, Joq came climbing down. One side of his face was red where his father had slapped him, and he wore a brooding, angry look that Laena hadn't seen before. Still, he hadn't shouted back at his parents. He seemed to have such a placid nature, she wondered if he was even capable of raising his voice.

He saw her, and he hesitated. Laena felt embarrassed, because she had obviously been eavesdropping. But Joq didn't seem to care. He was holding something in one hand while he clung to the rock face with the other. As he noticed her peering at it, he held it out to her. "Take this," he said.

Laena reached out for it and found that it was a small wood carving, delicately done. It was a miniature sculpture of a fish.

She shook her head. "No," she said. "Not me." She tried to hand it back to him.

He shrugged one shoulder, as if to say—keep it, what does it matter? Then he lowered himself down the rock face, much faster than she could move. He loped off into the shadows without looking back.

Laena watched him and wondered if he was doing what his father had said, going to see Worin. Was this why Worin had seemed so hostile—because she thought Joq was interested in Laena? If only Laena could speak the Fisher language fluently, she might be able to settle the whole thing. Even if she eventually decided to settle here among the Fishers, she certainly wasn't ready to pledge herself to a man, whether he was the son of the chieftain, or a dreamer who sat playing music all day, or anyone else.

She looked again at Joq's carving of a fish. It was really beautifully done, but she wished he hadn't given it to her, because she didn't know what the gift implied. Still, there was nothing she could do about that now. And so, feeling a deep weariness, she climbed up to her resting place.

Chapter 24

The next day, when Laena went to Nan's house for her lessons in language and healing, Nan wasn't there. Worin was alone in the big hut, hunched over a dish-shaped piece of rock, using a round stone to crush herbs on it. She looked up, saw Laena, and paused in her work. For a long moment, she was silent. Then: "What do you want?" she said.

Laena walked in, picking her way carefully. "Where's Nan?"

Worin shook her head. The motion made her lank hair swing away from her face, revealing the dark purple swatch that disfigured her left cheek and the left side of her forehead. "Nan has gone."

Something about Worin's voice made Laena feel uneasy. The woman made it sound as if Nan had disappeared; had ceased to exist.

"I don't understand what you mean," Laena said, crouching opposite Worin, less than an arm's length away. "Nan has gone—where?"

Worin eyed Laena, then deliberately went back to work crushing the herbs. She said nothing.

Laena felt a twist of anger. All the frustration and confusion of her new life in the village seemed to mount up inside her. She took hold of Worin's arm. "Tell me!" she snapped at her.

Worin jerked back. "Don't touch me!"

The two of them stared at each other for a long moment. *"Where is Nan?"* Laena said.

Finally, Worin lowered her eyes. "At Faltor's hut."

Laena stared at the woman. She wasn't ready, yet, to let this pass. "Why?" she demanded. "Why did you—why don't you like me?"

Worin set the round stone aside. She stood up, wiped the

palms of her hands on a hank of dried grass, then lifted the dish-shaped rock and poured the sap into a little leather phial. "You are ignorant," she said.

Laena stared at her in surprise. This was the last thing she had expected to hear. "I know more than you do," she protested. "Nan has taught me more."

Worin's face contorted in a grimace, and she banged the rock down. The sound was sudden, and it made Laena jump. "You can't even speak properly!" Worin leaned forward. Her lips drew back, revealing a jumble of discolored teeth. "I will be healer. Not you."

Laena sighed. She wasn't angry anymore; she actually felt sorry for the woman. She tried to decide what to say. Obviously, there was no point in arguing. "Maybe it's true," she said. "Maybe you will be the healer when Nan is gone. A good healer, I'm sure." She turned away, not wanting to deal with Worin any further. "I go now to see her."

Worin didn't say anything. She stood and watched Laena as she left the hut.

Outside, the sky was gray and the valley seemed even darker than usual. Laena walked along the narrow path beside the river, staring at the yellow-brown soil under her feet, not really thinking of anything at all.

Then, as she approached Fultor's hut, she suddenly wondered if Mertan would be there. He hadn't been, when she'd passed by in the opposite direction. That should have been a relief; and yet, to her surprise, she'd felt disappointed.

Now, as she approached, she saw him back in his customary place, working on his spear shafts. He was alone this morning; Turi was nowhere to be seen.

He was so engrossed, he didn't even notice her. But to get into the hut she had to push right past him. "Good morning," she said, feeling a new kind of tension growing in her chest as she looked at him.

He looked up, then stood quickly and stepped toward her. "Laena." He reached out and took her shoulders between his hands. When he bowed his head in the Fisher greeting, his face was so close to hers she imagined she could feel the warmth of him on her cheeks and forehead. "It is good to see you," he said, smiling.

She felt herself trembling. Why did her emotions still run

wild inside her like this? She wished she could control them. She tried to speak, but for a moment she couldn't say anything.

"Yesterday," he said, "you told Nan what I said? She explained?"

Laena nodded silently, not trusting herself to speak.

"You are happy that I will hunt for you?"

"I don't know," she said. How could she know? Being close to him made it hard for her to think.

His smile faded. He said something more, which she couldn't understand. She just shrugged helplessly. "I'm looking for Nan," she said.

Mertan gave a curt nod. "Nan went with my father to the hunting grounds. My father must say when the Fall Hunt begins. He looks for signs—the land, the sky, the animals."

"Oh. I see." Laena wanted to ask how long Nan and Faltor would be gone, but she didn't know how to say that. Well, she could go to Nan's hut again later, to find out if Nan wanted to teach her today. In the meantime, obviously, there was nothing for her to do.

"Laena!"

She hesitated. "Yes?"

"Will you walk with me this afternoon?"

She wasn't sure if she understood him. Did his words have some extra meaning? She was afraid to answer, in case she might be making a mistake. In any case, she didn't want to encourage him. He should be with Turi, not her.

And yet, she couldn't refuse him. "Walk, where?" she asked cautiously.

He gestured. "Up the valley?"

She felt terribly torn. She looked up at his face—and realized, with surprise, that he looked worried. Was he actually afraid that she would refuse him?

She didn't know how to cope with any of this, and she wasn't feeling strong enough to try. "All right," she said. "Yes, I will walk with you."

His smile returned, and his whole face seemed to glow.

"Come here, at midday. We will walk together." He reached out to her again—then stopped himself and dropped his arms back by his side. He solemnly bowed his head to her.

She bowed back, then flashed him a nervous smile and

hurried away. Had she made a mistake? Or should she take Nan's advice and make the most of her good fortune? She wanted Mertan, there was no doubt about that. The thought of lying with him and letting him take her was so exciting, it made her dizzy. He seemed gentle and romantic and enthralled by her. But how could she be sure?

Laena decided to go back to her cave and do the chores that she had been putting off. Maybe some hard work would stop her thoughts from chattering like this.

She found her way between the huts. They were built so close together there was barely room to pass between them. People greeted her in their usual friendly style, and she smiled and nodded and bade them good morning. But she was still thinking about Mertan: his face, the way his eyes seemed so alive, the way the light gleamed on his shoulders.

She started climbing to the mouth of the cave—and she found Joq's mother, Weeps, peering out at her. The woman was thin and pale, with large eyes that looked perpetually worried. "Laena!" she called.

"Good morning," Laena said, pulling herself from one handhold to the next. The last thing she wanted was a conversation.

"Come." Weeps gestured to her cave. "Here, please."

The Fishers were such social people. If Laena refused the invitation, she was afraid it might cause offense. On the other hand, she had been in Weeps's cave twice before, and it had been difficult both times to find polite things to say while Weeps pressed her to eat strange food that tasted bad.

"I am busy—" Laena began.

"Please." Weeps gave her a plaintive look.

Laena sighed. "All right."

The cave was much larger than hers. When she'd first visited it, Orleh had told her how he had spent years enlarging it for his family, working with flint tools, creating two separate rooms at the back and little cavities along the walls for storing necessities. Orleh was proud of the home he had built, even though Laena had learned that it was a mark of low status, among the Fishers, to be a cave dweller. The families who were truly respected occupied huts on the ledge beside the river.

Laena squatted just inside the entrance. She saw that Weeps was alone, and she guessed that Orleh and Joq were out fishing. Weeps had been working, powdering dried meat and mixing it with rendered fat and red berries. She quickly scraped a portion onto a piece of birchbark and offered it to Laena. "Please, eat." She bowed her head.

Reluctantly, Laena tried it. It had a sweet, pasty taste that seemed pleasant at first, but stuck in her throat. "Good," she said politely.

Weeps smiled and nodded. "Take more!"

"No. No, thank you."

Weeps's smile disappeared, and her habitually plaintive look took its place. The woman acted as if her whole life was full of disappointments.

"My son, Joq," she said. "He is a fine person."

Laena nodded. "Yes," she agreed.

"You like him?"

Laena hesitated, sensing a trap. "I don't know him," she said.

Weeps leaned over and laid her hand on Laena's arm. "Talk to him. You will like him."

Laena wondered if Orleh had told Weeps to do this. Orleh was a proud man, who thought he deserved better—a better place to live, a better wife, a better son. Yes; it made sense for him to try to set up a match.

"I'm sorry," Laena began, "but—"

"The Fall Hunt will be soon. You understand? You must choose a man."

Laena felt the words closing in on her like a prison. "I am not ready," she said as firmly as she could. "Why do I have to?"

Weeps tightened her grip on Laena's arm. "Talk to Joq."

Laena still didn't understand the Fisher language or Fisher etiquette well enough. She was afraid that if she refused outright, it might cause permanent offense. Well, merely talking to Joq wouldn't do any harm. "All right," she said. "I'll talk to him."

"Wonderful!" Weeps released Laena's arm. She pointed. "He is outside. By the river." She pulled Laena to the mouth of the cave. "See, there!"

In the far distance, a solitary figure was sitting on the riverbank. She guessed he was playing one of his flutes, though he was too far away for her to hear the music.

"I will talk to him," she said grimly.

Weeps patted Laena on the cheek. Laena knew that this was a great sign of affection among the Fisher Tribe. "You are a good person," said Weeps.

Laena forced a smile. "Thank you."

"Go now."

Laena climbed down the cliff face, feeling angry again— at herself this time, for not being strong enough or clever enough to deal with Weeps. The clouds had become lower and thicker, she noticed, matching her grim mood. She walked by the river, moving downstream, uncomfortably aware that Weeps must be watching from her cave as Laena emerged from among the huts of the village. "Joq," she called as she headed toward the lonely place where he had chosen to sit.

He acted as if he hadn't heard her. He was sitting on a rock near the point where the river spilled over a ledge and began its quick descent to the lower part of the valley. That was where Laena had met Horill, when she and Nan and Moru had first come here.

She started climbing up toward Joq, and she called his name again. This time she was sure he must have heard her, but he still didn't look at her. He set down his flute and stared in the opposite direction, with his hands resting calmly on his knees.

Laena felt tempted to turn around and leave. But she had given her word, and she had to go through with this. She sat down on a rock close to Joq. "Hey," she said.

He glanced at her and did not smile. "My mother told you to speak to me."

So, he knew, and he felt as embarrassed as she did.

He turned away, raised the reed to his lips, and started playing. The notes were quick and delicate, cascading effortlessly out of the tiny instrument. Despite herself, Laena felt impressed, touched by the music. "That sounds very beautiful," she said.

He paused and shot her a quick, cautious glance, as if he wasn't sure whether to believe her. "You think so?"

She shrugged, wondering why he should doubt her word. "Of course."

"I talk to the river," he said. "The river talks to me."

It was true, she realized. His music was like the water tumbling over rocks where the valley was steepest.

She wasn't annoyed with him anymore. Strangely, she found herself feeling sorry for him. "You're right," she said. "Your mother told me to talk to you. The Fall Hunt—"

He gave her an enigmatic look. "Don't worry, Laena. I don't need to hunt for you. Not for you; not for anyone. I'm happy alone."

She wondered if she had understood exactly what he meant. "You won't hunt for Worin?"

"Worin?" He laughed and shook his head. "Not for Worin. Not for any woman."

"You will stay alone?"

"Of course," he said as if it should be obvious.

They looked at each other. His face was so gentle, so innocent. Laena felt a pang, although she didn't know quite why. The things that mattered to most men didn't seem to matter to Joq at all. Hunting, fighting, showing strength, taking a woman—none of it touched him, somehow.

"I think you are a good person, Joq," she said.

He looked startled; and then he looked embarrassed. "You say kind things," he said. For the first time, he seemed unsure of himself.

"Maybe we can be friends," she said. Impulsively, she held out her hand.

He stared at her for a moment, looking even less confident. For a moment, Laena wondered if she'd used the wrong word. But then, tentatively, Joq took her hand. His touch was light but sure. "Friends," he agreed.

"Laena!" The voice came from somewhere by the river.

Laena looked and saw Moru with Horill and a couple of the other hunters. The little girl waved her arm, beckoning.

Laena turned back to Joq. "My sister. I must go."

He held up his hand. "Just a moment."

"Yes?"

"You have the wooden fish?"

She remembered the little carving. "At my cave," she said.

"You should carry it with you. It is good fortune."

Laena nodded slowly. "All right. I will."

"Good." He picked up his flute, and straight away he started playing his music again, as if she were no longer there.

Laena scrambled down the rocks. Moru was waiting for

her, while Horill and the other two men started walking back toward the village.

"Look, Laena!" the little girl held up a fish. It was half an arm's length, with a gash in its side. "Horill gave it to me."

Laena kneeled down beside the little girl and hugged her. "That's wonderful. We'll cook it and eat it."

Moru's happy smile slowly faded. "I'm still not sure how to take the bones out."

"Well—" Laena paused. "We'll do our best. We have to get the hang of it sooner or later."

Moru smiled again. "All right, let's go back to the cave."

Laena fell into step beside her, happy to feel that her sister was friendly again.

"Why were you talking to him?" Moru said, gesturing back at Joq.

Laena hesitated, wondering how much she should say. "His mother wanted me to speak to him. I like him. We agreed to be friends, that's all."

Moru shook her head in disapproval. "No one likes him. He's strange."

"Well, I like him. I don't have to think the same way that everyone else thinks. I can make up my own mind."

Moru narrowed her eyes. "You won't let him hunt for you, will you?"

Laena felt a wave of irritation. Even her little sister was interfering in her love life! "No, Moru. I won't let him hunt for me. In fact—well, Mertan wants to hunt for me."

Moru blinked. Her disapproval turned to an expression of disbelief. "Mertan?"

"Yes."

Moru stopped. She stared at Laena. "Mertan," she said again. "Are you sure?"

"Of course I'm sure." Laena put her hands on her hips. "Why are you so surprised?"

"You know what it means, don't you? It means he wants to be your mate."

Now Laena felt really annoyed. "Of course I know what it means! I'm older than you, remember?"

Moru slowly shook her head. "Turi will be furious. She's been—you know, waiting for him."

Laena studied the little girl. "How do you know all this?"

Moru resumed walking along the riverbank, toward the village. "Everybody knows," she said. "The same as everybody knows that Worin is waiting for Joq. But Worin, she's an evil person."

Laena sighed in exasperation. "She's not evil. She's jealous, and she's had a hard life, that's all."

Moru gave her a scornful look. But she said nothing.

Back at her cave, Laena used a flint knife to prepare the fish. Moru tried to show her how, from the lessons that Horill had shown her, but it was far more difficult than she'd expected. Between the two of them they got the job done, more or less. Soon the cave reeked, and then Laena's eyes began stinging as she started a fire and its smoke lingered inside instead of wafting out.

But Moru was excited by every part of the process, and when the fish was finally cooked, she ate it slowly, savoring every mouthful. Even Laena was able to enjoy some of it, knowing that she had prepared it herself.

In the afternoon, she looked out and saw Mertan standing out by the river. He was staring up at the mouth of her cave, and when he saw her looking at him, he waved to her.

He was waiting for her, she realized. The knowledge sent a new wave of anxiety and anticipation rippling through her, even stronger than before. Was she being foolish, building up her hopes like this? Would he still be interested in her when they understood each other better and she no longer seemed so strange and special to him? What would he want? What would he do?

"I have to go," she said to Moru.

The little girl heard the tension in Laena's voice. She frowned suspiciously. "Where?" she said. And then she saw who Laena was looking at, and her eyes grew round. "With *him*?"

Laena nodded. She started clearing up the mess that they'd made while they were cooking the fish.

"I'll do that," said Moru.

Laena stopped. She didn't know what she was doing or why she was doing it, she realized. She hesitated. "Do I look all right?"

Moru made a face. "You still keep braiding your hair."

"He likes it that way." Laena glanced around, and suddenly noticed the little carving that Joq had given her—the wooden fish. If it was a good-luck charm, she should take it with her. Quickly, she thrust it into the leather pouch at her waist.

"Don't keep him waiting!" said Moru.

The urgency in her voice made Laena even more anxious than before. She imagined Mertan getting tired of hanging around and walking off in disgust.

"All right. All right, I'm going." Laena moved to the mouth of the cave, groped for a handhold, and almost fell.

"Careful!" Moru called.

Laena cursed her own clumsiness, knowing that Mertan was watching her. What would he think of her, if she couldn't even climb out of her own home?

Mertan led the way upriver, where the walls of the valley closed in either side and it seemed there could be no way out of the deep cleft in the land. He moved quickly, and Laena had to hurry to keep up. But after a while she discovered that she still had the muscles and the stamina she had developed from her trek with Nan and Moru. Soon she was able to fall into an easy striding rhythm.

Eventually, they reached a place where the path became so narrow, the only way they could proceed was by stepping cautiously in single file. And then, just ahead, the path disappeared altogether. The canyon became a narrow crevasse through which the river surged and sprayed.

Mertan paused and looked at Laena appraisingly. "You are strong," he said. "Most women do not travel so well."

"Most women have not traveled as far as I have."

He nodded thoughtfully. "I would like to know about your travels. Will you tell me?"

"Of course."

"Good. But now, we must climb."

Laena looked up. A series of steps had been carved in the side of the canyon.

"This way," said Mertan, starting upward.

The first three steps were narrow and awkward, but as she followed him she found that the canyon opened out. Soon, there was an easy trail to follow.

They moved slowly, pausing often so that Laena could look at the view below. The canyon was a jagged gash in the land, its red rocks spotted with green vegetation, the river gleaming silver, wending its way past the tiny huts of the Fisher Tribe in the far, far distance.

Once again, Laena felt the sense of tranquility that had overcome her when they had entered the land of the Fishers. "Tell me," she said to Mertan, "is it true, your father's great-great-grandfather, Orwael—" She broke off, not knowing the word for "spirit" in the Fisher tongue.

"He is here," said Mertan, nodding gravely.

Laena looked around at the enchanted place as if, somehow, she could sense the old man's presence. She thought of her own father, and her mother, and the vision she had had of them in the green landscape where the sun was high in the sky. If the spirits of Mertan's people were here, where were hers?

He led the way further upward, and the rocky ground became sandy underfoot. Laena found herself walking through tall, dry grass, and there were wiry, stunted trees of a kind she had never seen before.

"The animals pass this way, when the season is right," Mertan said. "It will be soon now."

"The Fall Hunt," she said.

He nodded.

She didn't want to think too much about that. "Why do the Fishers hunt so little?" she asked, changing the subject. "Instead of eating fish, you could—"

"No." He frowned. "It is hard to explain in simple words. My father told me, and his father told him—if we hunt more, yes, we eat better. But there are not many animals here. If we kill them all, we must travel farther and follow them when they migrate, and then we cannot be Fisher People and stay in our homes all the year round."

Laena knew enough of the words to understand what he meant. She remembered her life with the Panther Tribe. That was how it had been, she realized. They had eaten all the game in their land, so they had to travel each year, following the herds.

Mertan led her up to the top of a craggy rock formation. There was grass on the top of it, so that it was a comfortable place to sit. Standing up here, they could look out over a wide panorama. There were rolling hills, to the north. To the south, just the other side of the Fishers' valley, the mountains rose up stark and severe, disappearing into the clouds that still filled the sky. These mountains were part of the same range that Laena had imagined climbing one day, on her way south. Now that she saw them more closely, she realized just how farfetched her idea had been.

"We will sit here," said Mertan. He turned and looked at Laena.

Evidently, she was supposed to sit first. It seemed odd that he was telling her what to do, but maybe it was just the custom of his tribe. Also, she reminded herself, he was the chief's son. It was natural for him to make decisions for others to follow.

She sat down, and then he joined her. The closeness of him made it hard for her to think of anything else. Her nervousness seized her again, and she felt shivery. Was he going to touch her? What was going to happen? She wondered suddenly if she should have come here at all. But he was a gentle person, wasn't he? He respected her. He was Faltor's son. He had avoided touching her this morning, after she had pulled away from him.

Laena couldn't decide what scared her more: the possibility that he would reach for her, or the possibility that he would not.

"You are very quiet," he said.

She jumped at the sound of his voice. "Just—a little nervous," she said.

He laughed gently. "You are safe here."

Something about his voice helped her to relax a little.

"Tell me now," he went on, "about your life before you came here to us."

Laena was glad to have something to think about. She started describing her childhood, as well as she could in the Fisher tongue. Once in a while, Mertan helped her with words that she wasn't sure of. And so, bit by bit, she told him the story of her life.

When the story was done, the sun had moved lower in the sky and all her nervousness had gone. She was able to look at Mertan and feel relaxed with him, warmed by his company.

He touched her cheek. "You have had so many troubles in your life," he said gently. "You have suffered so much."

Laena bit her lip. "Well—I suppose—"

"You can be happy here," he said. "With the Fishers. With me."

The words were so simple, but she felt overwhelmed by them. She looked at him, and tears pricked the corners of her eyes.

He reached for her and gathered her to him. He nuzzled her neck, and she let out a little cry of surprise as glowing, tingling sensations flooded through her. He seemed so strong and so calm, and all his attention was on her. She touched him tentatively at first, but then more boldly. She ran her hands over his body and felt the hardness of his muscles under his clothes. She slid one trembling hand inside his jacket and touched his warm, bare chest.

He smiled at her, and then he pressed his lips against hers. The pressure of his mouth, soft yet firm, made Laena feel as if she were dissolving inside, turning into a warm river that could somehow flow and merge with the spirit of the man beside her.

When he pulled back, she found herself gasping. Her face was flushed, and her heart was pounding. He looked into her eyes, and he seemed to know exactly what she was feeling.

And then, unexpectedly, he moved further away from her. "The hunt will be soon," he said softly. "Two days, maybe three."

She realized what he meant. The hunt was the time when a woman selected the man she would take as her mate. Then she could have Mertan—if she chose. But not until then.

She stared at him. She wanted him now, she realized. She wanted him more than she had ever wanted anything. She reached out to pull him to her, so he would kiss her again.

He took hold of her wrists, gently but firmly. "We must wait. You know, my father is the chief of our tribe. I must be true to the traditions of our people."

She nodded wordlessly. With regret, she saw that it was so.

"We can come back here again," he said. "Tomorrow, if you like."

Again she nodded. "Yes, please," she said.

"Look." He pointed to the distant mountains. The clouds were breaking up as afternoon faded into evening, and the sun was showing through, blazing red, casting a rich glow over the land.

"It's beautiful," said Laena.

Mertan looked at her. "It is an omen," he said softly.

Chapter 25

She went walking with Mertan every day after that. Nan chided her for taking so much time from her studies, but Laena barely listened. She felt as if her whole life—her whole world—had been remade. The discontent that she had felt in the past, always nagging at her, now seemed as if it had never existed. The tranquility she had experienced when she had first walked into the valley now seemed a natural part of everyday life, suffusing even the smallest tasks. She smiled as she swept sand out of the cave; she sang to herself as she prepared meals.

She still had to cope with some problems. Turi had screamed threats at Laena; she had burst into tears; she had grabbed Mertan and refused to let go of him; and she had even vowed to throw herself off the cliff at the end of the valley. As a result, she had roused so much sympathy among the other young people in the tribe that none of them would talk to Laena anymore.

Mertan told her not to worry, because as soon as she was paired with him she would have the same status that he enjoyed himself as the chief's son. She would find then that her worst enemies would suddenly want to be her friends. Laena wanted to believe him, for she certainly had no intention of sacrificing Mertan just to placate Turi and the rest of them.

Laena's neighbors were another problem. Orleh had visited Laena and told her, with gruff embarrassment, that if Worin paired with Joq, it would be a terrible humiliation. He begged Laena to choose Joq instead of Mertan. At first, Laena had tried to say no as politely as she could. In the end, she had pointed out that she herself would feel embarrassed, and stupid besides, if she rejected the chief's son and chose a misfit whose only ability seemed to be flute-playing. Orleh had scowled at her, and he'd turned his back and left without a word—a gross breach of manners among the Fisher Tribe.

The last of Laena's problems was Moru. Laena's romance with Mertan no longer impressed the little girl. Instead, she was jealous. At first Laena had found this hard to believe, but Moru became angry whenever Laena mentioned Mertan, and she became sullen when she saw the two of them together. She barely even spoke to Laena anymore.

Normally, problems such as these would have filled Laena with despair. But Mertan was such a source of joy to her, it eclipsed all the petty jealousies around her. If people resented her happiness instead of sharing it with her, that was unfortunate, but she refused to let it spoil her state of mind.

A week after she had first walked with Mertan on the hunting lands, Laena woke to sounds of singing. She looked out and saw the women of the tribe working by the river, preparing for the Fall Hunt, stowing dried food and necessities in leather packs. It would be soon now: probably tomorrow, if the weather was good.

Moru had woken before Laena, as usual, and had left the cave. Laena decided not to bother with breakfast. She felt so content she hardly seemed to need food anymore. She had all the energy she needed, even when she skipped meals.

She picked up the leather bowl of water that she kept at the back of the cave and brought it toward the light. She looked at her reflection in the water and saw herself smiling. There was a radiant quality to her face that she had never noticed in the past. For the first time in her life, she felt as if she might be a little bit beautiful.

Mertan had told her he would come for her today, around noontime. That seemed an unreasonably long time to wait. Laena felt restless and impatient—far too restless to go and sit with Nan and learn lessons while Worin watched resentfully from the shadows.

Laena climbed down to the riverbank and started walking away from the village. The day was bright, but the air was chill with the promise of autumn. She pulled her jacket more tightly around her and hugged herself, thinking that it would soon be time to wear her heavier furs.

She climbed the tumble of boulders beside the river,

moving quickly to warm herself. She headed for the place where Joq often sat—but when she got there, she found he was missing.

Laena felt disappointed. He was the only one of the young Fishers who seemed to approve of her romance with Mertan and hadn't turned against her.

She glanced around, then heard a shout from above, where the side of the valley sloped more gently and you could walk easily instead of having to climb on all fours. Up there, the land was high enough to catch the morning sun. Laena shaded her eyes and saw a figure waving to her.

She started climbing. It was heavy work picking her way among the loose rocks and shale, but she enjoyed the way it made her skin tingle and her heart pound. She felt very much alive, especially when she emerged into the sunlight.

Joq was sitting on a boulder holding a spear across his knees. She paused in front of him, breathing hard. "What are you doing here?" she said.

"Practicing." He nodded toward a rock a hundred paces away. A wad of leather had been tied around it to serve as a target, and Joq had used charcoal to draw the outline of a rabbit on the leather. Several spears lay nearby, where Joq had cast them.

"I didn't know you could hunt," she said.

"Only when I have to." He stood, took careful aim, and threw the spear that he had been holding across his knees. It flew true, hit the leather target, and dug in.

She walked with him across the steep, stony hillside. "Why don't you practice where the other hunters go?"

"Because they don't like it if I do better than they do, and they laugh at me if I do worse. It's easier here on my own."

She admired the little picture he had drawn. "Most men just draw a circle to aim at, don't they?"

He shrugged. "A circle doesn't please me." He retrieved his spear, then gathered up the others. "There are no circles in the real world. Animals, grass, trees, rocks—don't you think they are more interesting shapes?"

Often, when she talked to Joq, she found the conversation wandering off the topic. His mind was strange to her. He seemed to step back from the world and look at it like a man looking at a fish in a river, studying the way it moved. He acted as if he weren't a part of it himself.

"But—the sun is a circle," Laena said, pleased that she had found an exception to his rule.

Joq paused. Slowly, he smiled. "That's true," he conceded. "Although, the sun is not part of our world, is it? You can't touch it. You can't even look at it for very long." He started back to the rock where he had been sitting before.

She followed him. "What is the sun then?" she asked.

"How should I know?"

Laena sat on another rock, near him. "In my tribe, we used to have a legend that it was a fire that the great Panther had thrown up into the sky."

"That isn't true." He sounded as if there were no doubt about that at all.

'It *could* be," she said. She stared away, into the distance. "But I don't know if I believe the old legends anymore. You know I told you once about the vision that I had, of my parents—"

He nodded. "I remember."

Joq was the only person Laena had shared her secret with fully. She didn't want Mertan to know, in case he might think she was strange. She didn't want anything like that to come between them. But she had sensed that Joq would understand, and she knew he would never tell anyone.

"The sun was in a different place, in my vision," she said. "It was up there." She pointed directly overhead.

"That's impossible," said Joq. "The sun moves in a circle around us. In the summer, it's a big circle. In the winter, it's just a little piece of a circle toward the south."

"Of course," she said impatiently. "I know that. I just meant—" She trailed off. "Well, I think it's a mystery, that's all. The sun, the stars, and the land where souls go—all those things are mysteries."

He didn't laugh at her for talking this way. He ran the tip of his thumb lightly over the point of his spear and narrowed his eyes, staring into the distance. "It sounds nice, a land where the sun shines down from high above. It would have to be warm, wouldn't it? It's always warmest when the sun is high."

"You think that the place in my vision doesn't really exist?"

He shook his head. "I've never had a vision, so I wouldn't know. Maybe what you saw was a place that we go to after we die."

"Yes," said Laena. "I've wondered about that. It seemed so real—you know, I used to think it was my destiny to find it." She looked out across the valley and frowned. "It used to seem like the most important thing in the world. That was what gave me strength, when my life was really hard."

"But now, Mertan gives you strength." There was no hidden meaning in the words; Joq said them plainly and simply, as a fact.

"That's true," said Laena. "He does."

He smiled at her. "I'm happy for you, Laena. But I should be practicing." He stood up, selected a spear, and threw it. It flew wide of the target.

"You're not planning to take part in the hunt, are you?" she asked.

He shrugged irritably. "My father will be ashamed if I don't go. He'll be even more ashamed if I don't kill anything." He cast another spear, and this time it hit the target squarely. "I get sick of my father being ashamed of me all the time."

"You're really quite good," said Laena. "I think you could be a fine hunter if you wanted to."

"But I don't want to." He gave her his strange, enigmatic smile.

"Are you sure you won't hunt for Worin?"

"Never. Why should I? She's ugly and she's mean, and she even smells bad. But just because she doesn't fit in, and I don't fit in, people seem to think we should be paired with each other." He gave her a sudden suspicious look. "You don't think that, do you?"

"No," Laena said quickly. "I don't like Worin. She makes me nervous."

"So I'll stay on my own," said Joq. "And if any woman chooses me, I'll tell her to leave me alone." He laughed to himself. "And now I have to tell you to leave me alone, because you're distracting me, and it's spoiling my aim."

She wasn't offended the way he said it. He was just telling the truth, that was all.

She started down the hillside. "Good-bye, Joq," she called over her shoulder.

He threw the last of his spears. "Are you seeing Mertan today?" he called after her.

"Yes, I am."

He nodded. "Good. You're lucky to have him."

"Yes," she said. "I know."

Back at her cave, someone was waiting for her. Laena peered into the shadows. "Moru," she called, "is that you?" But even as she spoke, she knew that the figure was not her sister.

The person turned, and her face caught the light. Laena gave a little start of surprise. She raised her hand to her mouth. "Nan! What are you doing here? You always said—"

Nan gestured impatiently. "Yes, I said I didn't much like the idea of scrambling up a cliff. And I was right, I'm too old for it. But I had to talk to you, Laena. Privately."

Laena didn't like the tone of Nan's voice. "Is something wrong?"

"Maybe it is, maybe it isn't. Come in, come in, girl, I can't see your face against the light."

Obediently, Laena moved into the cave. She hunkered down opposite Nan, on her bed of woven grasses.

"Don't squat like that!" Nan complained. "I've told you, among the Fishers it's a sign you want to get pregnant and give birth if you squat that way."

"Yes, Nan, I'm sorry." She quickly sat down and crossed her legs. "You're worrying me, coming here like this."

"Well, you're worrying me, too." She peered at Laena's face. "Have you been eating? You've lost weight. Still walking with Mertan? Yes, I can see you are."

The woman's voice sounded harsh and critical. Laena felt confused. "You said I was fortunate that he should be interested in me, Nan. You said I should be thankful, and I should make the most of it."

"Well, yes, I did. And that's true." Nan sounded gruff. She folded her arms and grunted to herself. "But I've been thinking, maybe I spoke too quickly. You have to consider the alternatives."

Laena blinked. The notion didn't make sense. "What do you mean? Who else could there be?"

"Not who else, what else," said Nan. "Meaning, you could choose not to take a man at all, this year. Just a couple of weeks ago, you still weren't even sure if you wanted to stay here with the Fishers. Have you forgotten that?"

Laena tried to think clearly. "But, that was before— before—"

"Before Mertan started taking you for walks with him," Nan said. And there was something disapproving in the way she said it.

"Well—yes!" Laena shook her head in exasperation. "Nan, I don't understand this. Why are you picking on me?"

Nan reached out and patted her knee. "I'm not, Laena. I'm not. But you're young, and I see you making decisions that you'll have to live with for the rest of your life. And it worries me."

Laena leaned back against the wall of the cave. She needed to feel it hard and solid behind her. She felt strange— as if Nan's words had come to her like a blow that caught her where she least expected it. "Are you wondering if I'm going to make the same mistakes that you made, once?" she said. "I remember you told me, you married and regretted it, because your true nature—"

Nan held up her hand. "Yes. Precisely." She shook her head. "It's hard to know what's best, Laena, especially at your age. If you could wait for another year—"

"But Mertan is good to me," she said slowly. "He doesn't order me around. He is respectful, and kind, and gentle. And he's the chieftain's son. And if I wait for another year, I doubt he'll wait for me."

Nan gave a curt nod. "I realize that." She leaned forward. "But are you ready to spend the rest of your life here in this valley? Are you, girl? Are you ready to have children, too?"

She felt as if the words were pummeling her. She had asked herself those questions, just a few days ago. But somehow they had slipped out of her awareness.

"Think, girl!" The old lady reached forward, grabbed Laena's shoulder, and shook her. "Is this what you really, truly want?"

Laena felt stung. "Nan, I've never been so happy before. Why should I want it to stop?"

Nan sighed. She shuffled across and put her arm around Laena's shoulders. "Sometimes I have to speak sharply to people to get them to pay attention." She was quiet for a moment, brooding inside herself. "I'm fond of you, girl. I just want to be sure you've thought this through."

Laena looked up into the woman's face. "Nan, I'm really happy here, and I'm happy with Mertan. I truly am. Maybe I'm not a wanderer like you, after all. I never chose to be, you know. It was forced on me."

Nan patted her shoulder. "All right." She nodded to herself. "I just want you to be clear about things, that's all. Otherwise, I'd blame myself." She drew back and shuffled toward the mouth of the cave.

"Thank you, Nan," Laena called after her.

The old lady didn't answer as she moved cautiously out of the cave, and out of sight.

That afternoon, Laena sat with Mertan on the outcropping of rock that she had come to think of as their special place, looking out over the hunting lands to the mountains beyond. She tried to drown herself in the warmth of her feelings—and it felt good, leaning against him, sensing his strength as he held her to him.

It was true, what she'd said to Nan. She really was happier than she'd ever been in her life, and she really did like to think that she would never have to leave the Fishers' valley. In that case—why did Nan's words of warning keep coming back to her, distracting her from her happiness?

Well, most people probably felt nervous about pledging themselves. That was natural enough. "Do you think about the way things will be, after—after the hunt?" she asked Mertan.

He nodded. "Of course. I think of you sharing my home. And I think of holding you beside me each night." He smiled down at her.

Looking into his eyes, she could forget everything else. She imagined sitting like this forever, staring into Mertan's face. If that were possible, she knew she would never have any doubts at all.

Deliberately, she made herself look away. "You will want children," she said.

He shrugged. "Of course."

Well, there was nothing wrong with that. Every woman bore children sooner or later, unless she was an ugly misfit like Worin. Even Nan had had a child.

"Can I come with you sometimes, when you go out of the village?" Laena asked. "I know I won't want to stay at home all the time."

"Of course." He patted her cheek. "We can take walks together. We can come back here, if you want, and sit together like this."

That sounded reassuring; and yet, somehow, it wasn't what she'd meant. She found herself remembering the long trek with Nan through the lands of the Wolf Tribe; and her experiences before that. She had been terrified a lot of the time, and filled with grief over her misfortunes. Still, there had been something to be proud of in taking her destiny in her own hands and daring to strike out alone. "My life used to have so much adventure in it," she said, mostly to herself.

"You needn't worry about that anymore," he told her. "You're safe here, Laena. Orwael's spirit protects us. The river feeds us. You can feel safe in our village forever."

He kissed her, and a great yearning seized Laena. She pressed herself hard against him. Very soon, she realized, all the mysteries of her body, and his, would be revealed to her. She would couple with him. The thought made her feel dizzy, for at that moment she wanted him more than anything she could possibly imagine. At that moment, compared to the feelings that flooded through her, Nan's words, and the vision that had once seemed so important, meant nothing at all.

Chapter 26

Laena picked up her pack and looked at it for a moment, thinking of the many times and places she had worn it in the past. Its straps were shiny where they had rubbed across her shoulders, and its shape had long since conformed to her body, so it almost seemed like an extension of herself.

She slipped it on. It was heavy with spare clothing that she was bringing in case her garments became wet—trousers, a jacket, and a hood lined with wolverine, which was the best protection if the weather suddenly turned cold. She also carried pemmican and dried fish; a set of firesticks; some flint knives; sinews and bone needles; and a sack of medicinal herbs, in case her healing skills might be needed.

"The hunt only lasts three days, you know," said Moru. She was sitting at the back of the cave, watching as Laena prepared to leave.

"I know," said Laena. Mertan had described the rituals to her in detail. Today—the first day—the hunters would bring in as much meat as they could, to be stored during the winter months. Tomorrow, the young men would make ceremonial offerings to the young women who had come of age, and the women would choose their mates. And then, on the third day, there would be the ceremony of joining, with feasting and celebration.

Moru would see none of it, for she was still too young. This was the way the Fishers did things, but she resented it nonetheless. "You don't need to take so much stuff with you," she said in a scornful tone.

"No harm in being prepared." Laena held out her arms. "Come, now, you're my sister. Wish me good fortune. This is a special day. The next time you see me, I will be paired with Mertan. My whole life will have changed."

Reluctantly, Moru moved forward and let herself be

hugged. She was silent for a long moment, with her face pressed against Laena's chest. "I want to ask you something," she said finally.

"Ask me then." Laena tried not to sound impatient. She felt anxious, eager to be outside.

"Will there be room in your home?" Moru said. "I mean, when you and Mertan are living together. Will there be room, for—" She trailed off as if she couldn't bring herself to finish the sentence.

"For *you*?" Laena asked.

Reluctantly, Moru nodded.

Suddenly Laena realized how she had misunderstood the little girl's jealousy. Moru wasn't jealous of Laena having Mertan. She was jealous of Mertan having Laena. For the first time in her life, she was being separated from her older sister.

"There will always be room for you to come and visit," Laena said. "And Nan will take care of you the other times. You know that. I already told you that."

Moru still didn't look happy. She glanced around at the cave. "It'll be so lonely here, by myself."

"Well, you won't be up here unless you want to. You'll live with Nan, and I'll be close by. You'll see me whenever you want."

Moru pulled back. She didn't speak.

"I love you, Moru." Laena reached for her and hugged her again. "I always will. Remember that."

Moru turned away, sat down, and wrapped her arms around her knees.

Outside the cave, there was a growing murmur of voices as people gathered, getting ready to leave. "I have to go," said Laena. "But I'll see you soon. Good-bye, little one."

"Bye," said Moru.

Laena went to the mouth of the cave and saw that the day had begun. The sky was still dark purple, with the highest peaks around the valley catching the first orange light from the rising sun. She had to get outside. She glanced back one last time at Moru, then lowered herself out of the cave, down to the ground.

At the far end of the village, the hunters had already gathered in a band led by Faltor. As Laena watched, they set off upriver, walking quickly, shouting to one another, their voices sounding brash and loud, full of anticipation.

She went over to the group of women that had gathered by the river. Turi was there, and Worin, and others their age. Their mothers were with them, too, for there would be much work for women to do up on the hunting lands, gutting the game and bagging the meat so that it could be hauled back to the village.

Laena stood at the edge of the group, trying not to notice the hostile glances that she was receiving. She told herself that she wouldn't need to put up with this for much longer. She would soon have Mertan, and everything would be different. It had to be; she couldn't stand being treated like this for much longer.

Then she saw a familiar figure coming along the river path. "Nan!" she cried. She went running over to her. "Have you come to see me off?"

Nan eyed her sternly. "I've decided to come with you on the hunt, girl."

Laena paused in surprise. "But—you said you were getting too old for this kind of thing, and—"

"Never mind what I said." She eyed Laena sternly. Then she smiled, and the sternness went away. "You're the closest thing to a daughter, girl. And I'm the closest you've got to a mother. If you've really made up your mind to take Mertan as your husband, it's my duty to be with you and see you through it all."

Laena felt overwhelmed with sudden emotion. She quickly hugged Nan. "Thank you," she said, hiding her face so that the other women wouldn't see the tears in her eyes.

As the day brightened, the women moved along the riverbank, singing a ritual song as they followed the path that the hunters had taken a little while before. Their voices echoed between the narrow walls of the valley, drowning out the sounds of rushing water.

They climbed the steps in the rock that Laena had climbed so many times with Mertan, and soon they reached the high, open lands. Here, they set off toward the north and walked for another hour till they reached a place where a stream trickled down a shallow cleft and the grass was thick and soft underfoot. Trees grew nearby, serving as a windbreak and a source of firewood. It was an ideal spot to make camp.

The women set down their packs, and the youngest ones were sent to find kindling. Nan sat near Laena and told her it would be a good idea to build a hearth. For a moment Laena resented being told what to do. But then she realized that it would occupy her mind. She set to work, and soon had an area of bare earth with small rocks around it. Moments later she had a fire flickering, warming her against the chill of the morning.

Around her, other fires were coming to life. Laena saw that they had been placed in a circle, marking the edges of the camp. In the center, women now began work on large tree branches taken from the forest, stripping off small shoots and lashing the branches together to form meat-drying racks.

Laena went over and helped as much as she could, but it was clear that she wasn't really welcome. The half-dozen girls who were around her age simply refused to speak to her, and their mothers seemed embarrassed by having her among them. Weeps, in particular, didn't know how to deal with Laena, and couldn't even look her in the eye.

So Laena went back to Nan, feeling dejected again and grateful for the old woman's company.

"Tomorrow you will become one of them," Nan told her. "Tomorrow, they will accept you."

"You really think so?" Laena searched Nan's face for reassurance.

The old woman looked away. "I believe it will be so."

"You know, I used to be able to see the future," Laena said in a small voice. She stared at the snow-capped mountains in the far distance. "I used to have visions that warned me of bad things to come." She shook her head. "I haven't had a single dream since I started living here. None that I can remember, anyway."

"Maybe that means there are no more bad things in store for you." Nan seemed uncomfortable, as if Laena were asking for something that Nan didn't really have to give.

Laena turned back to the old lady. "But you told me once you'd had visions yourself in the past. Didn't you, Nan? Didn't you tell me that?"

Nan laughed, but there was no humor in the sound. She

looked even more uncomfortable than before. "I said something about it. Some dreams I had, long ago." She stood
up suddenly. "Look, here come the first of the hunters."

All the women had stopped work as three men came striding across the grassy land. The first of the hunters Laena
saw was Mertan. He was carrying a caribou around his
shoulders, its head lolling across his chest. Behind him came
two men dragging a musk ox between them.

The men came to the center of the camp and threw down
their game. They did a short ritual dance, imitating the animals they had slain to show respect for their spirits. Then
they stood tall and raised their clenched fists and shouted
their pride.

The women tied grass ropes around the rear legs of the
animals, hoisted them, and hung them from wooden tripods
so they could be drained and gutted. The women started
singing a new song, praising fate for bringing food for the
winter, and their chanting voices rose and fell on the cool,
clear air.

Mertan came over to Laena and Nan. He embraced Laena
quickly, then nodded respectfully to Nan. "A perfect start
to the hunt," he said. "Perfect!" His eyes were bright and
his face was flushed. His furs were hanging loosely around
his chest, and she saw that his skin was filmed with sweat.

"Congratulations on your kill," Nan said. "You found it
quickly."

He shrugged. "I am the best hunter." He said it as a fact
which everyone knew was true.

"Are there many caribou out there?" Laena asked. It
wasn't what she really wanted to talk about. All she wanted,
really, was to hold Mertan and feel his warmth driving away
her loneliness.

"The animals are nervous at this time of year," Mertan
said. He looked at her while he spoke, but she had the odd
sense that he was looking beyond her, somehow. Inside his
mind, he was still reliving the hunt. "They feel they should
follow the sun and migrate to the south, but our valley blocks
their way, and so do the mountains beyond. It takes skill to
sneak up on them when they're so wild." He stood up suddenly. There was a distracted look in his eyes. "I must hunt
more." His hand tightened on his spear. "There's much to
be done."

He nodded to her, then strode quickly away.

Nan looked at Laena and saw her expression. "He's a man," Nan said quietly. "He's doing what men do. He's the best hunter in the tribe, and he's proud of it. This isn't a time when he can sit and talk with you. It would be shameful to do that and let other men take the game and the pride that are rightfully his."

Laena nodded. She rubbed her eyes. "You're right," she said. "I understand that."

And yet, in a way, she didn't understand it at all.

The days were ending earlier now that summer was turning into autumn. After a while, true darkness fell over the land. Dozens of animals had been brought in by the hunters, and the women had gutted them, cleaned them, and stretched them over fires in the center of the camp. The men had gone back to their own camp, just the other side of the hill, but for the women the work was still not done. Before they could rest they had to build up the fires around the edges of their camp to scare off predators that might be lured by the smell of the fresh-killed meat.

Finally, it was time to eat, to rest, to sing songs and tell stories. The women invited Laena to sit with them, but she could tell they asked because they felt obliged to, not because they really wanted her company. And if that was the way it was, she wasn't willing to join them.

Feeling dispirited, she went off by herself. She lay down on the ground beside one of the fires at the edge of the camp, and she stared up at the stars.

Faintly, she heard the voices of the men singing a hunting song, not so far away. For some of them, this was their last night before being joined. There would be a lot of shouting and laughter and celebration.

It should have been a special time for Laena, too; and yet she didn't feel the joy that she had expected. She felt scared and lonely. "Will everything be all right?" she whispered, staring at the stars and listening to the women nearby and the men further away. "Tell me, what should I do?"

She remembered times in the past when she had asked her parents for guidance. In the end, they had always advised her to be strong; to be patient; to follow the pattern of things.

But what did that mean to her now?

* * *

The next morning, the older women continued the hard work of dressing the meat while the younger women prepared themselves for the choosing ceremony. They went searching for wild flowers, then combed their hair and wove the flowers into it. Some of them changed into fresh clothes that they had brought with them. Then they went to the stream and found red clay that they mixed with water and rubbed into their cheeks.

Laena tried to do what they were doing. She checked her reflection in a bowl of water, and she combed her hair, and she found a few flowers. But somehow she felt as if she were playing a part, not really being herself at all. The longer she had to wait for the ceremony, the worse she felt. Why couldn't she simply be joined with Mertan? Why were all these rituals necessary? If he truly cared for her, what did it matter whether she wore flowers, or whether her cheeks were pink?

Nan tried to talk to her, but Laena had trouble concentrating on the conversation. In the end, she excused herself and went off on her own again. She sat with her hands clasped tight around her knees, and she bowed her head and tried to think of nothing at all, as the morning dragged by.

Finally, Nan came and laid her hand on Laena's shoulder. "It's time," she said.

Laena stood up. She realized that all her muscles were knotted with tension, and yet she felt detached, removed from everything around her.

"Come," said Nan. "Since Faltor has no wife, and since I'm the oldest woman here, I've been chosen to lead the young women to the men's camp."

Laena nodded. She followed Nan, still saying nothing.

The other girls were waiting. All their excited talking and giggling and laughter was over now. They were so full of anticipation, they couldn't speak.

Worin was there, with her hair pulled forward to cover the birthmark on her cheek—not that it made much difference, Laena thought to herself. Turi was there, standing tall and elegant, with her jaw raised in proud defiance. There were three others whom Laena knew as Perri, Golin, and Lenna. None of them looked at Laena as she joined them.

Nan walked out across the open land, and the girls followed. The other women of the tribe had finished their work for the day, and they came along behind, at a respectful distance. The choosing ceremony was something that everyone wanted to see.

The sun burned brightly, and the day seemed fresh with promise, but still none of it seemed to touch Laena. She told herself she would feel fine, just as soon as the ceremony was over. It was the waiting that was making her so anxious and so tense.

The men's camp came into view. Four tall poles had been set into the soil, and animal skins hung from them, flapping in the wind. As Laena walked closer she saw Faltor standing tall in the center of the camp, with the older men behind him and the young hunters on either side of him—five of them altogether. Five young hunters, Laena thought to herself. Six young women, including her. She felt her stomach clench, knowing that before the end of the afternoon she would be paired, and one of the girls walking with her would be rejected and forced to wait for better fortune next year.

Nan led the girls into the men's camp, and she walked forward till she was just a couple of paces from Faltor. She stopped and bowed her head to him, and he bowed to her. "I bring you the young women of the Fisher tribe," she said.

Faltor smiled. Once again Laena sensed the serenity and the simple wisdom in him, though it did nothing to make her feel calmer now. "The young men have hunted well this year," he said. He spoke softly, so that his voice was almost lost in the wind. "They've set out their trophies, and they're ready for the women to choose among them." He turned and gestured, and Laena saw that a slain animal lay at the feet of each hunter. Behind them, the older men of the tribe moved closer, gathering around; and the older women went and joined them.

Nan turned to the six girls. "It is time for you to choose," she said. "Be cautious. Be wise. Your choice will last for a lifetime."

Laena had expected something more, somehow—a bigger ceremony, a song—something. But clearly, this was the moment. Even though she had imagined it countless times, she felt strangely unprepared.

She glanced quickly to either side, and she realized that for the first time, the other girls were allowing themselves to look at her. There was an air of tense expectation among them that became almost unbearable as they stood close together, with no one wanting to make the first move.

All right, Laena thought to herself, there was no point in pretending. They knew that she and Mertan had agreed to pair with each other.

She walked forward, feeling light-headed, as if she were drifting across the ground without quite touching it.

Mertan had warned her that it was considered good manners to admire each hunter's trophy. She paused in front of a musk ox. It was a fine beast, laid out on the ground as if it were still running, with its head tilted up and its eyes wide. A small gash in its chest showed that just one spear-thrust had brought it down.

Laena looked at the hunter standing beside this trophy. He was a fellow named Hurow, tall and broad-shouldered, almost as strong as Mertan. She forced a smile and moved on.

Behind her, she heard footsteps in the grass and knew that the other girls were moving forward to pay their respects.

The next man was Joq. Laena looked at the goat laid out at his feet—a small one, with a wound in its throat and another in its flank. It wasn't much, but still, Joq had done his duty as a man, and she felt oddly proud of him. She looked up at his face and smiled shyly. "Congratulations," she whispered.

He shrugged as if to tell her that it didn't matter to him, and as far as he was concerned, this whole affair was a waste of his time.

Laena moved on. And the next man in line was Mertan.

His prize was the largest, as she'd known it would be. It was a mountain lion that must have taken three men to drag here. Mertan stood behind it with his legs spread wide, his spear in one hand, his other hand on his hip. His chest was bare, regardless of the cold air, and she saw the muscles bunched under his smooth brown skin.

She looked up at his face and found him watching her, so proud, so brave, and so strong. She felt herself sway and she almost panicked at the thought that she might faint in front of him.

Laena was still vaguely aware of all the other people—the men and women watching, the other girls behind her, Faltor waiting at one side, Nan standing nearby. But none of them seemed real. She was only aware of herself and of Mertan standing opposite her. The crowd was totally silent, and the moment seemed suspended outside of time itself.

Laena knew what she had to say, because Mertan had told her. She should say to him: "Your trophy is a fine one, hunter. I would be honored to have you hunt for me."

Her mouth was dry, but somehow she managed to swallow, and she parted her lips. She saw Mertan smile in expectation.

She drew a breath. But she could not speak.

She stood there, swaying. She wanted him; there was no possible doubt of that. She wanted him more than she had ever wanted anybody.

But she could not speak.

She felt her cheeks burning. Why did it have to be so difficult? And then, suddenly, she knew that it wasn't just difficult, it was impossible. She felt a flash of understanding, and she knew what she had always known, though she had not been able to admit it before. "I'm sorry," she whispered to him. And she turned away.

There was a startled murmuring in the crowd. It grew so loud that Faltor clapped his hands and shouted for silence. He strode over to Laena and took hold of her arm. "Is something wrong?" he asked quietly.

She looked at his face. He seemed concerned, not angry with her, as she'd feared.

She shrugged helplessly. "I think I have changed my mind," she whispered.

He drew back, looking shocked. But within moments, he regained his composure. He nodded to her. "Make your choice freely," he said, loud enough for everyone to hear. "All of you, choose freely, choose carefully. Take the time you need."

His hand tightened briefly on Laena's arm, and then he left her.

"Laena!" Mertan called. He took a step toward her. "Laena, why—"

"Mertan, that is not the way!" Faltor's voice was suddenly loud, and Laena realized it was the only time she had ever heard him shout. "Stand by your prize," Faltor told him. "You know our customs, Son. Wait to be chosen."

Mertan stared at his father. He looked stricken. Slowly, reluctantly, he stepped back to his place.

Laena felt terrible for him. She had embarrassed him in front of his tribe. But at the same time, she felt overwhelmed with relief. She had done the unthinkable; and now she was free.

The other young women were moving forward, looking startled by what had happened, but eager to take advantage of it. Turi was heading straight for Mertan.

Laena retraced her steps. She stumbled once and almost fell. And then she was in front of Joq. She paused there, and he looked at her with an expression of wonder. She had done what he had only talked of doing. She had said no.

She looked at him, and she realized what had to happen next. It had to happen quickly, before she lost the courage that she needed. "Joq," she said, "your trophy is fine." And as she spoke the words she had to struggle not to smile, because she knew, and he knew, that his trophy was the smallest of all.

But she knew that it didn't matter. Hunting and killing were not the real tests of a man; they were not even the truest test of courage, necessarily.

Laena took a deep breath. "I would be honored to have you hunt for me," she said, and her voice was loud and true, so that no one could doubt that she spoke freely and from her heart.

Joq stared at her for a long moment. Bit by bit, he realized what she had said; and as the words made sense to him, he slowly grinned. His face was a picture of innocent, simple delight, like a small boy who had just been given a present that he never expected to receive. "Yes, Laena," he said. "Yes, I will hunt for you."

Laena felt the last of the tension drain out of her. She didn't know exactly what had happened, or why, or whether she had done the right thing. But she had done what she had to do, and it was over. The choice had been made.

She felt her knees give way, and Joq dropped his spear and grabbed her under her arms to stop her from falling.

He hugged her to him, and she realized that the only other time she had ever touched him had been when she clasped his hand and asked to be his friend. He felt much smaller than Mertan, but stronger than she had expected.

She looked at his face. "Are you sure?" she whispered.

"Of course I'm sure!"

"But you said—you said if any woman asked you—"

"Yes, yes. But I never dreamed that *you* might be the woman."

She smiled. She thought of the strange talks they had enjoyed together, and all the times they would have now to talk more. Joq, she knew, would treat her as an equal. He would value her not just for the present time, but in the years to come, because she was a prize that he had never expected to receive.

She turned her head and saw the other girls milling around among the remaining men. Her change of mind had upset everyone's plans. But at the same time, she could see that it made things easier for them. They wouldn't hate her anymore. They might even thank her.

Mertan was looking furious at the way she had spurned him. But Laena hoped that he might forgive her, as time passed. Turi was a beautiful woman, after all. She would be faithful and dutiful to him, in a way that Laena might have found difficult as the years wore on. In time, perhaps, he would realize that it was better for Laena to show her ambivalence now than later; and he would forgive her.

But there was one other person who looked as if she could never forgive Laena anything. Worin was standing a couple of paces away with a wild look in her eyes. Her hair had blown away from her face in the wind, and her purple birthmark looked so dark, it was almost black. Worin hunched her shoulders and lowered her head, and her lips pulled back from her crooked teeth till she resembled a snarling dog. She clenched her fists and spat on the ground.

Then, while Laena clung to Joq, Worin turned her back and strode away across the hillside.

Chapter 27

After the time of choosing, it was the time of joining. As the sun touched the distant mountains and the sky turned purple and gold, the people of the Fisher Tribe gathered around a big bonfire at the center of the men's camp. They ate fresh-killed meat and sang songs praising the hunters, offering thanks for the bountiful game, and wishing good fortune to those who had paired with one another.

Each young hunter sat with his young bride, and one by one, people came to pay their respects. Laena sat with Joq, feeling dazed. It seemed strange and frightening to think that they were to be joined as one. All she had done was speak a few simple words; and now her whole life was to be different, as a result.

Worse still, when she looked at Mertan, she still found herself remembering how he had felt when he held her. She found herself wanting him even now. She knew that the deepest part of her had made her turn away from him in the choosing ceremony, but still she felt a pang of great sadness and longing when she thought that she would never again have the thrill of being touched by him.

Well, it was too late now. Turi was sitting with Mertan, pressing close against him and laughing while she fed him scraps of meat from the lion that he had presented as his trophy. Mertan himself looked less sure of himself and less contented than Turi did, but he touched her with affection, and he smiled at her as well as he could. He tried not to look in Laena's direction, where she sat farther away from the fire, in the shadows; but a couple of times she found him glancing at her with a puzzled, lost expression.

Laena dragged her attention back to Joq, sitting beside her. He was smiling, holding her hand in his. She had made him far happier than she would have thought possible. His talk of wanting to spend his life alone had been just talk; there was no doubt of that now. But would she still please him as much a week or a year from now? And could he please her, in the days and years to come? Should Laena have done as Nan advised, and simply waited for a year?

Joq's parents came over to pay their respects. "This is a fine thing, a great thing," Orleh said. His voice was deep and thick with emotion. He clasped his hands in front of him and bowed his head. "Joq, I am proud. You have made me very proud."

Weeps pushed in front of him. "Thank you," she said to Laena. She paused, groping for more words. Then she spread her hands helplessly. "Thank you," she said again, sniffing back tears.

"It feels strange," Joq murmured to Laena after his parents had moved away. "I feel as if they've won a battle with me, and I've lost."

"That's foolish," said Laena. "You've lost nothing. You have much more now than you had before."

He slowly shook his head. "I feel as if they own me now. I finally did what they wanted. That means my life isn't really mine anymore."

She felt irritated with him. Here she had made the most difficult decision of her life, and he was worrying about getting along with his family. "You don't have to fight them all the time just to be independent," she told him. "Look, if you find it hard to keep them out of your life, I will help you to cope with them."

He looked down with embarrassment. At that moment he seemed quite childlike. "Thank you, Laena," he said. "You understand me very well."

It was true, she realized; she did understand him better than anyone else ever had. Maybe that was why she had been able to pledge herself. Even though he was so different from other men, she knew what he needed, and it was something that no other woman could give him. That knowledge made her feel secure.

But did *he* understand *her*? She wasn't so sure about that.

"So, you finally made up your mind." It was Nan's voice, jolting Laena back to reality. The old lady kneeled in front of Laena and leaned forward, studying Laena's face in the flickering light from the fire. "I hope you're happy now."

Laena felt uncomfortable under Nan's severe scrutiny. "I think I am," she said.

Nan turned to Joq. "Be good to her," she warned him. "You're lucky to have her. She could have chosen Mertan, but she chose you. Always remember that."

Joq's back stiffened, and his mouth tightened. Laena realized that Joq could never stand being lectured, by his father or anyone else. If someone told him what to do, he would always want to do the opposite.

Laena leaned forward, placing herself between Nan and Joq. "Thank you, Nan, for your good wishes," she said.

Nan turned back to her, and she patted Laena's cheek. "I think you made the right choice," she said. "It's best for you, and probably best for everyone else, besides."

"For everyone except for Worin," Laena said.

"Oh, I'll deal with her. Don't worry." Nan paused. She frowned as if there were something more that she had to say, but it wasn't so easy for her to say it. She edged a little closer to Laena. "You know, after I talked to you at your cave, I started thinking about things myself. I started thinking I might stay here. For good, I mean." Her voice was gruff, hard to hear above the crackling of the big bonfire and the talk and laughter of the people all around.

"What?" Laena leaned forward.

Nan sighed. "The trek that brought me here with you and Moru, it was harder than I expected." She shifted her position and winced as she flexed her limbs. "I'm getting a bit too old to go roaming without a home."

Laena remembered all the times she had had trouble maintaining the pace that Nan had set. "You always seemed so strong," she said.

"Maybe I seemed that way." She shook her head. "But I'm not as strong as I was. When I gave you that little lecture at your cave a few days ago, I think it was because I wasn't sure what I should do myself." She stared away, into the darkness. "Faltor is a kind man. A good chieftain. And the living here is easier than I've known it anywhere else."

"Would you and Faltor—" Laena hesitated. The idea seemed strange, but she had learned in the past Nan was capable of strange things. "Could you and Faltor ever be joined as husband and wife?"

Nan laughed. "I'll never join with another man. Never!

That I know.'' She paused, and a sly smile showed itself just at the corners of her mouth. ''I visit him in his hut, though, from time to time. When the mood takes me.''

Laena would have been shocked if she hadn't already gotten used to Nan's way of following her own code and talking frankly about it. She reached forward, seized Nan, and hugged her tightly. ''So you'll stay here,'' she said. ''That's wonderful! I was always afraid that you'd pick up and move on again, maybe next summer. I was afraid I would have to say good-bye to you then.''

Nan pulled free, looking embarrassed. ''Well, I'm not making any guarantees.'' Slowly, she got back up onto her feet. She brushed at her clothes, and the weakness she had shown was erased as if it had never existed. ''But as I say, I like it here, and they've told me I'm welcome to stay, because they need my healing skills, apart from anything else.'' She straightened her back. ''Now, listen to me. If either of you needs anything, you come and ask me, understand?'' She looked from one of them to the other. ''If you need—advice, or anything like that.'' She gave a curt nod. And then, without any further words, she turned and walked away.

''Why would I want advice from her?'' said Joq.

Laena heard the disrespect in his voice, and she turned on him. ''She's a fine healer, and she saved me when I was wandering homeless in the land of the Wolf Tribe. You could learn from her, Joq, if your pride would let you.''

He looked surprised by her sharp tone. ''Learn what?''

''How to be a healer, perhaps. How to speak half a dozen languages. How to save people's lives.'' She glared at him. ''I doubt that you know that much already.''

He pulled back from her, and Laena saw from his expression that she had wounded him with the sharp edge of her voice. He was really quite vulnerable, she realized. She felt suddenly guilty at having hurt his feelings. At the same time, though, she felt stronger, knowing that she could make him pay attention if she needed to.

''I'm sorry,'' Joq said. ''I just didn't like the way she spoke to me, that's all.''

Laena took his hand. ''Nan can seem a difficult person, but she's important to me. Try to be nice to her, Joq.''

''All right, I'll try,'' he said.

Faltor came to them then. He stood looking down at them for a moment, and Laena felt a wave of anxiety in case he was angry with her for spurning his son. But then he sat on the ground in front of them, and he smiled gently and reached out, taking their hands in his.

"This is a good thing that you have done," he said. His voice was deep and resonant, and full of kindness.

Laena blinked in surprise. "I was afraid that you—"

"Mertan will be happy with Turi. He has always liked her, and she is devoted to him."

"But I shamed him," she blurted out. "I shamed him in front of everyone!"

Faltor slowly shook his head. "No, Laena. You humbled him. That is a very different thing. In fact, it is a good thing. Tonight, he learned that even though he is the chieftain's son, he can't always have whatever he wants. If he learns that lesson well, one day it will make him a better chieftain of the Fisher Tribe." He inclined his head. "I thank you, for what you have done."

Laena marveled at his ability to look at things so quietly, so philosophically, without letting his feelings interfere with his judgment. She wished she could learn to be like that. At the same time she knew, with absolute certainty, it would never be possible.

"The joining ceremonies will begin in a moment," Faltor said. "Yours will be first, because the hunter with the smallest prize is always the first to be joined in our tribe. You will also need to pledge yourself to the Fishers, Laena. But I'm sure you realize that."

She nodded. "Of course."

"Very good." He got to his feet. "Come with me."

She and Joq stood up and followed him toward the fire, then slowly around it. One by one, the Fishers realized what was happening, and they started singing a new song, praising the young hunter and his bride. Laena felt herself blushing, with so many eyes upon her, so many voices raised to honor her. She wished this didn't have to be done so publicly. She had a brief vision of how she would really like it to be. She and Joq would sit in his favorite spot on the rocks overlooking the river; Faltor would come to them, ask them their intentions, and pronounce them joined. That would be so much simpler, and so much easier.

Faltor led them to a spot where some white stones had been placed in a circle. He gestured, and Laena and Joq stepped into the circle. Feeling self-conscious, Laena groped for Joq's hand and gripped it tightly. She wanted to glance at his face to see if he was feeling as nervous as she was. But it didn't seem the right thing to do. She held back her anxiety as well as she could and stared straight ahead at Faltor.

The chief held up both his arms, and the singing stopped. There was a long moment of expectant silence. "A girl has come to us," he called out, speaking louder than she had ever heard before. "Who is she?"

He looked at Laena, and waited.

"She is Laena of No People," Laena said. Her voice sounded strange in the stillness, as if it weren't really her voice at all.

"Very well, Laena of No People, do you pledge yourself to the ways of the Fisher Tribe, from this time on, for the rest of your life?"

"Yes, I do," said Laena.

She remembered when she had been among the Wolf People, and how hard it had been for her to renounce her Panther birthright. By comparison, pledging herself to the Fishers seemed much easier—perhaps because, in her own mind, she had done so already.

Faltor turned slowly, looking at all the people gathered around. "If anyone here objects, he should speak."

There was a long silence, broken only by the crackling and spitting of the fire.

"Very well," said Faltor. "Laena, I pronounce you a member of the Fisher Tribe."

There was a deafening shout of approval. As it died away, Laena heard a faint echo returning from the distant mountainsides, and she remembered when the Wolf People had shouted out their frightening wolf cry. She was glad she wasn't with them now; she was happy to be among these easygoing, friendly people.

"And now," said Faltor, "I ask you, Laena of the Fisher Tribe: have you chosen to be joined with Joq?"

It was all happening faster than she had expected. She should have known that the Fishers wouldn't stage an elaborate ceremony. She took a deep breath, and she wished she could be certain that her voice would not betray the nervousness that she felt. "I have chosen to be joined with Joq," she said. And now that the moment had actually arrived, she found her voice ringing out clear and confident, as if she had never known any doubt at all.

Faltor nodded slowly. He turned to Joq. "I ask you, Joq of the Fisher Tribe: do you accept Laena as your wife?"

There was a pause. For a moment, Joq seemed incapable of speaking. "I—" he began. His hand tightened its grip on Laena's. "I—yes, I accept Laena as my wife."

Faltor nodded again, smiling now. "Then Laena and Joq are joined as one, so long as each may live. Laena and Joq will live as one. They will renounce all others. All of us have seen this, and we will remember that it is so." He looked at them with compassion. "May you be happy, and may you have many strong children, and may everyone here wish you well in your joining."

There was another shout, even louder than before. People clapped and cheered, and some of the women threw flowers. Joq hugged Laena to him, and she looked around at all the people of the tribe, and she found herself crying a little, though she didn't know why. She was happy, yes; but more than anything, she was relieved that it was over.

Everyone was smiling at her, and the other girls came forward to hug her and congratulate her. Within just a few moments, she had made them all like her, she realized. No one resented her anymore.

She found herself wondering how they could act so differently toward her from one moment to the next. She was still the same person, wasn't she? Did they like her now, just because she had done something that was convenient? If that was so, it wasn't really *her* that they liked at all. They were just pleased that she wasn't making trouble anymore.

She felt a sudden, overwhelming need to run away from the smiles and congratulations. More than that, she wanted to leave so that she wouldn't have to stand and watch while Mertan was joined with Turi.

She took Joq's hand and dragged him back from the crowd and the firelight, into the night. "Come, Joq! Come with me!"

He followed her, though he seemed reluctant. "Where are you going?"

She ran across the grassy land, pulling him after her, on and on, till the bonfire was just a point of yellow light in the distance, and the landscape seemed vast around it. "Don't you have a retreat that we can go to?" she said, as she held his hand tightly in hers.

Mertan had told her once that it was customary for each young hunter to prepare a tent for himself and his bride where they would spend the night alone together after the joining ceremony.

"I don't—" Joq hesitated. "I mean, I didn't—"

"You didn't think you would be joined with anyone." She turned toward him. His face was faintly outlined by moonlight. She put her arms around him and pressed close, enjoying the warmth of his body in the cold night air.

"I *knew* I wasn't going to be joined with anyone," he said.

She stared at his features. "So why did you say yes to me, Joq?"

He was silent for a long time, looking away from her, trying to understand his own thoughts. "Because you're the only person who's ever really liked me, Laena." His voice sounded very small, and she saw that the defiance he had shown while she was getting to know him had just been a way to protect himself from the world. "You care for me." He paused. "Don't you?"

"Of course." She hugged him tighter.

"You aren't still thinking of Mertan? I thought—everyone thought—I mean, it's like Nan said, you could have been joined with the chief's son."

"But he wouldn't have treated me the way you do, Joq. He wouldn't have valued me as I really am. I was like a trophy to him. I was like the most special caribou that he could ever find and capture. It's different, with you. I feel like a real person."

He was silent for a moment. "I think I see." Then he gestured helplessly. "But what am I to you? I'm just an outcast who hates his family and sits on a rock and plays a flute all day."

She didn't want to hear this. "You can hunt when you

need to,'' she said quickly. ''And you don't have to be an outcast anymore. You can be a fine husband to me, Joq.''

''You think so?'' He sounded unsure.

''I'm certain.'' She willed herself to sound confident. The last thing she wanted now was to feel new doubts and fears.

She reached up and took his face between her hands. ''Tell me, Joq. Have you ever lain with a woman?''

He pulled back a little. The question had caught him by surprise. ''Of course not,'' he said, staring at her.

''I have never lain with a man,'' she said. ''So we will have to teach each other as we go along.'' She started untying the thongs of his jacket, and her fingers fumbled in the night. ''Help me, Joq.''

''You mean—now? Out here?''

''Faltor joined us with each other. You are mine, and I'm yours. Haven't you wondered what it feels like, to lie with a woman?''

He stared down at her fingers, as she worked to undo his clothes. He stood passively, with a strange look on his face. ''I've often wondered,'' he said softly. ''But, I never imagined—''

''Where else should we go?''

He hesitated. ''Back at the men's camp, I have a tent—''

''The ceremonies are still going on back there. So we will have to use this grassy hillside.'' She finally opened his jacket and slid her hands inside. His skin felt warm under her cold fingers.

Slowly, they sank down on the grass. It was damp with the first dew of the night, and the dew was freezing, turning to frost. She clung to him, pressing her body close.

He touched her face, like a blind man learning her features. His touch was very gentle.

She pressed her mouth to his, lightly at first. For just a moment she thought of Mertan and the overpowering yearning she had felt. But that was in the past now, and she must drive it out of her mind. She focused again on Joq—kind, gentle Joq—and found herself teaching him how to kiss her. Clearly, she was the first woman he had ever held like this. That made her feel good in a way that she never had with Mertan. Mertan had held other women, there was no doubt of that. Joq was different. He was hers alone.

His body was very tense as he lay beside her. His hands

trembled as he touched her. His breathing started coming in fast, shallow gasps.

"Shhh," she whispered to him. "We have all the time we need, Joq."

"But I want you," he said. His hands pulled her furs aside and he was suddenly grasping her naked body. She felt his palm on her breast, and it was her turn to gasp, not just with surprise, but with desire.

Joq rolled onto her and kissed her harder. She reached down, tentatively at first, then boldly. Her fingers slid across Joq's tight, hard stomach, between his legs. She touched him there and made a little sound of surprise. He was so large, so hard, and she trembled at the thought of him forcing inside her. How would it happen? Surely, the pain would be terrible.

He started groping down between her thighs. She guided his hand, and his finger probed into her. She cried out. "Be gentle!" she gasped.

"You're bleeding?" He pulled back.

"No. No, it's not blood, it's just—wetness. It happens. It happens when I get excited."

He touched her again, more tentatively this time. "What is this wetness for?" His voice was full of wonder.

Laena remembered some of the lessons that Nan had taught her. "It helps you slide into me," she whispered to him. Warm waves of desire were sweeping over her now, sparked by his touch. She clung to him and pressed her breasts against his naked chest. "Don't you want me?"

"Yes. Yes, very much." He touched her again, then rolled onto her. Instinctively, she parted her thighs. He fumbled, trying to guide himself in. She reached down to help, eager to know how it would feel, even while she feared it.

There was a sudden stab of pain, almost as bad as she had imagined. She cried out and clutched at him, digging her nails into his shoulders. "Gentle!" she gasped.

He didn't hear her. Either that, or he had grown too excited to stop himself. He thrust deeper, and she screamed. Her mind was a sudden turmoil—desire, fear, longing, dread. She closed her eyes and saw Mertan smiling down at her, so strong, so sure of himself, holding her with casual ease in his powerful arms.

"No!" she cried. It was Joq she had chosen, Joq who cared for her, Joq who would nurture her.

She opened her eyes and saw his face in the moonlight, inches from hers, staring at her, looking surprised by the intense emotion. "Laena," he whispered. He made a throttled, whimpering sound. Then he grasped her head between his hands and pressed his mouth to hers, and his body shook convulsively.

He slumped against her, and she realized it was over almost as quickly as it had begun. His breathing gradually quietened. She ran her fingers through his hair, then across his back. For a moment he had seemed quite fierce, pushing into her, breaking her open. And now he seemed harmless, almost like a child.

She wondered if there would ever be an end to all the surprises, all the confusion that life seemed to have in store for her. Maybe, as time passed, things would begin to seem more comprehensible, more predictable. She and Joq would couple again, and she could begin to understand her jumbled emotions, and enjoy the act that seemed so strange and frightening.

She hugged Joq to her, holding him now as if she feared that he might suddenly be plucked away from her. "Be good to me, Joq," she whispered, so quietly that he didn't even hear her. "Prove to me that I did the right thing when I chose you."

He buried his head in the curve of her neck, and kissed her there. "You're mine now, Laena," he said. He sounded as if he were still trying to convince himself.

Laena closed her eyes. This time, she didn't see Mertan's face. This time, she was just aware of Joq beside her.

"Yes," she said. "I'm yours now, Joq. All yours."

PART TWO

Chapter 28

She lay on a bed of woven reeds in the healer's hut, trying not to think about the pain.

She stared up at the amulets hanging above her. Joq had made them, and he had placed them there to guard her and comfort her. There was a plump little musk oxen fashioned from hardwood, ornamented with tufts of hair from the beast itself. There was a mammoth shaped from pieces of tusk taken from the part close to the bone—the strongest part, richest in magical power. And there was a little cat, its clay body blackened with charcoal. Joq had never seen the plains-dwelling panther in real life, so he had made his model with only Laena's description to guide him.

Laena stared up at the amulets and tried to believe in their power, but it seemed small compared with the power of the pain that seized her now. She closed her eyes and clenched her fists, gasping as all the muscles in her body knotted tight, tighter, claiming her with a will that seemed far greater than her own. She had known it would hurt, but she had never imagined it would feel like this.

She heard a rustle of clothing, and a cold, damp scrap of animal hide was pressed against her forehead. Bit by bit, the cramps subsided.

Laena opened her eyes and found Nan bending over her, her face half lost in shadow in the dimly lit hut. "Breathe slowly," she said. "Through your mouth. Slowly."

Laena willed herself to relax, and she took a deep breath. She smelled the herbs and potions that filled the leather pouches hanging on the rear wall, and she tasted acrid smoke from the fire burning in the center of the healer's hut. It was good to be here, surrounded by so many familiar objects and smells. "Thank you, Nan," she whispered.

The old woman patted Laena's cheek. "You're doing well. Everything will be all right."

Laena didn't try to answer. Talking was an effort, and she couldn't spare the strength.

Outside, Joq was chanting. The song had no words; it was to comfort her and pledge his power to her. Other voices joined him. Orleh was there, and Faltor, and a couple more that Laena could not recognize. She was glad of the support, but they couldn't take away her pain.

Nor could they take away the fear that she felt. The fear of what was about to be.

Nan's hands probed gently between Laena's thighs. She grunted with satisfaction. "The passageway is starting to open. The baby's head is there."

"At last!" Laena cried.

"Yes, girl. Be calm."

How could she be calm? She had waited so long. It had been three years since she had pledged herself to Joq. At that time, she had been afraid of conceiving a child. It had seemed scary enough just to join herself with a man and make her home here in a tribe that was not really her own.

But as time passed, she had found herself feeling more and more that she truly belonged among the Fishers, and she had allowed Joq to place his seed in her when they coupled together. She'd assumed that she would get pregnant straight away. And yet, nothing happened. Was there something wrong with her? She had felt as if she were failing Joq somehow, and he, in turn, began to feel as if he were not truly a man.

People in the tribe started gossiping. Worin spread a rumor that Laena was barren.

But then she finally missed a period; and then her belly started to swell; and then there was no longer any doubt about it. Suddenly, Laena wanted the baby—wanted it more than she would have imagined possible.

She heard liquid being poured into a cup, and she turned her head. "Nan, what is that?"

"Just a little something to dull the pain."

"Dreamwater?"

Nan didn't answer.

"I don't want it. You know I don't like it. I don't—" She broke off with a cry as another contraction seized her. She closed her eyes, trying to meet the pain and conquer it through her will alone. At the same time, she felt something touch her lower lip, and wetness flooded her mouth.

She tried to spit out the liquid, but the pain gripped her so hard, she couldn't keep control of her thoughts and actions. She coughed and gasped as warm, bitter juices trickled down her throat.

"I told you no!" she shouted as the contractions ebbed again. She felt tears in her eyes.

Nan pressed the wet hide against Laena's forehead again. "Shh, girl. The dreamwater does no harm."

Dreamwater was compounded from rare herbs and berries. It was one of Nan's most closely guarded secrets: a potion that would take a person away from her pain, into a state of euphoria.

Laena had drunk it only once before, after she had crushed a finger between two rocks. For her, the dreamwater had been more frightening than the pain. It had lifted her out of the world she understood, into another place that seemed almost, but not quite, real.

The cramps seized Laena again, and she screamed. Outside, the men heard her, and they chanted louder. Laena looked up, and the panther amulet looked down at her with its sightless oval eyes.

"I'm scared," she gasped.

"No, no. Everything will be all right."

Laena groaned. The edges of her vision seemed to lose focus. Was the dreamwater taking hold of her? She tried not to let it. Her pulse was fast and light, tapping inside her ears.

She turned her head—and saw, instead of Nan, a life-size panther standing beside the cot where she lay. It moved closer, and she felt its breath on her face.

Laena cried out.

"Easy, child." The voice came from somewhere else. "Not long now."

The words drifted like smoke. The world wavered in Laena's vision. She tried to reach out to the panther, to see if it was real; but her muscles wouldn't obey her.

Laena blinked. The hut was dissolving into green grass and blue sky. Suddenly she saw where she was, and she felt a jolt of excitement. She hadn't seen this special place since her vision three years ago. She was lying on the warm ground, and the panther was standing in front of her, almost close enough to touch, and it held a cub in its mouth.

She no longer felt afraid. She was filled with wonder. It had been so very long, she had begun to doubt if her vision had really meant anything after all. "What am I doing here?" she asked.

The panther dropped the cub into the grass. The little one struggled up onto its feet and made a helpless mewling noise, hunting blindly for its mother.

The big panther flattened its ears and growled at Laena, and its lips pulled back, revealing its fangs.

Laena's wonder turned to horror. "What's wrong?" she gasped.

"This is your place. Yet you have turned away from it."

Laena tossed her head from side to side. She didn't know where the voice was coming from.

"This is your place, Laena." The panther lowered its head and seized the cub in its jaws. It turned and loped away.

"Wait!" Laena cried. "I don't understand!"

The panther disappeared among the long, lush grass. She tried to get up, but she was still paralyzed. Then the sky turned from blue to purple above her. Darkness closed in, and she felt as if she were turning head-over-heels. Bright flashes of light flared around her.

"Push!" a voice told her.

She opened her eyes and found herself back in the hut. Nan had pulled her up so that she was in the birthing position, squatting with her knees wide apart.

"Push!" the healer shouted again.

Laena felt as if her whole body was ripping open. She was covered in sweat. She was trembling. She bore down as hard as she could, and suddenly it was a joyous feeling, thrusting, freeing herself at last. She pushed and pushed—and a great weight dropped out of her as the baby fell into Nan's waiting hands.

Laena slumped back and her shoulders met the rough wooden walls of the hut. She gasped for breath, looked down, and saw Nan clasping the glistening bundle. "Is it—" She couldn't speak. She was still gasping.

Nan used a pad of wet matted grasses to wipe the infant

clean. She cleared mucous from its face. Then she slapped the baby's flank, and it screamed.

"You have a son," Nan said. She beamed at Laena and held the baby out to her.

With shaking hands, Laena accepted the gift. She held the little squirming thing and stared down at it in amazement.

Outside the hut, the men stopped chanting. They started shouting and cheering excitedly.

Nan used two lengths of sinew to tie off the umbilical cord. Laena watched dumbly. There seemed to be blood everywhere. She looked down at herself. "Is everything—"

"Everything is exactly the way it should be." Nan slashed the cord with a flake of flint. She paused and drew back as a last spasm gripped Laena, and the afterbirth emerged. Then she continued cleaning up the mess.

Laena turned her attention back to her child. Nan had told her that it was important to feed the baby immediately. Not only did it benefit the child; it helped to stem any bleeding from her womb.

The baby closed its mouth around Laena's breast, and it started suckling. Laena felt a wave of relief. She hadn't realized before how fearful she had really been. Maybe her fear explained why she had had such a strange, disturbing dream just now—though she didn't want to think about that.

"I'll go outside to the menfolk," said Nan.

"Yes. But—" Laena hesitated. "Can you keep them out for a few moments more?" She felt overwhelmed by emotions that she couldn't even name. It still seemed almost inconceivable that she had become a mother. She had a baby, and the baby was healthy and strong, and everything was going to be all right.

She lay back on the bed of reeds, holding the baby against her. "A boy," she whispered, feeling his life and warmth. Again, she looked up at the amulets. The panther amulet dangled directly above her, almost close enough to touch.

The vision that the dreamwater had given her seemed suddenly unimportant, compared with the thrill of feeling her baby drinking from her breast.

Chapter 29

Joq sat cross-legged beside Laena, and he stared at the baby with an expression that she had never seen before. His eyes had a solemn intensity. There was not a trace of a smile on his face.

This wasn't the Joq she knew. Most of the time, during the past three years, it had been hard for her to get him to take anything very seriously. If she complained because he brought home fish instead of the meat that she loved—or if she told him he should spend more time improving the little hut that Faltor had given them to live in—Joq would listen to her, he would even agree with her, and then he would smile his dreamy smile and wander off and play his flute for a while, and she would realize that he hadn't really been paying attention to her at all.

Now, as he stared at his son, he seemed quite different. This was an event too big to smile at, too important to ignore.

Nan had left them alone together in the healer's hut, and the only sound was the hissing of the fire and the pattering of light rain on the roof. "Do you like him?" Laena asked, holding up the baby.

Joq said nothing. Very slowly, he reached out and touched his son's face.

"Don't you want to hold him?"

"Hold him?" Joq stared at her as if the idea would have never occurred to him.

"I'll show you how. Give me your hands."

He did so, with their palms upward.

She gently placed the baby in his arms. "Let his head rest against your shoulder. Like that."

The baby stared up at Joq with wide eyes. Joq stared

back. Laena found herself smiling: both Joq and the baby looked equally surprised.

"You like him?" she asked again.

Joq nodded slowly. Then, quickly, he handed the baby back to her. He stood up. "This is a special day," he said. "I didn't realize—" He broke off. "I really didn't know—"

"You didn't realize how you would feel?"

He stared once again at the baby. "My son," he murmured to himself.

"Our son," Laena corrected him.

He didn't hear her. He raised both arms and clenched his fists, like the victor of a battle. Then he let out a yell.

"I must tell everyone what a fine child I have." He was grinning now. His face was radiant.

"Go on then," she said.

He hesitated. "You do understand, it is the custom—"

"We must spend the first three nights alone with our child," she said. "You told me, Joq, a dozen times."

He nodded seriously. "This way, its spirit will bond with ours."

Privately, she thought it was a foolish notion. But she was a Fisher herself now. She had long since resolved to follow the customs whether they seemed sensible or not.

"So, I will go and tell everyone," said Joq. "Then I will come back to you, and we will stay here together."

He turned and strode out.

That evening, he fussed over her. Was she warm enough? Was she comfortable? Did she need anything?

It was good to have him there, so helpful and concerned. She was exhausted by the long labor she'd gone through. At the same time, it made her feel strange. This still wasn't the Joq she knew. In which case—who had he become?

She was too tired to worry about it. She quickly fell asleep, lulled by the warmth of the fire and the sense of security that she felt in the hut.

Much later in the night, she woke suddenly. She realized she had been having a dream, though she couldn't remember what it had been about.

In the dim glow from the embers of the fire she saw Joq stretched out on some dry grass that he had strewn on the floor beside their bed. He had insisted that she should have the bed all to herself.

She watched him sleeping and marveled at the way she had come to this place. Chance seemed to have played such a part in it. The loss of her parents, her fight with Gorag, her meeting with Nan . . . and yet, sometimes it seemed as if there was a pattern, and she had merely been following it. Fate had forced her onward, and had made her do what she had done. Even during the choosing ceremony, she hadn't felt as if she was acting with her own free will. The words had come out of her of their own accord.

The baby stirred, and cried.

Joq was awake in an instant. He sat up, looking concerned. "Is he all right?"

"Yes, yes." Laena smiled. "He's probably just hungry." She held the baby to her breast, and sure enough, he quickly quieted down.

The child lying against her was a comfort that drove away her thoughts of the past. What could be better, she wondered, than this? To have her child, and her husband, and be secure in this peaceful little village. Once again she told herself that the vision the dreamwater had given her was unimportant now. It was a relic from a bygone time; nothing more.

The next three days were filled with pleasure. Joq left her for only a short while each day, and when he came back, he always brought food. Nan visited, and she showed Laena how to wash the baby, how to wrap him to keep him warm, and how to tell the meaning of his cries. Laena felt her strength returning, and she truly felt as if a whole new chapter of her life had begun.

"Have you talked to Moru?" she asked Joq when he returned home on the second day.

"Of course. She says she can't wait to see the baby."

Laena frowned. "Really?"

Things hadn't been easy between them, during the past three years. First, Moru had been scornful of Laena for choosing Joq instead of Mertan. Then she had resented it when Faltor gave Joq and Laena a home of their own, and Moru had to share with Nan for most of the time. After a couple of years, Moru decided to move back to the cave that she used to share with Laena. She was old enough to take care of herself now. But she still seemed to feel resentful of Laena for abandoning her.

Finally, when Laena got pregnant, Moru became jealous. She was nearing her own time of womanhood, and it annoyed her that Laena was a center of attention.

"Everyone is excited," Joq went on. "They want to see how a baby looks that was mothered by a woman from the plains people." He drew himself up. "I've told them he's more beautiful than any child has ever been in the Fisher Tribe."

Laena realized that he was serious. "That probably isn't true, Joq," she said. "And some other mothers might take offense."

He shook his head. "No. It's true."

The baby cried then, as if he knew they were talking about him. He waved his arms, and refused Laena's breast. Already, she was learning his moods and mannerisms. When he slept, he often pressed one chubby little hand beside his cheek. When he woke, he raised his arms and clenched his fists, even before he made a sound. He cried one way when he was hungry, and quite a different way when he was uncomfortable. Already, he was a real person to her. Maybe the Fishers had been right, after all, and it was good to spend these days alone with just Joq and her child.

On their last evening in seclusion, Nan came and cooked for them. She served roasted rabbit, and she took care of the baby, playing with him while Joq and Laena ate together.

"So," she said when they finally sat back, sated. "The naming will be tomorrow."

This was a topic that Laena still didn't feel able to deal with. She glanced nervously at Joq and didn't say anything.

Nan gave Joq a hard look. "Have you made your decision?"

Joq glanced at Laena. He, too, looked uneasy.

Nan grunted. "Let me hear it. Come on."

Laena saw the muscles tighten in Joq's face. Even now, he still resented it when Nan interfered in any way. "I don't see—" he began.

"Joq wants to name the child after his father," Laena interrupted quickly. "But—I would like to name him after my father." It was hard to speak up for herself, because she knew how much trouble it would cause. And yet, she felt she had no choice.

Nan gave a curt nod. "Well then. That's clear enough."

Joq gave her a suspicious look. "What do you mean?"

Nan stood up. She put her hands on her hips and glared at him. "Laena has lost her parents. She lost her whole tribe. She came here with nothing in the world. There's no way you can deprive her of this small thing, keeping alive the memory of her people."

Joq stared at her. For a moment, he seemed too surprised to be angry.

"I'm sure when I tell Faltor, he'll agree," Nan went on. "And he's the one who conducts the ceremony."

Joq turned and stared at Laena. Then he stared at Nan again. Even now, he didn't speak. It wasn't his way to show anger. If she had a disagreement with him, his usual way of dealing with it was to walk away to some secluded spot and sit on his own for half of the day. By the time he came home, he had usually come around to her point of view. But he never actually argued with her.

"I thought you weren't close to your parents, Joq," Nan went on. "Isn't that right?"

Joq stiffened. "That's true," he muttered.

"So I don't see that it should matter to you if they're unhappy about this. Just tell your father that when Laena has a second son, that one can be named Orleh." She bent down and patted the baby's cheek where he lay near the fire, sleeping peacefully. "This child will be named Henik." She reached for her furs then and pulled them on. "I must go and see Faltor now." She nodded to them. "I hope you enjoyed your dinner, the two of you."

"It was wonderful, Nan," Laena said.

Joq was still staring at her, with his jaw clenched. And even now, he said nothing.

Later, Laena watched him as he lay with his eyes closed, pretending to be asleep. He would get over it, she decided. It would just take time.

She turned and looked at the baby beside her. She imagined speaking his name—the same name that brought back so many memories. It seemed strange, and not just because she had grown up knowing Henik as her father. The Panthers had never dared to name a child when it was only four days old. The reason was simple: once a baby was named, it was a real person who was part of the family and the tribe. If it died after that, it was a terrible loss.

But babies perished often among the Panther People in their trek across the plains. Under the circumstances, it made sense to be cautious and not name a child till it was one year old and seemed sure of surviving. Laena had to remind herself again that here among the Fishers, life was different: fate was not so cruel, and life was kind.

Still, as she lay with her baby, cradling him protectively, she found it hard to feel secure.

The next day, she woke to the sound of singing. She peeked through a crack between the posts that formed the wall of the hut, and she saw the people of the village already assembling outside in the gray morning light. Someone was building a big fire, meat was roasting over it, and the villagers were gathering around.

Well, Laena thought, they had been waiting for three days. It was only natural that they would be impatient now.

She felt Joq's touch on her shoulder, light and tentative. "How are you?" he asked.

"I feel good." She looked up at him. "And you?"

The grimness she had seen in him last night was gone. He smiled at her, and she saw the shy, boyish look that she had noticed when she first started getting to know him. "I've been thinking," he went on, "how it will annoy my father when he finds out that my son isn't named after him."

She raised her eyebrows. "Yes?"

"It pleases me." His smile grew broader.

She stood up and took Joq's face between her hands. She kissed him. "You know, one day, Joq, you should stop feuding with your family."

He laughed scornfully and turned away.

Well, Laena told herself, it was his affair. She started donning clothes over the simple undergarment she wore to keep her warm at night. She fussed with her hair, then impulsively decided to braid it. She'd fallen out of the habit during the past year or two, because Joq didn't seem to care either way, and the Fishers still seemed to think it looked odd. But today, she was conscious of her past. It would be a tribute to the tribe she had once known.

When she had finished, she picked up a bowl of water. But it was too dim in the hut for her to see her reflection. "Do I look all right, Joq?"

"Of course. You look beautiful."

"No, I'm serious. Look at me."

He paused and studied her face. "I'm proud to be your husband," he said. He turned to the baby, and his face took on its serious expression again. "I am especially proud to be the father of my son."

Laena wrapped the child in hide to protect him from the cold, even though it was springtime and the weather was relatively mild. She fussed with her hair some more, and she peered again through the crack in the wall. "Everyone is out there," she said.

"Because they are waiting for us," said Joq. The singing had grown so loud, he had to raise his voice to make himself heard above the noise.

"I'm nervous," Laena said.

"There's nothing to feel nervous about. You've seen other couples go through it. It's simple."

"Yes, I know. But that isn't what worries me." Laena looked down at the infant in her arms, so small and so precious. She realized she couldn't explain to Joq why it made her so anxious to give this little boy a name. "All right," she said, because she knew she had no choice now. "I'm ready."

Joq went to the door and pulled the flap aside. As soon as he did so, the singing stopped.

He beckoned to Laena, and shyly, she walked outside. She had been in the hut for so long, she found herself dazzled by the morning light.

A cheer went up from all the villagers. Laena paused, shading her eyes. Every single person in the tribe had come. That pleased her deeply. She knew this was a busy time for the Fishers, because it was the start of the spawning season, when schools of salmon swam upriver. Normally, the men would be out with their fishing spears at the first light of dawn. But here they all were, gathered around her with their families, smiling at her.

She felt herself smiling back at them, feeling proud and

happy. She started making her way slowly around the circle with Joq at her side, pausing for each person to look at the baby, and she smiled more as they all exclaimed over him.

"He is a fine child. A wonderful child," said Orleh. He had forced his way to the front, even though it was customary for women to be the first to set eyes on a newborn. He seized Laena's shoulders and gave her a little shake. "Wonderful!" he cried.

Just wait till you find out what his name is, Laena thought.

"Very pretty," said Weeps, peering at the baby's face. He was staring at the huge crowd of people with an expression of amazement. So far, he hadn't uttered a cry. "He has your eyes, you know. Very pretty."

"Thank you," said Laena. She moved on—and found herself face-to-face with Moru.

Her little sister wasn't little anymore. She was almost as tall as Laena, and even though her body hadn't filled out yet, it was clear she was going to be a beautiful woman.

For an uncomfortable moment, the sisters looked at each other. Moru seemed as if she were wrestling with something inside herself. "You have a good, strong child," she said at last. But her voice was low, and she didn't really look at the baby.

"Thank you," said Laena.

Moru shifted uneasily. "I won't stay for the ceremony." She took a step back. "I hope you don't mind. I have things that I need to do." She ducked her head then, and hurried away.

Laena watched her go and felt a deep pang of loss.

But there were many others pressing forward to take Moru's place. The women seemed excited; the men were calm and polite, and they paid more attention to Joq than to Laena. She moved on around the circle, and the sounds of the voices washed over her.

Then she found herself opposite Worin.

The woman had not grown any more beautiful in the past three years. Indeed, at this point, she almost seemed to take pleasure in her own ugliness. Her clothes were always soiled with mud, and her hair hung in matted strands across her filthy face.

She still helped Nan sometimes, though she seemed to resent doing the work, and the villagers obviously preferred having Nan care for them. Worin had never joined with a man, and she lived alone now in the last cave in the cliffs, right on the edge of the village. She seemed to be grimly biding her time, although what she was waiting for, Laena couldn't imagine.

Worin shouldered her way forward and peered at the baby. Then she looked up at Laena with a twisted smile. "So, you finally managed it." She narrowed her eyes. "Was the birth painful? Did it take a very long time?"

Laena felt a moment's anger. She didn't want this person here, casting a shadow over the special, joyful day. "If you have nothing pleasant to say, please don't embarrass us both," she said quietly.

Worin looked at the baby again. "He looks a little sickly to me." She prodded the child's cheek with her finger.

The child's expression changed as he looked up at her. He screwed up his eyes and started to whimper.

"He has colic." Worin nodded to herself, as if she were a healer confirming her own diagnosis. "He'll be a lot of trouble. I can see that."

Laena felt her anger demanding an outlet. But before she could speak, Nan pushed between the two of them.

"Enough of this!" Nan glared at Worin. "I'm ashamed of you. Come, Laena." She took her arm.

Laena glanced back and saw Worin still watching her. But then there was no more time to think about that, for Faltor was waiting, and the naming was about to begin.

He was standing beside a large, flat-topped rock that stood on a little rise in the land, overlooking the big fire and the crowd of villagers that had gathered around. He was smiling down at her with obvious pleasure, and she knew that out of all the ceremonies, this was the one he enjoyed the most.

"Let the father of this child bring him to me," said Faltor, raising his voice above the crackling flames and the murmuring of the crowd.

Everyone fell silent. Laena handed her baby to Joq, and he carried him carefully to the flat-topped rock. A square of fur had been spread across it, and it was there that Joq placed his son.

The baby lay on his back, with his body swaddled in skins but his arms and legs free. He wriggled and waved his arms. He had stopped crying, and he looked around as if he were surprised to find himself in this new place, with no one holding him.

Faltor picked up three tiny objects. One was a miniature hunting spear. Another was a fishing spear. The third was a smooth, white pebble.

"This child has come into the Fisher Tribe," he proclaimed. His voice echoed across the river to the steep wall of the valley, and back again. "He must choose."

He bent over the baby and held the three objects within reach.

The little child stared up with round eyes. He waved his fist, then reached for the white pebble.

An expectant murmur came from the villagers.

But the tiny fingers slipped over the pebble and didn't grasp it.

"His choice is not set," said Faltor. "His fate is undecided."

The villagers sighed.

Faltor set down the objects. "He will choose as time passes. His fate is open." He clasped his hands. "It is time now for the naming." Gently, he picked up the child. He raised him high and turned slowly, so that everyone could see him. "A name has been chosen," Faltor went on, and once again there was an expectant silence. "He shall be Henik, of the Fisher Tribe."

The people cheered—once, twice, and a third time.

Laena glanced quickly at the circle of faces. She picked out Orleh, and saw his expression of shock. He opened his mouth as if he wanted to object, but people all around him were still shouting their approval.

Faltor turned to Laena and placed the baby in her arms. "Go to your home, and live in peace, and be well, and be happy," he said with a smile that looked as if he wore it just for her. "It is a fine thing, Laena, that you came and joined our people."

"Thank you," said Laena.

He turned to Joq. "Be proud. And be a good father." He gave him a stern look.

Joq nodded. "I will."

Once again, Laena saw the serious expression on his face that had never been there before.

Chapter 30

Joq crouched beside the bed, sorting through his tools and his hunting gear. He coiled a braided line between the web of his thumb and his elbow, tied it off carefully, then stowed the bundle in his pack.

Laena sat watching him. She shifted Henik from one arm to another. The baby was growing heavy: she had to keep him in a sling now most of the time.

"How long will you be gone?" she asked.

Joq glanced around, then noticed a wooden toy lying on the floor. It was a model of a mammoth, the size of a man's hand. He had carved it for Henik a couple of months ago, right after the naming ceremony.

"What's this doing here?" He retrieved it and wiped dirt off it.

"It must have fallen off the bed," said Laena. In fact, each time she'd given it to Henik, he'd thrown it on the floor. Eventually, she'd just forgotten about it.

Joq put it carefully on the ledge where he kept his carvings. "He'll use it for teething one day," he said. He frowned at Laena. "It shouldn't be on the floor. We don't want him eating dirt."

Laena sensed the disapproval in his voice. "You didn't explain what it was for," she said.

"I thought it was obvious." He glanced around at the little hut where they lived. "You know, the hut is a mess these days."

"I was hoping you could help me clean it," said Laena. The baby was growing heavy in her arms. She placed him back on the bed. "I didn't realize you were going away again."

Joq grunted. "Cleaning is not a man's task."

Laena wiped her hair back from her face. She felt distracted and short-tempered, and she didn't understand what was happening between them. "Joq, you never used to say things like that."

"Like what?" He gave her a guarded look. He often seemed to do that these days.

"You didn't say—you know—that men do this, and women do that. You and I, we've always done everything between us."

He shrugged. "I didn't have a son before." He sat back on the earth floor and continued packing his things.

"But why should our son change anything?" Laena heard her own voice, and it sounded plaintive. She didn't want to nag him, she didn't want to whine at him. But she honestly didn't understand.

"I have to provide for him," said Joq, speaking slowly, as if she were simpleminded. He turned down the flap of his pack and tied the thongs. "I have to hunt, isn't that obvious?" He noticed the baby lying on the bed. "Hey, is he safe there? He could roll onto the floor."

"He's fine, Joq." To herself she thought—if Joq paid half as much attention to her as he paid to the child, she would have less to complain about.

He gave her another brooding look. "Sometimes I wonder if you really take care of him properly."

She stared at Joq in amazement. "How can you say such a thing!"

He shook his head. "I just wonder, that's all. When I see things in such a mess, here—" He tied a spare pair of boots onto the side of his pack, then picked it up. "I have to go."

She quickly moved between him and the door. "Wait a moment. Wait, Joq." She closed her eyes and rubbed the tips of her fingers across her temples. What could she say that would reach through to him, and not make him pull back from her even more? "We always used to have such an easy time together," she said. She took his face between her hands. "What's going wrong? I don't understand. You leave me alone here, you don't even warn me when you're going away—"

He jerked his head back. "It isn't my decision. The other hunters decide."

"But why should you have to do whatever they want you to do? Why don't you pay attention to me anymore?"

"I am a *man* now, Laena! I have a *son*!" He sighed. "You obviously don't understand." He shifted his weight from one foot to the other. "I have to go."

"For how long?" she clutched his sleeve. "You still didn't tell me."

"One night, two at the most." He was eager to get away from her, she realized. "Why do you always make such a fuss whenever I go hunting?"

"Because I hate being left here on my own!" She looked around at the little hut. It had seemed wonderful when Faltor had first given it to them. But now it was cramped and dim and dirty, like a prison.

"You should get out and visit," Joq said. "Spend time with the other mothers in the village."

Yes, the other mothers. All they ever talked about was their children and their husbands. None of them had ever ventured more than a day's hike out of the valley, and they never would. They didn't know what lay beyond the horizon, and they didn't even care about it very much.

"I don't have much to say to them," Laena said.

"You used to, didn't you?"

"No, Joq! You were the person I used to talk to most of the time."

"Well, what about Nan? You can certainly talk to her." Laena sighed. "Yes, I can. But she spends a lot of her time with Faltor now." She clutched at him again. "Don't you remember how it used to be for you and me? We used to talk together all the time. About all kinds of things. Why the world is built the way it is, and what happens to souls when people die, and why the sun is round—"

For a moment, he seemed to stop and think about what she was saying. "I was a dreamer," he said.

"Yes, you were! And I loved you for it!"

He looked down at the floor. "Well, I'm sorry." He wriggled his shoulders, trying to settle the pack more comfortably. "You know, it's difficult for me, too, Laena. The men never accepted me in the past. I have to prove myself now. That means trying really hard, as a hunter."

Laena nodded sadly. It was ironic, she thought, that she had always wanted him to take himself just a little more seriously. Now he was trying to turn into a man like Mertan, and all she really wanted was for him to be the way he was before.

Joq picked up his spears. "I'll tell Nan to come and visit," he said. "Would that be a help?"

Laena forced a smile. "Yes. Thank you."

"And I'll bring back some new boughs, for our bed. To make it more comfortable for you and Henik."

"Thank you, Joq. That's sweet of you."

He kissed her briefly, then glanced around for the last time. "You will try to clean the place, won't you?"

He walked out of the door without waiting for her to reply.

Laena sank back onto the bed beside her baby. She couldn't tell anymore, where the truth lay. Was it really important for Joq to hunt with the other men? Did it matter that the hut wasn't clean and tidy? Was she being moody and difficult? Was it her own fault that she didn't feel the same glow of happiness anymore? She honestly didn't know.

She lay with little Henik and clasped him close. Outside, she heard the usual sounds of a summer day. Children were shouting to one another by the river. A woman was singing as she laid fish on drying racks. Someone was beating a skin to soften it so that it could be made into clothing.

Laena considered putting on her sling and walking out with Henik. Maybe she should make the effort, the same way that Joq was trying to participate with the men in the tribe.

But she knew what the other women would say before they even said it, and the thought depressed her. Maybe she would try later, but right now, she needed some more sleep. For some reason, she seemed tired all the time these days.

Henik curled up against her stomach and made his own little sleepy noises. It was nice, having him there. She pulled over the bundle of sticks that she had made, to keep him from rolling off the edge of the bed. Then she allowed herself to slip into slumber.

She was very, very warm. So hot, she felt as if she must be lying close beside a huge bonfire.

She opened her eyes and found herself in a strange, bright place. The land looked yellow, the color of straw. Her body was wet with sweat, and her mouth was dry. She was gasping. "Where am I?" she cried, and the words hurt her throat.

"I see you're thirsty." The voice came from somewhere in the brightness. She couldn't see who was speaking.

Laena nodded weakly. "Very thirsty."

"Drink then." A cup fashioned from rough bark was pushed into her hands. The cup was heavy: it was all she could do to lift it.

"Drink!" the voice urged her again.

Laena struggled. Her muscles felt weak, and the cup seemed much larger than it needed to be. Finally, she managed to raise it to her lips.

The liquid wasn't water. It smelled sweet. She hesitated.

"It's good," the voice told her. "It will calm you."

Laena took a sip. And—yes, it tasted fine. It took away all the hurt from her mouth and tongue. It soothed her as it trickled down her throat.

"Drink more," said the voice.

Laena drained the cup.

Somewhere, she heard someone laughing.

Without warning, terrible cramps seized her stomach. She felt as if she were being skewered. She screamed in pain.

The laughter grew louder.

"Why?" Laena gasped. "Who are you? Why did you do this to me?"

The pain became a fire consuming her from the inside.

"Laena!" another voice spoke. "Laena, are you dreaming?"

Yes, she realized with sudden relief. Yes, it was a dream.

She struggled up from the terrible hot, bright place, and the pain fell away as she opened her eyes.

She blinked in the dimness of the hut and lay for a moment, gasping for breath. A dark shape was bending over her. "Who's there?" Laena cried. Her mouth was dry, as it had been in the dream. She winced as she tried to swallow.

"It's me, child." Nan's voice. "Whatever is the matter?"

Laena tried to calm herself. "A dream. I dreamed I was poisoned." Once again, she tried to swallow. "I need water."

Nan made an impatient sound. "I'm getting a little old to be fetching and carrying for you." But she bustled over to the leather bucket beside the hearth, and she came back with a cup.

Laena hesitated just for a second. It had been a dream, she told herself, nothing more. The water that Nan was offering her was safe to drink. She raised the cup and drained it greedily.

"What's all this about?" Nan sat down on the end of the bed. "Joq says you're out of sorts, so I dropped everything and came here, and now I find this place in a mess, and you look as if you've been spending all your time sleeping."

"I haven't been—very cheerful." Laena felt ashamed now that Nan was here. The old woman never complained, no matter what happened to her.

Nan patted Laena on the shoulder. "It's common enough to feel out of sorts when you have a young baby."

Laena blinked. "It is?"

Nan nodded. There was a distant look in her eyes. "All the extra chores, and your man leaves you on your own—I remember it quite well." She sighed. "So, what's to be done?"

Laena looked down at little Henik. He was awake now. When he saw her looking at him, he grinned. She picked him up and hugged him. "I'll be all right," she said. "I shouldn't be bothering you, Nan."

"Well, I'm here now, so I might as well make myself useful. Why not take a walk, girl? Clear your mind."

Laena hesitated. The idea seemed intoxicating. "But I shouldn't leave Henik."

"Why not? I'll take care of him."

Laena looked at her doubtfully. "What if he wants to be fed?"

"Then he'll have to wait till you get back. It won't hurt him. Go on, girl. Before I change my mind."

Reluctantly, Laena stood up. "Are you sure?"

Nan sat on the bed. She picked up Henik and put him in her lap. He stared at her, then at Laena, and his face took on a plaintive look. He let out a wail.

Laena shook her head in distress. "He's crying!"

Nan popped her thumb into Henik's mouth. After a moment he calmed down, and he began to suck quietly. "See?" said Nan. "I've tended to more babies than I can count, girl. Go on. He'll be here when you get back, good as new."

Laena forced a smile. "Thank you, Nan." And as she turned toward the door, she felt some of her burden fall away. "I won't be long."

Outside the hut, she paused and blinked in the brightness. The sky above the valley was clear blue, and the day was so warm she hardly needed her outergarments.

"Laena!" someone called. A woman nearby straightened from her labors and waved. "How's the boy?"

"Fine, thank you."

"Come and see us sometime."

"Thank you. I will." Laena started down the path, moving quickly, so that she wouldn't be trapped by a conversation.

The village was bursting with activity. Some of the women were grinding dried roots and seeds for spices. Others were mending clothes or sewing clothes for the winter season. The older women sat quitely in shaded doorways and talked to one another. Several of them greeted Laena as she passed.

Nearer the river, she saw three boys sitting cross-legged amid a litter of wood shavings, fashioning new fish spears from tree branches that had been trimmed and dried. Further on, two younger children sat near racks of gutted, split fish, feeding wet fragments of wood to the smudge fires smoking underneath.

In the river itself, a little boy with a toy fish spear flailed at reflections in the surface of the water. Two other kids were tossing stones at the drifting carcass of a dead salmon. "Hello, Tribe Mother," one of them called respectfully.

Laena bent and picked up a stone. One of the children grinned, nudging the other.

Laena squinted and flung the stone. The water heaved up around the fish.

"You got him!" the boy shouted.

"So I did." Laena smiled at them. "Didn't you think a mother could throw?"

They giggled with embarrassment and ran off.

Laena walked on along the river. Maybe if she had the same freedom as Joq, she thought, she would be happier. To go off roaming across the land for two days—how long had it been since she had done that? She and Joq had gone camping together, a year ago. That was the last time. And how sweet it had been, alone with him in the wilderness, sitting together, sometimes talking, sometimes making love, sometimes just enjoying things without saying a word.

She looked up and noticed a woman walking toward her. She realized with surprise that it was Turi.

Laena hesitated. Her first impulse was to turn around and walk the other way. Ever since the two of them had clashed over Mertan, Laena had never felt very comfortable talking with Turi—although, ultimately, they had both got what they wanted.

But maybe this was foolish. Now that Joq was spending so much time away, Laena needed to be more friendly with the women of the tribe. Why not start now?

She stopped and waited, and gave Turi a smile. "Out for a walk?"

Turi paused. She hesitated, then smiled back, although she seemed a bit cautious. "I like to take a stroll once in a while," she said.

"If I'm bothering you—" Laena began.

"No. No, not at all." She had put on weight, Laena noticed, and she didn't take the same trouble over her appearance that she used to. Well, mothering two babies could have that effect.

"Who's taking care of your children?" Laena asked as she fell into step beside Turi, heading back toward the village.

Turi shrugged. "One of the others. You know, Laena, we've hardly seen your baby—what's his name?"

"Henik."

"Henik, yes. An unusual name."

"My father's name," said Laena a little sharply.

"Of course, I'm sorry, I didn't mean any offense." And it seemed as if she was quite sincere. She touched Laena's arm. "You know, it was a long time ago when you came to the tribe and I thought you wanted to take Mertan. That's all forgotten now. You do understand, don't you?"

Laena nodded. "I understand." She tried to decide what to say that would seem friendly. "I hope you're happy with Mertan."

Turi laughed. "Oh, you know how he is. He spends most of his time hunting. That's what he loves the most."

Laena nodded to herself. She wasn't surprised.

"But I have two wonderful children," Turi went on. "Urami

and Toma. And that's what really matters.'' She looked at Laena. ''I'm happiest when I'm at home with them. Now you have one of your own, I expect you know what I mean.''

Laena wondered what to say. She certainly loved little Henik with all her heart. And yet—she loved Joq just as much. And she loved to get out and see the country, too. It seemed as if she wanted more than other women, though she couldn't say why.

''Joq's been gone a lot just lately,'' she said as they walked back into the village. ''To tell you the truth, I wish he was home more.''

Turi laughed. ''He'd just be in the way. You should be glad that he's started doing something useful.'' She gave Laena a speculative look. ''I used to wonder how you could put up with him, when all he did was sit around and play music all the time.''

The music was beautiful, Laena thought to herself. It was far more valuable than hunting for game. Why couldn't Turi understand that?

''Well, I have to go,'' Turi went on. ''But look, if you get lonely, just drop in and say hello. Anytime.''

Laena smiled, even though she felt empty inside. ''Thank you,'' she said.

She stood and watched Turi walk away. *I wish I could be like that,* she thought. Life would be so much easier.

Laena turned and started back toward her own home. As she came closer, she heard a baby crying. It was her baby, she realized, with a sudden stab of anxiety. How long had she been gone? It hadn't seemed very long. She squinted up at the sky. It was so hard to keep track of the time, down here in the valley where the sun stayed behind the mountains for most of each day.

She hurried into her hut, and as soon as she stepped inside the doorway, she saw that something was wrong. Nan was lying on the bed, not moving, and Henik wasn't on the bed with her. His screaming came from the darkest corner of the hut.

Laena's eyes adjusted to the gloom, and she saw there was another figure there. A woman squatting down in the corner, holding Henik, lifting something toward him.

''What are you *doing*?'' Laena shouted. She strode

across, seized Henik, and jerked him out of the woman's arms.

The woman looked up, and Laena saw her face.

"Worin!" Laena cried. She felt a sudden coldness spreading through her.

Slowly, Worin stood up. "I heard the baby crying," she said calmly.

"You *made* him cry!" Laena's voice was rising. She clutched Henik to her breast. "What were you doing to him? Tell me!"

"Nothing." Worin set down the cup that she had been holding.

"What's that, there?"

"A remedy." Worin stared at Laena. "It's to calm a baby with colic."

Nan stirred then. She rolled over and blinked. She saw Laena, then she saw Worin.

"She tried to poison him!" Laena shouted. She reached for the bark cup and seized it before Worin could take it away. "Did he drink any of this?"

Slowly, Worin smiled. She said nothing.

"Did he drink it?" Laena was screaming now. "Answer me!"

"Laena, Laena." Nan was getting up off the bed. She paused, wincing from the stiffness in her joints. Then she took a step forward. "What ever is all this fuss?"

"But I dreamed it!" And suddenly she realized it was true: the voice in her dream had been Worin's voice. "I dreamed she would poison my child!" Suddenly Laena started sobbing. "Nan, you have to help me!"

Nan muttered something. She pulled the bark cup out of Laena's hand and sniffed it. "Syrup," she said. She turned to Worin. "Where did you get it?"

"Over there." She gestured to the leather bottle that Laena kept in the corner of the hut.

"See?" Nan turned back to Laena. "She meant no harm."

Laena stared at Nan. "How can you be sure?"

"I know syrup when I smell it. Here." She turned to Worin. "Drink some of it yourself."

Calmly, Worin raised the cup, sipped from it, and swallowed.

Laena shook her head. The world seemed to be tilting around her. "I don't understand," she said. Her dreams were always accurate, always true.

Nan looked down at Henik. The baby had stopped wailing. He was staring at the adults, trying to understand what was happening. "There's nothing wrong with him," Nan said.

"But—"

"You're crazy," said Worin. She moved up and peered into Laena's face. "Do you realize how crazy you are?"

"That's enough, Worin," Nan said sharply.

"But it's true. I don't think she even deserves a child."

Nan drew a deep breath. "Worin! I will see you back at the healer's hut."

Worin stared at her for a moment. She turned then and walked out.

Laena felt weak. She slumped down on the bed, still holding Henik. "You fell asleep," she said to Nan. "I trusted you."

Nan eyed her for a moment. "Don't you ever sleep with your child?"

"Yes, but—"

"Worin could have crept in just as easily while you were asleep, Laena."

Laena shook her head. "No. No, I would have woken when the baby cried."

Nan seemed to lose patience. "All right, I won't look after him ever again. But Laena, you have to get a grip on yourself."

"Fetch Moru," Laena interrupted her. "Please!"

Nan paused. "What for?"

Laena clenched her fists. "I need Moru. I really need her, Nan. Please tell her to come here."

The old woman grunted. "She'll be with the men by the fishing pool. She'll be busy."

"Fetch her for me! Nan, it's all I ask."

Nan gave Laena an odd look. "All right. I'll tell her." She started toward the door. "But it's about time you understood who your friends are, Laena. I came here to help you. Even Worin wanted to help, in her own simple way."

"Please, fetch Moru!"

Nan left without another word.

Laena sat in silence, holding her child and rocking to and fro, feeling the time passing slowly, slowly. She suddenly felt very alone.

Finally, she heard footsteps outside. She looked up, hoping so much that she would see Moru's familiar face. And yes, here she was, walking into the hut.

Moru stopped and stood with her hands on her hips. She was breathing hard, and her cheeks were flushed from running. "What is it?" she said.

"Sit down," said Laena. "Please."

Moru remained standing. "Why? What's happening?" She frowned at Laena. "Nan said you were screaming. She said you were acting very strangely."

Laena carefully laid Henik on the bed. She stood then and took Moru's hands in hers.

Moru tried to pull back.

"No!" Laena said sharply. "Don't pull away from me."

Something in her tone made Moru hesitate.

Laena drew a slow, deep breath. "Are you still my sister?"

Moru looked uncomfortable. "What sort of question is that?"

"Remember, Moru, I helped you to survive out in the wilderness. And you saved me once, when Gorag was—attacking me."

"Of course I remember." Moru sounded sullen now. "Look, I don't see what all this—"

"You are my *sister*!" Laena gave Moru a little shake. "You're of my blood and flesh. I know you need your own life now. I know you have your own friends. I know you want to forget you were ever a Panther. But, you are still my sister."

Reluctantly, Moru nodded.

"All right, I need your help," Laena said more quietly. "I have no one else to turn to."

Moru blinked at her. "Why? I don't understand."

Laena searched for words. "I need someone I can trust. Joq is never here anymore. Nan is getting old. She fell asleep while she was looking after the baby, and Worin came in here, and—" She realized her voice was getting shrill again. Deliberately, she tried to calm herself. "I had one of my dreams."

Moru looked surprised. "I thought you told me—"

"Yes, I said I didn't dream anymore. For three years, I didn't dream. But during my birthing, I had a vision. And just this afternoon, when I napped, I dreamed that someone was being poisoned. Worin's voice was saying, 'Drink! drink!' And then I went out for a walk, and when I came back into the hut, Worin was *here,* trying to get the baby to drink from a cup—" She clutched herself. "She hates me for being close to Nan, and for taking Joq away. I don't trust her. And you've seen yourself, the things I dream *always* come true. You remember, don't you?"

"Yes, I remember." Moru no longer sounded doubtful or uncomfortable. She seemed thoughtful.

"I really need you, Moru. I wish you wouldn't turn away from me. It hurts me very much. And I need your help."

There was a long moment of silence. "It seemed as if you wanted to run my life," Moru said finally. "Half the time you were telling me what to do. The other half of the time, you weren't there. You were so wrapped up with your own affairs."

Laena stared at her. "Was that really how I seemed?"

Moru nodded. She stared back at Laena in silence.

Laena sighed. "I'm sorry, Moru. I thought you just didn't like me anymore."

Now it was Moru's turn to look concerned. "Why would you think that?" she said. She stepped closer to Laena. She wrapped her arms around her, and she hugged her close. She was silent for a long moment. "I suppose some of it really has been my fault. You know, there's this boy, his name is Rorah—" She hesitated. "It's a bit hard to explain. I get so wrapped up in thinking about him, it's hard to think about anything else sometimes."

Laena laughed. She patted Moru's hand. "I understand. Believe me, I understand."

Moru shook her head quickly. "Don't sound like that! Don't sound as if you know everything!"

There was a short silence. "I'm sorry," Laena whispered.

Moru stepped back. Bit by bit, she calmed herself. "Well, I'm sorry I snapped at you. And—I'm sorry I didn't stay for the naming ceremony." She looked down at Henik. "Is he all right?" She touched her forefinger to Henik's hand and watched as he closed his fingers around hers. "He seems so little."

"I think he's fine," Laena said. Once again, though, she thought of her dream. "I was so scared when I found him with Worin—" She shivered.

"Are you sure it was Worin's voice in the dream, talking to you?"

"Yes. At least, I think so."

"And Henik was in the dream?"

Now Laena paused and thought more carefully. "Well, no, he wasn't. Worin—or someone like her—was giving *me* the cup." She laughed self-consciously. "I suppose it doesn't make sense after all, does it? But when I saw her feeding Henik, so soon afterward, I—I went a bit crazy. You know, it's been such a strain, taking care of Henik all on my own."

"Henik," Moru said, as if she were testing the sound of the name. She leaned forward and stared into the baby's face, studying his features. "Do you really think he'll be anything like—like our father?"

"I don't know. We'll have to wait and see."

Moru nodded. She sniffed, and with astonishment Laena realized the girl was crying.

"You're not the only one who gets confused, sometimes," she said. "Sometimes I want people to leave me alone, and then I get mad at them for not talking to me. I hated you for being bigger and smarter than me all the time and—"

Laena sat beside her and hugged her. "It's all right. We're together again now."

Moru nodded. She wiped her eyes on the back of her hand. "All right." She straightened her back. "So tell me what I can do to help."

Chapter 31

As the day passed and Moru sat with Laena in the little hut, Laena found herself talking more openly, more closely with her sister than they had talked in years. She'd thought that the bond between them had been broken, but she realized now this was not the case. It had been weakened, that was all. It could easily be strengthened again.

Moru had to go back and work some more by the fishing pool that afternoon, but in the evening she returned to Laena, bringing with her the biggest of the salmon that she had cleaned and boned. "Remember that first fish we tried to cook?" she said as she roasted it over the fire. "It was so funny, trying to take the bones out. We couldn't even remember whether to start at the head or the tail."

Laena smiled at her. "I remember."

As the evening went on, Laena found herself explaining why she had chosen Joq instead of Mertan. She had never really confided this to anyone, least of all Moru, because Moru had seemed so full of anger at the time. But now, as Laena spelled it out, she found that Moru was a sympathetic listener.

"I didn't realize back then," said Moru, "what it really meant to link yourself with a man. All I knew was that you gave up your chance to have the chief's son. Everyone would have respected you, and they would have respected me, as well." She shrugged. "I was just thinking about it from my own point of view."

"The sad part is," Laena said, "that I chose Joq instead of Mertan, and now he seems to want to make himself more and more like him. All Joq wants is to be out with the men, learning to be a better hunter." She shook her head ruefully.

"But it seems to me," Moru said quietly, "you always

used to enjoy being on your own. Don't you remember how I used to go searching for you when you walked off into the hills?''

Laena smiled. ''Yes. I remember those times.'' She stood up. Outside, it was almost nighttime. The fire had died down, and it was very dark in the hut. She hunted around for the leather bottle of musk oil that she kept, poured a little into a stone saucer, and lit it with a stick from the cooking fire. The yellow flame cast a faint, uneasy light.

Henik made some little complaining noises. They had placed him in the sling that Laena kept near the fire. Moru picked up the baby and held him, and as he looked up at her face, he stopped crying and smiled at her. She smiled back, enjoying him now that she had allowed him into her world.

Moru turned back toward Laena. ''I remember you used to roam around a lot, too,'' she went on. ''You always wanted to see what was over the next hill. That's how we ended up here, isn't it? You wouldn't stay by the river, after Gorag—died.''

Laena nodded. ''That's right.''

Moru looked wistful. ''I always felt so small beside you, Laena. You could do everything, and I couldn't.''

Laena nodded. ''I understand.''

Moru looked down at Henik, who had fallen asleep in her arms. She carried him to the bed, taking care not to wake him. When she laid him there and he felt himself separated from her warmth, he made a little whimpering noise. She tucked a square of caribou skin around him, and he slowly quieted down.

Moru turned back to Laena. She gestured at the baby, and at the little hut. ''Compared with the things I remember,'' she said, ''this doesn't seem like you at all. I suppose I don't quite understand how it happened. I mean—why did you really want a baby in the first place?''

Laena tried to think back. It was hard, because her troubles at the present time were so big in her mind. ''Well, I wanted a man,'' she began. ''You understand that, don't you?''

Moru smiled shyly. ''I do now.''

''And then, after the joining ceremony, the other girls all started getting pregnant. And they seemed so happy. And everyone seemed to think it was the right thing to do. Nan had told me how to avoid having a baby—"

Moru leaned forward. "She did?" Her voice was alive with curiosity.

Laena remembered when she was Moru's age, eager to know everything about sex. She told herself to be patient. "When the man reaches his climax, he has to pull himself out of the woman. Or, there are some times of the month that are safer than others."

Moru opened her mouth to ask more.

Laena held up her hand. "I'll tell you about it, but not now. Let me talk about the baby first."

Moru gave an embarrassed grin. "All right."

Laena thought back to her first year with Joq. "Taking the—the precautions was troublesome. And it was hard for Joq. If he was a real man, he should be making me pregnant, you know? People started asking questions about it. Well, I was happy with him here, and I felt as if I was fated to stay with the Fishers. It seemed that a child would make things complete."

She trailed off into silence. She stared into the flame burning in the saucer, and she seemed to see herself in there somewhere—her old self, as she once was, always searching for something. That old self seemed a relic now—like her vision of the panther. It wasn't really her anymore.

"You really think you'll always be happy to live with Joq?" Moru asked. "You won't ever want to go roaming again?"

Laena thought about it for a moment. "It seems to me I should be able to have a little of both," she said. "In the summer, Joq and I often went out walking together. Sometimes we'd be gone for two or three days. That gave me all the roaming that I needed."

"So leave the baby with me, once in a while, and take a day off with Joq," said Moru. "I can get one of the other mothers to nurse him."

Laena stared at her. "Really?"

Moru looked down at Henik. She gently touched his face. "I don't mind learning how to look after a baby." A distant look came into her eyes. "You remember when we were very little, we used to play with make-believe babies? You rolled up some hide—"

Laena laughed. "I remember. But—are you thinking of having a baby yourself one day?"

"I was never a wanderer like you, Laena. I like it here. I don't need to go anywhere else. I fit in with the Fishers." She glanced at Laena. "When Joq gets back, tell him there's nothing to stop you from going out of the village with him the way you used to."

Laena thought for a moment, wondering how he would react. "He'll probably say he can't do it because he has to practice his spear-throwing. Something like that."

Moru shrugged. "So, you can practice with him. You once speared a big cat yourself, didn't you? When you were with Jobia."

Laena felt tears in her eyes again—but this time, they weren't tears of sadness. She went and sat behind Moru and wrapped her arms around her. "Thank you. Thank you, so much. You've given me back my strength."

"I think that's what sisters are supposed to be for," Moru said quietly. "I know that that's what you always did for me."

At this time of the year, if they had been out on the plains, they would have seen the sun lingering just above the horizon even at midnight. Even here at the bottom of the valley, there was a little light left in the sky. Still, Moru didn't feel like groping her way back to her cave through the dimness. Besides, it was warm and comfortable in Laena's hut. So she decided to sleep there.

As the sisters settled themselves on the bed, Laena remembered all the times they had lain close together out in the wilderness. As she slipped into sleep, she felt sure there would be no dreams to haunt her during this night.

She woke a long time later to sounds of shouting. At first she felt confused. "Joq," she called, "what's happening?" Then she remembered who was lying beside her. "Moru, wake up!"

Her sister rolled over and opened her eyes, and they stared at each other while they both listened. The shouts were distant, coming closer. They weren't shouts of fear; they had a triumphant ring.

"It must be the hunters," said Moru. "Coming back early."

"You think so?" Laena got out of bed and pulled on her clothes. Henik woke up and started to yell. She grabbed him and hugged him, trying to calm him.

Moru went over by the door and stood listening. "It has to be them." She tied the flap aside. "Come on, Laena! We'll meet them."

Laena quickly donned the pouch that she used to carry Henik. She slid him into it and made sure he was secure, then ventured outside.

Several of her neighbors were already standing there, staring down on the path that ran beside the river. The shouts were coming from that direction, echoing between the steep sides of the valley.

And then, through the dimness of dawn, Laena saw figures running toward the village. The youngest hunters came first, yelling and shaking their spears above their heads. Trophies were tied to every spear—horns and hooves from the animals that had been slain.

Next came the older hunters, led by Mertan. They moved in pairs, with poles resting across their shoulders. Butchered meat dangled from the poles, wrapped in animal skins that swung to and fro as the hunters took big, loping strides.

All the people who lived in the village were out of their huts now. They were shouting and clapping their hands. The din was deafening.

"I see Rorah," said Moru. "There he is!" She turned to Laena. "Do you mind if I—"

"Go to him," Laena said. "I'll wait here for Joq."

Moru gave her a big smile. "Thanks!" She turned away, then checked herself. "Don't forget what I told you to tell him."

Laena laughed. It was the first time she ever remembered getting advice from her little sister.

Then Laena saw Joq. She called to him. "Over here!"

He saw her and came running up. The skin of a caribou was bundled across his shoulders, wrapping the meat that he had butchered. He dumped it on the earth in front of her and stood there grinning. "It was such an easy hunt! The animals were right on the edge of the valley. Look at all this meat—we'll be eating well for the next month." He quickly hugged her.

Some of the younger hunters passed by. A couple of them

saluted Laena with their spears, even though it wasn't the custom to honor another man's wife this way. One of the youngsters was so proud he even held out his trophy for Laena to touch, as if she were a girl he was courting. Joq glared at him, but Laena just smiled and shook her head, while the people all around scolded the boy and told him to move along.

"I should help give out the meat," said Joq. He turned to follow the hunting party as it continued on into the village.

"Later," said Laena.

Joq looked down at the bulging caribou skin. "But if they think I have kept this all to myself—"

"Leave it outside our hut then. If anyone wants some, they can help themselves."

He hesitated, then nodded. "All right," he said. He seized Laena again. "You know," he said more softly, "I was thinking of you, out on the hillsides. You were right, you've spent too much time down here alone."

Before Laena could answer, Henik started crying. He'd been upset by all the noise and activity. She let go of Joq and cuddled the baby. "Come inside," she said over her shoulder.

In the hut, Laena gave the baby her breast, which quietened him. Then she went to the crevice in the stone wall where she kept her possessions. She found the ivory comb that Joq had carved for her, and she started tugging at the tangles in her hair, to give herself a moment in which to think.

Finally she turned around. "I've been talking to Moru," she said. She felt uneasy about confronting him like this, without any warning, especially since he had just come back from the hunt and seemed as if he was trying to make things better between them. But if she didn't say anything now, she knew that she'd keep putting it off. "Moru and I are friends again," she went on. "Real friends."

Joq gave her a surprised look. "I'm glad," he said.

"Moru even says she'll look after the baby," Laena went on. "So that I can take a day off once in a while. That way, you and I can go walking like we used to."

"Walking?" Joq paused a moment, thinking about it. "All right. That sounds good." He moved toward her.

She hugged Henik, keeping him between herself and Joq, like a barrier. "Wonderful," she said. "So—when can we do it?" It almost sounded like a challenge.

Joq stopped. He gestured uncertainly. "A month from now?"

Laena slowly shook her head. "I don't want to wait that long."

He spread his hands. "I have to practice. The other hunters are so much better than I am."

Laena saw that it was just as she had expected. "When you practice, you go off on your own sometimes, don't you?"

Cautiously, he nodded.

"Then take me with you." She tried to make the words sound firm and strong.

"Take you with me?" Joq stared at her. "But Laena, you know that isn't the custom."

"I don't care about customs!" Her voice was suddenly loud. "I killed a big cat with a spear once—remember I told you that? I survived with my sister, out in the wilderness. I know how to look after myself. If you're going to learn to be a better hunter, why shouldn't I?"

Joq stepped back, stung by her tone. "Laena—"

She felt herself getting angry. "If you won't teach me, I'll take one of your spears and teach myself."

He slowly sat down on the bed. He held his head between his hands. "No, Laena. Please, don't make this so difficult. A woman can't take a man's spear. It's not possible. The other men would never hunt with me again."

"I had my own spear once, you know. Till I let Nan have it, and then—" She trailed off, realizing that Joq was looking deeply unhappy. She saw she had hurt him, and a pang of guilt replaced her anger. She could never be angry with him for long; it hurt him too much. Also, she knew he genuinely wanted the best for her. It wasn't his fault that the customs of the tribe made it impossible for her to do what she wanted.

She went and sat beside him. She laid her hand on his arm. "I will never take your spears. I'm sorry I shouted at you." She paused a moment. The hut was quiet now. The noise of the hunting party had receded, and the villagers were back in their homes. "When I was little," she went on, "I used to play with a make-believe baby. Moru reminded me of that, last night. So let me practice with a make-believe spear. You can fashion it for me. That wouldn't offend anyone, would it?"

Joq turned and looked at her. He was silent for a long time. "You are a strong woman," he said. He sounded worried. "I can't stand against you, Laena."

She saw that this was his way of saying yes, even though he couldn't actually bring himself to say the word itself. She felt a little surge of gratitude. "It can be fun," she said, smiling at him, trying to infect him with her own enthusiasm. "You can make me a spear with—oh, an ivory head. Wouldn't that be all right? A toy spear. It wouldn't be a real spear at all. Then we can go off together." She squeezed his arm. "Remember the fun we used to have?"

He looked down at the dirt floor. "I remember. While I was away this time, I thought about it."

She nudged him. "Remember when we made love in Rocky Hollow? I teased you and I wouldn't stop, and you got fierce and pushed me down—" She reached up, loosened the thong, and opened the neck of her jacket.

She saw in his eyes that he remembered it just as clearly as she did. "I've always found it hard to resist you, Laena," he said.

Well, she thought to herself, that wasn't entirely true. Ever since she'd given birth to Henik, Joq had been gone so often there'd been hardly any time for lovemaking.

But she smiled at him as she loosened the next thong. "You're probably tired after the hunt," she said. "Too tired, I'm thinking."

He shook his head. "Not really."

She opened her jacket a little wider. "You're too tired even to look at me."

"You're teasing me again," he said.

"What if I am?" She lay back on the bed, and her jacket fell half open.

He lay beside her and slid his hand across her naked skin. Her breast was plump and round with milk for Henrik, and Joq caressed it lightly. "I want you, Laena."

"I want you, too," she whispered. She pressed his hand harder against her. "Let's see what a big, strong hunter you are."

He took her then, with a mixture of strength and tenderness. He was never rough with her, even when she teased him. And, Laena thought, his words had been true: she was a strong woman. Stronger than she had realized. It was hard for him to stand against her strength, even now.

Chapter 32

They went to a small, shallow valley—a private place carpeted with grass, rimmed with trees. The grass seemed to glow in the midday sun, and insects hummed in the shade from the trees. She was alone here, with Joq. The village was far away.

They had found this place almost three years ago, soon after she had chosen him. They had lain together in the grass, back then, talking, laughing, and making love. Laena thought of those moments wistfully, and wished she could lie with Joq like that now. But time was so much more precious today than it had been in the past. Her days in this private place had to be used for learning, not for loving.

Joq had bundled some long grasses together and tied them with a leather thong. He hung them from a tree branch, a hundred paces from where Laena stood. This, he told her, was her target. The ivory tip of her spear wasn't sharp enough to penetrate the kind of target that hunters normally used, made of leather stuffed with fur.

Laena felt the sun warming her. Overhead, a flight of geese honked, flying south. She waited while Joq stepped back to a safe distance, and then she raised her spear, holding it as he had shown her. She tried to ignore everything around her except the dangling bundle of grasses. She tried to focus on the target until it filled her entire awareness.

She steadied herself carefully, pulled back her arm, then paused, feeling the weight of the spear, trying to visualize it as a living extension of her body.

She took a deep breath, then hurled the spear.

Many days of hard work had led up to this moment.

At first, Joq had refused to make the spear for her. He still wanted to help her, and he was willing to teach her all she knew; but she had to make the spear herself. A hunter must always be able to build and repair his own weapons, he said. That was the custom, and there were good reasons for it. So Laena had set to work.

She painstakingly chipped a spearhead from the tip of an ivory tusk. Then, while Moru cared for Henik, Laena went out to some woods near the river valley and found herself a long, straight branch that had fallen from one of the trees.

Back at her hut, she tied the spearhead to the branch with sinew. This was much more difficult than she had expected: the shaft of the spear kept wiggling loose, and she had to pull the knots so tight, her fingers ached and throbbed. But finally, that night, she had her spear ready for Joq to inspect.

He turned it over in his hands, then suddenly thrust it into the face of rock that served as the rear wall of their hut. The sinew snapped and the ivory tip spun away, landing on the floor.

Joq frowned. He flexed the shaft of the spear in his hands, and it snapped.

Laena stared in horror at the ruins of her work. She felt as if he had betrayed her. "Why did you do that?" she cried.

He looked up at her and gave an apologetic smile. "A spear has to be really, truly strong. Otherwise, it's more of a danger to you than your prey. Imagine if your spear broke or its head came loose while you were trying to kill a fierce animal. The animal would be angry, and you'd be left without anything to defend yourself."

She shook her head, still feeling upset with him. "But this isn't meant to be a real spear. It's just for me to practice with."

He considered that for a moment. "That's true," he said. "But if you want to learn how it is to be a hunter, you must go through all the steps along the way. I was impatient myself, Laena, when I started learning. But now I can see there are no shortcuts."

She picked up one of the broken pieces of the spear and turned it over in her hands. "Even so," she said, still feeling resentful, "you could have told me how to make it, instead of letting me waste my time."

He went to her and put his arm around her. "I have to

teach you the same way that people taught me. The way to learn is by making mistakes. Otherwise, the lessons can be too easily forgotten.''

Laena realized she couldn't disagree with that. She had discovered the principle for herself, when she learned the art of healing from Nan. ''All right,'' she said, ''I've made my mistakes. Now, will you show me how it should be done?''

He smiled at her. ''Yes. Of course.''

The next day he went with her into the woods. A dead branch, he told her, could never make a spear shaft. She had to choose a healthy young tree whose trunk was thin, straight, and tall. Using a flint knife, he showed her how to whittle away the bark around the base of the tree. Without this protection, the tree would die. True, it would take days for this to happen—but there were other things to do while they were waiting.

Over the next few days, he taught her the skills of tracking. A simple set of footprints could contain countless clues. With enough experience, you could even judge the health of an animal from its tracks and dung. You could tell how recently the animal had passed this way, how fast it was traveling, how easy it would be to catch, and how hard it would be to kill. But even this wasn't the whole story, because the same set of marks could mean wildly different things depending on whether the weather had been hot or cold, wet or dry.

There was much more. They practiced crawling through the long grasses, stalking one another. She learned how to conceal herself in the contours of the land, and she learned how to use the wind as her ally. It would bring to her the smell of her prey at the same time that it concealed her own odor. It ruffled the grass, which helped to hide her movements. Even the faint sounds that the wind made could help her, if she used them to conceal the sounds she made.

Next, she learned patience. Joq took her to a part of the river where the summer mosquitoes swarmed, and told her that her task was to sit and watch the water while he floated chips of wood downstream. Each time she saw a chip, she made a mark on a piece of birchbark. At the end of the ordeal, he would check to see if she had made the right number of marks. There were long gaps in which nothing happened at all; yet she couldn't afford to look away for a second, in case she missed seeing one of the chips of wood.

It was a game that every young hunter had to play, and it was maddening. But at the end of the day, when she compared her tally with his, she found that they were the same. She had been determined to prove herself, and she had succeeded.

Many days later, Joq judged that the spear tree was ready, and he showed her how to fell it using a stone ax. Then it had to be stripped and shaped. All of this was work that she had to do herself. Joq hardly even touched the wood; he told her that a spear was such a personal thing, it must grow entirely from the hands of the person who would use it. The only exception, on a real spear, was its head. The special, mystical skills of a flintknapper were required to create a spearhead from a cobble of flint.

Laena smoothed the rough shaft of her spear with the gritty ashes of burned, pulverized bone. Then she polished it with animal fat, which helped to protect the wood and make it supple. Finally, she fastened the spearhead with tightly wound sinew, which she sealed with heated resin.

That night, Joq tested the new spear in just the same way as he had tested the old one. The point rebounded from the wall, and even when he bent the shaft over his knee, it flexed without breaking.

He laughed and placed the spear back in her hands. "Now," he said, "you are ready to learn the real art of hunting."

She hurled the spear, and it flew cleanly through the air. Her arm felt as if she had wrenched it half out of her shoulder, but she paid no attention. She held her breath and stared as the spear struck the bottom of the target, pierced the bundle of grass, and buried its head in soft ground just beyond.

For a moment, there was silence. And then: "Good!" Joq shouted. Was it her imagination, or did he sound surprised? He turned and looked at her. Yes, she decided, he was surprised—she could see it in his face.

"That was really good?" she asked. "I was aiming a little higher up—"

"No. Just hitting the target is good." He frowned at her. "Where did you learn to do that?"

She felt a warm glow that seemed to spread from her belly, out to her fingers and toes. She grinned happily. "I told you, I practiced a little, once."

He walked to where the spear had landed. He picked it up and returned it to her. "Try again."

To herself, Laena thought: *He thinks it was just luck.* And then she felt a moment of doubt. Maybe it *had* been luck. In truth, she had never really practiced with a spear.

Once more she stared at the target. It seemed much more daunting now than it had the first time. How could she possibly hope to repeat a performance like that?

Then she glanced at Joq, and she saw him watching her. She imagined how he would react if she missed this time around. He would come over and pat her on the shoulder, and he would smile at her the way men did when a woman failed to do something that they could do.

She couldn't bear that. She lifted the spear over her shoulder and bounced it lightly to find the balance point. She turned her attention back to the target and studied it with grim intensity, focusing her awareness as she had before. She forced her doubts out of her mind. She simply had to do as well as she had before. There was no other option.

She braced herself and threw.

The target fell to the ground with the spear embedded in its center. The force of the blow had broken the thong suspending it from the tree.

This time, Joq said nothing. There was a stiffness in his movements as he went and picked up the spear, pulled it free, then hung the target back on its branch. "Perhaps you should step back a little, this time," he said as he came and returned the spear to her.

That seemed unfair, and she wanted to protest. But when she saw the way he was looking at her, she simply gave him a curt nod and took several paces backward.

She paused, rubbing her thumb on the wood of the shaft. She felt more confident now, and with the confidence came a sense of power. She remembered the time when she had been out on the plain alone with Jobia, and she had taken his spear, and he had tried to take it back from her. She'd had the same sense of power then. She felt as if she were

freeing herself from something that she hadn't even known
was holding her a prisoner.

She raised the spear, focused on the target, then took a
running step and threw the spear with savage force, truly as
hard as she could. This time, the spear cut cleanly through
the center of the target and soared far beyond.

Laena turned and looked at Joq. She felt so pleased with
herself, and so proud, she couldn't help smiling.

He stood staring after the spear. For a long moment, he
didn't say anything. "You'd better go and get it," he finally
told her.

"All right, I will." Taking her time, she walked to the
long grass where the spear had come to rest. She had to
search a little while before she found it. She picked it up
and wiped it meticulously clean. The polished wood felt
different in her hands now. She understood at last why he
had insisted that she make it herself, and why men always
refused to let anyone else use their weapons. This spear was
not just a tool; it was a way to become more than herself.
If someone tried to take it away from her now, she would
fight almost as fiercely as if someone tried to take away her
husband or her child.

She returned to Joq with her back straight and her chin
held high.

"Perhaps that's enough for today," he said as she approached. "Moru will be waiting for you—"

"No," said Laena.

He stopped short. "But, Laena—"

"The sun is still high," she said. "I have a lot more
practicing to do." She looked him steadily in the eyes. "You
know how important it is for a hunter to practice, Joq.
You've told me so again and again, ever since Henik was
born."

He sighed, looking unhappy. "But you're not a hunter,"
he blurted out. "You're—"

"A woman," she finished for him. She felt a wave of
anger. She opened her mouth to vent it—and then realized
how hurt he was. He was looking dazed, as if she had hit
him.

She dropped her spear on the ground. "Joq, what is it?"

"Nothing." He turned his face away from her. "You stay
here. I'll go back to the village."

She put her hand on his shoulder. "Don't go. There's no reason for us to be at odds with each other."

He sank down on the ground, rested his elbows on his knees, and pressed his hands on either side of his face. He sat that way for a long moment, and then, finally, he looked up at her. "It isn't easy, Laena, to see that you're better with a spear than I am."

Now that he was admitting his own weakness, she couldn't be angry at him anymore. Instead, she felt a wave of guilt. He had been so helpful to her, teaching her everything. No other man would have given away his skills so freely. And no other man would have willingly admitted that a woman was better with a spear.

"I can't be better than you are," she said, sitting down close beside him. "I only just started. I had three lucky throws—"

He looked at her and managed to smile, now that she was being kind to him again. "You throw hard and well. If you practice, you'll be one of the best. Myself, I don't have that kind of concentration. I've tried to learn it, during the past few months. But it's something I just can't do well."

She took his hand. "Even if that's true, there are more important things than hunting."

He laughed, without much humor. "I thought I was the one who used to tell *you* that."

She gave him a puzzled look. "You did?"

He nodded. "It was when I was practicing with my spears, the day before the choosing ceremony."

She thought back and realized it was true. "Well," she said, "you were right. And that was why I chose you, because you had the courage to be different, and be yourself. Joq, if I had wanted a wonderful hunter, I would have chosen Mertan, remember? It's *you* that I care for, not your skills with a knife or a spear."

He nodded slowly. "I suppose that's true."

"It *is* true. Be what you are, Joq. Don't try to be something that isn't natural to you."

He reached for her then, and hugged her. "Thank you, Laena," he said. He looked into her eyes, tenderly now. He kissed her.

She slumped back under him. It suddenly seemed very important to unite herself with him. She still craved the feeling that the spear had given her, but she craved him, too. How would she be able to find a balance? That seemed a big question—far too big and difficult for her to grapple with now. All she wanted at this moment was to give herself to him, and close the gap that she had felt opening between them.

She took his hand and slid it inside her jacket. She pressed his palm against her breast. "Make love to me here," she whispered. "Like you did, when we were first joined. You remember?"

"Of course I remember." And she saw in his eyes, he wanted it as much as she did. He started pulling her clothes off, more roughly than usual. She surrendered to him, enjoying the feeling of being owned and taken by him. He took her quickly, with a wild, forceful spirit, and she marveled at the way she yielded to him.

Meanwhile, her spear still lay close by, with its wood gleaming amid the green grass.

When they went back to the village, something strange happened. Her sense of freedom and her closeness to Joq both seemed to slip away. As the valley closed around her and she saw the familiar straggle of huts beside the river, she felt as if the happiness that had leaped up inside her was being slowly dampened.

And then, of course, there were the comments from her neighbors.

"Killed anything yet?" an old man called to her, sitting outside his home, grinning.

"It's just for fun," Joq said as he walked past with Laena carrying her spear.

"Hunting isn't fun," a younger man shouted. She recognized him; he was Hurow, one of Mertan's friends.

"I'm sure that's true," said Laena. "But I haven't been hunting."

"You should be careful you don't stab your foot," someone else called, and she felt her face turning pink as people started laughing.

"Don't pay any attention," Joq murmured to her. "They're the same people who laughed at me all the time, when I was a child."

Laena didn't say anything, but her grip tightened on the shaft of her spear.

Back at their hut, she found a warmer reception. Moru had brought Henik out onto the path and was bouncing him on her knee. The boy was crowing with delight. As Moru bent over him, he reached up and seized hold of her dangling hair. "Ow, you're skinning me alive!" Moru cried. She started prying his fingers loose, but as soon as she succeeded, he seized hold again. In the end, they both slumped down, laughing.

"How was he today?" Laena said.

"Oh, he's . . . ouch! He's as strong as a bear, that's how he is." She finally managed to free herself. "He's nothing but trouble, but I have to admit, I'm enjoying most of it." She tucked her hair back, out of range of Henik's hands. "So, how was it? Did you hit the target?"

Laena glanced down at her spear, then glanced at Joq, standing beside her. She hesitated, choosing her words carefully. "I have a lot to learn," she said.

Then quickly, she turned and ducked inside the hut. She looked around, wondering where to put her spear. In the past, while she was making it, she had just stood it in the corner. Now, however, she felt a need to hide it safely. Just possibly, one of the hunters might come in and steal it—out of resentment, or as a joke. She couldn't imagine how she would cope with that.

In the end, she slid it under the pad of thin green branches that was their mattress. Then she ventured back outside.

She found Joq standing a little way away, talking with Mertan. Mertan nodded to him and moved on, and Joq came back looking concerned, as if he had just received some worrying news.

"What is it?" Laena asked.

He put his arm around her, and she felt the warmth of him. It was a while since their lovemaking, but the pressure of his body against her and the shape of him inside her still lived vividly in her mind.

"Benke was out on the highlands, near Blind Valley," he said. "He saw a herd of mammoth. Mertan is calling everyone together. There'll be a hunt tomorrow."

Laena absorbed the news. It made sense that the man named Benke would have been the one to find the mammoth. He was five or six years older than Joq, but he didn't have a family, and he spent a lot of time out on his own. The other hunters respected him as a scout, but they didn't really embrace him as a friend.

As for Blind Valley—she had only been there once, when she and Joq had been out together, just wandering. It was upstream from the village, a small dent in the land, open at one end and closed at the other, making it ideal as a trap for animals.

"Three of the men are going out tonight to join Benke and set fires across the valley entrance," Joq was saying. "That'll keep the mammoth inside. We'll go after them at dawn."

"Will it be dangerous?" she said, looking up at him.

He shook his head. "It should be fairly easy, in that part of the land. The valley is narrow—"

"Then why are you looking so worried?"

He gave her a brooding look. "Because I know what you're going to want to do."

There was a long silence in the little hut. In the end, it was Moru who spoke up. "I went out with the last hunt, Joq," she said. "Do you remember? Laena was pregnant back then, so she had to stay at home."

"Yes!" Joq's voice was suddenly loud. "And now she is a young mother. So she should still stay at home. She has a child, not even one year old."

Moru carefully tucked her hair behind her, out of Henik's reach. She was calm and composed, and Laena wished she could be like that herself, instead of feeling forever ruled by her swings of emotion. "I will stay here and look after the baby," Moru said to Joq.

"But you know quite well," he said, "it's against the customs for a mother to come on a hunt. Youngsters are the only girls who can help with the herding."

Laena sighed. "Joq," she said, "I don't see why I must always do what everyone has done before me."

He looked down, away from her eyes. "Because it will embarrass me," he said, so quietly that she could barely make out the words.

She moved closer to him. Why, she wondered, did everything always have to be so difficult? "You can tell the other hunters that you ordered me to stay at home," she said to him. She was trying to speak gently, trying to hold back the impatience that threatened to take hold of her. "Tell them that I refused to listen to you."

He raised his head and gave her a pleading look. "Laena, why must you—"

"Because I am who I am." She gestured helplessly. "Tell the other hunters anything you want, Joq. Tell them that I'm crazy, if you like. But I will be coming on the hunt."

Chapter 33

At dawn the next day, when the hunters set out along the path beside the river, they were tense and alert, striding quickly, their faces showing a mixture of excitement and apprehension. A mammoth hunt was a chance to be bold and brave, a hero in the eyes of the tribe. At the same time, though, a mammoth was more dangerous than any other beast: supremely powerful, and easily angered. Even when men were not hunting it, it could turn on them and gore them or trample them to death.

Behind the hunters came the people of the tribe who would serve as herders, to control the movements of the mammoth and make them easier to kill. There were youngsters here, chattering excitedly to each other; elders, scolding them to be quiet; and women who were free to join the hunt because they had no young children to care for.

And then there was Laena.

Joq had hardly spoken to her that morning. Moru had arrived to take care of the baby, and Laena had shouldered the pack of necessities that she always took when she ventured outside the village. She retrieved her spear from its hiding place under the mattress, turned to leave the hut, and found Joq standing between her and the door.

For a moment, they confronted each other in silence.

"Laena," he said finally, "if you care at all for my reputation in the tribe, please don't carry your spear today."

Laena's first impulse was to stand firm. "There is no reason," she said, "why I shouldn't bring this. It might even help to protect me."

Joq glanced at Moru, who was sitting and watching, saying nothing. Then he turned back to Laena. "It isn't a real spear. We agreed on that, didn't we? I helped you make it, which is more than any other man would have done. And you are coming on the hunt, which no other hunter would allow his wife to do. Isn't that enough, Laena? Can't you do this one thing for me, and leave the spear behind?''

It was Laena's turn now to look at Moru—for support, or for guidance.

"I think he's right," Moru said quietly, simply.

Laena felt the words as a sudden, unexpected slap against her. But then, reluctantly, she realized that Moru was trying to help her. Laena couldn't have everything her own way, no matter whether she was right or wrong. There had to be compromise.

She looked down at the spear in her hands. "All right, Joq," she said. "I will leave it here. Because you've asked me to." She turned then and stowed the spear back under the bed.

"Thank you," he said. And unexpectedly, he embraced her.

Now she walked near the end of the procession of villagers, through the dim gray dawn. Some of them glanced at her, wondering why she was here instead of caring for her baby. But no one spoke to her. Even Faltor, who had gathered everyone together before they set off, said nothing directly to her. Evidently, he felt it was not his business to interfere in the relationship between a husband and his wife.

The Fishers reached the place where they had to climb the narrow track up the side of the valley. Laena saw the hunters leading the way. As they climbed higher, they became a series of tiny hunched silhouettes against the deep gray sky. She recognized Faltor at the front, and Mertan immediately behind him.

Then she saw Joq, and she felt a pang. She still felt in her heart how much she needed and loved him. She watched him making his way toward the top of the valley, and she made a silent wish for his safety.

Then it was her turn to climb. She suddenly felt very lonely, surrounded by people who could never understand why she would abandon her child and insist on being here with them. Well, there was no point in dwelling on that.

By the time Laena reached the highlands at the top of the valley, the hunters were far ahead, striding across the low, rolling hills. The sun hung directly ahead of them, a pale, liquid disc almost touching the distant mountains. The sky around it was yellow-white, while the sky overhead was still so dark, she imagined she might see stars up there.

Laena hurried to keep up with the column of Fishers as they straggled across the grasslands. Some of the elders were falling behind, while the young boys were running, eager to see the place where the mammoths were trapped.

Finally it came into view: a pocket set in a steep hillside. Five fires had been built across its mouth, and their smoke rose lazily in the still morning air. The men who had set the fires came running out to meet the hunters, and there was a confusion of voices shouting to one another.

As Laena approached, she saw Faltor conferring with the hunters and nodding as they discussed their plan. Despite the chill morning air, most of the men started stripping off their outer robes. The folds of clothing could interfere with the speed or precision of a spear thrust, and could make them an easier target for the point of a mammoth's tusk.

The men's bare chests gleamed with nervous sweat. They steamed in the cold, damp air.

She saw Joq and pushed closer to him. He looked up, hesitated, then smiled awkwardly and beckoned her to his side. "In your pack," he said. "You brought the body grease?"

She swung the pack down and drew out a pouch of animal grease rendered and boiled with herbs and resin. It concealed a man's body smell, helped to keep him warm, and helped to prevent infection if his skin was broken. She opened the pouch, scooped out a handful of the grease, and rubbed it over his arms and chest. Around her, other women were doing the same thing for their men.

Finally, Laena brought out a smaller pouch in which the grease had been mixed with soot. She smeared this across Joq's body in a pattern that should help to conceal him from his prey.

"Be careful," she whispered to him as she finished.

"Of course." He eyed her gravely, and clasped her hands between his.

Mertan was waiting close by, still fully clothed. He would be coordinating the hunters, while Faltor took charge of the herders. Mertan shouted something, and the bare-chested men turned and echoed his cry, raising their fists in the air. Then they started running toward the mouth of Blind Valley.

Faltor gestured for the herders to follow with him. The youngsters of the tribe were quiet now. Their eyes were bright with expectation.

She glanced back for a moment. A small group of elders had made camp beside a brook further back. They would be overseeing the huge task of slicing and packing the meat when the hunt was done.

Laena climbed cautiously with the rest of the herders toward the fires that had been set in the valley mouth. She saw Benke standing there—the solitary man who had come upon the mammoth originally. He was standing like a guard at the mouth of the valley, as if he had somehow earned the right to supervise the hunt. "Ho!" he shouted as he saw Laena.

She hesitated, wondering whether to ignore him.

He came striding toward her. He looked older than his years; his face had been deeply marked by the passing seasons. "What are you doing?" he shouted to her. "Why are you here?"

She eyed him for a moment, wondering what to say. Whatever she said, it would start an argument. And she was in no mood for that. She wished Joq were close by, to deal with this man; but he had already run deep into the valley with the other hunters.

Laena decided that the best way was simply to say nothing. She started forward—but Benke grabbed her arm. "Your place is with your child!" he shouted.

She felt anger rising inside her. She opened her mouth to shout back—then stopped herself as Faltor came up beside her. "Laena has chosen to be here," the chieftain said calmly. "And Joq has consented to it. This is a private matter between them, Benke. It is nothing to do with us."

Laena jerked her arm free from the man's grasp. He glared at her, wordlessly, as she moved on past him. "Thank you," she said to Faltor when Benke was out of earshot.

"Do not thank me, Laena." He frowned down at her. "I am not so sure it's wise for you to be here today. As I say, it's a matter between you and your husband."

Still, Laena thought to herself, Faltor could have forbidden it if he had chosen to do so. But then she thought no more about it, as she passed through the plumes of acrid smoke and the mammoths came into plain sight ahead of her, clustered together at the far end of the valley.

She drew in her breath in awe. There were six of them altogether. Only one had the enormous, curling tusks of a mature male. Three of the others were adult females, and two were not yet fully grown.

The beasts were standing in a patch of tall, thick grass. Laena could see why they had been attracted to this spot. The days were already growing shorter. With winter not far off, the lush vegetation of the valley made a tempting meal.

The hunters were scaling the sides of the valley and moving around it, taking up positions beyond the mammoth, at the far end. Faltor, meanwhile, was posting the herders. "Laena," he called to her. "Take this." He reached into a large pouch that he was carrying and pulled out a thin tube of leather. She recognized it as a boomer—a noisemaker that the Fishers used to scare animals. "Your place will be high up the valley wall, there. By the stunted tree." He pointed.

She nodded, seeing that he had picked an especially safe spot for her, well out of reach of the beasts, even if they chose to stampede. She took the boomer from him. "They look strong," she said.

He nodded slowly. "This may take a long while."

"Couldn't we herd them toward our own valley, and over the edge?"

He shook his head. "Too far from here. They would probably try to break free, and if we tried to hold them back, we'd be trampled. No, we must keep them here and exhaust their strength." He patted her shoulder. "Go to the place I have chosen." Then he moved on.

Laena started climbing the steep, stony ground. The other herders were doing the same, fanning out either side of the entrance to the valley.

Laena reached the stunted tree and waited. At the far end, she saw the hunters scavenging rocks small enough to throw, and stacking them in piles.

Mertan stood and held out his spear, parallel to the ground. When all the others were ready, he gave a shout and brought the spear down.

Faltor signaled the herders, and they exploded into noise.

Some of them blew whistles made from bone. Some banged rocks together. Some shook rattles made of rawhide pouches stuffed with pebbles. Laena swung her noisemaker on the end of its thong, and it made an eerie moaning sound.

The mammoth jerked their heads and shuffled their feet, confused by all the people and the sudden noise. They wheeled around and started running toward the far end of the valley. But as soon as they came within range of the hunters, the hunters started pelting them with rocks.

The test of endurance had begun.

The herd of mammoth shied away from the hail of missiles and charged back toward the open mouth of the valley. Some of the herders had thrown more fuel on the fires, so great billows of smoke now blocked the exit. Everyone started shouting, making a wall of sound.

The mammoths hesitated, then wheeled again. One of the young ones stumbled as a rock hit its forehead. One of the females trumpeted in anger, and the fractured sound just added to the din. Slowly, the great beasts retreated to a point in the center of the valley, midway between the two groups of tormentors.

The beasts were safe there; but the Fishers couldn't allow them to rest. Faltor shouted orders, and four boys ran out into the dangerous open ground, swinging boomers like the one that Laena carried. The bull turned its tusks toward them, then suddenly charged. The boys quickly ran back to the safety of the smoldering fires, and the great mammoth stopped, bellowing in anger and thumping the ground with its front feet.

Laena heard a shout from below and saw Faltor gesturing for the herders to move deeper in. He seemed to want them as close as possible to the spot where the mammoths now stood.

Laena started picking her way carefully along the rocky ground. The steep slope was a mixed blessing, she realized. It kept her safe from the mammoths; at the same time, it was so severe that if she fell, she would have no way of stopping herself. She would roll to the floor of the valley, where she could easily be trampled to death.

She told herself not to hurry. She tested each foothold carefully, till she finally reached a safe resting place on a high ledge. The slope below her here was of sheer rock, almost vertical.

Once again, at a signal from Faltor, they started making noise. Once again, the mammoths shied away and retreated deeper into the valley—where they were met with another fusillade from the hunters.

Laena saw small spots of blood on the backs of the beasts where some of the missiles had struck. But Faltor had been right: it would take a long time before the men could safely try to kill them.

A spear flew. It struck the great bull on his shoulder and lodged there.

Laena heard an angry shout from Mertan, scolding the spear-thrower for his impatience. Meanwhile, the bull was angered by the wound. He charged unexpectedly toward the herders who had followed him into the valley.

They scattered in panic. Laena drew in her breath in dismay. She stared down at the running figures as the big bull mammoth thundered toward them. One boy slipped and fell, then rolled aside just in time to avoid being trampled.

The bull had broken through the line of herders. Only the fires lay between it and the plains beyond. The smoke and flames had deterred it before, but it was in an angry, desperate state now. It just might charge on through.

Faltor was the last man standing between the mammoth and its freedom. He hesitated. Laena found herself holding her breath, willing the beast to turn aside. It was thundering along, right beside the valley wall where she stood. It would pass right beneath her.

She started screaming and whirling her noisemaker—anything to divert the beast. Other people near her joined in. But the mammoth seemed not to hear them. It lumbered onward.

Faltor turned toward the valley wall. He started trying to climb his way to safety. But the wall was steep, and a rock came loose in his hand. He lost his grip and tumbled down with a cry of surprise. He landed on his back on the ground and lay there, looking stunned.

Get up! Laena screamed at him, inside her mind.

He struggled, but the fall seemed to have winded him. He was moving painfully slowly.

Meanwhile, the mammoth was still moving toward him.

Everything was happening too quickly. She screamed at it till her throat felt raw. She was the only person between it and Faltor now. Suddenly she knew that if the beast passed on by, and she failed to deflect it, and it trampled Faltor, it would all be her fault. She would blame herself for the rest of her life—and so would the tribe.

That was too much to bear. As the mammoth thundered beneath her perch, she realized she had to do something. Anything, to stop the beast.

Without thinking, she threw herself forward.

For an instant she saw people on the valley floor staring up at her in astonishment as she fell through the air with her arms and legs spread wide. Then she landed on the back of the beast, hard.

Instinctively, she seized hold of its thick, matted fur. A great wave of fear seized her. The mammoth was lurching from side to side as it ran, and she was almost thrown off. But she twisted her hands in its fur, wrapping the strands around her wrists. Then she screamed as loudly as she could, and tugged hard.

The beast was huge, but not so huge that it could ignore her completely. It turned its head, confused by the burden on its back and the shrill sound coming from up behind its head. It raised its trunk and trumpeted.

Laena screamed again, and jerked the mammoth's fur with all her strength. Meanwhile, she saw with relief, Faltor had rolled over onto all fours and was crawling out of the way. Someone jumped down, perhaps inspired by Laena's own bravery, and dragged him to safety.

The mammoth turned its head back toward the mouth of the valley. Laena had distracted it, but only briefly. Its main goal was still the same: to find its freedom.

The beast lurched wildly under her as it increased its pace. It charged forward, across the piece of ground where Faltor had lain just moments earlier. It headed for a gap between the fires, hesitated, then stampeded through.

It went thundering down the slope from Blind Valley. Laena saw the landscape moving past her, and she felt her pulse pounding. She stared with a mixture of astonishment and terror as she saw the elders in their camp scrambling to get out of the way.

Then the mammoth was running over the open grassland, leaving Blind Valley far behind.

Laena's body hurt where she had landed on the mammoth's back, and her arms felt as if they were being jerked out of their sockets. She tried to judge how high she was off the ground and what would happen if she swung herself down and allowed herself to fall. The drop wouldn't kill her, but the beast's feet might.

She thought of Joq, and she thought of Henik. Why had she done what she did? It had been an uncontrollable impulse. And it had been the right thing to do, for Faltor's life had been saved. But what of her own safety?

She heard faint shouts from behind her. The voices were almost lost on the wind. In any case, there was nothing that anyone could do to help her now.

The mammoth moved over the crest of a low hill and began to slow its pace. It was breathing heavily; she could actually feel the air surging in and out of its lungs.

Just ahead, she saw, was a patch of woodland. The trees were sparse but tall. Laena realized that the mammoth was heading directly for them, to take refuge among them.

It slowed to a walk and started pushing between the high branches. Dense foliage rustled around her, and boughs smacked painfully against her knuckles, her shoulders, and her head.

The mammoth pushed deeper in, where the trees grew taller and closer together. Laena wondered if the branches were thick enough to take her weight. This, surely, was her only hope.

She tried not to think about the sickening gap between herself and the ground. She tried to summon her courage. She balanced herself as well as she could, and reached out with one hand while she held on with the other.

The tips of her fingers brushed the highest branches of a nearby tree. It looked frail, but she was afraid to pass up this chance in hope of something better. Before she could have second thoughts, she lurched up and flung herself out from the mammoth's back.

She seized a branch in both hands. The wood was smooth and cool under her palms. The mammoth moved on, and she felt its fur slide out from beneath her, leaving her dangling with her legs kicking in empty air.

She moaned as she felt the branch bending under her weight. Desperately, she tried to haul herself along it, hand over hand.

But the branch was too weak. There was an agonizing fracturing sound as it slowly peeled away from the trunk of the tree.

Laena screamed as she plummeted down. She glimpsed a flurry of leaves rushing past her face. She saw the ground below her—and then she saw nothing.

Chapter 34

It was terribly cold. Her cheeks felt raw, burned by the cruel wind, and she tried to huddle deeper inside her furs.

But—she had no furs. She was dressed only in a thin leather coat. She shuddered convulsively as she stared in dismay at the drifting snow. Without her furs, she would quickly freeze to death.

She struggled up onto her feet. The wind threw snow into her face, and her eyes started watering, so she couldn't even see where she was going.

She needed shelter immediately, or she would die. She blinked away her tears, laid her numb fingers across her face, and peered through a slit between them. At first, nothing look familiar. Then, with a leap of recognition, she saw the Flat Hills that overlooked the winter camp of her people. The Panther People.

She stared running wildly through the drifts, cupping her hands over her mouth to warm them, at the same time that they warmed the air before it could reach her lungs.

"Turn," a voice spoke.

She stopped. She looked around, and she saw a tawny white panther sitting on a ridge behind her, outlined against the sky. It watched her with huge unblinking eyes.

"I want to go home!" Laena cried.

"This is not your home," the panther said. It started walking toward her, padding effortlessly through the snow.

Laena swayed as a rush of memories overwhelmed her. The trek across the plains; the Wolf Tribe; and Joq. "What am I doing here?"

The panther stopped in front of her. "You are lost."

"No, I was living with the Fisher Tribe—"

"You are lost," the panther said again.

The wind blew harder. "Help me!" Laena cried.

The panther eyed her for a moment, then turned and started heading back up the slope, taking great leaps through the drifts.

"No, don't leave," Laena cried to it.

"You can follow me, if you choose." The panther reached the ridge. It paused and looked at her one last time, then strode over the ridge, and was gone.

The sky up there was a vivid blue.

Laena felt a wave of fear. "Help me!" she shouted. The wind blew harder, making her shake and stumble. She lost her footing and fell on her back. She looked up, and there were faces above her, peering down from the sky. "Help me," she whispered again.

"She lives!" someone cried.

"Can you hear me, Laena?" A face loomed close. It was Weeps, Laena realized. Joq's mother.

"The panther." She tried to turn her head. She felt dry earth under her. She saw a canopy of leaves above.

"She's delirious," someone said.

"No. The fall stunned her."

"She's possessed, more likely."

Laena managed to focus on the person who said that. Worin, she realized. Inevitably.

Laena mustered her strength, as well as she could. "I fell," she said. "I fell from the tree."

Then everything slipped away again.

When she regained consciousness for the second time, the sun had shifted and it was late in the afternoon. But there were no more visions now, and everything was clear. She opened her eyes and saw more people gathered around her. Their faces were marked with concern and wonder.

"Hurts," she murmured. She tried to move, and her back protested. "Hurts!"

"Here." It was Weeps again. "Try to sit up."

Laena's training as a healer came back to her. She might have sustained some broken bones, in which case she shouldn't move. "No," she said. She shivered. "I'm cold."

"Take my coat." One of the elders laid his fur over her.

"We should build a fire," someone else said.

"Not here," said another voice. "You want to set fire to the forest?"

"Why hasn't her husband been brought here?"

"He came earlier, but he had to get back to the hunt," said another voice. Worin's voice again. The woman's blotchy face moved across Laena's line of sight. "Look, she's holding something in her hand." Laena felt fingers prying at her own. "Give it to me."

"No!" Laena made a fist.

"Leave her!" Weeps said. "She needs rest!"

Laena brought her hand slowly to her face. She opened her fingers. A tuft of coarse mammoth hair lay in her palm.

She heard a gasp from the people around her as they saw what she was holding.

Laena looked at their faces. They were so full of wonder at what had happened to her, they weren't concerning themselves with the practical questions. Evidently, if she wanted to find out if there was anything wrong with her, she would have to take care of it herself.

She slowly rolled onto her side, keeping alert for any sign of sharp, slicing pain. Her muscles hurt badly, but no more than she expected. "Pull my coat off," she told Weeps.

The woman kneeled beside Laena, clasping her hands nervously. "But you said you were cold!"

"Just pull it off. See if I'm bleeding."

Tentatively, Weeps did as she was told. "There are some wounds—"

"Are they bleeding?"

"Not now. The blood has dried."

Laena managed to sit up, and the world straightened itself around her. She pulled her coat back on, and winced as she flexed her shoulders.

"You must rest!" Weeps said.

"You've had a bad fall." That was Orleh, standing behind her.

"It's a miracle she wasn't killed," said one of the elders.

"A miracle!" said Weeps, clasping her hands.

There was a general murmur of agreement.

"We should take her back to the village," said Orleh. "Get Nan to look at her."

There was something odd in the way they spoke. Respect, Laena realized.

"Can you help me up?" she asked. All she really wanted

was to tell Joq that she was all right, and then get back to the village, to her child, and to Nan.

Immediately, there were hands reaching to her, lifting her under her arms. "Are you sure you can stand?" Weeps was close by, peering anxiously into Laena's face.

Laena winced. Her head still hurt. She tested her legs, and they felt barely strong enough. "I'm all right," she said.

Weeps and Orleh moved to either side of her. As Joq's parents, they seemed to feel it was their responsibility to look after her. And yet, Laena thought, they had never seemed to feel that way before—even at times when she had been sick.

They walked her slowly through the woods where she had fallen, and the other people who had gathered around came trailing after her. She realized she was retracing the steps that the mammoth had taken. Torn saplings, chunks of mud, and clumps of grass were scattered everywhere, testifying to the power and fury of its journey through the forest.

"Look!" One of the elders pointed up.

Laena craned her neck. The muscles protested, and she gasped with pain. Then she saw a fragment of her coat dangling from a branch high above.

"It's a miracle," Weeps said again.

They headed back across the hillside. As they neared Blind Valley, Laena heard the scream of an animal in pain. "How is the hunt?" she said.

"Almost done," said Orleh.

"I want to see Joq."

They went with her to the mouth of the valley. The herders were sitting by the fires now, resting from their day's work. Evidently, their job was done. But everyone stood up as they saw Laena approach, and she heard them murmuring to each other. Laena saw wonder in their eyes and faces.

"Here she is," someone called. "The one who rode the mammoth."

Laena shook her head, then winced as pain surged behind her temples. "Didn't ride it," she said. She wanted to tell them what had really happened—that she had acted on impulse, without really knowing what she was doing, in a moment of desperation, nothing more.

Meanwhile, she saw that the hunters were down among the beasts now. All of the mammoth were sprawled motionless on their sides, except for one, which was stumbling around, ringed by men with spears. Its coat was red with blood. Its eyes rolled as it tried to see a way to escape the circle of hunters.

One man darted forward and plunged his spear into its neck, just behind its jaw. The mammoth bellowed. It turned toward the man who had struck at it, but two others quickly ran up and thrust their spears into its flank.

The mammoth turned again. It tried to use its trunk to dislodge one of the spears.

"It's almost done," Laena said, half to herself.

Faltor hurried over to her. "Laena! Are you hurt? They said you were unconscious."

She looked at him, and suddenly felt glad and proud. "I'm all right now," she said.

He frowned at her. "What exactly happened?"

Everyone was staring at her again. She wasn't sure exactly what to say. "I saw that the mammoth was going to trample you. I had to stop it. So I jumped."

All around her, people gasped.

Faltor stared at her strangely. "Then you saved my life," the chieftain said.

Suddenly Joq was there, striding toward her. He looked tired and worn after his long day with the other hunters, and he didn't smile when he saw her. He just threw down his spear and stared at her for a long moment, with his fists clenched at his sides. "I told you," he said finally, "I told you it was dangerous. I told you not to come."

Laena blinked. This was not what she'd expected from him.

But then she realized there had been a plaintive note in his voice. And he wasn't angry; he was upset.

He stepped forward and hugged her close. "I'm so glad you're not badly hurt," he muttered with his lips close to her ear, so that only she could hear him. "All day, I've been worrying about you. I don't know what I'd do if anything happened to you."

The river valley was deep in shadow as Laena reached the village. Some boys had run ahead with news of her arrival, and Nan met her out on the path.

"Whatever is this?" She looked quickly into Laena's eyes, then felt her forehead. "Are you all right, girl? Tell me what happened."

Laena shook her head. "In a moment. Can we go to my hut, Nan? Moru should be there, looking after Henik—"

"I'll come with you," said Nan. "Just let me get my things." She ducked into the healer's hut, then came out carrying her pack.

Moru was already standing outside Laena's hut as they approached. "Laena!" she cried. "I was so worried! Some people said you seized hold of a mammoth with your bare hands. I didn't know what to believe. Are you all right? Where's Joq?"

"He's still up at Blind Valley. I just need to lie down." She trotted over to her bed. "Is Henik all right?"

"Yes, he's fine. See?" She held the baby up.

"Listen to me," said Nan. "I want some privacy. Moru can stay, but the rest of you should leave." She turned to Weeps, Orleh, and a cluster of other villagers who were peering in through the open door.

Reluctantly, they backed out. Nan secured the flap over the door, then went back to the bed. "Turn on your stomach," she said. And her swift, knowing hands started scarching and probing.

The examination didn't last long. "You've lost a bit of blood," Nan said, "but there are no broken bones, and the wounds aren't serious." She turned to Moru. "Hot water, please."

Moru had already been heating some water by the fire. She brought it quickly to Nan.

The old lady opened her pack, found a slab of bark, and scraped pulp from it into the cup. She stirred it, then held it out. "Drink."

Laena forced it down, even though the bitter taste made her stomach heave.

Nan hunted around, found Laena's food store, and put Moru to work shredding some meat to make soup. Then Nan went back to Laena and sat beside her. "So," she said. She folded her hands in her lap. "Now tell me."

Laena glanced toward the door. She was sure that there were people outside, listening. "I saw that Faltor was going to be trampled. I was on a high ledge. I didn't think about it. I jumped onto the back of the beast.''

"You *what*?''

"I jumped. I don't know why. I couldn't think of anything else to do. I had to save Faltor.'' She shrugged. "And I did.''

Later, the hunters returned, loaded down with the first of the meat, shouting their pride to the sky. Joq came to Laena and sat with her for a while, holding her. At times like this, it amazed her how gentle and loving he could be. It made her forget all the other times, when she nagged him and he ignored her, or when she told him what she wanted and he obstinately refused.

Outside the hut, Laena heard the sounds of celebration.

"I'll have to join them soon,'' Joq murmured to her. "There'll be a feast—''

"I know,'' said Laena. She clutched his arm. "Joq, I don't know how people are going to react to this. I mean, I saved Faltor's life. But it was rash and dangerous, and maybe foolish besides. I was lucky to live. And I'm a woman, I shouldn't even have been there—'' She trailed off.

Joq was silent for a long moment. "Maybe you should tell them that fate seemed to guide you, and you had to do what you did, because you felt you had no choice.''

Laena nodded slowly. She realized, in fact, that what Joq said was surprisingly close to the truth. She touched his arm and forced a smile. "Thank you.''

She slept for a while. Vaguely, she was aware of talking and shouting in the distance. And then she heard people singing songs.

She woke suddenly. Her muscles were aching even more than before, and her head was throbbing. For a moment she remembered her dream of the panther in the snow; but that was something she still didn't want to think about. She had enough to cope with, without that.

Outside, it was almost dark. Little Henik was lying close beside her, sleeping peacefully. She patted him gently, then struggled up off the bed. Her mouth was dry. She wanted some of the broth that Nan had made.

She sipped it at first, then drank it greedily. She suddenly realized that she was intensely hungry. The smell of roasting meat hung heavy over the village, and she imagined the feasting that was going on. How could she get some of the meat for herself?

Well, she was strong enough. She would put Henik into her pouch and take him with her.

Dressing was an ordeal. She had to pause several times and sit quietly till the pains subsided. Finally, she was ready to leave, with Henik in his pouch, snuggling against her chest.

She had to admit, though, that she was still weak on her feet. She looked around for something to steady herself. Maybe, she thought, she could use her spear. Surely, no one would object if she took it as a crutch.

Grunting with the pain, she stooped and dragged her spear out of its hiding place. Resting heavily on it, she made her way out of the hut.

For some reason, her vision of the panther suddenly came back into her head. She grunted with irritation. "Here is my home," she said to herself as she started down the path beside the little huts. "This village is where I live. It's more of a home to me than any other place has ever been." She hugged her baby against her. "Here is where I belong."

Her visions didn't seem to make sense anymore. Even the one about the poison in the cup seemed plainly and simply wrong. She wished her dreams would just go away and leave her alone.

She heard a new burst of cheering, and then the men of the village started singing one of their hunting songs. She imagined everyone gathered around, their faces flushed and glowing in the firelight. She suddenly wanted very much to be among them all.

And yet, still at the back of her mind, she heard the panther's voice.

Laena struggled on. She passed Faltor's hut and came to the open space where village meetings were held.

It was packed with people. Every living soul of the Fisher Tribe had gathered there. Laena stood for a moment in the shadows, watching as they all sang the hunting song. They cheered at the end of it, and one of the hunters seized a spit that was heavy with chunks of roasted meat. He started taking it around.

Laena pushed forward. "Can I have some?"

People nearby turned and looked at her. Gradually, the noise died down. Suddenly she found everyone staring at her.

"Here she is!" someone shouted. And then all the villagers were on their feet, and they were cheering.

Joq made his way toward her, struggling through the press of people. "Laena!" he cried. "You should be resting!"

"I just wanted some food," she said. She patted Henik, who had been roused by the noise and was starting to yell.

All around, people were beckoning to her, shouting for her to come forward.

Shyly, she hobbled into the firelight.

Faltor stood before her. He held up his arms, and gradually the commotion died down. "I must thank you, Laena," he said, loud enough for everyone to hear. "Thank you, for turning the beast away from me."

She looked up at him. He was smiling.

"She should sit with the hunters," someone shouted. "She deserves to."

Faltor held up his hands for silence. "She may sit with the *junior* hunters," he said. "After all, she has been practicing with a spear." And he gestured to the shaft that Laena was leaning on.

Laena looked again at Faltor, and she saw his talent as a peacemaker. All he wanted, she realized, was to find a path that would please everyone.

She hobbled over to a group of boys who were sitting behind the adult hunters. One youngster quickly jumped up and gestured for Laena to take his place. "Thank you," she said to him.

"No, I'm honored," he replied and bowed to her.

So she sat among them, and someone passed the meat to her. She seized a piece and feasted on it greedily. Everyone cheered her again, and Joq came and joined her. She looked around at the smiling faces, and she thought how strange it all was. That same morning, these people had disapproved of her, and none of them had wanted to talk to her. It was like the day of the joining ceremony, all over again. The only difference was that that time, she had done what everyone was supposed to do. This time, she had done what *she* wanted to do. Did that mean they accepted her as she really was now? She deeply hoped it could be so.

She looked around again. Some of the older people seemed less friendly, and she guessed they didn't approve of a woman getting so much praise and attention. In the future, she had no doubt, there would still be those who stood in her way.

But now she believed it was at least possible for her to achieve what she wanted. That seemed a huge achievement; and as she took her place among the young hunters, she felt deeply thankful.

Chapter 35

Time passed. Winter came, and snow crept down the mountain sides. Ice cloaked the river, the wind blew bitterly cold, and the sun hung so low in the sky that it was hidden behind the mountain peaks even at noon.

The arctic nights grew longer, then longer still. Eventually, as more snow fell and winter tightened its grip, darkness became constant. It was no longer possible to tell when one day ended and another began.

This was Laena's fourth winter with the Fisher Tribe, and she still found it hard to bear. Even in the summer, the narrow valley had tended to seem gloomy and dim. Now, it felt like a prison whose dark walls were closing around her.

She had grown up on the plains, under an open sky. Even in the middle of winter, there had been a faint trace of light to see by. But down here by the river, there was only a slim wedge of sky to peer up at, and as often as not, it was totally black. She felt as if the sun would never return again.

Even the people who had spent their whole lives there showed signs of strain, as the lack of light and the bone-chilling cold made it unwise to venture outside for more than a few moments. Some people became restless and irritable, squabbling incessantly. Others developed a kind of perpetual weariness, so that they slept almost constantly, waking only to eat.

Now that Laena was truly accepted by the tribe, she found herself sharing their lives and rituals more intimately than before. She ate with them, she huddled with them in their huts, and she listened to the legends and stories that the old people told, whiling away the endless dark hours.

The Fishers pressed her to join in the storytelling, and so she found herself reliving the past, trying to remember every tiny detail of her childhood and the years that had followed. She related the death of her parents; she talked about El-brau, the flintknapper; and she described how Gorag had betrayed her people.

She even said a few words about her dreams and visions. The people of the Fisher Tribe didn't laugh, as she had feared. Ever since she had saved Faltor's life, they realized she was unlike any woman they had known before.

One afternoon, as she changed the dry grass that lined Henik's leather diaper, Laena realized that she actually thought of herself as a Fisher now. At the same time, as winter ran its course and the days began to brighten, she found herself thinking how good it would be to walk again on the land around the valley. That was the last relic of her wanderlust: the desire to walk out under the open sky—before returning to the place that was her home.

The last of the big snowstorms had spent itself. The sun was up, and the sky was blue—for a short while, at least.

Thickly swaddled in furs, Laena climbed the side of the valley with three boy-hunters of the tribe. They moved slowly, cautiously, pausing to brush snow from each ledge before they trusted it with their weight.

Then they reached the place where the slope became easier, and one of the boys turned to her, his white teeth flashing in the light that reflected off the snow. "Race you the rest of the way," he said. His name was Orban, and he was the most adventurous of the three, full of young ambition.

"What if you lose?" said Laena. The daylight had cheered her, and she felt playful. "It would be a terrible thing, Orban, if you were beaten by a woman."

Orban laughed loudly. His breath steamed in the frigid air. "I can't lose. I kept myself fit during the winter, when everyone else was sitting around telling stories. I even practiced with my spear."

"Liar!" one of the others shouted at him. His name was Pulo. He was the largest and oldest, which made him feel he should be the leader. "It was too dark outside. You never threw a spear."

Orban turned on him. His eyes narrowed. "Don't call me

a liar, Pulo. I went out and built a fire, and I cast my spears at that.''

Pulo moved toward him. ''That's not true.''

''Hey,'' said Laena. ''Stop.''

They both turned and stared at her. As a mother, she had a voice of authority; but when she was out practicing her hunting skills with them, she was their equal. Sometimes, it was difficult for them to know how to deal with her.

She eyed the slope ahead. It wasn't steep enough to be dangerous, and the snow was thin. ''Come on then, Orban,'' she said. ''I'll race you. Go!'' And she started for the top.

It took him a moment to realize she'd accepted his challenge. ''Hey!'' he shouted.

She heard him scrambling after her. He was fast, but she was ahead of him, and she had spent a lot of her childhood racing up and down snowy slopes. She heard him breathing hard, and she heard the other two boys jeering at him.

Orban narrowed the gap between them by the time she reached the rocky rim of the valley. But she was still just ahead of him. She fell to her knees in the snow, just as he threw himself down beside her. For a moment, both of them lay gasping for breath.

''You cheated,'' he said.

She shook her head. ''I outwitted you. That's not the same at all.''

He glared at her, and she saw with surprise that he was genuinely angry. He was always unpredictable, veering wildly from one mood to another. ''You think you're so clever—''

''I know I'm clever,'' Laena said. ''I don't just think it.''

''She beat you, Orban!'' Pulo shouted, coming up alongside. ''She's a woman. A mother! And she beat you!''

''She beat you, too,'' Orban shouted back.

Laena sighed. The boys were always sparring with each other. She got up and walked ahead, ignoring the two of them as they started wrestling with each other. She deserved more than this, she thought to herself. She had practiced her hunting for two months, before winter set in. That had been her apprenticeship. She deserved to be with the men-hunters now.

"Laena-mother?" The third of the boys came up behind her. He was Olken, the youngest. He seemed shy and withdrawn, and Laena wasn't sure what to make of him.

"Laena-mother," he called to her again. He always used the respectful mode of address, even when she told him it wasn't necessary. "I have a question," he said.

"Then ask it, Olken." She nodded to encourage him.

He paused beside her. He was a plump boy with a wide, fleshy face that made his eyes and mouth look small by comparison. He frowned as he searched for the words that he needed. "I have a sister, Laena-mother." He spoke softly, and she guessed that he didn't want the other boys to hear. "Her name is Yara."

"Yes, Olken. I know your sister."

He gave a curt nod. "She says—she wants to come and practice here with us. She says if you can throw a spear, so can she."

"And what does your father say?"

Olken frowned. "My father says—no."

Laena tried to decide what she should tell him. Now that the Fisher Tribe had accepted her so fully, the last thing she wanted was to create dissent. "Tell your sister," she said, "that when I was young, my father also said no. I had to wait for many years, and I had to prove myself, before it was allowed."

Olken paused, looking deeply serious. "You proved yourself, when you killed a mammoth?"

It was amazing, how the stories of her bravery had been embroidered in just a few winter months. "Olken, I didn't kill a mammoth. I jumped on its back and turned it away from Faltor, that was all."

But he wasn't really listening. The truth, after all, was less interesting than the myth.

Orban and Pulo came up alongside. Either they'd settled their fight, or they'd forgotten about it. "Come on," said Pulo. "We don't have long."

It was true, Laena realized. The sun was low, and the cold was already starting to creep inside her furs.

Pulo slid his spear out of the sling on his back and laid it carefully on the ground. He took off his pack, got out his snow shoes, and laced them. "I'll go make a ball of snow. We can use that as a target."

Laena and the other two boys waited while Pulo went where the snow was deeper, rolled a big snowball, and set it on a ridge a hundred paces away. The landscape was dazzling, after the long months of darkness. Snow carpeted every flat surface and outlined every tiny outcropping of rock. Where it had gathered in drifts, it was as deep as a man was tall.

"All right!" Pulo called. "Try that."

They took turns casting their spears. Laena's muscles were stiff after months of inactivity, and her thick furs made her clumsy. She wondered if Orban really had ventured out and built a fire to aim at. It was possible, she decided. He could be single-minded when he set himself a goal. That was why she liked him, she realized: his determination lifted him beyond the modest ambitions of the other people in the Fisher Tribe.

Sure enough, Orban was the only one to hit the target the first time around. Laena felt irritated, more with herself than with him. After she retrieved her spear, she spent a minute just staring at the ball of snow, focusing herself properly while the others threw.

Finally she tried again. This time, her shaft followed a smooth, clean arc and hit the target squarely. The throw wrenched her shoulder, but she refused to pay attention to that. Pain was unimportant compared with proving her skill. That was the way it had felt in the fall, and that was the way it felt now.

It was Orban's turn to look irritated. No one said anything as they retrieved their spears, but she could see in his face his determination to beat her.

Still, it did him no good. He missed twice during the rest of the afternoon. Laena, however, didn't miss once.

Finally, Orban stopped in disgust. "This is pointless," he said.

Laena looked at him. She waited.

"I practiced in the winter. I really did." He kicked the snow, scattering it like silver sand. "I wanted to be a better thrower than you. But you're bigger and stronger, and you throw straighter." He turned and spat. "You should practice with the men."

Laena smiled. "Yes," she said. "I should."

* * *

Something seemed to have happened in the village while they were gone. Several people were talking excitedly outside the healer's hut.

"What's going on?" Laena asked them. "Is something wrong?"

"It's Inrei," someone said. "A stranger found him outside the village. He's hurt."

Inrei was one of the elders. He had never been very friendly to Laena, and she didn't know him very well, even now.

Laena tried to make sense of what she'd been told. Outsiders rarely came into the valley while the land still lay in the grip of winter. "What stranger was this?" she said.

"A man from the Wolf Tribe," someone else said. "He's with Faltor now."

Laena felt a momentary sense of foreboding. There was no sense to it; she just didn't like to think about the Wolf Tribe, and what had happened years ago. "What happened to Inrei?" she asked.

"He fell and hit his head. He's badly injured."

Laena hesitated, wanting to get back to her hut and care for her son. But the needs of an injured person came first. She was the only one other than Nan who had the skills of a healer. She shrugged off her pack. "Orhan," she said, "take this to my hut. And this." She gave him her spear.

He looked as if he was going to object.

"Quickly now!" Their spear-throwing was over; she was Laena-mother now, and he was a boy.

He gave a curt nod and ran off. Laena pushed into the healer's hut. "Nan? Can I help?"

Nan glanced up, but only for a moment. "Come here and hold him." Her voice was sharp.

Laena saw that Inrei was stretched out on the dirt floor. "Shouldn't we put him on a bed?"

"No. He'd move too much. Hold him!"

Laena squatted down. Inrei's hands were trembling, his body was quivering, and his heels were thudding on the dirt. His old face was pale, and his eyes were closed. There was a bloody dent in his forehead.

Laena seized Inrei's shoulders and bore down with all her weight. Nan wiped away the blood, revealing a jagged hole in the man's scalp. With dismay, Laena saw that a triangle of bone had broken inward.

Nan picked up a flint knife and delicately cut the skin around the wound, making a flap that she peeled back. She wiped away fresh blood, then tried to use a wooden spatula to pry up the bone that had been smashed inward.

"He fell?" Laena asked.

Nan nodded. She grunted with exasperation. "This isn't working." She tossed the spatula aside, then picked up a fist-sized stone. "Kneel on his shoulders, and hold his head."

Laena did as Nan said. Inrei's skin felt cold and damp. This kind of wound, Laena knew, could easily be fatal. Anywhere else in his body, it wouldn't have mattered so much.

Nan drew back the stone, weighed it carefully, then swung her arm and struck Inrei's forehead. The triangle of bone broke free. Nan tossed the stone aside and plucked the bone out.

Inrei spasmed more fiercely, then fell still. His chest moved under Laena in little spasms. He made muffled, throttled sounds in the back of his throat.

Nan gently spread the flap of skin back over the gaping wound, then used wooden tongs to pull a stone out from under the fire in the center of the hut. She touched the stone briefly against the edge of the wound, cauterizing it where blood was still flowing freely.

Nan drew back then. She washed her hands in a leather bowl of water, then wiped them on a square of animal fur. "Help me put him on that bed."

They shifted him as gently as they could. There was a blue cast to the old man's lips, but he was no longer in convulsions.

"Is there anything else I can do?" said Laena.

Nan shook her head.

"Did you see the stranger who brought him in?"

"Yes. He said the Wolf Tribe cast him out, and he was walking by the river when he found Inrei. He said he followed Inrei's tracks in the snow, and they led back here."

"They cast him out?" Laena frowned. "Do you know why?"

"I don't know anything more than I told you." Nan's

voice was gruff. Laena guessed that the old lady was upset that she couldn't help Inrei more.

"Can I go and look at the stranger?" Laena asked.

Nan shrugged. "Why not?"

Laena went back outside. She shivered, and not just because the air was growing colder as the brief daylight faded. She felt something undefined, something out of place.

Several people had been waiting outside the healer's hut. They pressed around her, asking about Inrei.

Laena knew better than to give a definite answer. It could quickly turn into a rumor, and just as quickly, it would become a fact that might have no link with reality. And then, somehow, she would be blamed for it. "You must ask Nan," she said, and she hurried away beside the river.

More people had gathered outside Faltor's hut. They were huddled together—for warmth, as much as anything else. "Can I see?" said Laena. "Please let me through."

Someone glanced at her, and she realized it was Pulo. "It's private," the boy said. "Just Faltor and the elders."

Laena grunted in irritation. "Come on, let me take a peek."

Reluctantly, he edged aside.

She pushed her way to the door flap. It was tied shut, but there was a crack between the leather and the wooden frame.

She peered in. The interior of the hut was flickering yellow, lit by a crackling fire. Laena saw Faltor sitting with his arms folded, deep in thought. The village elders were gathered with him—five old men, huddled in their furs.

Faintly, Laena heard the stranger talking. His voice was deep and resonant. It sounded commanding, even though he was having trouble speaking the language of the Fisher Tribe.

A gust of wind blew, and Laena felt a deeper chill gnawing inside her. She wondered why she felt so strange. Other travelers had come to the tribe during the past four years. Some had been traders; others had merely lost their way. They had told their stories, and they had moved on. None of them had brought any harm or danger.

She shifted so that she could peek across at the other side of the hut. The stranger was sitting there, warming his hands over the fire. His face was hidden by the collar of his furs;

but then he turned his head to one side, and Laena saw his profile.

Time seemed to cease around her. The ground seemed to ripple under her feet. *It can't be,* she thought. And yet, she had looked on that face so often, there was no way she could mistake it now.

The man she was looking at was Gorag, chieftain of the Panther Tribe.

Chapter 36

Laena ran to her hut. She fumbled with the outer flap over the door, then wrestled with the thongs that tied the inner one. At this time of year, everyone kept their doors covered with two or even three layers of heavy leather. "Moru!" she cried. "Quickly, let me in!"

Finally she found herself blundering into the warm, bright little room. Moru was holding Henik in the crook of her arm, looking at Laena with surprise.

Laena blinked in the light. She realized that her chest was aching, and her throat was burning from the cold. She was completely out of breath. She slumped down on the bed and held her head in her hands.

"What's wrong?" said Moru. "Orban came by, he left your pack and your spear, and he said you were at Nan's hut. Is Inrei all right? Joq went out looking for you—"

"Gorag has come to the village."

Moru stared at Laena. "What?"

"Gorag. He's still alive. He found Inrei injured, outside somewhere, and he brought him here."

"*Gorag?*"

"Yes! I just said so!" Laena stared at her sister.

Moru set the baby in his sling and seized her furs. Her movements were quick and tense.

"At first I couldn't believe it," Laena said, "but then I realized, we never really made certain he was dead. He's in Faltor's hut." She shivered. "I peeked in and looked at his face—"

"Give me your spear." Moru was quickly tying her furs.

Laena stared at her. "What?"

Moru stepped forward. "Give it to me!"

Laena stood up. She seized her sister by the upper arms. "No, Moru. Don't be foolish."

Moru wrenched her arms free. There was a wildness in her eyes. "Don't tell me what to do! I made a vow once, remember? I vowed he would die."

Laena stared at her sister in amazement. "You were just a little child then! Listen to me. If you attack him, if you even threaten him, people could take his side against us."

"We are Fishers!" Moru snapped. "The people here are *our* people!"

"Yes," Laena said patiently, "but that's why we must follow their code. The Fishers are peaceful. They never turn their weapons against each other."

Moru wasn't listening. She quickly dragged Laena's spear out from under the bed. The flaps over the door had been left untied; without a word, she tossed them aside and ran out.

Laena watched her, open-mouthed. She started forward— then remembered Henik. He was lying in his sling, staring up at her with surprised eyes. There was no way she could leave him unattended.

Laena cursed silently. She went to the door and peered out. "Moru!" she shouted. "Moru, come back!"

There was no reply.

Maybe she could take Henik with her. But it was very, very cold outside. She hesitated, caught in an agony of indecision. Then she saw a figure looming up in the darkness. It was Joq, she realized.

"What's happening?" He pushed into the hut. "Moru ran right past me."

"Joq, I have to go after her. Look after Henik." And she bolted out of the hut, ignoring his startled protest.

It was almost totally dark outside. She couldn't run, for fear of stumbling off the edge of the bank and landing on the treacherous, frozen river. She struggled along the narrow path, and her feet skidded on frozen mud. Twice she had to dodge around other villagers. Finally, she reached Faltor's hut. A few people were still gathered there.

"Moru!" said Laena, breathing hard. "Where is she?"

The villagers gave her puzzled looks. "She went in," someone said. "She didn't even ask permission."

Laena hesitated. There was a strong taboo against entering the chieftain's hut when he was conferring with the elders. But then she heard Moru's voice, shouting something.

"Let me past." Laena shouldered her way between the villagers. She pulled the door flap aside.

Moru was standing in the center of the hut, holding Laena's spear. It was leveled at Gorag—but Faltor had moved between them, using his body as a shield. He had drawn himself up to his full height and he was scowling, angrier than Laena had ever seen him. The elders were struggling up onto their feet and clustering around Moru. As Laena watched, one of them tried to pull the spear out of her hands. She elbowed him roughly aside.

Laena felt a deep sense of dread as she stared at the scene in front of her. "Moru!" she shouted. "Stop this!"

Everyone turned to look at her. For a moment no one spoke.

"All right, you may come in, Laena," said Faltor. His voice was quiet, but Laena heard outrage in it. "Come and speak sense to your sister."

Slowly, Laena entered the hut. "Moru. Put down the spear. Put it down! Now!"

Moru's grip tightened on the shaft. "I'm not your little sister anymore. You can't order me around." She turned back toward Gorag. "This man betrayed our people."

"This is *not the way.*" Laena seized the shaft quickly. She wrenched it out of her sister's grip.

"No!" Moru shouted.

Laena threw the spear behind her. She grabbed Moru by her arms, then hugged her tight. "Listen to me!"

Moru struggled. Finally she broke loose, looking wild and distraught. She clenched her fists as if she wanted to strike out at Laena. But then she looked at the others who had gathered around her, and her strength disappeared. She slumped down on one of the stools, rested her elbows on her knees, and pressed her hands to her forehead. Silently, she started crying.

"All right," said Faltor. He drew a deep breath, then moved away from Gorag. "Give me that spear."

Laena realized her only hope was to seem calm and obedient. She bent down, picked up the weapon, and handed it to him. He took it from her and laid it aside.

Laena felt Gorag looking at her. She turned and eyed him with a feeling of rage and disgust that was so deep and strong, it seemed to take hold of her stomach and twist her inside. He was just as ugly as she remembered, and he looked just as devious and untrustworthy.

But if Gorag had any idea of the reaction he stirred in her, he showed no hint of it. "Thank you," he said. He smiled as if he was genuinely happy that she had saved him from being attacked by her sister. "Who—are you?" He formed the Fisher words clumsily. His face showed no sign of recognition.

For a moment, Laena couldn't believe he was actually trying to pretend they had never met. "You know who I am!" she shouted at him in the Panther language.

Gorag shrugged and spread his hands. "No understand," he said.

Laena felt her rage mounting higher. "You are lying," she said, now using the Fisher tongue.

One of the elders gestured impatiently. "This is not right or proper. This man is our guest. These girls should not be here."

"You are correct," said Faltor. "But they *are* here, and we must settle this."

"No." The man wagged his old head. "They must leave."

"They will stay," said Faltor. "I have decided, and it is so."

For a moment, the old man seemed as if he would challenge the chieftain's authority. Then he muttered in disgust and sat down. Grudgingly, the other elders joined him.

Faltor turned to Laena. "Are you sure you recognize this man?"

"Of *course* I recognize him!" She stared at Faltor in amazement. "I grew up in his tribe. He was my chieftain. I know him better than I know you."

"Very well. And Moru—you are sure, also?"

"Yes!" she shouted, staring up at him, her cheeks streaked with tears.

"Mistake," said Gorag in the Fisher tongue. "Must be mistake."

Faltor inclined his head. "We will ask you to speak in a moment." He turned back to Laena. "You believe this man committed crimes against your people?"

Laena drew a deep breath. Moru had already fallen victim to her own anger, with repercussions that were as yet unknown. Laena couldn't let herself make the same mistake.

With great difficulty, she fought her rage and brought it under control. "I have told you the story," she said to Faltor in a voice that trembled with emotion. "Gorag led my people to their deaths. He abandoned them while he saved himself. He murdered Elbrau—a man who was a dear friend. And the day I came of age, he—tried to force himself on me."

"My name not Gorag," Gorag said. "My name Alcor."

"Liar!" Moru screamed.

"Please!" Faltor held up his hand. "Laena will finish speaking first."

"Moru defended me from him," Laena went on. "She hit him with a stone. We thought he was dead, and we left him in the river." She shook her head in exasperation. "But I told you all this, long ago. You must remember."

Faltor sighed. "Yes, Laena, but we must be very clear about the facts of this matter. This man came here bringing Inrei, who needed help. We are grateful for that. He says he is from the Wolf Tribe—"

"Wolf People speak like Fisher people," said Gorag. "So, I understand your language."

"Liar!" Moru shouted again. She started up onto her feet.

"That's enough!" Faltor snapped at her. He strode to the door, pulled the flap aside, and peered out. "Banra! Jinkil! Come in here." He stood aside as two hunters strode in. There was barely enough room for them in the crowded space. "Banra, take Moru to the cave where she lives. Stay with her and make sure she doesn't leave. Jinkil, take Laena to her hut. Stay with her and Joq and their child. I will not have this bad behavior in my home."

"But what about Gorag?" Moru cried out as Banra took her arm. "He's the one who should be placed under guard."

"He will be," said Faltor. "He will be watched, I promise you. But we can't settle this while there is so much anger. We will deal with it tomorrow, in the manner of the Fisher Tribe, after I discuss it with the elders." He looked at Moru, then at Laena, and Laena thought she saw just a hint of regret in his eyes. "Both of you must go now. This is not your place. Not at this time."

"This is an insult," Joq said as Jinkil brought Laena into the hut. "Jinkil, we have hunted together. You've known me all my life. How can you be here in my home, treating us as if we are a danger to our own people?''

Jinkil hunkered down by the door and rested his spear across his knees. He was a big man, slow to talk, slow to act, but honest and loyal. Squatting on the floor, he looked as solid and as immovable as a boulder. ''Moru took a spear into the chieftain's hut and threatened his guest,'' he said. He made a little gesture, as if the conclusion were obvious.

Joq looked at Laena, then back at Jinkil. ''Don't you believe what Moru and Laena have to say about this stranger?''

Jinkil shook his head. ''That's not the point, Joq. When one person threatens another, we are all threatened. You know this is so.''

''Of course.'' Joq nodded patiently. ''We can never allow violence among the people of our tribe. But this man Gorag is an outsider, and Laena says he's a murderer.''

Jinkil shrugged. ''We'll find out tomorrow.''

Laena took Joq's arm. ''Let him be,'' she said. She felt weary now. Things had turned out far worse than she feared, and arguing wasn't going to make it any better. She turned to Jinkil. ''I must feed my baby, and then we will sleep. Are you warm enough there?''

He blinked at her. ''I'm all right.''

''Very well then.'' She turned to Henik, picked him up, and took him to the far corner of the hut. Behind her, she heard Joq mutter something. Then he went to the bed and lay on it with his back turned.

At the end of the long night, when the sky finally lightened above the valley, Nan came to the door. Jinkil stood respectfully to let her in. He must have suffered stiff, cold limbs during his vigil, but he hadn't complained. It was his nature to do exactly what the chieftain said; anything else was unthinkable.

Joq had been sitting and playing one of his flutes. When he saw Nan, he tossed the reed aside and jumped up. ''How long do we have to be trapped in our home like this?'' he cried without any preliminaries.

Nan gave him a measured look. ''Where are your manners, young man?''

Joq clenched his fists. "It's not right—"

"Sit down and be quiet. I can only stay here a short while, and I have to talk to your wife."

Joq stepped back, blinking as if she had slapped his face. But her tone of voice left no room for argument.

Nan walked over to Laena and hugged her. For a moment the two of them stood with their arms around each other and their eyes closed, saying nothing.

Finally, Nan pulled back. "Your foolish little sister—"

"I know," said Laena.

Nan shook her head. "Men will say that this is why women should not be allowed to have weapons. That's not the point, of course, but—" She sighed. "We'll try to make the best of it."

"Are people talking about us?" Laena asked.

"Are they?" Nan laughed without humor. "A young girl forcing her way into the chieftain's hut is scandal enough. When she threatens a man with a spear, and her sister comes running in as well, and neither is a Fisher by birth—" She spread her hands. "What do you expect? And this is the worst possible time for it. Everyone's restless and edgy after the long winter."

"But I saved Faltor's life last year," Laena said. "Doesn't that count for anything?"

"Of course. Of course it counts. That's why we want to resolve this with justice, Laena." She gave her a steady, meaningful look, as if she were trying to tell Laena something. Then she took Laena by the shoulders and gave her a little shake. "Listen carefully," she said. "In the middle of the day, when it's warmer outside, they will test the truth. With the hot stone. You understand?" Her eyes narrowed. "It's a custom I told you about once."

Laena thought back, and she remembered. A stone was heated in a fire, then touched against a person's tongue. The tongue of a liar would blister; the tongue of a truthful person would not. That, at least, was the way it was supposed to be.

Laena felt a wave of anger. "They think I'm a liar?"

"No!" Nan's voice was sharp. "They want to prove that you aren't. Then there can be no rumors, no arguments, no more complaints about the way Moru acted. You see?"

Laena shook her head. "Surely, Faltor believes me."

Nan glanced cautiously at Jinkil, then back at Laena. "Maybe he does. But he must follow the customs of the tribe. Where there is a dispute, it has to be resolved so that absolutely everyone is satisfied."

Laena closed her eyes. She didn't want to have to go through with this.

Nan shook her sharply again. "Laena! If you pass the test, and everyone sees that you pass it, then everything will be all right. You see?"

Laena nodded. "I see."

"So. You'll be all right." Nan released her.

Joq had been listening with an expression of growing anger. "But, this is wrong!" he shouted.

Nan turned to him. "Joq, there is no right or wrong here. There is only the will of the people. And your chieftain serves them."

"Then he's wrong, too!" Joq blurted out. He suddenly seized his spear, raised it, and thrust it down, sinking its point into the packed earth of the floor.

Nan turned back to Laena. "You'll be all right," she said again. "Just remember what I told you, that time, long ago."

"What about Inrei?" Laena asked as Nan turned to go. "How is he?"

Nan paused. Her face became troubled. "He died during the night. There was nothing I could do for him." She gestured for Jinkil to open the door flap. "I must leave now."

At noon, when weak winter sunlight touched the mountains overlooking the valley, Laena wrapped her baby against the cold and walked out, escorted by Joq on one side of her and Jinkil on the other. All the villagers were emerging from their homes, heavily muffled against the fierce cold. They gave Laena quick, nervous glances, and they said nothing.

Weeps and Orleh were waiting for her near the meeting place. Weeps held out her arms, and for a moment Laena imagined that the woman wanted to comfort her. But that was not the case. "Give me Henik," Weeps said. "I'll look after him, dear."

Laena considered refusing. But this was not the best time

to be rebellious. It seemed outrageous to her that she should have to prove herself, but clearly there was no other way.

She hugged Henik and kissed him. Then, reluctantly, she handed him to Weeps. "I'll be back for him soon enough," she said.

Weeps nodded grimly. "I hope so," she said. Quickly, then, she turned away.

"You think my wife is lying?" Joq shouted at his mother.

"Quiet," said Orleh. He gave Joq an angry look.

"Why should I be quiet?" His voice was getting louder.

"Please, Joq." Laena gripped his arm. "Please, for my sake, don't make this worse."

He turned toward her, looking as if he were in pain. "Laena, you know, if you fail—"

She shrugged. "If I fail, I will be cast out. But why should I fail? Don't *you* think I'm telling you the truth?"

"Of course you are!" He looked stricken.

"Well, then," said Laena, "everything will be all right."

For a moment he looked as if he would cry. "I never want to be without you," he said suddenly.

Laena felt moved by his strong, simple sincerity. She reached up and stroked his face. "I won't fail," she told him. "Just believe me."

"Come," said Jinkil. He had been waiting patiently. "It's time."

Joq seized Laena and hugged her. He squeezed her so tightly, she felt as if he would crush her. Then he turned away without another word.

Laena went with Jinkil into the meeting place. Almost all the villagers had already gathered there. Everyone was heavily muffled against the cold, and a big fire burned brightly, melting the frozen mud around it. Faltor stood with his arms folded, staring solemnly out above the flames. Moru was already standing to his left. Laena went and took her place close by.

Moru seized Laena's hand. "I'm sorry," she whispered. "I should have listened to you. But I spent so many months hating Gorag—"

"Shh. That was yesterday. We have to concern ourselves with today."

Moru blinked back tears. She nodded dumbly.

Laena embraced her sister and used the opportunity to

move her lips close to her ear. "Do you remember, long ago, Nan told us how truth can be tested with a hot stone?"

Moru nodded. "Yes, I remember."

"You remember what Nan told us about it?"

"I think so." She hesitated. "Moisture on the tongue—"

"Yes," said Laena, afraid that someone might overhear. "So, there is nothing to worry about."

"But if we fail—"

"We won't fail."

There was no more time for talk. Gorag was led in by a pair of hunters, and he was placed at Faltor's right. He looked amiable and self-assured, and he smiled and nodded to everyone gathered around, as if he couldn't understand what all the fuss was about. If Laena hadn't known him, she would have thought he was a decent, innocent man.

"My people," said Faltor. His voice was loud above the crackling of the fire, and the villagers ceased their murmuring. The only sound was of a crying baby. Laena looked quickly and saw Weeps holding Henik; but Henik was lying peacefully. It was someone else's child who was fretting.

"Inrei's spirit has left us," Faltor went on, more quietly now. He took a beaded leather wristlet from his arm and threw it in front of him, into the fire. This was his tribute.

The crowd stirred. Everyone started casting mementos into the flames—necklaces, tools, whatever a person carried that had meaning to him. Laena realized that Inrei had already been cremated here, while she had been kept in her hut.

Gorag watched the ritual. In the Panther Tribe, out on the plains where resources were scarce, possessions had been far too valuable to be donated to the dead. But he evidently understood what was happening. He kneeled down, opened the pack that he had placed at his feet, and took out a finely made spearhead. He held it up, then cast it into the fire, and there was a murmur of appreciation from the crowd.

"This is the fire of Inrei's spirit," Faltor said, his voice carrying far in the silence. "The smoke of his burning will carry him back to the wind that made us all. But I ask, before he goes, that he will help us find the truth in a matter that now troubles us deeply."

Faltor stooped and picked up two long sticks. Using them as tongs, he squatted down and pushed three round, white stones toward the edge of the great fire. He backed away from the heat, shielding his face with his hand.

"Now," he said. "We will hear Laena speak."

Laena glanced quickly at the faces turned toward her, and she saw tense expectancy in every one. She tried to ignore the crowd, and she looked up at Faltor, hoping to find the kindness and understanding that she had seen so often before. But she searched in vain; his face was expressionless. *He has to seem that way,* she told herself. *Otherwise, his people will think he's taking my side.* Still, she felt a hollowness in her stomach.

"Who is this man?" Faltor said, gesturing to Gorag.

Be strong, Laena told herself. *Speak clearly, and show no doubt.* "He was the chief of the Panther Tribe," she said. "I have told you about him, many times. He betrayed my people, he murdered my friend, and he tried to force himself on me."

Her voice was loud, and it sounded self-assured. People murmured to one another, and she saw they were impressed. *So they should be,* she thought to herself.

"You could be mistaken," said Faltor, more gently now.

Laena drew herself up. "I was born into his tribe. I saw him every day, through my whole childhood, till the day I became a woman." She felt more sure of herself now. "There is no possible doubt. He is the one."

"Very well." Faltor bent down, reached for the wooden tongs, and plucked the first stone from the fire. Its heat made the stick smolder.

Laena knew what she had to do. Nan had explained that a person who lied would have a dry mouth, so it would be more easily burned. To pass the test, her tongue should be as moist as possible. Her saliva would protect her from the heat of the stone.

That had sounded simple enough. But now she faced the reality, and she was scared. She felt her knees quiver as Faltor raised the stone toward her, and she tried desperately to moisten her mouth. She imagined that she was chewing a large, succulent lump of meat. She imagined its juices flowing.

"Hold out your tongue," Faltor said. His voice was soft; and now, as Laena looked up at him, she saw the compassion she had searched for.

Still, it couldn't help her escape the ordeal. Laena thrust out her tongue and closed her eyes.

She felt the heat of the stone on her face. She smelled the scorching tongs. Then there was a brief contact, and a hissing noise. She felt a little stab of pain, as if she had pricked her tongue with a shard of flint.

Then it was over.

She opened her eyes and found Faltor bending close, studying the skin at the tip of her tongue. "I see no mark," he said.

Two of the elders stepped forward. They, too, inspected her. "No blistering," one of them said. The other nodded his agreement.

Laena felt a great wave of relief. She would not lose her tribe, or her child, or her life. She experienced a sudden, desperate need to sit down; but she denied it. This was still no time to show weakness.

Faltor turned to the people gathered around. "Her tongue spoke truly."

There was excited murmuring, and some shouts of approval. But Faltor held up his hands. "We still have two more stones," he said. He turned to Moru. "It is your turn."

Moru nodded. She seemed calm now that the moment had come.

"Why did you enter my hut," Faltor asked, " and raise a spear against this man?"

"He abandoned my parents, he killed my sister's friend, and he led our tribe to its death." She shouted the words and stared around as if challenging anyone to doubt her.

"But this man says he doesn't know you," Faltor said.

"He is a skilled liar. That is what makes him so dangerous."

"You will not even consider that you are wrong?"

She shook her head. "I apologize for entering your hut and for raising a weapon. But, I am not wrong."

Faltor nodded. He retrieved the second stone. Moru thrust out her tongue without being asked to do so, and Laena watched, feeling her stomach clench. She saw Faltor bring the hot stone close to her sister's face. Moru stood with her eyes closed, unflinching. There was a tiny hiss, and then Faltor tossed the stone aside.

He examined her, then motioned the elders forward. Each one peered closely. "She is not burned," Faltor said at last.

This time, the people were noisier. They were turning toward Gorag, shouting for him to be cast out.

"Wait!" Faltor shouted the word. He held up his arms. "There is still one more stone!"

Gradually, the people quietened. Faltor stood with his arms raised until, once again, there was complete silence.

He turned to Gorag. "Tell us," he said, "who you are."

Gorag glanced uneasily at the people gathered around the fire. "I am Alcor, an innocent man." He spread his arms. "I am a trader. I carry fine tools and spearheads from tribe to tribe."

Faltor gave a curt nod. "So you have told us. You still claim this is true?"

"Of course! Why should I lie?" Once again he seemed a picture of total innocence.

"How is it you were out traveling at this time of year?" Faltor went on.

"Life is changing, west of here," he said. "Each summer is warmer than the last. The seas are rising. There is less land for animals to graze on. There are more people, and there is less food. The Wolf Tribe let me stay with them through most of the winter, but when the days started growing lighter, and their stores of food were almost gone, they told me to move on."

Laena listened and realized that this, at least, could be true.

"I found a cave," he continued. He had everyone's attention now. They were listening carefully. "A bear was sleeping in the cave. I killed the bear and stayed there for several days. Then, when I was out gathering firewood, I found your friend." His face turned solemn, as if the death of Inrei troubled him still. "He had fallen and hurt his head. I wanted to save him, so I carried him here, following his tracks—" He shrugged. "The rest you know."

Faltor shifted impatiently. "But who are you? Isn't it true that your name is Gorag?"

"No. I am Alcor." He looked genuinely puzzled.

"You were not the chieftain of the Panther Tribe?"

"No. No, this is all a mistake."

"You do not know Laena here, and her sister, Moru?"

"I have never seen them before," said Gorag. He gave a nervous cough and covered his mouth politely with his hand.

"Very well," said Faltor. He bent down and picked up the last of the stones. It had been sitting beside the flames for much longer than the others, Laena realized, and it must be correspondingly hotter. Was that an accident? Had Faltor tried to arrange the test so that she would be favored by it?

"You agree to be tested by the stone," Faltor said.

"Of course." And Gorag thrust out his tongue.

Faltor dabbed it with the stone, then held Gorag's chin and peered at his tongue. There was a long, deep silence. "I see no burn," Faltor said finally.

The elders murmured to each other in dismay. They stepped forward to check his judgment, but already the crowd was pushing forward and voices were being raised in anger and confusion. Laena glimpsed Gorag holding up his hands, as if he wanted to keep the people away from him. She saw a small black pebble fall at his feet. Had someone thrown it?

"Witchcraft!" The voice was shrill, and Laena knew at once who it belonged to. Yes; there was Worin, pointing at her, staring at her with a face full of hate. "The Panther woman is a fraud! She is a witch!"

"Quiet!" Faltor shouted, but this time his people were not so easily calmed. "The stones have failed," he called out over the heads of the people. "I will devise a different test. We will return here again tomorrow." He turned to his hunters, who were glancing uneasily at each other. "Jinkil, Banra, take Laena and Moru to the cave where Moru lives. They will remain there together. Quickly now! Mertan, take our visitor to your hut."

"Who is the liar?" someone was shouting. "We need to know who lies!"

"Tomorrow," Faltor said. "We will settle this tomorrow. There's no need for haste. No need for violence."

"A witch," Worin screamed again. "Cast her out! She is a witch!"

Then Jinkil seized Laena's arm and hustled her away from the meeting place.

Chapter 37

The cave smelled damp. It was horribly cold. The sky outside was fading from gray to black as the short day ended, and there was barely enough light for Laena to see her sister's face.

The two of them huddled together, saying nothing, while Jinkil made a fire. The sputtering, crackling wood drove away some of the gloom and spread a little warmth, but Laena still felt desolate. "It seems so unfair," she murmured to Moru as they hugged the yellow flames.

"Blame me, not fate," said Moru. "I caused all the trouble."

"No," said Laena. "It was fate that brought Gorag out of our past. He provoked you. Don't blame yourself."

They lapsed into silence. The tang of wood smoke mingled with the musty smell of the furs and the comforting presence of her sister's body, and Laena tried to forget that she was being held prisoner by her own tribe. She remembered all the times that she and Moru had traveled together, first on their own and then with Nan. Those times had been difficult, and she had feared for her life; and yet now the memories seemed comforting.

"I still don't understand," Moru said after a while, "how Gorag passed the test."

Laena rubbed her eyes. They were sore from the smoky fire. "He must have heard about the test, or seen it done somewhere." She thought for a moment. "I saw something odd, just after the elders examined him. A pebble fell at his feet. But no one seemed to have thrown it."

"Maybe he sucked on it," said Moru. She sat up, and some life came back into her voice. "He could have sucked it to help wet his mouth, so his tongue wouldn't burn. Laena, he cheated! Should we tell Faltor?"

"It makes no difference." Laena hugged her sister. "There's no proof."

"But I speak truly! I always do!"

"Hush." Laena tried to quieten her. "You saw how Gorag behaved. He didn't show any anger. He seemed good-natured when we accused him. He even made a tribute to Inrei's spirit." She sighed, feeling despair taking hold of her again. "He's an outsider; and yet, in a way, so are we. They want to believe us, but they want to be sure, too. That's why they want to test the truth."

A faint shout came from outside. It sounded like a woman's voice.

Jinkil had taken up a position near the mouth of the cave. He peered out. "Who's there?" he called.

"Help me up." It was Nan's voice. "I've brought some food."

Jinkil reached down, and there were sounds of hands and feet scraping across rock. Finally, Nan struggled into the cave, panting from the exertion. "I *swore* I'd never come up here again," she complained. "I was too old for this climb four years ago, when you were still living here, Laena." She crouched near the fire, set down a leather sack, and started pulling provisions out of it.

Laena watched without much interest. She realized that Nan was being kind, but it didn't really change anything.

"Here." Nan set out chunks of freshly roasted meat and a leather bottle. She paused and looked at Laena and Moru. "I declare, the two of you look like a pair of orphans, huddled together like that."

"We *are* orphans," Moru said. "Had you forgotten?"

Nan looked annoyed. "Listen to me. This will all be settled tomorrow. You can count on it."

"I'm not hungry, anyway," said Laena.

Nan glared at her. "You need your strength."

Laena pulled the furs up around her face. "Nan, I'm tired of having to be strong."

"Laena!" Her voice had a sharp edge. "You listen to me!"

Laena realized, suddenly, she had had enough of being lectured. "Why should I have to listen all the time? No one listens to *me*."

"That's no way to talk to an elder. There're some things I can tell you—"

Moru leaned forward. "You already promised everything would be settled today, Nan."

"Faltor knows we're not lying," Laena said. "I'm sure of it. So why doesn't he just say so, and order Gorag to leave the village? That would be the end of it."

Nan gave her an angry look. "A good leader doesn't impose his will on his tribe. He finds out what the tribe wants, and he helps them to achieve it. That's how the Fisher Tribe maintains its peace and harmony."

Laena's hands tightened on her furs. She felt a wave of frustration. "But a leader is supposed to lead, isn't he? He gives people something to believe in. He doesn't trail along after them like a—a lost child."

Nan gave her a measured, warning look. "You should speak a little less loudly," she murmured. She nodded toward Jinkil, sitting at the other side of the fire. He wasn't looking directly at them, but from his expression, he didn't like what he heard.

Laena realized that once again, the old lady was right. Her anger drained away, leaving her with nothing but her despair. "The trouble is," she said, "I can see that some people are going to turn against me again. They're going to think the worst of me no matter what I do. They say I'm a witch—"

"That's just Worin. No one takes her seriously."

"I'm not so sure." She broke off, because she couldn't hold back the tears any longer. She missed Henik terribly, and she craved the strength that came from having Joq beside her. "I want my husband, Nan. And I want my baby. Why did Faltor banish me here in this cave? It's all so wrong."

"He put the two of you here for your own safety," Nan said. She sighed. "Look, I'll do what I can." She started shuffling toward the mouth of the cave. "I care about you. You know that. But I'm not the chieftain, and I can't tell people how to make up their minds."

Laena didn't answer.

"I'll do what I can," Nan repeated.

"Thank you for the food," Moru called after her.

Nan nodded. "I'll bring you more in the morning."

Jinkil lowered her out of the cave, and then she was gone.

Laena felt deeply weary. "I'm going to try to sleep," she said.

Moru started tearing at one of the chunks of meat. "You don't want anything to eat?"

"No." She curled up on the bed of boughs, remembering all the nights when they had slept here alone together. "I just want to forget about things for a while."

Moru opened the leather bottle. "How about some of this? It's redberry, and it's warm. She heated it for us." She poured a measure into a birchbark cup and held it out.

"No," Laena said again.

"I'll take some." It was Jinkil's voice. "I could use it."

Laena lay with her eyes closed while Moru and Jinkil devoured their share. Food didn't seem very important anymore. Nothing seemed important, so long as she was in exile here.

Someone was talking to her. "I'm sorry, Laena," the voice was saying. "I can't help you now. No one can help you. You must help yourself."

She realized with a shock that she was sinking into deep, dark water. She was in the river. The ice had all melted, and the water was surging around her, lapping at her cheeks. It was terribly, terribly cold. She had to struggle to breathe.

A face loomed over her. It was Faltor, she realized, and the voice, too, had been his. But his face was huge; it seemed to fill the storm-torn sky. "I cannot help you," he said again, and the words boomed and echoed between the mountains.

Laena felt herself being lifted by the black water and swept downstream. Something brushed across her face, and she realized it was a root dangling from the riverbank. She seized it, and it sliced into her hands, but still she managed to hold on to it. "Please!" she gasped.

Now, when she looked up, Faltor's face had changed. It was webbed with wrinkles. His hair was longer, and it was white. "I have protected you." His voice was old and tired. "For many years, I protected you. But now you must protect yourselves."

She felt a spasm of fear as she realized that she was no longer looking at Faltor, but at the face of Orwael, his great-

great-grandfather. The knowledge made her tremble inside, for she had never confronted a spirit before. "If you cease to protect us," she said, "we will die!"

The water heaved under her. She felt as if she were riding a huge wave. The root was dragged out of her hand, and she was flung forward. Directly ahead, huddled close together on the riverbank, she saw the huts of the Fisher Tribe, looking frail and vulnerable. They seemed to race toward her, and Laena saw what was about to happen. "No!" she shouted.

Her voice was lost in the rushing and roaring of the water. The river surged up and overflowed its banks. It seized the huts, dragged them off their shelf of rock, and swept them away.

Laena heard people screaming. She saw faces in the flood, men and women struggling helplessly as they were sucked under the churning surface.

And then, inexplicably, she was on the shore. She was wet and shivering, but she was alive. "It is time," said a voice.

She turned and saw with amazement that the landscape behind her was transformed. The river snaked placidly between grassy banks. The sun was high above, and the sky was blue. The white panther was standing close by, with its cub frolicking in the grass.

"Laena, it is time," the panther said. "You will have to leave. It is the only way." The panther lowered its head and lifted its cub gently in its jaws. It turned and started walking toward the south.

"Wait!" Laena called after it. She tried to move, but her limbs seemed paralyzed. "Please, wait!" As she watched the panther go, she felt she was losing something infinitely precious, more valuable to her than life itself. She struggled against the invisible hand that seemed to pin her immobile.

Then the ground shifted under her. She felt herself being lifted. Was the flood coming again? No, she realized, this was not a dream. She opened her eyes and she was back in the cave. She was shivering, her skin felt numb from the cold, and her bones were aching. The fire had almost burned out. She blinked, wondering if Jinkil had allowed himself to fall asleep. Surely not. He would never—

Hands lifted her again, under her arms. She was being dragged toward the mouth of the cave.

Laena's dream was still vivid in her head. She struggled to understand what was happening. "Moru!" she called.

The figure who had been dragging her suddenly drew back, and Laena heard a grunt of surprise. Hands released her. She thumped down onto the cave floor.

Her muscles were throbbing and tingling from the cold. She struggled up onto her elbow, trying to see the mysterious figure who was still looming over her. But then, without warning, he seized her around the throat. His hands clenched hard. *Who?* she asked herself. And then, just as quickly, she knew.

Fear swept the last of her drowsiness away. She saw the face of her attacker in the faint firelight, and yes, there was no doubt that it was Gorag now.

His hands were as powerful as a tourniquet around her throat. Her head started throbbing, and the pain was intense. She seized his wrists and tried to drag them apart. But he was far too strong. She tried to gouge his face with her nails, but he lowered his head and managed to avoid her grasping fingers. And all the time, his thumbs were on her throat, pressing harder, deeper, so that she wanted to scream with the pain. But she couldn't scream. She couldn't breathe. Little flashes of light started sparkling inside her eyes. She felt herself getting dizzy.

He had come here to kill her. He could have already killed Moru. That thought created panic—then rage that overwhelmed her fear. She groped desperately on the floor of the cave and found a loose piece of rock. She flailed wildly and struck Gorag on the side of his face. He grunted, and his grip faltered for a moment.

Laena struck him again, and again. He gasped in pain, and she felt warm, wet droplets spraying across her cheek. His hands released her.

She took a desperate breath and tried to struggle up off the ground. But she was still dizzy. She fell painfully on her side.

Gorag was fumbling for something under his furs. He pulled out his hand, and a flint knife gleamed in the faint firelight.

Laena tried to throw herself past him, toward the mouth

of the cave. She lost her balance and rolled into the remains of the fire. Gorag seized her ankle, but she kicked out and felt her heel hit his face. She reached for Jinkil and dragged herself toward him. "Wake up!" she shouted.

He didn't stir. Was he dead? Either way, Laena realized he wasn't going to be any help to her. She scrambled forward, lost her balance, and found herself suddenly plummeting into the night.

There was a horrible moment in which her head felt as if it would burst, and she was falling freely, turning as she fell, with the dark landscape of the valley spinning around her. Then her shoulders thudded into deep snow. For a moment she lay on her back. She tried to shout for help, but her lungs wouldn't work properly. The impact had winded her.

Clumsily, she tried to sit up. She reached out and found something beside her. Something warm. A person's face.

Laena gave a little cry of horror. She peered into the darkness, and she managed to draw a shaky breath. "Moru?" she called.

The body didn't stir.

Laena shook her furiously. "Moru! Wake up!"

She heard a scrabbling noise from directly above. A large black silhouette was climbing down the cliff toward her. "No!" Laena shouted.

Gorag's black silhouette pushed away from the cliff. He spread his arms, fell on her, and knocked her backward into the drift. Once again the knife was in his hand.

"Help!" Laena screamed. "Help me!"

"Quiet!" He seized her by the hair and pressed his knife against the side of her throat. "Be quiet, and I'll let you live."

He was speaking in the old Panther tongue. She looked at his face looming over her, and she remembered all the times he had lied to her people. "No!" she screamed. With a spasm of pure fury, she reared up and butted him with her forehead.

He grunted with pain, and Laena pulled free. "Help!" she screamed again.

He groped for her in the darkness. Laena rolled away and managed to struggle onto her feet in the snow. Then she saw a light—faint at first, sputtering and flickering. Someone was emerging from one of the huts, a hundred paces away, holding a torch made of oiled twigs. She heard him call out: "What's happening out here?" It sounded like Mertan's voice. But he was too far away. He wouldn't even be able to see her.

Laena turned, fearing another attack from Gorag—but she found him raising his hands, shielding his face from the faint torchlight, retreating toward a dark gap between two huts. He didn't want to be recognized, she realized.

Laena went after him, floundering through the drifts. She was dazed, she was scared, but she couldn't let him escape; couldn't let him evade justice yet again. She threw herself forward, seized the collar of his coat, and jerked backward as hard as she could.

Gorag flailed his arms and staggered to one side. He regained his balance and whirled around, breathing heavily. He raised his knife as a warning to her.

She was desperate to hold him here for a few precious moments, till Mertan or someone else from the tribe had time to come upon them and see what had happened. But he scythed his arm, and the flint blade was a gleaming streak aimed at her face.

Laena ducked below the swinging blade. Then she lunged forward, butting him in the stomach. He fell backward, slamming into the hut behind him.

He made a growling sound in the back of his throat, levered himself away from the hut, and tried to slash at her again. She made as if to duck a second time—but then, instead, she reached up and grabbed his wrist. She bit into it with all her strength.

Gorag yelled and groped for her face with his free hand. Laena clenched her jaw as hard as she could, and tasted his blood. She felt his tendons bending under her teeth. And finally the knife fell out of his hand.

She felt an urge to bite deeper and still deeper—but he was far stronger than she was, and she had to be quick. She let go of his wrist, dropped down onto her knees, and groped in the snow till her fingers found the flint knife.

He roared with rage and started after her, but she quickly backed away, holding the knife up near her face with its point toward him. She was trembling, she realized—shaking all over. Breath was rasping painfully in and out of her lungs. "Stay away from me!" she shouted at him.

His lips pulled back from his teeth. He groped in the snow, found a heavy rock, and raised it in both hands. Then he moved forward, raising the rock to hurl it at her.

Laena flung herself forward. She glimpsed his throat, naked and unprotected. She clenched her hand around the knife, brought her arm up, and stabbed the blade into the side of Gorag's neck. The knife thrust deep, driven by her wild fear and rage. It thrust so deep, she couldn't pull it back out, and she lost her grip on it.

Blood started surging around the flint. Gorag slumped down, shouted in outrage, and tried to hold his hand over the wound.

There were more voices behind Laena. She turned and saw Mertan leaping toward her through the deep snow. "Laena! Laena, are you all right?"

"It's the stranger," someone else was saying. "He attacked her."

Suddenly everyone was around her. Mertan's hands caught her under her arms, steadying her. She blinked in the brightening torchlight, and she looked at their faces. She was dizzy, still shaking all over and gasping for breath.

But she hadn't forgotten her sister. She pointed to the snow below the mouth of the cave. "Moru. Moru's lying there. He may have killed her. And Jinkil, too, up in the cave." She managed to pull free from Mertan, and she stumbled through the drifts. The wavering light made the world fearsome and strange, so that solid rocks seemed to waver around her like heat mirages. "Moru!" she cried. And then she almost tripped over her sister lying in the snow.

"Here." It was Mertan's voice. "Let me see her."

"Fetch Nan!" Laena shouted. "Quickly! Fetch Nan!"

"Hush, child." Nan was suddenly there beside her. She gave Laena an anxious, searching look, then squatted down, reached out, and touched Moru's face. She felt the side of her throat. "She lives." She turned quickly. "Take her to the healer's hut."

Two young hunters stepped forward. "Is she dead?" one asked.

"I already said she's alive," Nan snapped. "Take her to the hut, put her by the fire, and keep her warm."

"You're sure she's all right?" Laena clutched at the old lady. "Nan, is Moru all right?"

"Yes! Be calm, Laena. Whatever has been happening here?"

Laena turned. "Don't let Gorag get away!"

"Calm down now." It was Faltor's voice. His face loomed over her and Laena gave a little cry, remembering her dream. It had been true, she realized: there was no one to help her. She had to help herself.

"Why are you out of the cave?" Faltor demanded.

Laena was still half out of her mind with the fear of what had almost happened to her, but she still felt angry at the injustice that she had had to endure. "Gorag attacked me." She turned and saw him still lying in the snow, clutching his throat, his face contorted with pain. "I warned you about him, but you wouldn't listen to me. You wouldn't listen!"

Faltor took a step back, looking shaken by the force of her outburst. "Where is the stranger?" he said.

"There!" She pointed.

Faltor turned and looked. His face became even more troubled, and Laena suddenly saw him more clearly than she ever had before. *He's scared,* she realized. *He hates violence. He'll do anything to keep the peace—because he's afraid of the alternative.*

"People, go back to your homes," Faltor said, turning to the villagers who were gathering around. "We will settle this calmly and quietly—"

"No!" Laena shouted. "No, we should settle it now, in front of everyone!"

Suddenly, there was silence. The villagers stared at her. No one seemed to believe she could have spoken the way she did.

Laena felt a moment of misgiving. Was she making the same mistake that Moru had made, letting her anger lead her into even worse trouble? No, she told herself. She had to seize this moment; otherwise, it would slip away from her, and anything could happen. The people would see her, still alive, and Gorag, wounded by the knife she had wielded. There was no way of telling what conclusions they would come to, if no one told them what had actually happened.

She reached back and found the cliff behind her. She

steadied herself against its cold, hard surface. "Look at him!" she shouted. She pointed at Gorag. "He came into the cave where we slept. He killed Jinkil. He dragged Moru out and threw her into the snow. He came back for me, and he would have taken me, too. He attacked me with a knife. And there was no one to help me. You were all asleep in your homes. I had to defend myself against him."

The villagers started murmuring to each other.

"Laena, please," Faltor said, but his voice was barely audible among the voices of his people.

"Help me," Gorag called out to them. "I'm bleeding. Please, help!"

Nan pushed forward. "Let me near him."

"Laena attacked me," Gorag said. His voice wavered. "I had to defend myself."

"Does anyone here believe that?" Laena stared into each person's face.

Their voices died down. There was a sudden, worried silence.

Laena searched their faces, feeling desperate. Finally, she saw Mertan. "Tell them!" she cried.

"It's true that the stranger tried to attack her," Mertan said. "She managed to take the knife away from him, and then he tried to kill her with a rock. She struck at him in self-defense."

Laena looked up at him. She felt a wave of relief. "Thank you," she said with deep gratitude.

"You fought like a cat," said Mertan. "I couldn't get close enough in time to help." He shook his head. "I've never seen a woman fight that way."

A hand touched Laena's arm. "Laena, are you all right?"

She turned quickly. "Joq!" she cried. She threw her arms around him and held him, so grateful for his presence.

"I can't stop the bleeding," said Nan. She was kneeling beside Gorag. "I'm afraid that if I pull out the blade, it will just get worse."

Faltor was looking around uneasily. "Where is Tornan?" he said. "Tornan was guarding the stranger. Someone go and find Tornan."

"I'll go," said Banra. He hurried off among the huts.

"Don't forget about Jinkil," Laena said. "Up in the cave."

"I'll go to him." It was Orban who spoke up. The boy quickly scaled the cliff and swung himself out of sight. There was a moment's pause, and then he looked down at the villagers gathered below. "He's alive. But I can't wake him."

"What's going on here?" Joq asked. His eyes were wide.

Laena tried to clear her head. There was so much to explain. "I'll tell you everything in a moment." She clung to him, trying to quieten the tremors that still gripped her body.

Banra came running back. "Tornan's in a stupor. He just lies there and mutters in his sleep."

Suddenly Laena remembered the vision that had come to her when Henik had been only a few weeks old. She'd dreamed of a cup being raised to her lips—a cup of poison. Then, she'd thought the cup had been for Henik. Now, she saw what the dream had really meant. "The food and drink!" she cried. "Moru and Jinkil consumed it. Probably Tornan, too. But I didn't." She turned to Nan, still kneeling beside Gorag in the snow. "How can this be?"

Nan looked up at her. "I don't understand."

"Did anyone help you prepare the food?" said Laena.

Nan hesitated. Her eyes moved uneasily.

Suddenly, Laena knew. Suddenly, everything made sense. "Worin!" Laena shouted the name. "Where's Worin?"

There was a moment of silence. Then: "I'm here," said a voice.

People turned and saw her, and instinctively, they drew back from her. She was a strange, ominous figure in the flickering torchlight. Her eyes glittered as she eyed the other villagers. Her ragged furs hung around her stooped shoulders. Her face was lined with suspicion.

Laena realized that Worin had only just arrived; her cave was furthest away, and it had taken her a while to reach the scene of the conflict. She had no idea yet what had happened.

"Who's that in the snow?" Worin asked.

"It's Gorag," said Laena, watching the woman's face in the dim, flickering light.

Worin paused carefully. "You mean, Alcor. The stranger."

"No!" Laena shouted. "He's no stranger. He came and tried to kill me, because he knows who I am, just the same way that I know who he is. But I turned his knife against him.''

Worin didn't speak. Her face suddenly seemed frozen. "Let me see," she said, finally, in a hoarse voice. She suddenly pushed forward. "Let me see!"

Laena felt a new suspicion. "Why should you care?"

"I want to talk to him! Let me talk to him!"

Nan stood up. Blood had saturated the snow in a wide arc around the prostrate figure. Nan wiped it off her hands. "I don't think I can save him," she said quietly.

"No!" Worin's voice was a sudden shout. She stumbled forward and threw herself down. She seized Gorag's shoulders and shook him fiercely. "No!" she shouted again.

Gorag stared up at her with wide eyes. He made helpless sounds. One of his hands fluttered in the snow beside him, but he no longer had the strength to raise it. Blood was still flowing freely from his wound, and his face was deathly pale. Once again he tried to speak; and failed.

"Gorag!" Worin cried out to him.

His eyelids drooped. His chest spasmed and he made an awful coughing, croaking sound. Then his eyes closed, and his head slumped to one side.

"Gorag!" Worin called to him again in a voice that shook with anguish.

Now she uses his real name, Laena thought to herself.

Nan laid her hand on Worin's shoulder. "He's dead," she said. "I couldn't save him. The blade cut his neck where the blood flows most freely. You know yourself, Worin, there is no help for that."

Worin's hands clenched on Gorag's shoulders. She made a strange keening sound, and then, without warning, she seized hold of the knife still embedded in his neck. She wrenched it with both hands, using all her strength, and dragged it free. She stood up, and her birthmark seemed to glow red in the light from the torches. Her skin was smeared with Gorag's blood, and her face was wet with tears.

People cried out in alarm and started backing away. Laena started moving with them—but she was exhausted, and she stumbled in the snow. She reached for Joq's arm, and her fingers brushed his sleeve. She felt herself floundering and falling, and she saw Joq looking down at her with surprise.

As Laena landed on her back in the drifts, she saw Worin

striding forward, the snow spraying around her feet, her furs flapping around her. She threw herself forward and knocked Joq aside. She landed on top of Laena, forcing her deeper into the snow. "You took Joq from me," she shouted, "and now Gorag!" She raised the knife high.

Laena was pinned under the woman, flat on her back, and stunned with surprise. She raised her unprotected hands against the knife. "Stop her!" she cried out.

Worin brought her arm down, slashing with the blade.

There was a movement that Laena saw only from the corner of her eye. Joq pivoted quickly, bringing up the point of his spear. It struck Worin in the chest, with enough force to knock her aside.

Her hand plunged harmlessly into the snow, still clutching Gorag's knife. She twisted around and screamed.

Laena struggled to sit up. She glimpsed the faces of the villagers, horrified by the bloodshed they had already seen, staring down at her now in a state of shock. She shared their shock and horror; but she was already groping toward an understanding of what had just happened.

Laena turned and found Worin squirming on her side, clutching at the spear embedded in her ribs. The woman's eyes were wild with pain and rage. She screamed again, and the terrible piercing sound reverberated in the valley.

Laena felt Joq's hands under her arms, lifting her up. She stared into his face. "Thank you," she gasped.

"Help me!" Worin cried. She screamed again.

"Can you stand?" Joq said to Laena.

"I think so."

He turned quickly to Worin and seized hold of his spear. "Listen to me!" he shouted at her.

"Help!" she gasped. There was a bubbling sound in her throat.

"Let me help her." Nan was pushing forward, with the rest of the villagers pressing close behind her.

"No." Joq's grip tightened on his spear, and he glared at Nan defiantly.

"Joq." It was Faltor's voice. "Stop this now. We must have no more violence, no more pain. No matter what Worin has done, we must help her." But his voice sounded plaintive where it had once been commanding, and again Laena saw how the conflict had taken away his ability to act.

Joq shook his head. "We have to know," he said. He turned back to Worin. "Why did you attack my wife?" He clenched his hands tighter on the spear, as if he would thrust it deeper if she didn't answer.

"Joq!" Faltor cried out in dismay.

"We have to know!" Joq shouted.

Worin was tossing her head from side to side. "I need help." She made a liquid coughing sound.

"No help till you tell me!"

Laena felt a chill. She'd never seen Joq so angry, and she'd never imagined that he could ever act like this.

Worin clenched her teeth, fighting the pain. She stared up at Joq's face, and she saw no mercy. Clearly, he meant what he said, and at that moment, no one had the courage to defy him. "All right," she gasped. "I'll tell you. I went wandering. Alone. No one cared, because you all despise me."

"You met the stranger, Gorag?" said Joq. "In the cave where he was hiding, outside the village?"

"Yes. He had been cast out. By the Wolf Tribe. He was kind to me. He had heard of the Fisher Tribe. He wanted—to live here with me."

Laena moved forward. "And you believed him?"

"He cared for me!" Worin cried.

"Please, let me help her now," said Nan. "Joq, you must let go of that spear."

"No!" shouted Joq. "There must be more." He leaned over Worin. "You visited Gorag, and you were his lover. And then, one day, the two of you saw Inrei walking alone."

Worin started sobbing. "Gorag hit Inrei," she mumbled through her tears.

The villagers cried out in dismay.

"Tell us!" Joq demanded.

"Gorag said it would look like an accident. He said he'd bring Inrei in, and you'd praise him and let him stay."

"So he killed Inrei, and you knew." Joq's knuckles whitened on the shaft of the spear.

"What does it matter now?" Worin was weeping. "What does any of it matter?"

Laena turned to face the villagers. "I understand it all," she said. "Gorag came to the village, and then he saw me and my sister, and he feared we would turn you all against him. So Worin drugged Moru and me and our guards. He was going to carry us out of the village and make it look as if we'd run away. And if I'd consumed the food and drink myself, his plan would have worked.'' Laena felt a wave of anguish. ''I told you all!'' she shouted. Her face felt wet, and she realized she was crying herself now. ''Last year, I saved your chieftain's life. You are *my people*. But you doubted my word and you weighed it against the lies of a stranger.'' She turned on Faltor. ''Why? Why didn't you believe me?''

Faltor averted his eyes from her. He was silent for a long moment. ''Perhaps you are right,'' he said. ''Perhaps we should have given you more of our trust.''

Joq let go of his spear and wiped his hands on his furs. He gestured to Nan. ''Help her now,'' he said. He no longer seemed fierce. In fact, his face was pale and deeply troubled, as if he felt shocked by his own actions.

''No! Leave me alone!'' Worin's shrill voice sounded unexpectedly. She tried to push Nan aside.

''Worin—'' Nan's face was lined with concern. ''Please.''

''Leave me,'' Worin shouted again. ''I have nothing now.'' She seized hold of the spear that was still embedded in her chest. Before anyone could stop her, she braced herself, then jerked her arms forward.

The spear plunged deep, and Worin gave one last despairing cry.

Chapter 38

Back in the comfort of her hut, Laena huddled under a heap of furs. For a brief time she had been oblivious to the cold night air. But now that the fear and the fighting were over, she found herself chilled to the core of her being. She saw again, inside her mind, the knife in Gorag's hand. She felt his hands on her throat, and she saw his face scowling at her. She shuddered and hugged herself, wishing she could drive the images out of her head.

Joq built up the fire, and he comforted Henik, who had been left alone in all the confusion and was crying at the top of his voice. When the baby was finally quiet, Joq brought Laena some hot broth. He sat beside her and embraced her, giving her his silent reassurance while she sipped the gruel.

When she had drained the bowl, she set it aside and nestled against him. She slid her hand inside his jacket and felt the strength in the muscles of his chest. "You protected me tonight," she said, remembering how fierce he had been, and still feeling strangely confused by it. "You were—you were violent, Joq."

He shrugged as if he preferred not to think too much about what she was saying. "One of the others would have helped you, if I hadn't been there. Mertan——"

"But you *were* there, and you were the one who actually did it." She searched his face. She knew it better than her own, and yet, at this moment, she wondered if she really knew him at all. "I never guessed you could be so fierce."

"Perhaps I never guessed, either." He sounded unhappy. She was talking about something so deep, so personal, he didn't know how to discuss it. "When I saw you in danger— I couldn't bear it. Something happened inside me. No one should ever hurt you, Laena. No one. It's so wrong, I can't explain it. I just lost control of myself.''

''You did the right thing, though.''

''You truly believe that?'' He gave her a brooding look.

''Of course. There was no other way.'' She kissed him gently on his cheek. ''Don't worry, Joq. It's over now. You saved me, and you forced everyone to face the truth.''

She lay beside him quietly, thinking of all the times she had clashed with him, and her demands for independence, humiliating him in the eyes of the other hunters. ''Sometimes I wonder why I should be so important to you,'' she whispered.

''Because you accept me as I am, and you care for me.'' His hands slid over her skin, tentative at first, but becoming bolder. He drew her to him, and she felt the heat of his body. He kissed her hard.

She tried to respond, but all her muscles felt limp. ''I don't have much strength left,'' she confessed.

''Tonight, I have enough strength for the two of us.'' He rolled onto her, and she felt his fingers searching between her thighs. His other hand closed on her breast. Usually, he waited for her to make the first move, but not this time. He was almost forcing himself on her. And yet, to her surprise, she found herself getting aroused by it.

She arched her back and gasped as his finger slid into her. Exhausted as she was, she felt new warmth spreading down across her abdomen, and she felt herself getting wet inside.

And so, she surrendered. She lay back, she opened herself, and she clutched his shoulders as he thrust into her. After all the times she had had to be strong, it was a relief, this once, to feel helpless. She breathed the heavy musky scent of him, and she felt her spirit mingling with his, more intimately than in many months. He had been there when she had needed him most, he had been loyal beyond her wildest dreams, and she loved him for it.

Their lovemaking was brief but intense. Afterward, in the glow from the fire, she fell into a stupor. She finally felt safe and at peace.

For just an instant she remembered the dream she had had before Gorag had attacked her. She saw, again, the flood washing away the homes of the Fisher Tribe.

But this was not the time to think of such things. With a great effort of will, she pushed the memory aside. With one arm around Joq, she slipped into a blessedly dreamless sleep.

Moru came to the hut early the next day, when the sky was still halfway between black and blue, and Laena was crouching beside the fire with Joq, eating a big breakfast of dried meat while Joq played with Henik in his sling.

"Sister!" Laena exclaimed as Moru untied the door flap, entered the hut, and stood there smiling.

Moru ran to her. Laena jumped up, and the two of them hugged each other tightly while Joq sat watching. They stood for a long moment, savoring the contact and the closeness.

"You're all right?" Laena said, finally pulling back and looking at her sister's face. "I was going to go over to Nan's hut, to see if you'd woken up. Did anyone tell you what happened? Were you hurt? Did Worin's sleeping potion—"

"I'm all right." Moru spoke calmly, firmly, smiling at Laena's concern. "My shoulder hurts, and I have a headache. But that's all. And yes, Nan told me what happened."

There was a moment's silence. Laena touched her sister's cheek. "I'm so glad you're safe." She drew a shaky breath. "You understand, I killed him this time, Moru. There's no doubt about it."

Moru's face turned serious. She gave a quick nod. "I went out a while ago, and I saw the body in the snow. I had to see for myself."

"Of course." Laena took Moru's hand, and she squeezed it tightly.

"They're building a fire now," Moru went on, "so that Gorag and Worin can be burned together."

Laena wondered if she wanted to see that. No; she had seen enough blood and death. She very much wanted to put it all behind her. "Did Nan find out how Worin drugged you?"

"Half of Nan's dreambrew powder is missing. Worin must have mixed it into our food and drink." Moru turned away. Beneath her obvious pleasure at seeing Laena, something seemed to be nagging at her. "Joq," she said. Her voice sounded artificially bright. She forced a smile. "I hear you

were a hero last night. You saved my sister. I'm so grateful
to you.''

"I did what any husband would do," Joq said quietly.

Laena stepped up and touched her sister's shoulder.
"Moru, is there something—"

Moru turned quickly to face her. She hesitated, then gave
up her pretense of good cheer. "Faltor wants to see you,"
she said in a tight voice. "Nan told me to fetch you. I don't
know what it's about."

"Oh." Laena had been fearing something like this, ever
since she had woken up that morning. Faltor had apologized
to her last night in front of the tribe, but still, she had defied
the chieftain as no one ever had before. She was a young
woman, not even a Fisher by birth, and she had shamed him
in front of his people. Could he simply accept what had
happened, without anger or resentment? Or would he want
some sort of public judgment, like the truth-telling ceremony all over again?

There was only one way to find out. "So let us go and
see him," she said. She turned to Joq and held out her hand.
"All of us," she said.

Farther away, at the center of the village, a big fire was
crackling in the meeting place, and acrid smoke was drifting
in the still, cold air. Laena guessed that even now, the bodies
of Gorag and Worin were being fed to the flames. But she
told herself not to think about that.

Nan was waiting outside Faltor's hut. She took Laena's
hands in hers and squeezed them, while she looked into
Laena's eyes. "It's—good to see you," she said. The words
seemed to imply something more: a confused mixture of
emotions that Laena couldn't begin to disentangle. But Nan
was already turning to Joq, and then to Moru, greeting them.
"And young Henik, as well," she said, patting the baby's
cheek, where he peered out from a thick bundle of furs.
"So, the whole family is here. Come inside, all of you."
She opened the door flap for them.

Laena wanted to grab Nan's arm and ask her to say what
was really on her mind. But really, there was no need. She
would find out for herself soon enough.

They walked into the dimness of Faltor's hut. He was
waiting for them, looking restless. "Sit," he said, gesturing

quickly at the wooden posts ranged in a circle. He seemed deeply preoccupied. Laena remembered his calmness in the other times she had sat before him. Even when she had burst into his hut, and Moru had been holding the spear against Gorag, Faltor had been steady and measured in the way he spoke. But now, she saw, his equanimity had been shaken.

She sat between Joq and Moru and took Henik in her arms, comforting him as he stared at his new surroundings. Nan seated herself away to one side, and for a moment there was silence as Faltor gave each of them a brooding look.

Laena felt the silence pressing on her. It made her anxious, and she had to do something to break it. "If I may speak," she ventured, "I want to apologize, for the way I spoke to you last night. I was upset—"

"You feared for your life," Faltor corrected her sharply.

"Well, yes," she said. His fierceness made her lapse back into an uneasy silence.

He clenched his fist and pressed it against his chest. "I was at fault, not you. You were right, Laena. You deserved my trust. If that man—Gorag—had killed you, I would have been to blame."

Laena felt confused. She didn't know what to say. This was different from what she had expected, and it actually seemed wrong for a chieftain to speak this way. "You—are a wise leader," she said. "You are not to blame—"

He glared at her. "Speak truly now! Truly you know, there was some fault on your side. Laena, and you, Moru, both violated the customs of our tribe. But the bigger fault was mine." He shook his head, still looking troubled. "We have always lived in peace here. The spirit of my great-great-grandfather has protected this tribe from outsiders who came to harm us. Consequently, I never had to deal with—with the terrible things that we saw last night." Abruptly, his shoulders slumped. The strength seemed to have ebbed from him. "I still don't understand how the spirit failed us this time."

He lapsed into silence and bent his head, staring blankly at the packed earth beneath his feet. Laena and Moru exchanged a quick, questioning glance. Joq sat motionless, looking surprised. Nan was huddled in her furs, fretting with a loose leather thong, avoiding everyone's eyes.

Finally, Faltor seemed to gather himself. He looked up at

Laena. "You may hunt with the men, in future. Obviously, you deserve to. No one will speak against it now." He made an impatient gesture. "I regret I wasn't willing to act on what you said about Gorag. I regret the violence and the terrible bloodshed." He paused, staring over their heads, as if he could still see Gorag bleeding in the snow, and Worin dragging the spear into her own chest. He grimaced. "There must be no more killing and dying here. No more." He sighed. "I can think of nothing else that needs to be said."

Was that really all? Laena was filled with new confusion. She wasn't sure what she had expected, but she had expected—something. She realized that Faltor didn't really know how to cope with what had happened. He was an honest man, a wise mediator, and a kind chieftain who knew how to preserve harmony among his people. But he had never had to deal with the violence of an outsider such as Gorag. And, she saw, he had no idea how unsafe his tribe might really be.

Joq stood up, and Moru. Joq tugged at Laena's arm, for it was rude to stay in the chieftain's hut after they had been dismissed. But Laena remained seated. "If you please," she said, "there is something I must say."

Faltor raised his eyebrows. "Yes? You may speak."

Laena tried to gather her courage. This, she knew, would be difficult. But it was the best time to say it, and for the sake of her conscience, she had to make the effort. "Before Gorag came into the cave where I slept last night, I had a dream. I saw our village swept away by a terrible flood."

Laena sensed Joq turning and looking at her in surprise. From the corner of her eye, she saw Nan look up sharply. Faltor merely seemed puzzled. He waited for her to go on.

Laena drew a deep breath. "I have had dreams like that in the past," she said. "And they foretell the future. Always. I dreamed the death of my father, before it happened. Again, when I was traveling with Nan, I dreamed the death of a young boy who was with us then."

Faltor turned to Nan. "This truly happened?"

"Well, yes, it did." The old lady sounded reluctant. "I believe Laena has—a talent. I don't know if all her dreams speak truly, but at least once, I saw it happen."

Faltor turned back to Laena. He was no longer brooding and preoccupied. His face was uncomprehending.

"For a while, recently, I doubted my talent," Laena went on. "I had a dream of Worin offering a poison cup; and I thought it meant she was trying to poison my child. When that turned out to be untrue, I decided that I shouldn't pay attention to my dreams anymore.

"But then, last night, I saw that even my dream of Worin offering a cup was true; because Worin was the one who tried to drug me, so that Gorag could drag me out and abandon me to die in the snow."

She paused, waiting for that to sink in.

"I see," Faltor said softly.

Laena spread her hands helplessly. "So, now I am telling you about my dream of the flood, because I fear that it, too, will be true."

There was a long moment of silence. Faltor's face was unreadable. "I must be sure I understand this," he said slowly. "You are telling me that the river will overflow its banks and sweep us all away."

Laena heard the words, and when he said them, and she felt him looking at her steadily, it all began to sound foolish. How could she be sure of herself? What if the dream had misled her? What if she had misinterpreted it, the same way she had misinterpreted the dream of the poisoned cup, initially?

And yet, it had been so clear. "Let me tell you exactly what I saw," she said. "I saw your great-great-grandfather's face." Her voice was unsteady under the force of Faltor's steady stare. "He told me that he could no longer protect your—our—people. And then I saw the flood. A great wave, so big that it even swept the huts away." She stopped, wondering whether to mention the panther that had urged her to follow it south. No; Faltor had never even seen a panther. It would stretch his credulity to the limit. "That's all I have to say. Except—it was very real. In every way. I saw the water sweep the huts off the bank, and I saw the people drowning. Many, many people. It was truly a terrible dream."

Faltor slowly shook his head. "But the river has *never* overflowed its banks. Every year, it flows the same."

Joq coughed politely. "I have noticed," he said, "the water flows a little higher each spring. The weather is changing, as people say. The winter ends a little sooner—'' He trailed off, sounding embarrassed. It was odd, Laena thought, that he could have been so fierce last night, but he was shy now, confronting his own chieftain.

Faltor turned to him. ''How do you know these things?'' he demanded.

''Well,'' said Joq, still sounding embarrassed, ''I used to spend a lot of time alone. I watched the sun, and the river, and the seasons. I saw the snow on the mountains melting earlier each year, and I made marks in the riverbank where the water flowed highest.''

Faltor rested his elbows on his knees. He rubbed his hand across his jaw. Then he turned to Nan. ''What do you make of all this?''

Nan drew back a little. She didn't seem happy about being asked to decide where the truth lay. She looked at Laena, then at Faltor. ''A flood could come,'' she said cautiously. ''Such things sometimes happen. But a huge wave, in a river like this, seems hard to believe. And who's to say when it may be? A dream may be a True Thing, but it could be a glimpse of something that's years in the future.''

The simple sense in Nan's words seemed to give Faltor what he needed—something to cling to. His back straightened. He nodded decisively. ''So, there may be nothing to worry about,'' he said. ''In any case, if the worst came to the worst, a little water shouldn't harm us. Why, it should be no worse than a heavy fall of rain.'' He looked at Laena. ''Isn't that so?''

Laena stared at him in dismay. ''It wasn't like that at all,'' she said.

Faltor grunted. ''All right, I will think on this some more. But in the meantime, please say nothing about it to anyone. People are distressed enough already, after all the bloodshed. It would be pointless to worry them further. Don't you agree?''

Laena wished she could convey to him the power of what she had seen. ''I really did see a giant wave,'' she said. ''It was so powerful—''

''My people have dwelled here for generations,'' Faltor interrupted her. ''You see for yourself, there is nowhere else for us to go. Should we uproot ourselves and move up into the mountains, just because of your dream?''

Laena felt the weight of his words. "We might take some more modest precautions," she said in a small voice. "Maybe move as many people as possible up to the caves—"

"I have already said I will think on this some more." His tone of voice made it clear: he had been generous with her, he had forgiven her for defying him the previous night, and he had taken more than his share of blame. There were limits to his tolerance, and she was now beginning to try his patience. "In the meantime, Laena, there is no reason to cause panic by telling people what you dreamed. Now, do you agree?''

Laena realized it was hopeless to argue. She opened her mouth to speak. The words seemed to stick in her throat, but finally she got them out. "I agree," she said.

Outside Faltor's hut, she took Joq and Moru by the hand and drew them close to her. "I have to ask a favor," she said, giving each of them a searching look.

Moru nodded. Joq looked at her strangely, as if he no longer knew quite what to expect. She had confided in him about her dreams; but always, she had told him about visions she had had in the past. Never before had they affected him personally.

"Until the thaw is over," said Laena, "we should all move into Moru's cave. That way, if my vision is true, we'll be safe from the water."

Moru took a moment to consider what Laena said. Then she shrugged. "All right," she said. More than anyone else, she had seen the truth of Laena's visions in the past.

"I don't know if I can really believe—" Joq began.

"No!" Laena said sharply. "I don't ask you to believe me. I'm just asking you a favor, that's all."

Joq paused thoughtfully. "I suppose it can do no harm. Of course, people will ask us why we're leaving our hut. And we can't tell them the truth, without breaking your promise to Faltor."

"So we'll make an excuse," said Laena. "We'll say— we'll say that Moru hurt her back when Gorag threw her from the mouth of the cave, and she needs us to care for her, and she doesn't want to leave her home."

"I suppose that would do," said Joq.

"Thank you." Laena squeezed his hand, feeling a wave of relief. "Thank you, Joq."

She was interrupted then by a shout. She turned and saw Mertan striding toward them. "Laena! I've been telling everyone how brave you were!" He walked up, grinning. Then he nodded to Moru, and to Joq. "You should have seen how she fought that man." He touched her arm tentatively, as if she were no longer the same as everyone else and must possess some special power. "Come on. The cremation is done, and people are still gathered around the fire. You have to tell everyone in your own words, how it happened."

"Mertan," said Laena, "I really don't want—"

"You have to!" Mertan seized her hand. "They need to know. And they all want to see you."

"It would probably be best," Joq murmured to her. "You know how rumors tend to twist things, if people aren't told the truth."

Laena sighed. "All right." She turned to Joq and Moru. "But you two will come with me. Yes?"

They nodded their assent.

She started following Mertan to the meeting place. It was going to be hard for her to describe what had happened, because it would force her to relive the awful experiences. Still, she would do her best to tell people everything, just as she had after she rode the mammoth.

Then she remembered her promise to Faltor, and she corrected herself mentally. She couldn't tell the villagers everything. She couldn't tell them about the one thing that mattered most: the disaster that she now feared would claim the village and most of the people who innocently lived there.

Chapter 39

The days that followed were easy; and yet they were hard.

It was easy now for Laena to be among the Fisher Tribe. The people were ashamed for having doubted her, and they tried to atone for it in dozens of little ways. Mothers were happy to help with her chores and eager to look after her child for her. Elders brought her gifts of food and clothing. One of the hunters gave her his best spear, and some of the young men shyly asked if she would teach them her fighting skills. Her story of her struggle in the snow with Gorag became a legend embroidered with so much fanciful, far-fetched detail, some of the younger children began to seem a little bit afraid of her.

She had always wanted respect. Now she had more of it than she could possibly need. At the same time, though, she was still deeply troubled, for she couldn't forget her vision of the flood. She would be talking to one of the people—a young hunter like Orban, or a mother such as Turi—and suddenly she would see the person's friendly, smiling face overwhelmed and swept away by a torrent of churning black water. The threat of it was never far away from her thoughts, and it darkened each day, even as the days grew longer and brighter with the promise of spring.

Laena yearned to tell everyone the fate that might lie in store. She went to Faltor and begged him to reconsider the vow of silence that he had imposed on her. But the chieftain refused to change his mind. He argued that the flood could not possibly come so long as the river still wore its shell of ice. He told her, as he had before, that a flood would be a trivial matter for people who were accustomed to living by the river. He said that his people needed a quiet, healing time after all the bloodshed and strife, and there was no point in spreading panic among them.

So Laena turned to Joq. He was willing to believe that there might be some truth to her vision, because he had seen for himself the gradual changes in the river and the climate during the past few years. Still, even he found it hard to imagine a catastrophe as violent as she foretold. He moved with her to Moru's cave, as they had agreed. But that was the most he would do.

More days passed, and the thaw began. Ice that had been firm underfoot became soft and treacherous. Bare rock and earth emerged from beneath the veil of white, and life stirred in the world after the months of frozen stasis.

As always, the transformation lifted everyone's spirits. The Fisher People smiled and laughed more readily, and they worked cheerfully at chores which they had avoided during the winter months.

Laena was the only one who found no joy in the spirit of spring. The river's icy crust was starting to break into a mosaic of floating fragments, revealing the water below—and, strangely, it was running lower this season than ever before. This was the opposite of what she had expected, yet it still troubled her. On the mountain slopes all around, she could see the snow rapidly melting. Where was all the water going? Why wasn't it finding its way to the river, as it usually did?

Each night, she lay awake on her pallet while Joq slept soundly beside her and Moru slumbered on a simple bed deeper in the cave. She stared into the darkness, waiting in fear, listening for the first sound of rushing water. Finally she would fall into a fitful sleep—only to wake with a start, well before dawn, convinced that she had heard the onset of the flood. Once again she lay in the darkness, listening. But all she heard was the steady breathing of Joq and Moru, Henik making little noises in his sleep, and the fire hissing near the mouth of the cave.

This morning, as the very first gray light touched the highest snow-covered peaks around the valley, she prayed in her head to the white panther, begging for guidance. Had she misinterpreted her dream? Was she haunted by phantoms of her own making?

She stared into the semidarkness, hoping for some sound or sign. But no images flickered to life in her mind, and she heard nothing but the voices of a few villagers who had woken early and were rebuilding their fires, ready to begin the new day.

So, there was no comfort for her; no one to tell her where the truth lay. She slid off the pallet, taking care not to wake Joq. She slung a water bag over her shoulder and swung herself out of the mouth of the cave. She could at least make herself useful fetching water from the river.

A couple of shadowy figures were moving around among the huts. They waved a silent good morning to her as she passed by. Ahead of her, she saw a figure standing on the riverbank, and she realized it was Orban, the young hunter.

She wondered what he was doing there alone, staring up at the peaks whose highest rocks were a faint gray outline against the black sky.

"Are you watching the dawn break?" she said, pausing beside him.

He glanced at her, then once again he peered into the twilight. "I think I hear a rock-slide. Listen."

Laena wasn't really interested, but she knew she should be polite. She paused and turned her head, trying to discover what he had heard.

Somewhere, a baby was crying. In a hut nearby, a mother was scolding her daughter for being slow to do the morning chores. In front of Laena, the river was making faint chuckling, trickling noises.

Then she heard it: a faint, faint rushing sound.

"You're right, Orban," she said. "It does sound like an avalanche." She turned away.

"But listen! It goes on and on."

It was true, she realized. The sound wasn't ending. And maybe this was her imagination . . . but it seemed to be growing fractionally louder.

Laena felt a prickling sensation across her neck and shoulders. She peered toward the east, where the frosty crescent of a quarter moon hung above the steep walls of the valley. There seemed to be some smoke or dust drifting in the far distance against the dim grayness of the sky.

Suddenly, more than anything else, she wanted to be wrong. She took hold of Orban's arm and clutched it tightly—so tightly, he cried out in surprise. The rushing noise was growing louder; there was no doubt about it.

He suddenly pointed at the surface of the river, right in front of them. "Look!" he said. The water was trembling, like water in a bowl that someone had jostled.

There was no doubt now in Laena's mind. Even so, she still didn't want to believe it. *Please,* she thought again, *please let me be wrong!*

She peered upriver. In the faint dawn light, she glimpsed something gleaming in the darkness, like ice. But it couldn't be ice; not now. As Laena stared with a deepening sense of dread, she saw that it was moving and surging.

Her vow of silence meant nothing now. "It's a flood," she said, fiercely shaking Orban's arm. "Do you understand? The whole village will be swept away. Are you listening? Warn people! Then climb for your life!"

There wasn't time to wait and see if he understood. Laena turned and ran among the huts. She cupped her hands around her mouth. "Wake!" she shouted. "Wake! The river is flooding! We'll all be drowned!" She ran to Faltor's hut, her feet skidding through the snow and slush on the muddy bank. She pried at the door flap with fingers that had grown clumsy with fear. "Faltor! Nan! The flood is coming! Get up!"

There were muttered exclamations from inside the hut, but she had no time to linger. She strode to the river and peered again upstream. She could see clearly now. A wall of water crowned with white foam was sluicing between the valley walls, bearing down on the village.

Behind her, voices were shouting confused questions. Orban was running among the huts, urging people awake. Laena hesitated, wanting desperately to save all the villagers. But there was no time. She had Henik and Joq and Moru to think about.

"Wake!" she screamed again as she ran back to the cliff face. "Out of your homes! Wake!"

The roaring was no longer faint and distant. It was loud and fearsome. Laena seized a handhold in the cliff and felt the rock trembling under her touch. She hauled herself up, wrenching her muscles in her panic, and she saw Moru peering down at her from the mouth of the cave.

"Get inside!" Laena shouted.

Behind her, villagers were emerging from their huts, milling around in confusion. The wave was clearly visible upriver, three times as tall as a man, engulfing small bushes and plants on the valley walls. People started screaming. Some of them ran to the cliff and mindlessly tried to climb sheer stone. Others ducked back into their huts as if the fragile buildings would protect them.

Strong hands seized Laena's wrists and dragged her into the cave mouth. She saw Joq's face outlined by the glow from their fire, and Moru beside him. He hugged Laena, opened his mouth to speak—

The ground shook. The roaring was suddenly so loud it seemed to press in on Laena's ears. Black water burst into the mouth of the cave. The force of it threw Laena backward onto the floor. She was suddenly engulfed, submerged under the ice-cold torrent. She couldn't see; she couldn't breathe.

Blindly, she groped for Henik. Her hands touched his sling. The water surged again, dragging him with it, but she managed to seize hold of her child. She clutched him with one arm and groped for the wall of the cave with the other. She managed to jam her fingers into a crevice just as the water reversed its flow and started trying to suck her away with it.

Her head broke above the surface. The fire had been engulfed. The cave was dark. She took desperate gulps of air. Henik, in her arms, started coughing and screaming.

The wave had passed, Laena realized. As quickly as that, it was all over. Trembling and gasping, she floundered and splashed her way to the cave mouth as icy water sluiced out around her ankles. Laena looked out, dreading what she might see.

The great wave had passed by, but the river was still twice its normal height. Uprooted trees were rolling in the flood as it swept down on the valley. More than half of the huts were gone, instantly erased by the huge surge of water. The huts that remained were still half submerged in the torrent. Laena glimpsed pale shapes—faces in the dark water, drifting downstream, shouting futilely for help, exactly as she had foreseen. Other villagers were clinging precariously to poles and posts that protruded above the surface. A lucky few, like Laena, were peering out of their caves.

Henik was screaming now, with all his might. He was shivering in her arms, and Laena realized that she, too, was frighteningly cold. Her outer furs were completely soaked. She ducked back into the cave, fumbled with the thongs, and threw off the furs. The water had closed around her so briefly, it hadn't penetrated to her undergarments, which were mostly dry. Still, she and her family would be doomed if they couldn't start a fire.

In the darkness of the cave, she couldn't see anything or anyone. "Joq!" she cried. "Moru! Where are you?"

"I'm here," Joq called from deeper in the cave. "Moru's hurt. She hit her head."

Laena started searching for the little leather pouch that Joq had made to hold their firesticks and some tinder. The valley was often damp, so Joq had done his best to see that the pouch would be airtight. His craftsmanship now mattered far more than it ever had before.

Laena stumbled to and fro. Everything had been thrown around by the flood. Nothing was where it was supposed to be. The wooden branches of their bed were scattered everywhere.

"Help me, Joq!" She was having trouble holding Henik in one arm while she rooted through the debris. "We have to start a fire."

She heard him stumbling toward her. His hand touched her shoulder briefly. "Are you all right?" he said. "I think Moru was knocked unconscious when she fell."

"Find the firesticks!" She couldn't keep the panic out of her voice.

"Here," he said. He pressed the pouch into her hand.

She felt a wave of relief. The pouch was still closed. "Hold Henik." She found his arms, put Henik into them, then squatted down. Calm, she told herself. Be calm. This might be the only dry tinder left in the entire village. She might have only one chance.

She found the stack of clothing that they kept at the side of the cave. Many of the garments had been swept away, but a couple still remained. She unrolled one and found that it was still dry inside. She used it to wipe the water from a small area of the floor.

Carefully, feeling her way in the dimness, she arranged the firesticks and tucked tinder around them. She started work then, swiftly rolling the stick between her palms.

"I should get outside and help people," Joq said.

"No!" she shouted. "You'll freeze. Take off your wet furs. Otherwise they'll soak through. It's cold enough to kill you if you aren't properly dressed."

He hesitated. Her voice had been commanding.

"Listen to me!" Laena shouted.

Joq nodded. "You're right." He started pulling off his furs.

At the back of the cave, Moru groaned softly.

"Please take care of her," said Laena, "and the baby. Once we have a fire, we can take it to other people and dry them out."

She heard Joq shuffling past her. But she was barely aware of him. All her attention was focused now on the sticks in her hands.

A dim orange glow showed in the darkness. Laena added a tiny amount of tinder, then redoubled her efforts.

A spark. A flicker. And finally, a flame.

She added more tinder with trembling fingers. She seized the twigs that had been part of their bed, shook water off them, peeled away the bark with her teeth, and fed the tiny dry shoots to the flame.

It blossomed before her; and its yellow light helped to drive her fears away. Even though her dream had come true, she could believe now that her family would survive.

In the grayish half-light, bedraggled figures clutched each other for warmth. The flood had gradually drained away, but the river was barely contained between its banks, and the village was a wasteland of mud and tumbled debris. The people of the Fisher Tribe were staring around blankly as if they still couldn't comprehend what had happened to them.

While Joq stayed with Henik and Moru, Laena hurried from cave to cave, carrying burning twigs, spreading the gift of fire. She urged the people to shed their wet clothes and dry themselves. Finally, she ventured down into the village itself. "Quickly," she called to the first person she saw. "Gather as much wood as you can. Shake off the water. It'll still be dry underneath if you work fast. We have to build a big fire."

"All right. Right away, Laena."

She recognized the voice, and she realized it was Orban. So, he had survived. But how many others had not?

They amassed a pile of wooden debris. It burned reluctantly at first, but then, as the flames penetrated, the fire grew fierce and tall. Laena left Orban to tend it, and she strode among the ruined huts, taking people by the arm and physically thrusting them toward the fire. Most of the villagers still seemed in shock, unable to think for themselves. Many were openly weeping, calling the names of relatives who had been carried away by the water.

"You'll die of cold if you stay in here!" Laena shouted when she saw a figure poking around in the tumbled remains of a hut near the center of the village.

The figure straightened and turned toward her. "Nan. Nan is missing."

With a shock, Laena realized that the person she had been talking to was Faltor. He stood clutching himself, shivering uncontrollably, his wet furs clinging to his tall, thin frame.

"I'm sorry," Laena stammered. "I didn't realize—"

It was his turn to recognize her then. "No," he said. "I am the one who's sorry. Laena, I have failed again, failed my people. But how could I believe?" He rubbed the back of his wrist across his eyes, and Laena realized that he had been crying.

"You think Nan is still in here?" Laena asked.

"Yes. Yes, she must be."

Laena picked her way across a heap of wet logs. The roof of the hut had fallen, so that she found herself walking over a heavy carpet of reeds matted with moss. "I don't see her," she said. The sky was gradually brightening, and as she looked around, she saw there was no way that Nan could possibly be there.

"But she has to be here!" Faltor's voice was shaking with emotion.

Laena took his arm. "She's gone," she said. Gently, she guided him out of the ruins of his home. "You must save yourself now." It seemed strange to be speaking this way to the chieftain of the tribe. But if he was no longer able to cope, it was her duty to help him.

As the sun rose, Laena found herself organizing everything. None of the Fishers had experienced a life-threatening disaster before. She was the only one who had learned from experience how to deal with such a situation, and how to survive. She felt self-conscious at first, telling everyone what to do. But they needed to be told, and there was no one else to tell them.

She remembered how her mother had kept her busy after the massacre of the Panther People. It had worked then. It would work now.

Laena made sure that Moru's head wound was of no danger, then assigned her to take care of Henik. She got Joq to form a search party, looking for villagers who might have swum to safety further downstream. She told Weeps to organize a group of women, gathering all the food that remained in the various stores around the village. And she told Orban to lead a group of young hunters, taking timbers from the huts that had been destroyed, using them to shore up the buildings that still remained.

Laena herself set up some rough and ready beds for the injured. If Nan was truly gone, Laena was the healer now. Not that there was much she could do; the healer's hut had been flattened, and it would take time to pull the wreckage apart and salvage any medicines that had been left untouched by the water. So Laena made hot compresses with leather slashed from the hem of her own robe, and she placed the injured close to the fire, and she hoped for the best.

Finally, when everyone had been cared for, she toured the village. In her mind, she was counting the survivors. Pulo, the strongest of the boy-hunters, had been drowned. Joq's parents, Orleh and Weeps, had survived—their cave had sheltered them. Jinkil, who had guarded Laena during the trouble with Gorag, was still alive, though his face and body had been bruised when the flood threw him against the cliff. Banra and Tornan, two of the other hunters, were missing.

Mertan and his wife Turi were gone, and so was their son, Toma. All of them had been swept away—a fact which plunged Faltor still deeper into a state of grief and guilt. But their one-year-old daughter, Urami, still lived. The waters had thrown her up onto a ledge in the wall of the valley, where she had been found and rescued by Joq's search party.

Laena returned to the fire. Gradually, the Fishers were recovering from their state of shock. They were talking among themselves, exchanging warm, dry garments, and caring for each other. With relief, Laena saw that the most critical part of the emergency was over. No more lives would be lost now. She could finally allow herself to relax a little.

She sat down on a piece of wreckage, and her feelings, which she had thrust aside, suddenly swept over her like the tidal wave itself. She trembled as she saw, again, the destruction of the village. She felt tears starting down her face as she thought of Nan. Why hadn't the old woman listened to Laena's warning? And why hadn't Laena tried harder to persuade her to seek safety? She blamed herself for not insisting that Nan relocate in one of the caves, as Laena herself had done. She could never forgive herself for that. She would bear the loss of Nan as a burden that would last for the rest of her life.

She slumped forward, staring into the flames. Again and again, she lost the people she loved. Again and again, it was foretold in a vision. Was there no escape from the cruel cycle? Was there nothing she could ever do?

Time passed, but Laena wasn't aware of it. She saw the ruined village, and she remembered the lesson she had learned years ago—that nothing was permanent, nothing could be trusted to endure. She had imagined that the Fisher village was different, and it would last forever. She had told herself that her dreams no longer meant anything, and were just a relic of the past. But that had been wrong; and now there was no longer any way for her to avoid the implications.

Laena felt a hand on her shoulder. She looked up and found Joq standing close by, with his face streaked with mud, and his furs ragged and torn.

Laena forced her own concerns aside. She stood and embraced him. "Are you all right?"

He nodded. "I was concerned about you. I saw you sitting over here, looking so overwhelmed—"

"I was just thinking about Nan. And about the past. About all the times of suffering, and the people I've lost." She shivered. "I feel so helpless, sometimes. No matter what I do—"

"No!"

The word was loud, and it surprised her. She blinked at him.

"Never say that," he told her, more gently. "Laena,

you've saved countless lives here today. You saved me, and Henik, and your sister. You shouted a warning when the flood was coming, and you saw what needed to be done afterward. No one else knew what to do. We could have *all* died here, if it wasn't for you.''

She was silent for a while, realizing that there was some sense in what he said. Yes, it was true, she had helped the Fishers to survive; but still, she wished she could have done more.

Joq drew her down beside him, and kept his arm around her. For a moment he watched some of the villagers dry their steaming clothes while others continued poking around in the debris of their homes. Faltor, meanwhile, was sitting on the opposite side of the fire, hunched forward, just staring blankly into the flames.

''You know,'' Joq murmured to Laena, ''I doubt he'll want to be the chieftain after this. I don't think he has the strength anymore.''

Laena wondered if it might be so. Faltor had never been a strong leader, and now that he believed his people were unprotected by the spirit of his ancestor, he would have even less confidence. The knowledge stirred something inside Laena—something that had never really lived before. ''Are you saying that I should—'' She trailed off. She couldn't bring herself to finish the sentence.

''You've already *been* leading them,'' said Joq. ''They will need your guidance just as much tomorrow as they do today.''

Laena looked at the ragged people, and at the devastation. It was such a huge catastrophe, and she was just a young woman with a baby who was less than a year old. How could she believe that she was capable of leading a tribe to overcome a crisis such as this? And even if they were willing to put their trust in her—did she really want that kind of responsibility? To rebuild the village would take the rest of the year, at least, and would be a huge task. Even then, the Fishers would still be living under the load of their own grief. And another flood could come.

The panther had spoken to her three times now, in her dreams. Each time, it had given her the same message. Could she continue to ignore it? If there truly was a warm, green place, where security was something real and her parents might somehow be alive—what was she doing, defying fate, turning away from her destiny, and lingering here in this narrow valley?

At the end of the afternoon, all the villagers gathered again around the fire. The children were strangely silent, looking up at the adults with wide, questioning eyes. Some of the women were still weeping over the loss of their husbands or their parents. Most of the men, too, had been touched by grief. The disaster had been so unprecedented and so sudden, it would take months or even years for everyone to come to terms with it.

Meat was skewered on sticks, heated over the flames, and passed around. Many of the food caches had been spared by the flood, so food, at least, was no cause for worry. The people ate ravenously, and they ate in silence, burying their grief in the simple pleasure of eating.

Finally, Faltor stood up. He still looked bowed and beaten as he surveyed the remnants of his people. "We are few now," he said in a voice that sounded infinitely weary. "We were protected, and now we are abandoned." He paused, searching for words that would enable him to continue. "There is a rumor that I have heard. The rumor says that one of us dreamed of the flood, and warned me about it. But I refused to listen." He paused again, and sighed. "My people, the rumor is true. Laena told me of her dream. She begged me to let her warn you all, but I couldn't allow it. It was too terrible to believe."

People started murmuring uneasily to one another. Many of them turned and stared at Laena. She kept her eyes fixed steadily on Faltor, and said nothing.

"I fear that I have failed you all," said Faltor.

There were some muttered protests.

"No," he insisted, "I failed you. I trusted in the spirit of Orwael, which watched over us for so long. But that spirit is no longer there to protect us." His voice was shaking. "Our world has changed, and I, as your leader, can no longer say what we should do." He turned unexpectedly toward Laena, and spread his hands. "You, a young woman—you have shown more strength, more wisdom, than any of us, in these strange times. Have you had any other visions of our future? Tell us, Laena, what you would do now.''

And then, without another word, he sat down.

For a moment, there was complete silence. Everyone in the tribe was staring at her, shocked by Faltor's speech. They had lost their loved ones and their homes; and now, evidently, they had lost their chieftain. Laena represented the only hope they had left.

She felt their attention like a heavy, suffocating weight. She hadn't expected this to happen so soon, if indeed it was going to happen at all. She was unprepared and embarrassed.

Time felt liquid around her. She remembered being paralyzed in her dream, while she watched the panther walking away. This was the same feeling. She struggled with it. She couldn't let the opportunity escape her. And yet, she was scared to say what was truly in her heart.

She heard people starting to shift restlessly as she sat immobile. Faltor was waiting for her. But he wouldn't wait forever. She had to speak. She had to!

She turned and looked at Joq beside her. He, too, was waiting expectantly; and she could never let him down. He smiled at her and squeezed her hand, as if to show his faith in her. And that, finally, renewed her courage.

She turned back and faced the villagers ranged around the flames. She clenched her fists, till her fingernails bit into the palms of her hands. "I think it is time," she said, "to leave this place."

It took a moment for people to comprehend her words. She saw them reacting, one by one. Some drew back in confusion; some stared at her with astonishment.

"Hear me!" she cried, gaining more courage from the sound of her own voice. She struggled up onto her feet. "When I was a young child, my world was destroyed. Now I see your world, and it, too, has been ripped apart. The seasons themselves are bringing these changes, wrecking your lives as surely as they wrecked mine."

"What would you have us do?" someone shouted. It was Orleh, she realized—Joq's father. He sounded angry. "Where do you suggest we go? Gorag—the stranger—he told us things are worse among the Wolf Tribe. They don't even have enough to eat."

"Yes," said Laena. "And that means, sooner or later they will come here looking for food. The legend of Orwael won't keep them away forever. There will be more fighting, and more suffering. The Wolf hunters are fierce people. I've seen them myself. They could easily kill us all."

She paused, watching people slump under the burden of truth in her words.

"There is nothing for us to the north or the west," she went on, more quietly. "We must find a new land. We must travel south."

This time, the villagers cried out in dismay.

"Listen." Laena held up her hands. Gradually, bit by bit, silence returned. "When my parents were taken from me by the river, I experienced a powerful vision. It has stayed with me ever since. I saw an empty land that was lush and green, warmed by the sun. I saw my parents living there in peace. I saw blue water and a blue sky. There is no doubt in my mind that this land exists.

"Once before, I set out in search of it. But I was too young then. I wasn't strong enough, or skilled enough. Fortunately, I met Nan. It seemed as if she had been sent to me, to give me what I needed to pursue my dream. She was a hard teacher, but a good one; and she brought me here."

Laena broke off for a moment. It was hard to talk about Nan; she felt the emotion rising up in her throat, choking her. But then she remembered how Nan had always managed to seem so strong. It was Laena's duty now to do the same.

"Nan has left us," Laena said. "So, from this moment on, I must stand alone. Three times, while I have lived here, I have had more visions of the land to the south. Each time, I pushed them aside. But they can't be denied any longer. This flood is the clearest sign that it is time for me to fulfill my destiny."

She paused and looked slowly around at the people. They were staring at her as if she had entranced them. They really wanted to believe, she realized. She was offering them hope at a time when they had little else to live for.

"I want you to come with me," she went on, speaking softly. "All of you. I truly believe I can guide you out of this terrible time of suffering, into a world of plenty." She paused. How could she convey to them the vividness of what she had seen? "I'm not just a dreamer; you have seen that. I know how to survive. I'm strong. I wouldn't walk into the wilderness if I wasn't certain of the prize that lies at the end of the journey. But I need your strength, too, for this great task."

She realized that that was all; there was nothing more to say. She sat down abruptly, and there was total silence. Laena felt scared, though she did her best to conceal it. She had never put herself in such a vulnerable position. This time, she didn't even dare to look at Joq.

Gradually, the villagers started talking among themselves. The talk became a torrent of words, and the noise rose around Laena. She bowed her head and stared directly in front of her, refusing to meet anyone's eyes.

"Quiet. People, quiet!" It was Faltor, on his feet again. He held up his hands. "Laena." He turned to her, and there was an imploring look on his face. "Laena, we cannot leave. We are Fisher People. This is our home—"

His challenge merely renewed her strength. She stood up to face him. "I felt that way, too, when I was forced to leave my own land. But if I hadn't left, I would have died." She stared steadily at Faltor. "Twice now you have turned away from the truth I have offered you. Surely, you won't turn away for a third time."

Once again the babble of voices rose up around her. Some of the elders were openly angry, outraged at her presumptuousness for telling them where they should live. "In any case, it's not possible!" one of them shouted. "There's no way to go south from here. The mountains block every path. Everyone knows that."

Laena had expected to hear that, and she wasn't sure that she could counter it effectively, since she herself had not explored the territory that lay to the south. But before she could speak, a man stood up whom she recognized as Benke. He was the one who had found the mammoths in Blind Valley last year. And he was the one who had protested at Laena being allowed to participate in the hunt. Did that mean he was still prejudiced against her? She wasn't sure. She hadn't spent a lot of time talking to him, because he seldom talked much to anyone. He was a quiet man who often went wandering on his own. The other hunters respected him because he probably knew more than anyone about the land surrounding the valley of the tribe.

Gradually, the villagers fell silent as they realized that Benke was waiting to speak. One by one, they turned and looked at him.

"It's true," he said, "that the mountains block our path to the south." He nodded toward the tall peaks that stood beyond the valley that the Fishers called their home. "But if a person went a way east, and *then* turned south—I think there might be a way through."

There were some murmurs of dissent.

"I'm not saying I think it's a wise idea," Benke went on, holding up his hands. "I'm just saying—it might be possible."

He sat down, and the villagers started arguing among themselves even more furiously than before.

"Enough," Faltor shouted again. This time, there was some strength in his voice. He waited a long moment while the noise slowly died down. "This is too big a thing to decide now. We need to think, and we need to rest. Tomorrow, after everyone has had time to talk things over, we can meet here again. And then we can decide." He turned to Laena. "Do you agree?"

She was almost tempted to refuse. If the villagers had more time, she sensed they would tend to back away from the challenge she had given them.

But when she looked around at their faces, she saw she had no choice. They were too confused and scared right now to make a lasting decision. Even if they bowed to her will, they could easily change their minds overnight.

"Very well," she said. "We will meet again tomorrow."

"Good." He sounded relieved that the decision had been postponed. "Go to your homes, my people. Care for each other, and restore your strength."

Everyone started standing up. Laena turned to Joq. She saw, with surprise, that he looked shaken. "I never realized," he said. "I never thought you could—you would—"

"It was you who gave me the courage to step forward," she pointed out. "You told me they needed a new leader. That was what you said."

"Yes." There was a strange look in his eyes. "Yes, I know, but—"

"And years ago, I told you about my vision. When we were sitting by the river, don't you remember?" She seized his arms and gave him a little shake.

"Of course I remember." He held up his hands. "I just didn't realize—how forceful you would be. Laena, you're my wife! That's how I think of you, as my wife. Not as—" He trailed off helplessly.

They didn't have time to talk any further. The villagers were crowding around Laena, asking her to tell them again about her vision, demanding to know where this wonderful land could be, how they could ever find it, and a dozen other questions.

She felt exhausted and she longed for some rest, but she saw how important it was to reassure everyone and make her vision as real for them as it was for her. So Joq and Moru took Henik back to the cave, and Laena stayed by the fire, calmly repeating what she had already told them, trying to give them the confidence that she almost felt herself.

Later, when she had done all she could to persuade the people to put their trust in her, she broke away and went in search of Benke. He was a cave dweller, and he lived alone. She found him sitting cross-legged at the back of his cave, slowly sorting through a heap of flints. "Benke?" she called, peering past the smoky fire that burned in the cave mouth. "It's Laena. May I speak to you for a moment?"

"Yes," he said matter-of-factly. He didn't bother to look up.

She hesitated, then slipped in past the fire and seated herself opposite him. The floor of the cave was cluttered with bric-a-brac—tools, squares of hide, flint knives, spear shafts, thongs, clothing, scraps of wood, and simple drawing scratched into curls of tree bark. She couldn't imagine what he needed them all for.

"The flood played havoc here," he said, still without looking at her. "I'm trying to set everything back in order."

"I see," she said, though she thought it would have made better sense to throw out most of the objects he was hoarding. "I'm sorry to interrupt you. But—I need to know more about what you said earlier. About the way south. None of the other hunters has traveled as far afield as you have. No one else seems to think that my journey is even possible.''

He laid a cobble of flint aside. Warily, he met her eyes. ''I didn't say it was possible,'' he told her. ''I just said that there might be a way. Most people tend to forget, but east of here, our river is fed by another one. It flows from the mountains to the south. Some call it the Ghost River. If a group of people followed the path it takes, it might take them up through the mountains.''

Laena found herself leaning forward, hanging on his words. ''You really think so?'' she said quickly.

His face was half lost in shadow, so that she could barely see his expression. ''It could be,'' he said cautiously.

She hesitated. ''Would you want to come on this journey yourself?''

''I've been thinking about that.'' He moved his head so that he seemed to be looking past her. ''You know, I was married, once.''

Laena wondered what that had to do with it. ''People have told me,'' she said. ''Five years ago, your wife died in an accident—''

''We had only been together for a few months. But I never chose to marry again. That's why I'm a wanderer. I've learned to enjoy my own company.''

What was he trying to say—that there was nothing to tie him to the village and stop him journeying with her? He acted as if he would be giving away something precious if he came right out and gave her a specific answer. Maybe it was because he was a proud man, and she was a woman, younger than he. In that case, he might not be such an asset in her adventure after all. ''If you did come with us,'' Laena said, ''I don't know how you would feel, following me as the leader of the group. There was a time, not so long ago—''

Benke gave a curt nod. ''At that time, no woman had ever proved that she was worthy of the privileges you wanted.'' He shrugged. ''You have proved yourself now. You have my respect.'' He paused, rubbing a piece of leather between his finger and thumb. ''But I wonder if enough people will follow you. And—they may not like the idea of following the Ghost River. No one has been there, except for me. But still there are legends—''

''I've heard them.'' Laena was beginning to feel impatient. He talked so slowly, as if there were all the time in the world, and no need to get to the point. She could be here all night, trying to get him to deal directly with her questions. "Surely, they're just myths," Laena went on. "Stories that people tell in the winter when there's nothing else to do."

"Maybe so." He leaned against the rear wall of the cave. "When I saw the Ghost River, there was certainly nothing strange about it."

Now he had her attention again. She leaned forward. "Did you follow it far?"

He gave her a wary look and paused for a moment before answering. "There was no reason to." His voice was gruff.

"But you could have, if you'd wanted to?"

"Well—the terrain there is rough. There are steep, dangerous slopes to climb."

Maybe he didn't want to admit he had turned back because the going was hard. Still, he wasn't ruling it out. If there were several people helping one another, and if they had a strong motive to force them on—well, that might be enough to conquer the most difficult terrain. "When I traveled through the lands of the Wolf Tribe," she said, "a hunter told me how they climb steep mountains there. They use long, thin strands of knotted mammoth hide, strong enough to take a man's weight. They tie the hide around outcroppings of rock and haul themselves up it. Have you ever tried such a thing?"

Benke stacked some small leather sacks in a methodical pile. "Never," he said, reluctantly. He was a proud man; it was hard for him to admit that she might know more than he did.

Laena felt disappointed. He wasn't really an explorer; he was just a wanderer who enjoyed solitude because he had never come to terms with the death of his wife. The Fisher Tribe were homebodies, for the most part. Their valley and the nearby hunting grounds gave them all they needed, so they seldom bothered to venture farther. Compared to them, Benke was an adventurer; that was why they respected him so highly.

Still, Laena thought to herself, their respect could be useful if Benke would cooperate. "You know, the future of the tribe may be in doubt, if everyone stays here and we don't try to start anew," she said, staring directly into Benke's face.

He met her eyes and nodded gravely. "There may be some truth to that."

"Even if you decide not to travel with us yourself," she went on, "could you tell anyone who asks you, that you think my plan has a chance of success? I know they will respect your opinion."

He thought about that carefully. "I suppose that would be my duty to the tribe, to say that. But if they want to know exactly how it could be done—it's best I don't mention the Ghost River. I should just say what I said in the meeting, that the best way to go is east, then south."

"Good," she said. "Thank you." Impulsively, she reached out to take his hand.

He pulled back, avoiding the physical contact. "I'm happy to help you this much, in your venture." He spoke stiffly, formally. "And now, Laena, if you don't mind, I have a lot to set in order here."

All right, she thought to herself, *stay here in your cave, hiding from the world.* "I'm sorry I interrupted you, Benke," she said to him, matching his formality with her own. "And I thank you again for your wise advice."

She left him then, feeling newfound confidence in her own plans. While she had been talking to Benke, something had occurred to her: that the Fisher People used mammoth hide to lash the heavy poles together that supported their huts. In the aftermath of the flood, with everything in disarray, it should be easy to salvage some lengths of hide from the ruined buildings.

Much later, when it was almost dark, Laena returned to her own cave and found Moru taking care of Henik while Joq sat playing one of his flutes. For a moment, Laena paused and listened to the music. It calmed her, and she felt suddenly glad to have him and her sister to come home to.

But then Joq saw her. He stopped abruptly and tossed the little reed aside. "Let me take care of the baby now," he said.

"No, go on playing," Laena urged him. "It was beautiful."

He shook his head. There was something odd about the way he wasn't looking her in the eye. "Moru wants to talk to you," he said. He took Henik in his arms and retreated with him deeper into the cave, leaving Laena alone with her sister beside the fire.

For a moment, they looked at each other, saying nothing. Laena felt a tense premonition, though she couldn't say exactly what she feared. She waited, fretting with the hem of her furs.

"I should have known," Moru said finally, "that you had never really given up your dream." She shook her head, then winced and touched the spot where she had bruised her temple. "You are strong, Laena," she went on, so quietly that Laena could hardly hear her above the hissing of the flames. "You are stronger than I am." Moru looked out of the mouth of the cave, across the ruins of the village. "I wouldn't have been able to help everyone, and know what to do, the way you did today."

"You were injured," Laena objected.

Moru held up her hand. "That's not the point." She paused, searching for something deep inside herself. "What I'm saying is—if you make this great journey, pursuing your dream, Laena—I don't think I will be able to come with you."

Laena blinked. She felt a sudden hollowness inside her. "Moru—"

"I'm sorry." She said the words quickly, defensively. "I just can't face it. We don't even know that it's possible, Laena. The mountains are so tall, no one has ever climbed them. No one! And you have no experience—"

"Benke said he thought there might be a way," Laena pointed out, calmly, logically.

"No." Moru shook her head firmly. "No, I've made up my mind. You're my sister, and you've always helped me, and you've cared for me, and I love you dearly, and I believe in you. But I can't bear to uproot myself again."

She really sounded as if she meant it. Laena felt an overwhelming wave of sadness. And then, just as quickly, she felt stony resignation taking its place. She had lost her tribe, and her parents, and Elbrau, and Nan. If she was going to lose her sister now, it would give her great pain; but she had survived her other losses, and she would have to survive this one, too.

Still, she had to be sure that there was nothing she could do. She took her sister's hand. "Think of the things we've been through before, you and I. You were brave then, and you weren't as old as you are now. If you need my strength, I'll share it with you, gladly." She squeezed her hand tighter. "Come on, Moru. I know you can do it. Can't I change your mind?"

Moru started crying then. "Laena, Laena, why can't I ever change *your* mind?"

Laena drew back. So that was it: Moru was trying to make her abandon the plan. "I've given my reasons," Laena said, with less warmth in her voice. "They're good reasons. You can see that. This place isn't safe for us anymore, and there's a better land waiting for us beyond the mountains."

Moru slumped against the wall of the cave. She closed her eyes. "You don't really know that. You say you do, but you don't. No one has ever crossed the mountains before. Not even the strongest hunter. Doesn't that mean anything to you?"

"My visions have never lied," Laena said simply.

Moru was looking sullen now. She was still young, Laena realized; still young enough to want Laena to stay and look after her.

Suddenly Moru gathered herself up. "I can't!" she blurted out. "I can't leave. This is my home. This is where I belong, and I will *stay* here."

Laena sighed. "So be it," she said softly.

Moru stared at her as if she could hardly believe what she'd heard. "You mean, you'll just abandon me?"

"I've told you," Laena said, "why I must go."

Moru let out a little sob. She turned away and huddled down in her furs against the wall of the cave.

Laena wondered whether she should go to Moru and hold her and try to comfort her. No, she decided. It was too late for that.

She heard a movement, and she found Joq crawling out from the back of the cave, joining her by the fire. He sat down close beside her, without speaking.

"Is Henik sleeping now?" Laena asked.

Joq nodded.

She tried to read his face, but failed. He was her husband, and she wanted to believe that she could count on him without needing to ask him how he felt; and yet, she was no longer certain. She looked inside herself for the strength she needed—to ask for what she wanted, and to sustain herself if he refused.

"Well, my husband?" she said at last. "I'm sure you heard what Moru just told me. How about you? What's your decision?"

He put his arm around her, and he hugged her against him. "Long ago, I told you, I would never want to live without you. I must confess, I don't share your vision, Laena. But if you are determined to pursue it, I also know that I can't change your mind." He gave her a faint, sad smile. "So, I will stay by your side, and I will do whatever I can."

Until that moment, Laena hadn't realized how much emotion she had been holding in. She had been steeling herself, forcing herself to be strong—as strong as Nan had been, and as strong as her mother, before her.

Now, suddenly, the emotional gates were opened and she felt herself crying. She clung to Joq, burying her face against him, sliding her arms inside his furs and hugging him as hard as she could. "Thank you," she said, "I was so afraid you wouldn't come with me. Thank you."

He lifted her face between his hands, and he kissed her. "You don't need to thank me. I think you're right, that the valley isn't safe anymore. And I don't see anyone else who has the courage to lead our people anywhere else." He kissed her again, and his hands clenched tight on her shoulders. "Over and over, I keep wishing that none of this had happened. But it has happened, and we have to face it, and do something. Maybe this isn't the right thing to do; but maybe it's the *only* thing to do. Certainly, no one has been able to suggest anything else."

His words warmed her, all the more because he seldom spoke so openly. She felt grateful to him, and yet—she found herself wondering what she would have done if he had refused to come. She needed him; she cherished him; she truly loved him. But would she have sacrificed her vision for Joq? Or would she have sacrificed Joq for the sake of her vision?

She thrust the thought aside because deep down she knew the answer: she had lived here happily, but only by turning away from the center of herself, the deepest truth in her being. And she couldn't do that anymore. As soon as she had voiced her feelings to the tribe, she had felt a tremendous sense of rightness: that this was exactly what she had been placed on Earth to do.

Not even Joq could keep her from it now.

Chapter 40

Once again, Laena sat by the fire in the meeting place. A new day was dawning, and one by one, the villagers were gathering there.

She thought back over her years among the Fishers, first as an orphan searching for food, shelter, and a little kindness, then as a member of their tribe, and now, suddenly, as a fighter, a seer, and a leader. She could never have imagined such a thing was possible; and yet, looking back, there seemed to be a pattern leading inexorably to this time and place. There was no longer any doubt in her mind: someone, or something, had intended her to be here and do what she was doing. The only question now was whether the people of the Fisher Tribe would be brave enough to take up the challenge that she had given them.

She and Joq sat close together, holding little Henik between them. Moru was nearby, but she said nothing and Laena knew there was no point in trying to talk to her. So she waited, trying to be calm and patient, while the villagers emerged from their homes and came to warm themselves and join together as they had joined so often in the past.

Laena greeted all of them as they arrived. Some of them came over to her and took her hands in theirs, and thanked her for what she had done the previous day. Others seemed embarrassed, as if they didn't know what they should say. A few seemed reluctant to speak to her. But all of them acknowledged her now as the most important figure among them. It was clear from the way they watched her, and from the respectful looks on their faces.

None of them, though, said anything about the great journey she had proposed to them. It was as if the topic was too big, too difficult to deal with in a few informal words. The meeting would decide the matter; and so, they deferred it till the meeting began.

There was a tight knot of tension inside her, growing still tighter. She yearned to ask some of them what they had decided during the night. But she didn't dare speak of it. If she seemed to be looking for their support, it would weaken her as a leader. She had to seem calm and strong—so strong, she didn't even need to know whether they were pledging themselves.

She saw Faltor emerging from the ruins of his hut, and she especially wanted to know what he himself had decided. That would determine how he was going to organize this meeting, and how the great decision would be made. Always, in the past, he had tried to sense the will of his people, and then obey it. Would he do things any differently now? And what if half of the villagers chose to stay, while the others were just as determined to follow Laena on her quest?

But there was no point in asking those questions. Faltor would do whatever he had decided to do. It was too late to influence him now.

He walked to the people in the meeting place, moving slowly, wearily. Still, he paused just for a moment and smiled down at Laena, laying his hand briefly on her shoulder, before he turned to the rest of his people and raised his hands for silence.

"Last night," he said, "we all had time to reflect on Laena's plan. Last night, I know, there was talk in favor, and talk against, and husbands who wanted to make the great journey that she described, and wives who felt it would be wiser to stay here and rebuild our homes as best we can."

He paused for a long moment. He looked a little stronger than he had the previous day, and his voice was clearer. He had reached a decision, Laena realized. He had a clear idea of what should be done.

"My people," he went on, "I have thought long and hard on this. On the one hand, I see that Laena is right: our valley will never be as safe for us as it once was, and our village is in ruins. Also, I have learned to trust Laena's insight, her boldness, and yes, her visions."

Again he paused. This time, his strength wavered. He had

lost not only Nan but his son, his son's wife, and his grandson, Laena reminded herself. She looked at the faces around the fire, and all of them were staring up at Faltor with expressions of sympathy.

"The trouble is," Faltor went on, "I am a Fisher. My family has always lived here. I have always lived here. I fear I am too old to change."

Laena felt a stab of dismay. Surely, after everything that had happened, he wasn't going to tell his people to ignore her? Surely, he wouldn't turn away from her for a third time?

He turned to her and spread his hands. "I'm sorry, Laena," he said. "I cannot join you on your journey."

Laena felt Joq stiffen beside her. She clenched her hand quickly on his arm, to stop him from speaking. She willed herself to say nothing, and to show nothing. Not yet; not till she was certain that Faltor had said all he was going to say.

Some of the villagers started murmuring uneasily. Others looked relieved. Faltor ignored them. He walked slowly around the gathering till he came to one of the women, holding his granddaughter, Urami, on her knee. Faltor stooped and picked up the little girl in his arms.

A young man stood up. Laena saw that it was Orban, hotheaded and impatient as ever. "What do you suggest we should do?" he demanded. His voice was loud, but there was a tremor in it. "You say it isn't safe for us to live here anymore, and yet—"

Faltor straightened. He glared at Orban. "Quiet!" he shouted.

Orban stopped talking. He glanced uneasily around, and sat back down, with his face turning red.

Faltor nodded. "If you are patient," he said, "I will tell you what I have decided." He moved slowly back around the group, till he came to Laena. He paused, holding Urami, who squirmed in his arms and made little protesting noises.

"I have lost all my family except for this little girl," said Faltor. "She was spared from the flood by a miracle, and I've wondered why this should be. I think the answer is that she was destined to start anew. Laena, I want you to adopt Urami and take her with you on your journey to a new land. Let her stand in my place, as an emissary from the Fisher

Tribe. Let her learn the same courage that you have shown, to do what others are too old, or too afraid, to do.''

He stooped then and offered his grandchild to Laena.

Laena felt numb at first as she received the little girl and held her. Of all things, this was the last that she had expected. It was unprecedented. It was overwhelming.

And then she felt a sudden wave of dismay, as she realized the implications. Her journey would be arduous enough with Henik; to travel with a second young child might strain her resources to the limit. Urami and Henik were not entirely weaned. Laena knew from her own experience trekking with the Panther People across the plains how vulnerable such young children were, and how much of an additional burden they would add.

At the same time, she realized she couldn't refuse Faltor's gesture. He was making a sacrifice, he was bestowing an honor upon her, and even more than that, he was trying to help her by making it easier for other people in the tribe to join her, even though their families might be opposed to it. If Faltor was prepared to divide himself from his own kin, why shouldn't others do the same?

Laena gathered Urami into her arms and stood up. The child was slightly older and slightly heavier than Henik, and she was full of life. She wriggled and waved her legs, and when Laena smiled down at her, Urami smiled back.

"I'm deeply honored," Laena said to Faltor. "I will treasure your child as if she were my own. I will care for her, and protect her, and do everything I can to bring her to the land I've foreseen, where she can live in safety and happiness."

Faltor reached out and stroked the little girl's curly black hair. "Tell her about the Fisher People, when she grows older. Tell her about our tribe, and Orwael, and this village in the valley."

Laena nodded gravely. "I promise I will." She sat down then, clutching Urami to her breast.

"Very well." Faltor turned and surveyed his people, He rubbed his palms slowly together. "This is a matter for each person to decide, as I have done. Anyone may choose to stay here with me, and cope as best we can. Anyone may choose, instead, to go with Laena in search of a warmer, safer world. But the choice must be made now. There is no time to waste." He had erased the emotion from his voice.

He sounded brusque. "For those who go on the journey, it must be completed during the summer months. Otherwise, the travelers will die. There can be no doubt of that." He turned slowly, surveying the crowd. "So: who will step forward? Who will join Laena's quest?"

Once again, Laena felt herself clenching up inside. This time, the tension grew till it was like a cramp, gripping all her muscles. She deliberately stared straight ahead, not meeting anyone's eyes. She waited. And she waited.

Faltor shifted uneasily. "Joq. Will you go with your wife?"

Joq nodded. "I will." He spoke with simple, calm assurance.

"Who else?" Faltor's voice sounded more demanding now. "Does no one else have the courage to begin again?"

Orban stood up. "I'll go," he said.

"No!" His mother reached up and seized his sleeve. She had lost her husband in the flood, and Orban was the last of her family. "I told you, no!"

Orban glared at her. "He said that it's each person's choice! I'm of age. I'm free to choose." He jerked free from his mother's grasp, strode swiftly around the fire, and stood close beside Laena. He folded his arms, ignoring his mother as she started weeping, rocking to and fro, and clutching herself.

Meanwhile, there was a growing bedlam of voices, as husbands urged their wives to come and mothers begged their sons to stay. Several people were standing up, moving forward. Laena realized that one of them was Benke. It was happening, she realized, with a wave of relief. It was actually happening!

But even now, the situation was not entirely clear. There were more voices raised in protest, and more tears being shed. The arguing and the complaining rose in a wave that seemed as big as yesterday's flood. It surged and buffeted the people, and Laena had to force herself to be patient. Little Urami started whimpering, and Laena hugged the child close and crooned to her, trying to shield her from all the noise.

Finally, when the big fire in the meeting place had burned down to half its original height, the arguing was done. Faltor had waited as patiently as Laena; now he stood up again and raised his hands for silence. "It has been decided," he said. "This we have seen, and it is so." He paused, surveying the people who had gathered around Laena and Joq.

The ones who had pledged themselves—who had resisted the begging and pleading of their families, and had stayed true to their decision—were few in number. There were just three men and three women. No more.

There was Orban, the brash, ambitious young hunter. He could be headstrong, which was a danger; but there was no doubting his loyalty to Laena.

There was Jinkil, who had guarded her during the trouble with Gorag. He was slow-moving but cautious and strong, and he, too, could be loyal to a leader.

Lastly there was Benke, whose value Laena still couldn't estimate. He had knowledge that could be useful, and he would help to reassure the others—but whether he would be able to cooperate with her, she didn't know.

Then there were the three women:

Perri, who had been at the same joining ceremony as Laena, and had chosen Jinkil as her mate. She was shy and simple in her ways, and Laena knew that the only reason she was coming was because her husband had told her to.

There was Newa, whose husband and children had been swept away by the flood. She had nothing left to live for among the Fisher Tribe, and she had a need to believe there might be a place where she could start anew. Also, by a stroke of good fortune, her breasts were still making milk—for her youngest son, who had been swept away. If she could bring herself to feed Urami, that would help.

Lastly, there was Fayna. She had lost her brother, but her parents still lived. They had begged her not to leave; but she had defied them with the same rebellious spirit that Joq used to show toward his parents. She had come of age a year ago, but she had refused to choose a man. She had been waiting for a young hunter named Pelor, this year—but now he had been lost in the flood, and she had no one. And so she, too, was ready to make the journey.

Laena surveyed them, and decided that even though they were few, they were the best she could hope for. All of them were strong, and all of them were still quite young. Benke was the oldest, but she doubted he was more than five years her senior.

"There can be no time for second thoughts," Faltor said. "There will be no more arguing, no more pleading." He gave the older relatives a long, hard stare. "The decisions here are final. We have seen, and it is so."

He turned to Laena. "We will give you our best furs, our best spears, and all the food we can spare. By tomorrow morning, I want you all to leave on this journey of yours."

A rising murmur of protest started among the people who were staying behind.

"No," said Faltor. "It must be done quickly, if it is to be done at all."

And Laena saw why: if too much time was allowed to elapse, it would be too easy for doubts to creep in.

And so, there it was. Laena rose to her feet. "Thank you," she said to Faltor. "Thank you, for your wisdom. Thank you, for your fairness. We will never forget you."

There was a cheer from the villagers; but it was a half-hearted one. Many of the people were still overcome with grief or anger at having their families further torn apart after they had already been decimated by the flood.

"I have done what I can for you, Laena," Faltor said, much more quietly, so that only she could hear the words. "I hope you feel I have made up for my failings in the past."

"Of course," she said, feeling deep gratitude to this kind, gentle man. She could no longer resent him for the times when he had refused to listen or refused to act. He had followed his conscience, and he had done the best he could. What more could she ask than that?

She turned to the six young men and women who had pledged themselves. "We have a lot to do," she told them. "Benke, we'll need your advice on the paths leading to the east and south from here—those that are known. We'll need to pack as much food as we can carry. And we'll need any supplies that we can dig out of the remains of the healer's hut."

They all nodded their agreement. She felt them staring at her with a strange intensity. They were depending on her, she realized. They had put all their faith in her.

Was she worthy of it? She felt a pang of self-doubt. The journey she was planning would be the most extreme test of skill and endurance. There would be only eight of them to shoulder the burden, care for each other, and protect the children. Perhaps someone would be injured; perhaps someone would even die on the treacherous mountain slopes. Would they have to be abandoned, as Gorag had once wanted to abandon Jobia's mother, Heese? And how could Laena cope if a man or a woman died because they had decided to share her quest? What if something happened to Joq, or even Henik?

But then she reminded herself of the alternative. If she and her followers stayed here with the Fisher People, they would be taking a far greater risk in the long term. They could never defend themselves against the Wolf Tribe, or any of the other threats to their survival. Ultimately, she believed in her soul, they would perish.

And so, there was no real alternative.

Faltor aided Laena as much as he could. He strode around the camp, shouting instructions, goading people into action, keeping everyone busy, so that there was no time for misgivings. She was deeply thankful to him, because she had her own problems to cope with.

"Please, please don't do this terrible thing!" Weeps cried as Laena started gathering up her own possessions and stowing them in her pack.

"You could come with us," she said, trying to keep her voice calm and quiet.

The woman started crying. "I'd die!" she wailed. "I know I'd die!"

She was sitting in the mouth of Laena's cave, blocking most of the light so that it was almost impossible for Laena to see what she was doing. "Listen," Laena said patiently. "I have given my reasons for going. If you really care for Joq, you should be happy that he'll have a chance to begin again in a new land."

"*He'll* die!" Weeps cried. She started sobbing hysterically. "Orleh, Orleh, come and tell her. Tell her that it's wrong."

But Orleh was already occupied, in his own cave, shouting at Joq. Laena could hear him: "I'm not just losing my only son, I'm losing my only grandson!"

And so it went on.

Other families were going through similar upheavals elsewhere in the village, as afternoon faded gradually into evening. Twice, Laena had to break off and go to each of the people who had pledged themselves to travel with her, so that she could lend them courage to stay true to their decision.

"I'm afraid I'm using up all my strength before I even set out on this journey," she confided to Faltor when the light was fading and only the highest peaks still glowed orange around the valley.

Faltor was playing with his young granddaughter, holding her on his knee, smiling at her wistfully as she tried to snatch a piece of bark that he dangled in front of her on a leather thong. "It is sometimes hard," he said, "to be a leader."

His quiet words were like a reprimand. She realized now what he had had to endure in the past, and she wished that sometimes she hadn't judged him so harshly.

He cradled Urami in one arm, then turned and patted Laena's shoulder. "Remember this. If you are fierce, your people may respect you. But if they see you are kind, they will love you, which is worth more. And if they see you are wise, they will follow you, which is the most important thing of all."

That sounded simple enough; maybe even too simple. But as she thought about it, she saw that it was true. "Thank you," she said. "Thank you for all you have done for me."

He bent his head. "I wish this could be a happier time," he murmured. He turned back then to the little girl in his arms.

Moru had avoided Laena for most of the day. She had retreated to the place where Joq had once sat and played his flutes, and she ignored anyone who came and called to her.

Finally, when it was almost dark, and Laena's party had completed all their preparations, Moru came to the cave. For a little while she lingered in the entrance, where Weeps had sat—a hunched figure, bulky in her furs, just crouching there and saying nothing.

"Have you come to say good-bye?" Laena asked finally. She had been sitting with Joq, huddling against him, enjoying the warmth of his body while little Henik lay between them, breathing gently, fast asleep.

"Yes," said Moru.

Laena started to disentangle herself from her husband and son, so that she could go to her sister.

"No. Stay there." Moru's voice was unsteady. "I'm sorry, but it has to be this way."

Laena paused. "What do you mean?"

"I have to be separate from you now, Laena. You know, even when we didn't get along for a while—even when you seemed to think that I had my own life and I didn't need you anymore, even then—" She trailed off.

Laena waited patiently. "Yes, sister?"

"I still felt your presence," Moru said. Her voice was muffled now. "Your strength. You were like Nan, always so strong. So much stronger than me."

Laena felt a deep sadness. "That's not the way it was at all," she said. "I was weak, and I was always afraid."

"No, that's not true!" Moru sounded hurt, and angry, and tormented. "You were the strong one, and I always did what you asked. But this journey of yours, this is something I can't do. So I have to learn to be strong now myself. And the only way I can do that is to be on my own. Otherwise, I know I won't have the courage." She drew a shaky breath. "So, I have to go now, Sister, and I won't be able to see you in the morning. I'm sorry, and I hope you understand."

Laena felt tears welling up, pricking her eyes. She realized that a part of her hadn't quite believed that Moru would stay behind. A part of her had assumed that her younger sister would follow her, as she'd always ended up following Laena in the past.

Suddenly it felt as though something were being physically taken out of Laena's body, a piece of her being removed from her chest. She leaned forward and clumsily reached out. "Moru, no! Please don't do this!"

Moru hesitated for just an instant. She gave Laena a distraught look, as Laena's fingers touched her cheek.

Then she pulled back quickly. "I will always remember you, Laena. Always! And I'll teach the young ones what you did for the Fisher Tribe." She drew another shaky breath. From her voice, it was clear that she, too, was crying. "Good-bye now," she said. And quickly, before Laena could touch her again, she scrambled out of the cave.

Chapter 41

And so, the next day, after the last farewells had been said and the last tears had been shed, there were just ten of them setting out along the riverbank. Four men, four women, and two young children, ready to put themselves against the vastness of the world that lay beyond the land they knew. For Laena, there had never been a moment when she felt so bold and proud. And yet, there had never been a time when she had felt so fearful for the future.

They followed her in single file, walking along the riverbank. Not so long ago, this in itself would have amazed her: to have four grown men looking at her as their leader. So much had changed, she thought to herself. If only Nan were still here, to see this now. Would she approve? Laena liked to think so.

Laena felt Henik squirming in his pouch, strapped across her chest. Joq had tied it tightly, and Henik wasn't used to being so snug. She hummed softly to him as she walked, and she stroked the top of his head, under his fur hood.

She was uncomfortably aware of how heavily loaded they all were. Her own pack was a burden weight on her back. And it was relatively small, compared to the loads that the men were carrying.

For a while, everyone moved in stoic silence, and Laena realized they were feeling not just the physical load but the burden of the journey itself, stretching into the unknown. The village still lay within reach behind them, seeming safe compared with the terrain that lay ahead.

But as they marched on, and the village became hidden by the twists and turns of the valley, Laena felt the mood of the party lighten around her. They were shedding their past, feeling stronger now. Their future could be just as rich with rewards as it might be burdened with hardship and danger.

Meanwhile, the valley itself was a constant source of wonder, transformed out of all recognition from the way it had always looked in the past. The steep sides were coated with brown mud where the flood had come surging through. The vegetation looked limp and bedraggled, and small trees had been tossed carelessly here and there.

Then, as they rounded the next curve in the river, they saw how the flood had come about. There had been a rock-slide, which wasn't unusual during the spring thaw. But this had been a major event, so that huge boulders still partially blocked the river and water gushed out between them where it couldn't flow over the top.

"See, the slide must have happened a month or more ago, and it took trees down with it." It was Joq's voice, coming from directly behind Laena. She paused and turned to him, and saw him surveying the walls of the valley. "Then the river washed the trees up against the pile of boulders. That made a barrier. There might have been a second slide, on top of the first. In the end, the whole river was blocked."

"That would explain why it flowed lower, at first, this season," said Orban.

"But the water would have built up behind the barrier," said Laena. "And then, finally, the barrier broke, and it all came surging through in a great wave."

They stood for a moment, staring with awe and dismay at the wreckage that Nature had caused. Some of the fallen trees were so large, six men working together would not have been able to lift one.

Laena began to feel uneasy. This was a bad idea, she realized—to allow her people to feel cowed by the forces of the natural world, even before they had left the security of their valley. "We must see this as a sign," she said, making her voice loud and strong.

They turned and looked at her.

"The flood was a message," she went on. "It was a sign that we should leave the valley and set out on this journey." She hesitated, groping for words. She felt their attention on her, and she realized they expected more from her. "It was also a sign that we must proceed in harmony with the world," she went on. "If we go against the flow of things, we may be crushed. But if we move cautiously, in harmony with Nature, its power can help us on our way instead of standing against us.''

She watched their faces. Would they believe her? She wasn't even sure if she believed herself. She had never been a leader before. She felt self-conscious and unsure of herself.

But she saw in the faces of the group that they took her seriously. Benke moved a little closer. His face was weather-beaten by the seasons, and there were deep wrinkles around his eyes, as if he had spent most of his life squinting into a cruel cold wind. ''I think you speak truly,'' he said. ''Sometimes, on a slope covered in ice, it can look as if there is no safe path to take. But if you stop and look, often you can sense a way that was not clear at first. The way is there, hidden just below the surface. And then, the land is not your enemy anymore. It is your ally. So, that's the secret of our journey. To find the way that we were intended to take, and not force ourselves against the land.''

Everyone nodded, and Laena saw how much they trusted Benke's practical knowledge of the terrain.

''See, there,'' he went on, ''the rockslide has opened up a new path to the top of the valley, and it looks easier than the old one, farther on.''

Laena looked where he pointed. She could barely make out a zigzag trail. It looked more hazardous, to her, than the path they normally took. This was the kind of thing she'd been afraid of, when she'd imagined him in her group. Should she trust his judgment, or should she stand against him? He could easily resent her, if she did. And it would divide people's loyalties. On the other hand, if she let him lead the way now, it might make her seem less of a leader.

She made her decision impulsively. ''Go ahead then, Benke,'' she said. ''Show us the way.''

He stepped forward, and she realized she had done the right thing. If she was willing to lend her authority to someone else in the group, that showed how confident she felt of her own position. No one would respect her less for that. They would respect her more.

''Perri,'' she said. ''You follow Benke. Jinkil, you walk behind Perri. Then Newa and Orban, and Fayna and Joq—

so that if any of the women misses her footing, a man will be behind her to break her fall.''

''What about you?'' said Joq. ''If you walk behind the rest of us, there'll be no one to catch you.''

She shook her head. ''I spent my whole childhood climbing steep hillsides. I won't fall.''

He glanced doubtfully at Henik in the pouch on her chest, but then he shrugged. ''All right,'' he said.

The others were already starting the climb, in the order she had suggested. Laena followed after them. In reality, there had been no slopes as steep as this in the land of the Panther People, but she needed to demonstrate that she could take care of herself.

As it turned out, the climb was easy. Benke had been right: the trail was there, if you had the skill to discern it. Reluctantly, Laena had to admit that she had underestimated him. She made a mental note to watch him closely—not just to learn from him, but to see that he took no unnecessary risks. Clearly, everyone felt more confident as a result of having him in the group. And that alone would increase their chances of success.

Later, around noon, they rested. They had walked a long way east, past Blind Valley, where the mammoths had been trapped and slain, and into an area which Laena had never seen before. The land here was unwelcoming: gravelly and barren, loose underfoot, with only a few weak clumps of grass struggling for life on the steep gray slopes. The Fishers seldom bothered to come here, for it had nothing to offer them. There were no animals to hunt on the barren slopes, and no water to quench a man's thirst.

Nor was there any wood to build a fire. The travelers had to huddle together for warmth while they made a quick meal from the smoked meat in their packs, and Laena fed Henik and Newa suckled Urami. So far, the children had been no trouble. But how they would react to weeks and months of travel was impossible to guess.

Orban was the first to finish eating. He always ate fast, as if he was impatient to be done with it. He wiped his hands on his furs, glanced around at the bleak land, and grunted discontentedly. ''Laena-mother,'' he said, ''when do we start moving south?''

Laena looked at him, then at the others. It was time, she decided, to tell them exactly what lay ahead. "Benke," she said quietly, "I would like you to explain the first part of our journey."

Benke gave a curt nod. He gestured for the people to move back, giving him some space. Then, using the shaft of his spear, he draw a wavy line in the gray gravel at their feet. "This is the valley of the Fisher Tribe," he said. He pressed the shaft into the ground, making a dent. "This is the village." He glanced around, making certain that everyone was paying attention. The only sound now was the wafting of the wind and an occasional whimper from Urami, who was still being nursed by Newa, but seemed to be pining for her real mother.

Benke shifted his spear a little way along the line. "Here is where we saw the rockfall. Just a little further, the valley gets so narrow there's no way to walk farther along it. At that point, there's the path we usually climb to our hunting grounds."

"But I know all this," said Orban. He shifted restlessly. "Even the women know this."

"Orban." Laena gave her voice a sharp edge.

He glanced up at her, and realized what he had said. "Forgive me, Laena-mother," he muttered, suddenly shame-faced.

Laena wondered if it would always be so easy to make him back down. She hoped so; he was too headstrong, and it bothered her. "Go on, Benke," she said.

The scout nodded. "Very well. From our hunting grounds, we moved east, to where we are now, in the Gray Lands." His spear traced the route on the ground. "But understand, the river is still nearby." He went back to the wavy line and extended it parallel with the path they had taken. "A bit further on, we can get back to the river, because the valley widens out again." He smiled faintly. "By that time, our water bags will be empty."

"Have you been this far before?" Orban asked. His voice sounded tense.

"Yes." Benke grunted. "Don't worry, young man. We will not die of thirst."

Orban drew himself up. "I wasn't—"

"In fact," Benke went on, "we will have more water

than we need." He dragged the shaft of his spear, showing
where their path would bring them back to the river. Then
he extended the river a little further east; and then he drew
a line from it, to the south. "There is another river that
flows into our river. It comes down from the tall mountains
that lie to the south and block our path. If we follow that
river, perhaps all the way to its source, I think we may find
a path through the mountains." Again he paused and looked
at them all.

Now the silence seemed uneasy. Laena noticed Orban
glancing at Jinkil, then at Joq. "That's the Ghost River,
isn't it?" he said. "I have heard—"

"You've heard stupid legends," said Laena, speaking
quickly, determined to take control of the conversation.
"Tales that people tell in the winter about monsters and
people who eat their dead." She made a sound of disgust.
"Has anyone actually *seen* the Ghost River?" She looked
around.

Again, people exchanged glances; but no one answered.

Laena turned to Benke. "You have seen it. Tell us."

Benke nodded. "It's just a river. The land is very steep,
very rough. The hunting is poor. And the stream runs so
fast, even the salmon avoid it. There's no one living there.
Without food, why would anyone choose to make their home
in such a place?"

"So," said Laena. "That is the path we will follow."

For a long moment, no one spoke. Then Fayna raised her
hand. "I have a question," she said.

Laena looked at her. The young woman had barely said
a word through the first half of the day. Laena had assumed
she was still grieving for the brother she had lost in the
flood, and the parents she had left behind at the village.

"What's your question?" Laena said.

"No travelers have ever come to us from the Ghost
River," Fayna said. "No one, ever. How can that be?"

Laena spread her hands. "Maybe the land is so un-
friendly, no one has ever chosen to go that way."

Fayna was silent for a moment. She seemed to be mulling
it over. "But if no one lives there, and if no one has ever
crossed the mountains—what can there be, in the land beyond? Will there by anything for us to eat? Will there be
anything at all?"

"I already told you my vision," Laena said. "Somewhere to the south, there is a land far more beautiful than anything we have seen before."

"But how far will it be?" Fayna persisted.

Laena told herself to be patient. The questions were inevitable, and they had to be answered. "I can't tell you that," she said. "I don't know. No one knows."

Fayna frowned. "You told us—"

"I told you I have faith," Laena interrupted her. "I believe with all my soul, I will find the land of my visions sooner or later, because it is part of my destiny. And if you follow me, you will find it, too. But I can't tell you exactly how, or exactly when. You must have faith in me, and be patient. I'm sure there are many unknown things ahead of us, and many mysteries that we will uncover."

Fayna watched Laena for a long moment. Finally, unexpectedly, she stood up. "In that case," she said, "we should not waste any more time discussing this. We should go and see for ourselves."

She was testing me, Laena thought to herself. *She wanted to be sure that I was sure.* And evidently, Laena had passed the test—this time, at least.

By the evening, they reached a dip in the land where some small trees grew. Laena had been afraid that they wouldn't get beyond the slopes of bare gray gravel before darkness fell, and she was relieved when the little pocket of green came in sight. She sat down and watched as the rest of her people moved ahead, gathering dry wood and poking around in the bushes, searching for any signs of wild life.

There was a sudden shout from Orban. He raised his spear and threw it in one quick, savage motion.

Laena peered into the twilight, trying to see what he had seen.

Orban ran forward, grabbed the shaft of his spear where it had fallen, and raised it high. A rabbit was impaled on the tip, still kicking. "Here, Laena-mother!" he shouted to her. "See, a good omen!"

Laena clapped her hands. "Good, Orban. Let's start a fire. This is a fine place to camp."

"Very good," said a voice. "They're all happy now."

Laena turned quickly and found that Joq had come up silently beside her.

"You know, Orban speaks truly," Joq went on. "You really are Laena-mother. You're a mother to all of them."

Something in his tone of voice made her uneasy. "What are you saying, Joq?"

He laid his arm gently around her shoulders. "I watched how you dealt with them today. Calming them, disciplining Orban, renewing their confidence—just like a mother. You did it very well."

She found herself feeling embarrassed. "All I did—"

"You don't need to say anything. You were a true leader." But then he frowned. "I just worry what happens, if the children ever find out that the mother doesn't know quite as much as she seems to."

"So you should keep my secret with me, Joq," she murmured. "Don't let them know that I have doubts, and I lack experience, and I may make mistakes."

He tightened his grip around her shoulders for a moment, then let her go. "You can trust me, Laena," he said. "Just as I trust you. Remember, though: speak truly to me. I'm not one of the children. I'm your husband."

Chapter 42

The next day, as Benke had promised, they found their way back to the river—the same river that flowed past the village, further downstream. The valley here was wider, but its walls were so steep they were like cliffs. The bottom of the valley was flat, and the river snaked among lush green vegetation. There were trees growing down there, Laena realized.

Cautiously, Benke led the way down an erosion channel that he had discovered on one of his previous visits. "This place is not quite as welcoming as it seems," he called over his shoulder. "There are hardly any animals that make the journey down."

Laena shrugged mentally. If the land had been more hospitable, people would have already settled here. Her party was carrying enough food for three weeks, at least. She wasn't going to start worrying about that for a while.

When they reached the floor of the gorge, she moved to the head of the group and led the way ahead, pushing through dense groves of spruce trees. Jinkil was the only one carrying a fishing spear, for he had more experience as a fisherman than any of the others. He moved along the riverbank, watching for any telltale silver flicker under the surface. But he only cast his spear a couple of times, and the one fish that he caught was so small he tossed it aside with disgust.

At noon, they reached a place where the gorge opened out wider than before. And there, around a rocky promontory, they came to the Ghost River.

For a long moment, everyone stood and stared at it. Finally, Perri spoke. "Why, it's no different from our river," she said.

People laughed then. There was something reassuring in Perri's simplicity, and Laena was thankful for it.

Benke led them to a shallow stretch of water, where rocks served as stepping stones. And then they were on the opposite side, moving upstream along the Ghost River, leaving the old river behind them.

All too soon, the terrain became as severe as Benke had warned them that it would be. The walls of the gorge closed in, and the flat land at the bottom, either side of the river itself, became cluttered with boulders and slabs of fallen rock. The trees thinned out and disappeared, and dense, thorny brambles took their place. Finding a way forward became an arduous, frustrating process.

The walls of the gorge rose even more steeply than the river at its bottom. Laena glanced up once in a while and felt a sinking sensation as the land seemed to be closing in around her. And directly ahead, the mountain peaks seemed to loom taller than ever, blotting out the sky.

By nightfall, everyone was feeling the strain. Fayna and Orban had started snapping at each other. They were both quick-tempered any impatient, and they argued over any small thing—even when Orban let go of a bramble branch too quickly, and it snapped back and scratched Fayna's arm. Meanwhile, Joq had gone into one of his silent moods, which always bothered Laena, because it usually meant he was nursing a resentment. Jinkil was being surly, ordering Perri around and complaining when she didn't move fast enough to obey. And both of the babies were shouting their discontent.

The only ones who seemed calm were Benke and Newa. Benke had retreated inside himself, and walked some distance away from the rest of the group. Newa, meanwhile, was still grieving for her lost husband and child, and she hardly seemed to notice her surroundings. Her face was flushed with the effort of the journey, but she said nothing when Laena called a halt. She simply sat on the nearest boulder, opened her furs, and nursed Urami till she finally ceased her wailing.

Laena realized it would be foolish to try to travel any further that day. She found a small area where the ground wasn't too stony, and she got Joq to help her clear a few large rocks out of the way. "This will be our camp tonight," she said, and no one argued with her.

Later, after they had built a meager fire from dried brambles, the travelers huddled together under the moonlit sky. Laena remembered years ago, how she had urged Moru along the riverbank when they had briefly journeyed south after leaving the camp where they had stayed with Gorag. She had sung songs to the little girl, to take her mind off the journey. And so, here among the Fisher People, in this inhospitable corner of the world, she started singing one of those same old songs.

When she finished, there was silence among her companions, as there had been before. But it was a different kind of silence now. There was serenity that hadn't been there before.

"Was that the language which you used to speak in your tribe on the western plains?" Fayna asked her quietly.

"Yes," said Laena. "And that was a song we sang as we made the great journey from our winter camp to our summer camp, and back again."

"You have traveled far in your life." That was Benke's voice; and for the first time, Laena heard some genuine respect in it.

"One thing my traveling taught me," said Laena, "is that a hardship today becomes a thing to smile about tomorrow. We will pass through this valley, and our way will get easier. I have no doubt of that."

She felt Joq shifting beside her, and then his arm snaked around her, hugging her to him. It was his way of apologizing for being so silent, she realized. Once again, she had been a mother to them all. She had found a way to keep them in harmony, despite everything.

But it had been an effort, and she didn't know how many more times she could find the resources to do that. What if the journey took many months? Could she be a peacemaker, and a leader, and a source of optimism, for all that time?

I never really wanted to be a leader, she told herself. *All I wanted was to find the place of my visions.*

But she saw now she couldn't have one thing without the other.

The next morning, as they continued on along the steep, stony bank of the river, they heard a steady roaring sound from up ahead. For a moment, Laena felt a twinge of fear. She remembered the sound of the flood, moments before it had engulfed the village. She looked around quickly to see if there was a place to climb to safety—but the walls of the gorge were as sheer as ever, allowing no refuge.

She turned to Benke. "When you came here before—"

"I didn't come this far," he corrected her. "But I think there's no cause for alarm. I think the sound we hear is just a waterfall."

Laena gave an embarrassed laugh. "Of course," she said. "You're right."

So they moved onward. And the sound of the water grew gradually louder—and louder still.

They found their way through a zig-zag twist in the gorge; and then, finally, they saw what lay ahead. At first Laena thought there must be some trick of perspective confusing her eye. There was a huge tumble of stone—so huge, it made the rockfall that they had seen near their old village look like a few stones that a child had tossed down.

This rockfall completely blocked the gorge, and it towered up, and up, filling the V-shaped gap between two mountains that stood on either side of it. The boulders themselves were massive—each of them taller than a man. Meanwhile, the river had carved its own path among them, so that it cascaded down in a wild, ragged, roaring torrent. White ribbons of water surged over the great stones with furious energy, and Laena realized that the ground was actually trembling under her feet.

Faintly, she heard a grinding sound above the noise of the water. She looked up, just in time to see a boulder roll free, high in the tumbled edifice of stone. It bounced down, shattering smaller rocks into a hail of gravel. It disappeared briefly among the white cascade, then reappeared, smashing into the chute below. The stones beneath Laena's feet quivered, and she flinched, curling her arms protectively around Henik where he lay against her chest.

She glanced at her people where they had gathered around her. All of them were staring at her in dismay.

"So, we must turn back," Jinkil said finally. There was no pleasure in his voice. He sounded angry at having to admit defeat.

Privately, Laena had been thinking the same thing. But when she heard Jinkil say it, she found herself instinctively reacting against it. She looked again at the towering mass of boulders, and she slowly shook her head. "There may still be a way," she said. She shouted the words, so they could be clearly heard above the roaring of the water.

Jinkil looked at her as if she was crazy. "What are you talking about?"

Laena slung her pack down from her shoulders. She opened it and hauled out the knotted lengths of mammoth hide that she had salvaged from the village. "Orban," she said, turning to the young hunter. "If Jinkil helped you, you could get up onto one of those lowest boulders, couldn't you?"

He hesitated only for a moment. "I could," he agreed with her.

She nodded. She'd been sure that he would be too proud to say no. "All right," she went on, "then Jinkil could help Joq up there. Yes?"

Joq nodded cautiously. He didn't say anything.

Laena passed the hide-rope to Orban. "Benke could join you, and then the three of you could pull the rest of us up with this. See, the boulders at the bottom here are the biggest ones. Farther up, we should be able to climb with less trouble."

Jinkil had been listening carefully, still with an expression of grim doubt. "How do you expect the women to manage a climb like that?"

"I am a woman," Laena said, facing him calmly. "And I see no problem. Do you, Fayna? Do you, Newa? Or Perri? Didn't we all expect to do some climbing on a journey like this?" She waited for a moment, while the woman exchanged uneasy glances. "All right," she said, "if it's impossible, then we'll try some other route instead. But we try it first."

Joq nodded. So did Orban. Jinkil said nothing, but she could see that he wouldn't back away from the challenge if the other men were willing to tackle it. And the women seemed reluctant to speak out against the men.

For a moment, Laena felt annoyed with them. It seemed wrong that she should be leading such a timid group on this great adventure. The Fisher People simply weren't the stuff that heroes were made of. They could be brave, but they were seldom bold.

Well, they would have to learn to be. "Let's get started," she said brusquely. "We need to reach the top before sunset, and it's already almost noon."

She walked toward the immense rockfall without looking back, as if she had total confidence that they would follow her. For a tense moment, she heard nothing but the sound of the waterfall; and then, thankfully, she heard footsteps coming after her, crunching across the fragments of loose stone littering the ground.

It would be best, she decided, to climb as far away from the torrent as possible. The stones would be drier and less likely to be dislodged by the force of the water.

She selected a giant boulder that had come to rest snug against the wall of the gorge. "All right, Jinkil," she said. "Help Orban up onto it."

The big man nodded. He bent forward and braced himself with his hands on his knees. Orban jumped up onto his back, then moved forward till his feet were on Jinkil's shoulders. Jinkil slowly straightened up, and from there, Orban pulled himself onto the top of the rock.

It actually seemed easy, now that they were confronting the task. The height of the rockfall was intimidating, but if they took it one step at a time, and if they were careful, there should be no trouble.

Within a few moments, Orban, Joq, and Benke were all standing on the great boulder. "Pull Jinkil up now," said Laena, throwing them the rope. "If it takes his weight, it will be safe for the rest of us."

She stood and watched as the three men took a firm grip on the knotted cord, and Jinkil started hauling himself up.

"How did you learn how to climb mountains, Laena-mother?" Orban called to her, as Jinkil joined them on top of the boulder.

"I was taught by a young man named Sordir, in the Wolf Tribe," Laena said. She would be foolish, she decided, if she admitted she had never actually done something like this before. Her people needed as much confidence as possible to make the climb.

"There's no room for more people on this rock," Joq called down to her.

"So, Jinkil, help the men up to the top of the next one. Then haul the women up with the rope."

They did as she said. She had a moment of anxiety herself, as she knotted the rope under her arms, clutched Henik against her, and allowed Jinkil to hoist her into the air. If the rope failed, or if Jinkil slipped, she imagined herself plummeting backward onto the stony ground that lay below. But then, within moments, she felt the top of the boulder under her feet, and she found herself looking into Jinkil's wide, grinning face.

Fayna came next, and had no trouble. Newa followed, with her eyes closed tight and her face looking pale. She smiled, though, when she found herself standing on top of the boulder. It was a smile of relief.

Last of all was Perri. "Tie the knot tight," Jinkil called down to her, as she looped the rope under her arms.

She fumbled with it, and Laena saw that her hands were trembling.

"Tight!" Jinkil shouted again. "Make sure it's tight!"

"It *is* tight," she shouted back.

"All right," Jinkil grunted. He started hauling her up, more quickly and more roughly than he had the others. Laena looked on, expecting Perri to start whimpering or screaming. But something had stirred in her; a defiance that she'd never shown before. When she found her footing alongside Jinkil, she said nothing. She simply untied the rope and handed it to him. And Laena noticed that the woman's hands weren't trembling anymore.

From there, the travelers moved up to the top of the next boulder, and the next. They were piled steeply, but there was always a ledge to stand on between one and the next. Newa confessed that she was afraid of heights, but she managed to avoid looking back, and she continued in the same way that she'd started—with grim, stoic determination countering her fear.

After a while the stones became smaller. Laena roped everyone together, so that if one person fell, the others could bear the load. From here, they scrambled up the rockfall side by side.

It was easier than any of them had expected, but it was still grueling work. Laena's pack seemed to grow heavier and heavier on her shoulders, and she was constantly afraid of falling forward onto Henik, who was still nestling against her chest, staring up at her with wide, startled eyes.

The smaller stones were sharp-edged, cutting into her mittens, and they were loose underfoot. Several times, she slipped and felt the rope jerk tight around her waist. The sun beat down on her, and she felt herself sweating. She loosened her furs, but there was no way to shed them. Whenever she looked up, she saw the distant mountain peaks high above, topped with snow; and she knew that in the days to come, she would need all the warmth she could get.

Gradually, as they neared the top, the roaring of the water diminished. The slope became easier, and they were able to move from the rockfall onto the mountainside that had spawned it. There was room to pause and rest here, and sit for a minute, looking back the way they had come. The view was dizzying, and Newa wasn't the only one who had trouble looking at it for long. The slope that dropped away below them was frighteningly steep, and Laena realized that even though the climb had seemed easy, it had been dangerous. If two or three of them had all happened to lose their footing at the same moment—she imagined the bodies rolling, tumbling, dragging each other down, leaving a trail of blood across the stones. She shuddered. The image was too real, like something out of a vision. But it hadn't happened, and maybe (she thought to herself) it *couldn't* happen. If she was destined to reach the green and sunny place, how could she die here on this remote mountainside?

Late in the afternoon, they finally reached a point on the mountain where they were higher than the rockfall itself. A large lake had built up behind it, but the level of the lake was a long way below the highest stones, because the water was able to escape through the chute that it had carved for itself.

Laena looked ahead and saw that it would be easy enough to follow a ridge that ran around the lake, to the river that flowed in at the opposite end. Even there, though, there was no easy way down from the ridge to the water.

Benke was looking at her, and she realized that he was sharing her thoughts. "Our water bags are almost empty," he said. "We didn't fill them before we climbed. And we drank on the way up, to quench our thirst."

Laena said nothing. It was her fault, she realized. If she was the leader, she should have looked ahead. But while she had been climbing the rockfall, with the constant thunder of the waterfall in her ears and wet spray drifting on the breeze, it had seemed as if water was the least of their worries.

She looked again at the lake. The water was a bright, rich blue, shimmering in the sun. "There has to be a way down to it," she said, half to herself.

Everyone now understood her concern. Together, they stood and studied the land that sloped away from the ridge where they stood. The valley was bow-shaped; it curved up from the lake till its sides were almost vertical. Down beside the lake itself, the slope was gentle and the travelers would have no trouble walking and finding a place where they could spend the night. Grass was growing there, and a scattering of thin trees. but up here at the rim, they found themselves perching above a sheer wall of gray rock.

Laena looked back. If they retraced their steps, they could get back to the waterfall and refill their water bags from there. But as soon as she imagined the task, she rejected it. The journey down would be much more frightening and dangerous than the journey up had been. She was sure that Newa wouldn't be able to manage it; and she wasn't even sure that she could tackle it herself.

"I have an idea," said Joq.

She turned to him. "What?"

"See the ledge down there, directly below us? It runs diagonally down, to the place where the walls of the valley aren't so steep. It would take us to a point where we could get down to the lake."

Laena tried to weigh the possibility. It was difficult, because she had so little experience of anything like this. The ledge was twice as far below her as the height of a man, and there was nothing but bare rock between it and her.

"We can lower the lightest people from here down to the ledge, using the rope," Joq went on. "Then we can drape the rope around that rock." He pointed to an outcropping that was firmly set on the ridge where they stood. "The men who are left up here can climb down the rope. When we've all descended, we pull the free end of the rope, and it slips around the rock and follows us down. That way, we'll still have it if we need it farther on."

She looked at his face. He seemed to think it would be

easy enough, regardless of the fact that none of them had ever done such a thing in their lives before.

She wondered what she should do. What would her father have done? Or Faltor? Or Nan?

"We should take a vote," she said finally. "We can follow this ridge all the way around the valley, and hope there's an easier way down at the opposite end. But that won't be easy. And I'm sure we can't make it all the way before darkness falls. Meanwhile, we need water. So should we do as Joq says?"

She paused and waited. For a long moment, no one spoke. Benke was looking away across the valley, as if he imagined that he could shift himself down there by the power of his mind alone. Jinkil was looking in the opposite direction, studying the line of the ridge, and eyeing the steep mountain slope that fell away from its outer edge.

Orban was shifting his weight restlessly from one foot to the other, staring down at the ledge and flexing his hands as if he were rehearsing the run down the rope. Perri was waiting calmly; Fayna seemed deep in thought; and Newa was sitting on the flat top of the ridge with her eyes closed, hugging little Urami, saying nothing at all.

"All right, we do it Joq's way," Jinkil said, breaking the silence. But he didn't sound happy about it.

"Yes," Orban said, "let's try it."

"Benke?" Laena queried him.

He drew a deep breath, then nodded quickly, still looking away. He was scared, Laena realized. She wondered why. He had shown little sign of fear while they were climbing up here.

She turned to the women. "Fayna? Perri? Newa?"

Reluctantly, they all nodded.

"All right." Laena assessed the situation. Orban was impatient; he'd be more likely to make mistakes if he had to wait too long. Benke was scared; he should be the last one down the rope. She planned it out in her head. "Jinkil, Joq, you two lower Orban, then Benke. That way, they'll be ready on the ledge to guide the rest of us down."

Joq hesitated. "Wouldn't it be better—" he began.

"No," she said, staring steadily at him. "This way is best."

He frowned. Clearly, he wanted to ask why. But then he

thought better of it. "All right," he said, untying the rope from around his waist.

"Careful now," Laena warned them. The ridge that they were on was barely wide enough for two of them to stand side by side. She got a sucking feeling in her stomach whenever she glanced down. "No mistakes now," she said as she untied the rope from her own waist. She felt suddenly insecure, knowing that if she slipped, there was nothing to save her.

Benke, she saw, was trembling. She couldn't embarrass him by mentioning it; but on the other hand, she had to concern herself with his safety. She placed her hand lightly on his shoulder. "You should sit till it's your turn," she told him quietly.

Clumsily, he squatted down.

"All right, Jinkil, tie the rope around Orban, under his arms." She waited while he did so. "Joq, hold the rope with Jinkil. Get down on the ridge, as low as you can, and brace yourselves."

A part of her mind was strangely detached from what was happening. She noticed how the men were obeying her without question, and once again she felt abstractedly surprised. They trusted her, she realized. Maybe it was because they thought she had climbed mountains before; or maybe it was just because she managed to sound confident, and they needed someone to trust, so that they wouldn't be confronted with their own fears.

"All right," she said. She personally checked the knots that Jinkil had tied. "Lower yourself as far as you can, Orban. Then Jinkil and Joq will let you down the rest of the way. Be cautious now."

He grinned and nodded. "Yes, Laena-mother." He turned quickly—and bumped against Joq, who had squatted down behind him. Orban flailed his arms. He shouted out in surprise.

Fayna stepped forward. She was nearest to him. She seized the neck of his furs, steadying him, till he regained his balance.

"I said be cautious!" Laena shouted. She found herself trembling—with anger, and with fear. She wasn't sure what she'd do if she lost one of the menfolk, so early on the journey. Worse still, if Orban had fallen over the side, and

Joq and Jinkil had tried to save him by holding on to the rope, he could have pulled them both down with him.

But she couldn't let herself think about that.

Orban turned on Joq. "That was your fault," he shouted, "squatting down behind me like that—"

"Orban!" Laena stepped forward. She seized the neck of his furs and shook him. "I said be cautious. If you had listened to me, you wouldn't have put yourself in danger. It was your own fault. Never shift the blame onto others."

His face changed as she harangued him. He bowed his head. "All right, I'm sorry," he said.

Slowly, she calmed herself. "We depend on you, Orban," she said, more quietly. "There are only a few of us. We can't afford to lose anyone, especially if he's young and strong like you."

Slowly, his shoulders straightened. "I understand," he said.

"Good. So, are you ready?"

"Yes." He nodded. "Ready."

She watched as he turned, moving carefully now. He kneeled on the ridge, then swung his legs down over the side. He lowered himself till he was hanging by his hands. Jinkil and Joq took up the strain in the rope, then started paying it out, and Orban slid away below. "All right!" he shouted up a moment later. "I'm standing on the ledge."

Laena felt a wave of relief. Maybe, she thought, this would work after all.

It was Benke's turn next. He could no longer conceal his fear as he positioned himself on the edge of the ridge with quick, jerky motions. Joq and Jinkil eyed him doubtfully, but neither of them said anything.

Laena squatted beside him. "Lower yourself," she said, pitching her voice low. "And everything will be fine."

He hesitated. Then, with a sudden spasm of his arms, he pushed himself over the side.

The motion caught Joq and Jinkil by surprise. The rope snapped suddenly tight in their hands. Joq almost lost his grip, and swore. There was a cry from Benke, below.

Laena peered over the edge and saw him swinging wildly from side to side. "Are you all right?" she shouted.

"He hit his knee," Orban called up. Benke, meanwhile, was clutching his leg between his hands, grunting with pain.

Bit by bit, Joq and Jinkil paid out the rope.

"I have him," Orban shouted. And then: "All right. He's down."

"Benke, are you badly hurt?" Surely, she thought to herself, it wouldn't be serious. Just a bruise, or a graze.

Benke gave a little gasp of pain as he tried to stand on the wounded leg. Orban caught him and held him.

Laena imagined trying to tell Orban how to treat a serious wound. It was out of the question. She turned to Joq and Jinkil. "Lower me next," she said. "I may need to help him."

"But—" Joq began.

"Right now," she said as the rope was untied below and she hauled it up. She knotted it quickly around herself. Then, before she could allow herself time to think, she sat on the edge of the ridge, with her legs dangling into space. "You'll have to stand behind me," she said to Joq and Jinkil. "I can't turn around against the face of the rock. Henik's in the way."

At that moment, as if he had been roused by the sound of his own name, the baby started wailing.

"Hush," she murmured to him as the two men positioned themselves behind her. "Hush, Henik. Everything's all right."

The rope tightened under her arms. It became painfully tight. And then she felt it lifting her, as the men pulled it. She felt herself swinging out, and she gave an involuntary cry.

Henik started screaming. Laena turned slowly on the end of the rope, and the world rocked around her. She hugged her child and clenched her jaw, refusing to allow herself to panic as Benke had done. Slowly, slowly, she felt herself being lowered. The men were being very cautious, and she was glad of that—but she wanted so desperately to feel the ledge under her feet. *Please*, she thought. *Please let this be over!*

Then Orban's hands touched her ankles. "I have you, Laena-mother," he called up to her. "Easy, now."

She looked down and saw his face, and she managed to smile at him. "Thank you, Orban," she gasped as he guided her down. She clutched the rockface and turned herself to one side so that her pack wouldn't be wedged behind her.

And then she was on the ledge, which was actually wider than it had looked. The rest of the drop below her was still scary, but not as bad as the view from the ridge had been. She was safe now, she told herself. Safe.

She fumbled with the rope and threw it off. Then she saw Benke, sitting on the ledge a little way away, clutching his leg.

He looked up at her with a strange, tormented expression. "I'm afraid," he said, "it may be broken."

Chapter 43

Laena tried to examine him, but it was almost impossible, squatting beside him on the ledge. Meanwhile, behind her, she heard Newa crying out in fear as she was lowered over the side; then Fayna coming down, venting a little gasp of relief as her feet touched solid ground; and then Perri, who was strangely silent, as if it were a matter of pride for her not to show any fear.

"Tell me what happened," Laena asked Benke. "Was it the height—"

"The height meant nothing to me," he said, angrily.

"Then what—"

"I am my own master. I never ask for anyone's help. I never put myself in the hands of other people." His face became grim. "I can't think of anything worse than to be held like that, like a—a dead animal, on the end of the rope."

Laena realized she had been wrong: he wasn't a wanderer just because he had never recovered from the death of his wife. He sought solitude because he simply didn't know how to trust other people. But even if she had known that, would it have changed anything? "I think your leg may not be broken," she tried to reassure him. "Even if it is, we can wait for it to heal—"

He laughed sourly. "Spare me your kind lies, Laena-mother. Your time is too valuable to waste days or weeks waiting for me. In any case, I wouldn't want you to. It's already bad enough that I have lost face among the menfolk. I wouldn't want them to despise me as a cripple, as well."

Laena turned away, feeling conflicting emotions. She felt sorry for Benke, but angry with him, too. Or was she angry with herself? Whose fault was it, anyway, that Benke was hurt? She honestly didn't know. But she was determined to avoid any more accidents. She squinted up. "Joq, are you next?"

His face peered out over the edge of the rockface. "No," he called down to her. "Jinkil isn't sure he can hold me well enough on his own. So we're stringing the rope around the outcropping. He'll climb down, and then I'll follow."

"All right," she said. She glanced at the others, standing along the ledge, and found them looking anxiously at her. They were unnerved by Benke's accident, and they wanted her to tell them it was going to be all right.

Well, they would have to wait. She stood and watched as the rope was thrown down. The two ends of it dangled side by side, just above her head.

Jinkil swung himself over the edge, and his bulk blotted out the sky. She heard his clothes rustling and his moccasins scrabbling over the rock. He gripped the two lengths of rope in his mittened hands, and he let them out slowly, edging himself down, breathing heavily and grunting with the effort.

Laena reached up and clutched one of his ankles. On the other side of him, Orban did the same. Together, they guided Jinkil down. And then he was standing beside them, his face wet with sweat and smudged with rock-dust. He wriggled his shoulders, centering his pack. "That wasn't so hard," he said. He wiped sweat out of his eyes. "But it wasn't so easy."

Laena looked up apprehensively. Joq was lighter than Jinkil, but he was nowhere near as strong. And he had already used a lot of his strength lowering the others.

"Here I come," he shouted down.

Everyone watched in tense silence as he started his descent. He let out the rope—too fast! He shouted in surprise and fear as he fell, but then he tightened his grip and managed to stop himself with a sudden jolt that made the rope quiver.

He hung there for a moment, swinging from side to side. Jinkil reached up, but Joq was beyond his outstretched hands. "Just a little farther," Laena called up to him.

Cautiously, he let the rope slip. Once again, it slid too easily in his grasp. He yelled—and he found himself falling down between Jinkil and Orban. Quickly, they grabbed him. They held him, barely, and they had to struggle for a moment to keep from falling off the ledge. Then, finally, they set Joq's feet down.

For a long moment, no one said anything. Joq was gasping for breath, wide-eyed with fear. He flexed his hands and winced. "The rope cut through my mitten," he said. "I couldn't control it. I tried, but I couldn't." Gradually, he calmed himself.

"All right," Laena said, "we're all safe now. Orban, can you slide past me? Benke will need to lean on you."

Orban nodded. "Right away."

"What about the rope?" Joq said.

Laena paused. "What?"

"Shall we bring it, or not?"

"Of course we should bring it. That's why you looped it around the rock up there, so you could haul it down."

"Yes." He was giving her a worried look. "But—well, if we take it down, there'll be no way we can go back the way we came. If it turns out that Benke is really hurt badly—"

"Pull the rope down, Joq," she said. She said it flatly, as if there were no possible room for argument.

"Wait!"

It was Newa who had spoken. Laena looked at her.

"What if—" She sounded agitated. "If we fail—if we need to get back—"

It was already too late. Joq had tugged on the rope, and the free end was sliding around the outcropping above. It came snaking down, looping into his arms.

"Don't worry, Newa," Laena said. "We won't fail."

They carried Benke down to the lake, where grass grew thick and lush in soft earth and the water made faint lapping noises. Everyone gathered around as Laena kneeled beside the injured man and peeled back his trousers of caribou hide. Already, she saw, the knee was badly swollen, and the skin was bright red.

She opened her pack and pulled out a square of mammoth fur. Nan had always said that there were special healing powers in it, though Laena never knew whether the old lady had really believed that. She gave it to Perri, who was nearby. "Soak that in the lake, then bring it back and press it against his knees. We have to cool his leg to ease the swelling.''

Laena turned back to Benke. She felt around the joint, and moved it tentatively. "It's not broken," she said.

She heard people sighing with relief.

"But you will need to rest," Laena went on.

"No." Benke started struggling to sit up. "Find me a branch, and I'll use it as a crutch."

"Lie down!" she snapped at him. "I am a healer. You must pay attention."

He blinked in surprise. Probably no woman had ever spoken to him like that before. Slowly, he did as she said.

Perri came back with the wet mammoth fur and pressed it against the knee. Laena nodded her approval. "It's late in the afternoon. We're all tired. We can camp right here. Tomorrow, we'll see if Benke's leg is strong enough." She glanced around. "Do you all agree?"

There was a murmuring of assent.

When the sky was almost black, she left her child with Perri, sitting with the other travelers beside the little fire they had built at the edge of the water, and she took Joq's arm. "I need to talk to you," she whispered. Together, the two of them walked away in the darkness.

They found a place to sit on the soft ground, as the stars filled the sky above the bowl of the valley and the water gleamed in the moonlight.

"Tell me now," Laena said, "if I am still a wise leader. With one man already injured, and no way we can get back to the place that we think of as home."

Joq looked at her for a moment. "Are you blaming yourself for what happened to Benke? Is that why you're upset?"

"Of course I blame myself!" Her voice was a whisper, but it was full of emotion.

"Then you're asking the wrong question," Joq murmured to her after thinking for a moment. "The real question is whether this journey itself is wise."

She stiffened. "What do you mean? I thought you believed—"

"Yes, I believe. When I think of what you have done in the past, and I remember how you foresaw the flood, of course I believe in your vision. But it's hard, Laena, to travel like this, not even knowing where we are going or how long it will take to get there.''

"I see.'' She hunched forward, hugging her knees against her chest. "Well, this *is* a wise journey. You must trust my judgment in that respect.''

He shrugged. "In that case, everything you have done so far is also wise. You guided your people over an obstacle that would have stopped other travelers. You chose to cut off our way back, so that everyone has to be committed now. I can't fault you for that.''

Gradually she felt some of the tension leave her. "You still don't sound very happy about it,'' she said.

He sighed. "I'm just hoping that when we reach our goal, it turns out to be worth all the effort.''

"It has to be,'' she murmured.

The next day, Benke's leg was slightly less swollen, and Joq carved a crutch for him out of a tree branch. The ground beside the lake was smooth and even, so progress would be easy for a while, at least till they reached the far end of the valley. After that, it was hard to tell. The snowy peaks still stood in the distance, serving as a constant reminder of the greater challenge that lay in store.

Jinkil surprised everyone with a breakfast of fresh fish. "The lake's full of them,'' he said, grinning. He stripped off his boots and leggings, which were soaking wet from where he had waded in the shallows. He threw four plump salmon onto the ground beside the fire, and gestured for Perri to start cleaning and gutting them.

"Strange,'' said Joq, "there were so few fish in the river, while up here—''

"They breed in still water,'' said Benke. "And remember, before the great rockslide, the lake would not have been here. Fish could have swum all the way upstream—''

"And then as the lake formed, they made it their new home,'' said Joq.

"No animals, though,'' said Jinkil, holding his moccasins by the fire till they started steaming in the cool morning air. "No tracks, no droppings.'' He turned and gave Benke a speculative look. "How do you explain that, eh?''

There was something challenging in the way he said it. And Laena didn't hear the same amount of respect that he'd shown the previous day. She realized that Benke was right: he had lost face among the men.

"I don't know where the animals are," Benke said stiffly. He turned and looked out over the water, and once again he was a solitary figure, cut off from the others.

Everyone was feeling stiff and weary after the previous day, and Laena wanted to give Benke as much rest as possible. So she let the morning slip by. She sat with Newa for a while, watching Henik and Urami crawl and tumble in the grass. The bowl-shaped valley blocked out the wind and trapped the heat of the sun, so it was warm here, and peaceful.

"You were brave yesterday," she said to Newa.

The young woman gave her a quick, uneasy glance, then looked down at the ground in front of her. "I wasn't. I was terrified."

"Yes, you were scared of the height. But you didn't beg us to turn back, and you didn't scream or cry. That was when you were brave."

Newa shook her head. "I made my own private pledge, Laena. When I lost my husband, and my child—" She stopped for a moment and closed her eyes. Her face showed sudden, sharp tension. And then, gradually, she relaxed. "It's still hard to think about that." She opened her eyes again. "But I told myself, they must have been taken from me for a reason. And the only reason I could find was that it freed me to come on this journey, and care for little Urami." She shrugged fatalistically. "So, there's no way I can turn back."

Laena rested her hand on Newa's shoulder. "I'll try to be worthy of your faith," she said.

Newa laughed dismissively. "I'm the one who isn't worthy, Laena. I wish I had even half of your strength."

They're all the same, Laena thought to herself. *They all seem to think that I'm stronger than they are.* Maybe it was just because she absolutely believed in her journey. In her heart, she certainly didn't feel strong.

A little later, she bandaged Benke's leg with dry hide, wrapping it above and below the knee so he would be unable to bend his leg. "We'll lighten your pack as much as we can," Laena told him. "And we'll move slowly. Remember, you're much more useful to us if you take care of yourself than if you make your injury worse and become unable to walk. So if you want to serve us well, you won't try to hurry.''

The corners of his mouth turned down. He gave a curt nod. Still, she saw, it was hard for him to take advice or instructions from her.

Around noon, they started on their way. Orban and Fayna quickly moved ahead, and Laena decided to let them go—there was no way she could rein in their impatience. Everyone else kept pace with Benke as he hobbled along, grim-faced, staring straight ahead and saying nothing.

''Still no tracks,'' Jinkil said a little later. ''Look there.'' He pointed to a stretch of mud sloping gently into the water. ''A spot like that, it's a natural place for animals to come and drink. The mud should be full of tracks. Deer and caribou, elk, bear, wolf, fox, maybe even bison.'' He shook his head. ''Doesn't make sense.''

''Maybe when the rockslide blocked the lower end of the valley, the animals were trapped here,'' said Perri.

Jinkil gave her a sharp look, as if he hadn't expected her to join the conversation.

''They could have starved to death,'' she went on.

''Grass.'' He pointed at the ground. ''Seems to me there's a lot of grass here for deer to graze on.''

''But the big animals could have eaten all the deer,'' said Perri. ''Then there was nothing left, so they died.''

Jinkil scowled. ''Now, you listen to me—''

Once again, Laena saw, it was her duty to keep the peace. She didn't know exactly what was happening between Jinkil and his wife, but it couldn't be allowed to turn into a pointless argument. ''We don't know yet,'' she cut in, ''what's at the other end of the valley. There's not much cover here. The animals might prefer it where there are more trees and bushes. Couldn't that be?''

Jinkil eyed her for a moment. ''Maybe,'' he said gruffly.

Privately, Laena didn't believe her own explanation. The deadness of this land was eerie. At the very least, there should have been some sign of squirrels and rabbits. Suddenly she wondered if this was why the Ghost River had gained its name. Had some unknown traveler managed to journey here long ago, and returned to tell stories about a place where no animals lived?

Her thoughts were interrupted by a shout from Orban. He was standing in the distance, with Fayna beside him. Both of them were pointing at something on the ground in front of them.

"Maybe they found something. A dead rat or something," said Jinkil.

But when they finally reached Orban, in a small patch of bare earth that had been baked hard by the sun, they found a human footprint.

They had left themselves no way back, and the sides of the valley curved up so steeply, there was no way out either side. So Laena and her people moved forward—cautiously.

At the top of the valley they found trees growing densely, and a lot of underbrush. "This'll give us cover," Jinkil muttered as he pushed ahead. "But it'll make noise."

Laena was following him—not because she feared exposing herself at the head of the party, but because she wanted to protect Henik. He was still slung across her chest, staring around at the woodland scenery, chewing on a wood carving of a turtle that Joq had given him. Laena remembered the day that Joq had made that carving. It had been during the winter, when there was barely enough light to see by, and everyone was restless for something to do. It seemed years ago now; part of a world that had seemed so vital to her at the time, yet had never been as real and permanent as she imagined.

Jinkil stopped abruptly, and she almost bumped into his backpack. He pointed wordlessly, and she saw a trail ahead of them, snaking between the bushes and shrubbery, under the canopy of leaves.

Laena beckoned to the people behind her, and everyone gathered around. They squatted down, close together. "Follow the trail?" Jinkil whispered. "Or try to cut around? I vote we cut around."

"The trail looks old," Laena said, pitching her voice as low as she could. "It was well-traveled once, but not recently. See, the weeds growing in it—"

"I already saw them," Jinkil said, though she doubted that he had. "So maybe we follow the trail—"

"Or the river," said Joq. The water was flowing close by, chuckling over a steep bed of stones, on its way to feed the lake below.

"But if there was an easy way beside the river, people wouldn't have made this trail," Orban put in.

Laena sensed them sparring with each other, trying to show their skill as hunters and trackers. And why was that? Because they weren't deferring to any one person as the leader.

She stood up. "We will follow the trail," she said.

There was a moment of silence as her people stared at her. "I still say," Jinkil began, "if we circle around—"

"Benke can't manage difficult terrain. And the trail is not well used. So, we will follow the trail." She turned to Perri. "Take Henik from me, so I can be free to throw my spear if I need to."

Perri stood up, looking surprised. "Are you sure—"

Laena realized they had been thinking of her so much as Laena-mother, they'd forgotten her skills as a hunter and a fighter. Well, maybe that was her own fault for mothering them too much. She slipped Henik's sling off, and handed him to the other woman. He let out a little cry of protest, and Perri moved quickly to stroke his head and calm him.

"Let him suck on this," said Laena. She gave Perri a little plug of leather. "Now, I'll lead. Jinkil, you're the strongest—be ready to help Benke, understand?"

"All right." He gave her a curt nod. He was deferring to her—because now she was acting like a leader.

"One thing," Laena whispered to them, "Some tribes are warriors; some are peaceful. But if strangers enter their land and start throwing spears, any tribe will fight back." She paused to let them think about that. "We must not be the first to attack," she said. "There are too few of us to start a battle. Understand, Orban? Don't throw your spear unless you see me throw mine."

He drew himself up. "I will be cautious, Laena."

"Good." She gave him a smile. "And if we can sneak past this tribe, whoever they are, without them seeing us— so much the better. This is no time to be heroic and brave. This is a time to survive in any way we can."

She turned then and started forward.

The trees reminded her of the forest around the camp of

the Wolf Tribe. She remembered their lookouts perched on high branches. If the people who lived in this valley were as well-prepared and as warlike as the Wolves, they would kill her and her people quickly and easily. There was no doubt of that.

But she pushed that thought aside. She would survive, she told herself, and her people would survive, because it was their destiny. That was something to cling to, as she crept along the trail, hunching forward, listening for the slightest sound in the undergrowth. She felt her mouth turning dry, and her skin prickling. A twig cracked, and she stiffened and turned—but it was only Newa, who had never been trained in the skills of a hunter.

"Laena." The voice was a whisper from directly behind her.

She turned and found that Orban had moved up. She looked at him questioningly.

"I smell wood smoke."

She paused and sniffed the air. He was right, she realized. "So, we are close to them," she murmured to herself. She paused, scanning the forest, wishing there were a way to circle around as Jinkil had suggested. But the undergrowth was even thicker here. And through the trees, she could see the rocky sides of the valley closing in, allowing little room to maneuver.

She edged forward and saw that the trees thinned out ahead. She took another dozen paces, then paused and studied the view. Up at the top of the valley was a rocky table which overlooked the river, tumbling past it. Half a dozen tents stood on the little flat area of rock—tents of a kind that she had never seen before. Each one seemed to have been built by leaning five or six tall poles together, so they met in a point at the top. Animal hide was stretched around the poles, daubed with red and black designs—pictures of animals, and hunters with spears.

Laena beckoned Jinkil to join her. "Tell me what you see," she whispered to him. He had the mind of a fighter, and more experience than Orban or Joq. If there was danger, he would be more likely to sense it.

"The grass up there is worn thin," he muttered. "They've lived here a long while. There's smoke coming from one of those tents, but only one of them. Meat-drying rack there hasn't been used in a while. See that bone pile? They don't bother to bury anything. A lot of flies. And the place smells bad. The way I see it, these people are savages, and there aren't many of them. Maybe they killed the people who built the camp, and took their place.''

Laena nodded slowly. She had noticed many of the same details herself, but hadn't drawn the same conclusions. Of course, Jinkil's conclusions could be wrong. ''We might be able to creep around behind their tents,'' she whispered, pointing. ''They don't seem to have a lookout. Why should they? This valley is almost impossible to get into.''

Jinkil narrowed his eyes. ''Move around the wall of the valley there? And out through the notch at the end?''

''Yes,'' said Laena.

He rubbed his jaw. ''What about Benke?''

Laena realized that she'd momentarily forgotten about him. ''How about if you carry him across your shoulders, if someone else takes your pack? We just need to get past those tents. We'll be out of sight as soon as we pass through the notches between the mountainsides into the land that lies beyond.''

''All right, I could carry him,'' Jinkil agreed. ''But he's got a pack of his own.''

''So Joy can carry two packs—his own, and Benke's. We can sling them on a spear across his shoulders. And Orban can carry two packs—his own, and yours. That frees you to carry Benke.''

Jinkil grunted. ''Doesn't give us much of a chance if we have to fight.''

Laena glanced back. The rest of her people were waiting, hunkering down in the bushes, watching her, wondering what she was talking about with Jinkil. ''Do you see any other way?'' she asked him.

He thought for a moment. ''Attack,'' he said. ''Leave the babies here with Benke. Give everyone else a knife or a spear. Creep up there, surround the tent that has the smoke coming out of it, then slice it open all at once and kill the people inside before they have a chance to kill us.''

Laena felt a strange coldness inside her as she imagined doing what Jinkil said. The plan was logical, in its own vicious way: it would give them the greatest chance of survival. And hadn't she said that survival was their first concern?

But then she remembered Jalenau's men, who had come and massacred the Panther People. Maybe Jinkil was right, and the simple folk who dwelled here in their strange cone-shaped tents were nothing more than savages. All the same, if she butchered them, she'd be doing the same thing as the warriors who had butchered her own tribe. And that knowledge would live with her for the rest of her life.

"I'm sorry, Jinkil," she said. "I can't sacrifice strangers who may be harmless. I can't turn myself into a murderer. I'm not sure that any of us would really want to do that."

He shrugged. "In that case, we have to do it your way."

She watched his face for any sign of resentment. But he seemed quite prepared to follow her instructions. "Let's tell the others," she said.

She went with him back to the rest of the people, and she explained the plan. No one raised any objections, probably because no one could think of a better way. But Benke looked unhappy as his pack was taken from him. "You should let me get by on my own," he whispered. "You all move ahead. I can follow at my pace."

"The caribou that lags behind the herd is the first one to taste a hunter's spear," said Orban.

Benke shook his head vigorously from side to side. "I don't want anyone's help."

"I am the leader," Laena said calmly. "I have decided. Jinkil will carry you. We need you too much to leave you behind."

Benke looked up at her, and his face twisted into a miserable grimace. But he saw the determination in her eyes, and he lapsed into silence.

Very soon, they were ready. "It looks to me," Laena said, "as if there's another valley just beyond this one. The mountains come down in a notch, which is where the river flows through. Once we get past the tents and through there, we should find more cover."

"I could go ahead and scout it for you," said Orban.

Laena hesitated. "No. You'd have to go out, and back; and that would just give the people in the tents two extra chances of noticing us. No; we'll do this together."

She led the way forward to the very edge of the trees.

Now that she had made the plan and was following it, she felt strangely calm. She eyed the stony ground that lay between her and the tents. Then, boldly, she started out across it, hunching forward, moving in a zigzag path between stones and bushes that offered a small amount of cover.

She heard the others following her. Their feet thudded into the skimpy grass. Their breath came fast. Their clothes rustled, and the leather straps of the packs creaked faintly. She wanted to glance over her shoulder and see that Perri was there, with Henik; but she forced herself not to. All her attention had to be focused on the tents.

She circled around behind the tents, climbing as high up the wall of the valley as she could. The ground was steep and stony here, and small stones rolled underfoot. Twice she almost fell.

There was the sound of someone stumbling behind her. She imagined Jinkil falling under the weight of Benke. But then she heard a high-pitched cry.

For an instant she thought it was a woman's voice. Then she realized: it was a baby. She stopped and turned. Perri had slipped and fallen on her side. She had cradled Henik to protect him, and he was safe in her arms; but the leather plug had come out of his mouth, and he was screaming now, even as Perri struggled back onto her feet.

Instinctively, Laena wanted to go to her child. But there was no point in that. The most important thing was still to move past the tents as quickly as possible. She started running over the rocky ground, and she heard her people following her, panting with the effort.

The deep notch in the land, marking the end of the valley, came closer. She saw the river tumbling through it, sparkling in the sun. There was another valley beyond, just as she'd thought. There were trees there, and bushes—

An ugly, guttural cry came from her right.

She whirled around. A figure was standing outside the tents. He was a hunched, scrawny figure, draped in ragged animal skins. His hair stood out around his head, thick with dirt and grease. His face was gaunt. He was holding a spear in one hand, and as she looked at him, he threw his head back and gave another guttural cry.

She froze. Her calmness, she realized, had been an illusion. She felt her pulse thumping fast. The savage was staring directly at her, standing beside the big bone pile that Jinkil had noticed. Would he attack? He was holding his spear with its point down. He wasn't coming toward her. His intentions might be peaceful. How could she tell?

Then another man came out of the tent and joined the first; and then another.

Suddenly, Laena knew what she should do. "Joq, Orban! Put down your packs! Jinkil, set Benke down on the ground!"

She waited just long enough to see that they were following her instructions. Then she turned back to the three savages. They were standing about a hundred paces away, no more than that. And she was higher up than they were. She knew, without a moment's doubt, that her aim would be true.

"Kill them!" she screamed. Quickly, she drew back her spear. She took a moment to focus on one of the savages. He was raising his own spear now. But he would not be able to throw it.

Laena swung her arm in a swift, clean arc. Her shaft flew out and down. The gaunt man gave a cry of fear; and then he fell backward, clutching his chest, with blood flowing out of him.

His two companions howled—in fear or rage, it was impossible to tell. "Kill them!" Laena shouted again. Jinkil was already throwing his spear, and Orban and Joq were only a moment behind. The wooden shafts sang through the air. One of the savages turned to run, and was struck in the center of his back. He fell on the ground and lay there screaming. The other man was speared twice, once in the chest and once in the neck. His knees buckled under him, his head lolled back, and blood started flooding the front of his ragged clothes.

Laena stood staring. It had been so quick, and so simple. So terrible simple. Suddenly, she found herself shaking. "Jinkil!" she cried. "Stop him from screaming!"

The savage who had been struck in the back was still shouting in pain, clumsily trying to crawl to the tent that he had emerged from.

Jinkil started down the hillside, reaching for his flint knife.

"Careful!" Laena called after him. "There may be more of them."

"They'd be out here by now, if there were," Jinkil said. He strode forward till he reached the fallen man. He hesitated; and then, quickly, he cut his throat.

Laena was still trembling. She was remembering how it had been when she had watched the massacre of her own people, and she was reliving the emotions that she had felt then. The disbelief, and the horror—and the desire to run as fast as possible, as far as possible from the scene.

"Quickly," she cried out. "We must leave this place."

Jinkil turned to face her. "We need our spears. We could use theirs, as well."

"All right. Get the spears. Then we must go."

Jinkil didn't hurry. He stepped over the dead bodies, pulled the shafts free, wiped blood off them, then gathered the weapons that the savages had held. Finally, he paused and peered into the tent that they had come from. He grunted with surprise.

Laena stood watching, feeling an agony of impatience. She felt terrible, having to stand here and look down at the men whose deaths she had caused. She couldn't look at her own people. She was sure they were staring at her, wondering why she had given the command to kill. "Jinkil!" she shouted again. "We must go!"

He emerged from the tent, dragging something. It was a person, Laena realized with dismay. A woman, in even worse condition than the men had been. She was so weak, she could barely stand. She made a terrible keening sound and held up her hands as if the sunlight were too bright for her eyes.

"Leave her!" Laena shouted. "Leave her there, Jinkil!"

He squinted up, looking puzzled. Then he looked down at the pitiful creature in his hands. "She could die of starvation," he said.

"No. She won't die. Believe me." Laena turned away then. She couldn't stand to watch anymore. She started toward the notch at the end of the valley, not bothering to look and see if her people were following her.

They gathered in a little copse of stunted trees. Jinkil set Benke down, then grabbed some grass and started methodically wiping his mittens. They were soaked with blood, Laena realized.

Joq was staring at her as if she were a stranger. Orban looked uneasy. Newa and Fayna were pale and obviously scared. The babies were whimpering. Strangely, Perri was the only one who seemed untouched by what had happened.

"I don't understand." Orban was the first to speak. "I thought you said—"

Laena held up her hands. "I know what I told you. Didn't any of you notice the bone pile outside those tents?"

"I saw it," said Jinkil. "I was the one who pointed it out to you."

"Yes," said Laena. "But those bones were human bones. And not just in the pile; around the drying racks, as well. Do you see?" She looked around. No one yet seemed to understand. "Some time in the past," she went on, "the valley was blocked by the rockfall that we climbed. After that, the tent people couldn't get out, and no more animals could get in. So the people killed all the game that was in the valley. That's why we found nothing alive there. And after that, the people started feeding off each other."

Everyone was silent. They understood now; and the look of disapproval was gone from Joq's eyes.

"There were still fish in the lake," said Jinkil.

Laena spread her hands. "You saw how primitive those people were. Maybe they never learned how to use a fishing spear."

"You're right," Orban said finally. "They had turned into cannibals. But the ones we saw were weak. Do you really think they would have attacked us?"

"Maybe not right away," said Laena. "Maybe they would have pretended to welcome us. Or maybe they would have let us go by. But sooner or later, they would have come after us and tried to kill us. They had already eaten most of their own kin. Do you think they would have thought twice about devouring strangers?"

There was another long, uneasy silence.

"All right, what now?" said Joq. He looked at the new valley they were in. The terrain was rougher here. A few stunted trees grew amid stony soil. And further up, there was a scattering of snow.

"We shall proceed," said Laena simply.

"Yes," said Joq. He hesitated, as if there were something he wasn't sure he should say. "But—maybe there's no way out of this valley. If there was, the tent people would have found it and taken it, instead of turning against each other."

There was a renewed gust of wind, blowing Laena's hood back and lashing her hair into her face. Carefully, she readjusted her clothing and pulled her furs more tightly around her. "I still believe there will be a way," she said. "We are more determined, more resourceful than those people back there."

"We'll need to be," Jinkil muttered. "If they killed all the game in the lower valley, they'll have killed everything in this one, too."

"We have food that will last us many days," Laena countered him. "Look up there." She pointed into the distance. "The peaks are lower ahead of us than on either side. That's where the river comes from. That's where the pass will be. If we have the courage to climb up there, there's no telling what we may find on the other side." She paused a moment. "And frankly, we have no choice. Remember, there's no way back."

Benke struggled up from where he had been lying on the ground. "Enough talking," he said. "We should use the daylight that we have left." He steadied himself against his makeshift crutch. "I'm ready to go on."

Maybe he was just trying to salvage his lost pride, Laena thought to herself. She was grateful to him, though. If a man with a crutch and a damaged knee was willing to tackle the challenge, how could the others refuse?

She went to Perri and retrieved Henik from her. She donned the sling, then went to Jinkil. "My spear," she said.

"Here." He handed it to her. He had cleaned its tip, but she saw there were still a few smears of blood. Well, so be it. She had killed a man, and there was no point in trying to pretend otherwise.

She turned then and started up the rocky slope.

Chapter 44

They camped that evening in the scant shelter of some boulders. Laena could see why the tent people had chosen to live in the lower valley: it was a sanctuary compared to this. The wind blew incessantly, bringing chill air from the slopes of snow that lay further on. The mountains on either side were frighteningly steep, funneling the wind and blocking out the sun. Even now, there was still some light in the sky; but where she sat with her people, crouching around the fire they had built from the meager supply of deadwood, they were in deep shadow.

Laena could see that everyone was depressed and demoralized by this barren place. "We should turn in early tonight," she said, "and start early tomorrow. Maybe then we'll come to a place that's less grim than this."

Jinkil opened his pack. He was the one who was carrying their skin tent. It was really not much more than a big, thin leather blanket, with thongs around its edges. He grabbed a rock and started banging sticks into the ground, pausing to tie one of the thongs to each stick, so that the leather would be anchored against the wind.

Soon everyone was huddling under it. Laena had slept like this many times in her childhood, when her tribe had migrated across the plains; but for the Fisher People, it was a new, unpleasant experience. She heard them grunting and muttering, trying to avoid each others' knees and elbows as they lay sandwiched together. At first, everyone was cold; but within a short time, it became oppressively hot.

"Loosen one of the thongs holding the skin," Laena said. "Our body heat will suffocate us, otherwise."

She heard someone grunting, squirming around, and tugging at a knot. Finally, a trickle of fresh air came seeping in.

"I've traveled like this many times," she said. "Trust me: you'll soon get used to it."

"I doubt that." It was Benke's voice, and she realized that for a man who valued his solitude, this was a particularly difficult way to spend the night.

"There's no other way, Benke," she said to him.

He didn't answer.

"Let's try to get some sleep." It was Joq's voice, from behind her. He sounded weary, and he wasn't holding her close as he normally did. He, too, had spent a large part of his childhood away from other children. Well, Laena thought to herself, he would simply have to adapt.

She curled herself around little Henik. He, at least, seemed to have no complaints. He had been well fed and was sleeping soundly. Laena cuddled him against her, taking comfort from his presence. And yet—something felt subtly out of place.

Then she realized: always, while traveling with her people, she had slept close to Moru. Even when the little girl had been only a year old, Laena had lain next to her as she was lying next to Henik, now.

Laena felt a stab of unexpected sadness. She wondered where Moru was, and what she was doing, at that precise moment. Maybe she, too, was trying to sleep. Maybe she was thinking of Laena, as Laena was thinking of her.

Laena felt suddenly, deeply alone. She felt herself crying. She'd thought she had managed to harden herself to the loss of her sister, but evidently she had been fooling herself. A thousand little memories suddenly crowded into her mind— of the way Moru ate her food, the way she smiled, the way she hugged Laena when they hadn't seen each other for a while, or the way she waved good-bye.

This must be what it was like, Laena realized, for the other people around her. All of them except Benke had separated themselves from their families, or had lost people they loved in the great flood. Worse still, unlike Laena, none of them had ever uprooted themselves from their homes before. Abruptly, she realized how frightening and sad this journey must be for them.

She told herself to be a little kinder to them in days to come. What had Faltor told her? She could almost hear him speaking the words: "If you are fierce, your people may respect you. But if they see you are kind, they will love you, which is worth more.''

Remember that, she told herself as she finally slipped into sleep.

The next day, everyone looked worn and weary from their night under the tent. She moved among them, putting in a friendly word here and a smile there, trying to encourage them. But she saw how their attention kept turning toward the mountain peaks that loomed ahead, and she knew what was on their minds. If it had been uncomfortable sleeping here, how would it be on those inhospitable, snowy slopes?

One thing encouraged her: Benke's knee was improving. It had been badly bruised, nothing more. He still needed to keep his weight off it as much as possible, but within a few days, it should be completely healed.

She was tempted to wait where they were and put off the ascent until he had regained all his strength. But she knew that the waiting would be hard on everyone's nerves; and she doubted that Benke would stand for it, anyway. So she didn't even mention it as a possibility.

She helped to build a fire for people to warm themselves. She made sure that everyone ate a hearty breakfast. And then, the real trek began.

By noon, they were walking across a thin layer of snow. Most of it had been blown down from higher slopes, but those slopes were no longer very far away. There were traces of ice at the edge of the river, and the ground seemed hard underfoot, as if it were still frozen.

The valley narrowed to a deep V-shape. The trees became sparse, and finally disappeared. Even the grass vanished as they climbed higher. And then the valley terminated in a craggy face of rock. Here, finally, was an explanation why the tent people had not tried to escape at this end. There was no obvious way out.

Still, the face of rock was not a vertical wall. It slanted, and it was crisscrossed with fault lines which were wide enough to serve as secure footholds. If a person was determined—if a person believed that something better might lie beyond the mountains that reared up so ominously—then the ascent didn't seem quite so forbidding.

Even so, it was hard to know how to approach the task. The river was no help here; it ran down the rock in a dozen different paths that split and rejoined. Nor could Laena see what she would find at the top of this slanting face. It curved away from her, hiding its summit from view.

Her people squatted on the ground, resting. Their breath steamed in the cold, damp air. No one said anything. They watched her, and they waited.

Laena scanned the slanting rock. At one side of it, almost on a level with her eyes, she saw a mark in the stone, like an arrow pointing upward.

She peered at it more closely. With surprise, she realized that it had been scraped into the stone with a flint held by a human hand. Clearly, it pointed along one of the faults in the rock, showing that this was the way.

"Look," she called. "Others have been here before us."

Benke was the first to join her and examine the mark. "This seems a good omen," he said cautiously.

She felt irritated by his grudging tone. "We should tie ourselves together," said Laena, "as we did before." She started stringing the rope between them. "You go first," she told Jinkil. He was the strongest; if someone fell, he would serve as an anchor. Or so she hoped.

And so they started the climb.

It was really not so much worse than climbing the rock-fall. The main difference was that it was colder here, and as the wind veered, icy water from the river blew across their faces in sheets of spray. Still, all of them had learned to cope with the cold, during their lives. They didn't like it; but it was certainly nothing new.

They followed the diagonal gash in the rock, and it took them steadily upward. Where it finally ended, Jinkil paused, trying to decide which way to turn. Then he saw another arrow scraped into the stone, pointing along a fault line that would lead them back in a zigzag path. He had to stretch to reach it, but once he was there, he was able to help the others across.

Laena wondered about the mountaineers who had marked this trail. Where were they now? And had they ever returned this way? In one sense, she was infinitely grateful to find that a path had been marked. At the same time, though, it troubled her to know that she was merely following in someone else's footsteps. Would there be another encounter with another tribe, like the savages in the cone-shaped tents? That was something she didn't want to think about.

She looked back to see how the others were managing the climb. Benke was between Joq and Orban, and they were giving him help, which he received in silence. Perri seemed to be managing well enough, and had taken on the burden of carrying Urami. Newa was still haunted by her fear of heights, but Fayna was staying close beside her, steadying her and encouraging her as they moved higher. Really, the climb was not so frightening, so long as they faced the rock, moved in small steps, and didn't look back at the drop behind them. It was a matter of endurance more than anything else.

Late in the afternoon, they finally reached the top of the slanting rockface. Another valley opened out beyond it, much steeper than the last. It was a deep furrow angled into the side of the mountain, mottled with snow and ice, with the river snaking down its center.

"That surface looks treacherous," Jinkil said, eyeing the mosaic of white.

"Then we'll go up the ridge," said Laena. "Here. Look." She pointed to a pile of stones. There weren't many of them, but clearly, they had been stacked by someone as a marker. And wedged in them was a fragment of wood, pointing the way.

So they continued. The ridge had been blown clean of snow, and the rock was ragged and pockmarked, providing many safe footholds. Once again, the climbing was not too difficult, though it was strenuous, and they had a harder time helping Benke, since Orban and Joq had to position themselves ahead of him and behind him.

Eventually they reached a small plateau where they could pause and rest and eat some of their rations. From here they could see all the way back down the valley, even to the dwellings of the tent people, which were tiny specks in the far distance. The lake lay behind that; but the rest of the view was shrouded in haze.

Laena squinted up at the sky. There were wisps of cloud, but it looked to her as if the weather would stay dry. She sensed that her people wanted to stop here on this little table of rock, and she was inclined to agree. Her arms and legs were weary with the effort of pulling herself up the mountain.

But then she remembered how Nan had always urged her on, and how she had found strength inside herself that she had never known she possessed. So she told them, kindly but firmly, it was too early to camp. She insisted that they had to continue. She saw some of her people exchanging grim glances, and she sensed that they wanted to speak out against her. But when they looked at her and saw her smiling at them, gently urging them on, somehow they couldn't bring themselves to argue with her.

Once again they found markers to guide them. Wherever the trail turned, there was a tiny cairn or a scratch mark. The path twisted seemingly at random, and yet in hindsight, Laena saw that it was carefully planned. It always took the gentlest slopes and the safest traverses, and always it came back to the river.

As the sun dropped behind the peaks to the west, they had crested a ridge that almost looked as though it was the highest point on the pass between the peaks. But as they dragged their weary bodies up and over it, they found that it opened into yet another steep valley, with even taller standing peaks beyond. She heard Joq and Orban groan as they saw the climb that still lay ahead, and Newa cried out in dismay.

But there was a sheltered area which Laena saw would make an ideal resting place. Some snow had drifted into it, but she could soon get rid of that. "Here," she shouted. "Help me, somebody." She pulled a square of hide out of her pack and used it like a scoop, throwing the snow aside.

Eventually, Joq came and shared the toil. After that they all spread the skin tent, anchored it, and crawled under it. The stony hollow allowed them much more room than they'd had the previous night, and they were soon warm enough, even though there was nothing here to make a fire.

For a while there were few words spoken. Everyone felt disappointed by discovering how much more climbing still lay ahead of them. They complained to each other about their aching muscles, and the weight of the packs on their backs. Laena listened for a while, saying nothing.

Finally, she decided she had heard enough. "You sound

like old women," she said, "with all your aching backs. Have you forgotten why we're here?"

There was a silence. Were they angry with her now? She couldn't tell.

"This is the greatest adventure our tribe has ever known," she said. "Our children and our grandchildren will remember us for this, and thank us for making it possible for them to live anew, in a land free from danger and strife. Have you forgotten this?"

"Laena is right," Joq said after a short, thoughtful pause. "Instead of complaining about the climb, we might be thinking more about the future."

"You should think about what we've achieved, too," she said. "Newa, with your fear of heights—did you ever imagine you could do what you've done in the past two days? Perri, Fayna—what would you prefer, to be here on this great adventure, or to be back in the village, huddling in a hut and cleaning fish?"

"I'm sorry, Laena." It was Newa's voice. "I was complaining too much."

Other voices began echoing her.

And so the talk turned—from complaining about their hardships, to speculating on the way ahead, and what the people of the Fisher Tribe would think if they could see Laena and her people now.

But there were some other tensions in the group. Perri and Jinkil were barely speaking to each other, and the few words they exchanged were cold and harsh. Perri had always been a dutiful wife back at the village. Now, she seemed to be turning into a different woman, challenging Jinkil where she had yielded to him before. Laena didn't understand why, and there was no discreet way to ask. Sooner or later, though, she could see it would cause trouble.

Orban and Fayna were sparring with each other, arguing over every tiny detail—but it seemed more good-natured than before, which encouraged her. Orban had been saving himself for a girl who had been lost in the flood. Fayna was a year older, but she shared the same impatient, rebellious spirit. Laena wondered if the two of them would find each other attractive. If so, how would the joining ceremony be done? Would she be called on to do it, as the leader of the group? That was a strange thought.

Benke was still the misfit, sitting in silence, ignoring the press of people around him. Yet even he had company of a sort: Newa was still nursing her grief. She barely spoke and tended to gravitate to the edge of the group. That tended to place her near the wounded man, though he hardly acknowledged her presence.

Laena looked at Joq. He was a barely visible silhouette in the semidarkness under the tent. He had started arguing about something with Orban—some incident that had happened a year ago, during a hunt that they had both been on. Who had thrown the spear that lodged in a tree, and who had climbed up to retrieve it? It wasn't a serious disagreement. They were goading each other, laughing.

Laena felt happy to be paired with Joq. He was always loyal, and almost always good-natured toward her. And she actually felt encouraged by the way that the journey was progressing. Her muscles were tired, but it was a familiar feeling, reminding her of those simpler times when she had trekked with Nan. She remembered the time when Moru had told her that she had a natural need to wander, and she realized that her sister had been right.

The next day they climbed with a new spirit of determination. If the climb was going to take longer than they had realized—well, there was no turning back, and they only had a limited amount of food in their packs. Clearly, they had to move with as much speed as possible.

The markers still showed the way. Laena had learned to trust them totally, for they had never led her away from the path that took them inexorably higher.

That afternoon, they approached the snowy ridge that they had seen the night before. She felt the sense of growing anticipation in her people, as they toiled up the last part of the slope. And then she felt their anger and their disappointment as they found that there was yet another ridge still ahead, even higher than the one they were on.

They camped on hard-packed snow that night. Laena had to show them how to shape it into blocks and build a circular shelter, curving the walls to make a domed roof. They lined the bottom of the shelter with their skin tent and slept in a huddled mass. This time, there was no way to take their minds off the trek and lighten the mood. There was just a somber sense of united purpose—and growing fear.

The next day, the way ahead was deeply covered in snow. If there were any more markers, they were hidden. At first, Laena felt disconcerted. But she had learned from the markers they had passed. Up here in the mountains, the best way wasn't necessarily the most obvious way. It was usually the safest way, or the way that avoided the steepest slopes. Stretching in front of her was a seemingly featureless expanse of ice, which surely could be traversed if they cut steps into it with their spears. But at once she knew that the climbers who had placed the markers would never have taken that path. It was too easy to become fatigued by the weary routine of chopping the ice; too easy to allow just one little slip which could drag the whole party down across the slope, with nothing to hold on to to save themselves. No, the right way was to double back along a ledge that was twice as long, but far safer.

None of the others disputed her judgment. By this time, they were beginning to understand how big the task was that they had chosen to tackle, and they were well aware of their own lack of expertise. Once in a while there were some angry words, debating other paths that should have been taken on the very first day they had set out. Sometimes, someone complained about the lack of preparation, or the recklessness of striking into the unknown like this. But through it all, they followed Laena, imagining that she had far more experience than they did.

Fortunately, Benke's leg was strong enough now for him to climb unaided. But other people were developing ailments of their own. Newa was suffering chronic headaches from snow-blindness; she hadn't understood the need to shield her eyes from the dazzling slopes. Laena made eye patches of thin leather with slits scored in them so that Newa could see just enough to keep her balance while the rest of the party led her onward.

One of Joq's hands was frostbitten where his mitten had been sliced open by the rope, days ago. Fayna seemed to be on the verge of exhaustion, though she refused to admit it. And Henik was constantly crying and fretting, though Laena couldn't find anything physically wrong with him. Maybe, she thought, he was just expressing what everyone else was feeling: the fear of the prospect of being stranded here in this rocky, frozen wilderness.

They spent another night on the snow fields, and another. Each was colder than the last, because they were still climbing relentlessly higher. Laena noticed that no one shared their food anymore; they were hoarding it now. And since the river was frozen, the only source of water came from melting ice in their mouths, which meant they were constantly thirsty.

On the fifth night in the snow, Laena found herself lying beside Moru in yet another snow-shelter while the wind whispered around it and the cold seeped deeper into her bones. "We need fuel for the fire," Moru was saying, and Laena started arguing with her, trying to explain that there was no fire, no fuel, nothing up here but rock and snow. Then Moru struck Laena across the face with more strength than her tiny body could have possibly possessed. "Sleep!" Moru shouted. "You're crazy with fatigue, Laena. You're scaring people."

Laena blinked. Joq shook her roughly. "Come out of it," he said—and she realized she had been hallucinating.

Everyone rested the next day, because she saw they had all been pushing themselves too hard. In any case, the weather had suddenly turned bad. Sheets of freezing rain swept across the slopes. The gray clouds thickened and sank lower till they cut off all visibility, and the travelers found themselves stranded in an eerie, featureless gray world. Laena realized how lucky they had been so far with the weather. And she prayed that it wouldn't stay this bad for long.

That night, while the others slept, she lay listening to the rain lashing their little shelter. She found herself wondering whether she was still following the right path—whatever that might mean. The mountains seemed endless, and far more formidable than she had ever imagined. She remembered Nan laughing at her, in her childhood, for thinking she could journey south. She remembered the elders of the Fisher Tribe telling her that she was crazy, and that she would lead everyone to their deaths. Why had she thought she knew better? Why couldn't she accept that older people might actually know more than she did?

She silently begged the white panther to return to her and

speak to her as it had before. But even when she slipped
into sleep, there was no dream to comfort or guide her. She
was truly alone here with her companions, in the fierce,
bleak mountains.

But the next day was brighter. The rain stopped and the
clouds lifted, at least enough for Laena to see the way ahead.
Her people were well rested and refreshed, ready to con-
front the snowy slopes again. Nevertheless, she still felt
empty inside, full of the doubts that had plagued her during
the night. No one knew, of course; only Joq seemed to sense
her mood. But she resisted his questions, and she quickly
roped everyone together, smothering her feelings in the simple, practical tasks that had to be done.

The next slope, at least, was easy. There were lateral
ridges across it, like giant steps just under the snow, leading
up to a gap between two taller peaks.

Near the top, though, she found herself stumbling. She
tottered forward, flailing her arms, and she fell flat on her
face in the snow with a little shout of surprise. Fortunately,
that morning, she had given Henik to Perri, so the only
thing that was injured was her pride.

Laena struggled back up onto her feet and brushed the
snow off her furs. Everyone was looking at her, but no one
was laughing. They knew how much they depended on her.
If she was showing signs of weakness, or if she had hurt
herself in some foolish way, it would endanger them all.

"I tripped," Laena said, still wondering how it had happened. After all the difficult slopes they had tackled, it
seemed absurd to have fallen on this one. But she had felt
as if something had snagged her boot. She retraced her
steps, peering at the snow—and saw something like a thin,
dark line embedded in the drifts.

"Look!" she cried, brushing the snow aside. "Here!
Look!"

It was black and hard from exposure to the sun and wind;
but it was leather, clearly enough. A rope, like the one they
had been using themselves, but finely made from braided
thongs.

Laena heaved on it, and it came up out of the snow. She
saw that it extended further up the slope, and she started
pursuing it, moving eagerly now.

It led toward a crevice in the nearest face of rock. No; it

didn't just lead there, it actually disappeared inside the crevice.

Laena hesitated. She stood for a moment, breathing hard. Her breath rose around her as plumes of white. There was something ominous about that crevice; and yet, she knew, she had to see what it concealed.

There was barely enough room for her to squeeze in. A tiny space existed between three faces of rock. Water had gathered in the bottom of it, and had frozen into a solid block of ice. Laena looked down, and she saw something there; something murky and dark and hard to see.

She crouched and wiped away the frosty mist that her breath deposited on the frozen surface, She peered closer—and she saw that embedded in the ice, with their faces turned up toward her, were two men.

For a long moment, Laena stared at them. The wind howled through the crevice behind her, but she didn't hear it. She was overcome with a mixture of grief and awe. These, surely, were the climbers who had placed the signs marking the trail for others to follow. She guessed the men had come originally from the tribe down in the valley. Like her, they had hoped for a better place beyond the mountains; or they had been desperate to find a way to escape their valley after the avalanche had sealed it off. Either way, they had left signs behind them in the hope that other people of their tribe could follow.

And then they had taken shelter here—maybe the same way that Laena had sheltered from the storm the previous day. But they had not been so lucky, or so well prepared. They had brought insufficient food; or maybe the weather had turned bad for days or weeks at a time, stranding them. Ultimately, they had succumbed.

"Thank you for showing the way," Laena said softly, hoping that somehow, somewhere, the vanished spirits of the men would hear her words.

"What's in there?" Joq was calling from outside. There was no room for him to get in; she was blocking the narrow entrance.

Without knowing why, Laena felt a sudden need to keep this place as her own secret. There was something sacred about it, and something personal, as if she had already come to know the spirits of these men during the long climb, and it was not something she could share.

"There's nothing here," she called back. She quickly brushed some snow onto the thick slab of ice. "Just a broken spear and an empty pack."

"Hey!" The shout came from further away. It sounded like Orban's voice. "Hey, come and look!"

Laena backed out of the crevice. She turned and found that Orban had clambered to the top of the ridge. He was waving wildly, pointing ahead. All the others were turning and hurrying to join him. The crevice, and the rope in the snow, had already been forgotten.

Jinkil climbed up alongside Orban, and Laena heard him give a great bellow of surprise. Then Fayna joined them both, and she cried out in pleasure. Laena wondered what they could possibly have seen—and then, instinctively, she knew. She clambered up the slope, moving fast and recklessly. When she got to the top herself, it was no surprise to her to see that the next ridge was lower than the one they were on; and the one beyond that was lower still. The mountains subsided in front of them, dropping away into a bank of haze. And somewhere down there, in the far distance, was a hint of green among the white.

Chapter 45

It took as long to climb down out of the mountains as it had taken to climb up into them. By the time her people found themselves walking on bare stony ground instead of snow and ice, they were ragged and worn, light-headed with exhaustion, their hands stinging with frostbite and their faces ravaged by the cold. By the time they reached grassland and found a stream flowing through it, they were tormented by hunger and thirst.

The euphoria that they had shared at the highest ridge was long gone. So were most of their supplies. They fell down on the ground, cupped their hands in the stream, and drank deeply, feeling infinitely thankful that they no longer had to suck fragments of ice that stung their frostbitten lips.

Then they followed the stream, and it led them into the green valley that they had seen in the far distance, days ago. The valley was so wide and so long, it seemed like a whole new land in itself. Its floor was not flat, but contained gently undulating hills and ponds of clear water that had gathered from melted snow. Best of all, there were animal tracks in the thin soil; so now they knew they would not starve.

Daylight was fading when Laena and her people chose a spot where they could make camp. The men were too weary to go searching for game, and darkness was closing in. So they ate the last of their rations, built a small fire mainly with twigs and animal droppings that they found close by, and lay down without even bothering to spread the skin tent. There was nothing that anyone needed to say; they were thankful to be alive, grateful that the ordeal was over, and desperate to rest.

This time, she was in a featureless gray place—like the gray cloud that had engulfed them up in the mountains. She felt as if she was hanging there, touching nothing. Yet the panther was lying at her feet, so close she could actually feel the warmth of its body. And there were two little white cubs with it now, nestling against its belly, looking up at her.

Laena felt a rush of wonder. The panther seemed happy to stay close beside her now, without turning its back or walking away. "I did what you asked of me," she found herself saying. "I tried harder than I have ever tried at anything in my life, and I did it. I brought my people across the mountains."

"Yes." The panther yawned and stretched its forelegs, then lolled back, licking its paw. "You have returned to the path, Laena. But still, if you look around you, you will see that your journey is not over."

She felt a moment of black surprise; then distress. The emotion lifted her up as if she were a leaf spinning on a gust of wind. "I tried!" she cried out. She threw herself forward, wanting to seize the panther, to stop it from escaping her ever again. But the grayness faded, and she opened her eyes, and it was morning.

At first she felt confused, unable to recognize her surroundings. Then she saw the mountains looming over her—the mountains that she had somehow managed to cross—and she was overwhelmed with relief to be here amid the tall grass, frostbitten, exhausted, but alive. The echoes of the dream still resonated through her, but she managed to shut them away, out of her mind. She had done what she had set out to do, she told herself. What mattered now was to make sure that she and her people were safe. They needed food, they needed a proper shelter—

She heard a shout. Quickly, she sat up. This new land had seemed empty of human life, but that could have been an illusion. There was no reason to feel safe or complacent. She turned—and she saw Jinkil striding up the grassy slope with a caribou draped around his neck, its head lolling across his shoulder, and blood dripping from a spear wound in its neck. "Hey!" Jinkil was shouting. "Hey, wake up!"

She felt surprised to see him like this, and even more surprised to hear him calling out so cheerfully. He had become more and more grim during the last days of the descent, to the point where he hardly spoke at all. He had acted as if everything were his adversary: the mountain slopes, his own rations of smoked meat, the weather, his wife, and his companions. But now, he was grinning.

"It was a straggler," he said, throwing the animal down. "Separated from its herd." He flexed his shoulders and stabbed his spear into the ground. "We'll eat well now."

Laena stood up. Everyone had been roused by Jinkil's shouts and the promise of food. "Let's have a cheer for this man, who got up before dawn to hunt for us all," Laena said.

They stood and cheered him; but Jinkil shook his head. "Listen," he said, holding up his hands. "Listen to me."

Gradually, they fell silent.

"I don't make speeches. You all know that." He hesitated, reached inside his furs, and scratched his chest. "Listen. We had some tough times, up there." He squinted up at the mountains, made an expression of disgust, and spat on the ground. "But she was right. She brought us through. Look at us, we wouldn't be here if it wasn't for her."

There was a moment of silence. Laena felt suddenly embarrassed. Jinkil was not a man to give thanks to anyone. His clumsy words meant more, somehow, than any eloquent speech would have. She found, with surprise, that her eyes were wet. "Thank you," she started to say—but she never had a chance to finish. Everyone was gathering around her. They were congratulating her, taking her hands, telling her how wonderful she had been to them all.

The previous night, she realized, they had been too tired, too bruised by disappointments and deprivation to trust their good fortune. But now, with the prospect of meat to fill their bellies, they could finally let themselves believe that the ordeal was over. And she was the one to whom they gave their thanks.

Laena was crying openly now. Something about their gratitude took her strength away. But even as they praised her for her courage and her kindness and her strength, a part of her mind was detached and untouched by the scene, looking down as if from a distance, and remembering the dream that she had tried to forget. She had learned the hard way never to ignore her visions. She treasured the smiles and the kind words from her people; but at the same time, she felt a new foreboding.

* * *

They ate, and they slept; and then they ate again and slept some more. On the second day, they felt strong enough to start exploring the new land, to find how far it extended and how much it had to offer them.

There seemed to be no break in the mountains encircling it. There were peaks to the east and to the west, even taller than the peaks that lay behind them. Ahead, far to the south, were still more mountains. The wide, shallow valley was a refuge rimmed with towering rock and ice.

The soil here was thin, supporting tall grass but hardly any trees. Laena realized she would have to show her people how to use wood sparingly, as her old tribe had done; otherwise, they would quickly strip the place bare.

They soon found tracks of caribou, bears, foxes, and rabbits. How had the animals found this valley and populated it? She guessed there must be an easier way into it through the mountains that lay to the south. But there was no sign here of other human beings. So far as anyone could see, she and her people had this place to themselves.

They ate, they talked and laughed, and then they hunted. She could have gone with them in search of game, but she chose not to. She had roamed enough for a while, and she needed the time to sit with her son and with Urami, to watch them playing together, to repair her clothes, to stitch proper tents out of new animal hides, and to think. Most of all, she needed to think.

That turned out to be less easy than it seemed. Now that her people felt that their ordeal was over, they treated her with an almost superstitious reverence. They brought her gifts; they smiled shyly and offered to do chores for her; and then, inevitably, they asked for her advice.

Laena was playing with Henik, helping him to take a few hesitant steps on the bank of the river that flowed past their camp, when Perri came and sought her out. "Laena-mother," she said, bowing her head. "There's something I must ask you."

Laena pulled Henik into her lap. He and Urami had suffered less than anyone during the trek across the mountains, probably because they had been cared for with such constant concern. There were marks on his back where he had chafed in his sling, and some of his fingers showed slight signs of frostbite. But he was plump and happy now, staring up at her, smiling as he tried to grab her braided hair.

Laena looked at Perri. "You can ask me anything," she said. "Although, I may not know the answer."

Perri did not smile. It seemed as if she could no longer believe there could be anything that Laena might not know. She seated herself cross-legged, with her back straight and her shoulders square. Her posture had changed since the journey through the mountains. Laena remembered Perri as a woman who walked with her shoulders slumped, as if she felt constantly burdened by her life. She seemed far stronger now than when they had started. "It's a problem with my husband," she said.

Laena felt surprised to be asked for advice on such a personal subject. She felt unprepared, too, and unfit for the task. After all, she was no older than Perri, and she doubted she could be very much wiser. But she was the leader of her people. If they had questions, they were liable to come to her for help; and if they came to her for help, she couldn't simply turn away from them. "I've noticed," she said cautiously, "that Jinkil often seems to anger you these days, and you seem to anger him."

"Yes." Perri said it clearly and simply, without any of the shyness that she had shown in the days back at the Fisher village. "He's a strong man, and I used to respect that. He would give orders, and I would obey, because—because that was the way it was. My father had been a strong man, too. And his father before him."

"Were you afraid to say no?" Laena asked.

"I suppose I was. Yes. But back when we started climbing the rockfall at Ghost River, something happened. Maybe you remember, everyone else went ahead of me, onto the first of the big rocks. For a moment I found myself left behind, looking up at you all, and feeling scared, because I'd never dared to do anything like this before, and I wasn't even sure that I could. But then I looked at you, Laena, standing so confidently, and then Jinkil started shouting at me, and—I hated myself for being so weak. I vowed to do something about it. Maybe I couldn't be as strong as you, but I could be stronger than I had ever been before."

"I see," said Laena. Henik was getting tired of the game

of playing with her hair, so she set him on his feet. She helped him to balance, then let him go. He took a couple of hesitant steps forward—then fell down in the grass with a little cry of frustration.

Laena nodded toward the little boy. "We all need to learn to walk on our own, without anyone helping us. It's a natural part of being alive."

"Yes," said Perri. "I see that now. But Laena, my husband—"

"He still orders you around," said Laena. "Or at least, he tries to. I understand the problem, Perri. But what do you want me to do?"

"Well, I was wondering." Perri hesitated shyly. "If you could tell him—tell him how your own husband respects your spirit, and gives you freedom—" She trailed off.

Laena tried to imagine saying that to Jinkil. He would be outraged. He would see it as intolerable interference. He would become more angry and stubborn than ever. No; there had to be another way.

"A difficult journey can change people," Laena said. "It seems to me, you're not the same person now that Jinkil married. In a way, then, he didn't marry you. He married someone else. So perhaps—perhaps you should not feel married to him anymore. Perhaps you should not *be* married to him."

Perri looked shocked. "How can that be? A marriage lasts for the rest of time, Laena-mother. That's what a marriage *is*."

"That is what a marriage *has been*," Laena corrected her. She felt more sure of herself now. What she was saying sounded intuitively right to her. "There are only ten of us here in this new land," she went on. "We have to start anew. The laws that we grew up with may not work for us here. We must invent new ones of our own. I think you should ask Jinkil if he would like not to be married to you anymore. He would be free then to choose another mate instead—if anyone would have him."

Perri's lips were parted. She was staring at Laena with round eyes. "Do you think he will—"

Laena felt her patience slipping. All she really wanted was to play with her son. Was it really her job to solve such personal problems? "I don't know what he'll do! Just ask him, and see what he says. But don't tell him I told you to ask him. Do it for yourself.''

Perri edged back, chastened by the sternness in Laena's voice. ''Yes, Laena-mother. Thank you.'' She stood up, and she hurried away.

Fayna was the next one to come looking for help. This time, Laena was sitting out in the sun, mending the seams of her furs, while Henik and Urami crawled through the grass like little animals, surprising each other and giggling. Meanwhile, Newa and Perri were working at skinning a fox some distance away.

''Laena-mother,'' Fayna said solemnly, ''there's something I must ask you.''

''Yes, Fayna?'' There was no escaping this, Laena realized. She should get used to it, because it was going to keep happening for the rest of her life—at least, so long as she was the chosen leader of her people.

''You know, I never married, back in the tribe.''

''I know that, Fayna.'' Laena chewed on the end of a leather thong to soften it. A memory came back to her—of Moru scolding her, telling her that she should soften leather in the way that the Fishers did it, by wetting it with water and pressing it with a stone. Poor Moru! Laena still missed her sister deeply. But she had decided not to think of the past, and so she pushed the memory away. She looked, instead, at the young woman sitting in front of her. ''Tell me why you didn't marry,'' Laena said. ''You were old enough, last fall.''

Fayna shrugged restlessly. ''I don't know. None of the men pleased me. Or maybe I was just rebellious. I didn't like the way my parents kept pushing me.''

''And now?'' Laena prompted her. ''You favor Orban?''

A sly smile crept onto Fayna's face. Her eyes made little darting movements. ''I might,'' she said. ''He's more mature than he used to be. I think he realized, on our journey, what he can do, and what he can't do. I like him. But—''

Laena set aside her sewing. ''Shall I guess? He wants you. Yes, I saw the two of you sneaking away together last night, when everyone else was bedding down. And I know how it feels, Fayna, when a man wants you.''

The smile left Fayna's face. She gave Laena a skeptical

look, as if she didn't think it was possible for Laena to indulge in such wild emotions. "The point is," Fayna said, "if we want to marry—I'm not sure we would, but if we did, at the Fall Hunt—well, there isn't a Fall Hunt, and there isn't a ceremony." She looked at Laena with her head on one side. "Will you be marrying people? Or what?"

So there it was, the same question that Laena had already asked herself. But even now, she didn't have an answer. If her people wanted new rituals—or if they still wanted the old ones—it was up to them to decide, not up to her. And here in this new place, no one could possibly know, yet, how they wanted to shape their lives.

But she had to give Fayna some sort of response. "Here's what I think you should do," she said, leaning forward and speaking quietly, so that there was no chance of being overheard. "Don't think about marriage; at least, not yet. We are not properly settled. Everything is still uncertain."

"All right." Fayna nodded earnestly.

"And when Orban wants you—well, it might be best to refuse him. At least until you're more sure of how you feel."

Fayna looked doubtful. "I'll try."

"But if you find you can't refuse him," Laena went on, "there are some things I must tell you which I learned myself from Nan, years ago. It's too soon for any of us to start having children here, Fayna, so you must understand how to have sex with a man and not get pregnant."

Fayna blinked. She opened her mouth to speak; but she could think of nothing to say. Evidently, this didn't fit with her conception of Laena as a mother and a healer and a leader; not at all.

"Do you want to know these things?" Laena asked.

"Oh, yes!"

"Then listen carefully." And she started passing on the wisdom that she herself had learned from the wise old woman she tried not to think about anymore—because when she remembered her too clearly, it made her feel too sad.

So it was that Laena found herself acting as though she were a chieftain, though she hardly felt she had the right to do so, and the advice she gave was unlike the advice of any chieftain she had ever heard of. Did that mean it was bad advice? She honestly didn't know. All she knew was that her people had risked their lives for the privilege of starting anew. They had earned the right to control their own destinies, and she was not going to stand in their way.

Perri spent a couple of days sewing a new tent, then moved her meager set of possessions into it, leaving Jinkil on his own. Jinkil came to Laena, full of righteous rage, and asked how such a thing could be permitted. Laena felt the force of his anger, but she didn't let him see that. She drew herself up and told him that in this time of change, any person should be free to follow his or her conscience, because the laws that had been made by the Fisher Tribe were no longer meaningful. In any case, she said, Jinkil might be happier on his own, without Perri confronting and defying him. And why didn't he approach Newa, who seemed to admire his strength in her own quiet, shy way? If Jinkil wanted a different wife, it was up to him to do something about it.

"I'll have to think on this," Jinkil said; and he spent the next two days sitting alone on a hill close to the camp, meticulously cleaning and sharpening his spears and knives, without speaking to anyone. On the third day, he went out and killed a small mountain cat, brought it back, placed it outside Newa's tent, and asked her if she would prepare it for him and eat it with him. She was surprised and confused, but when Laena said she should feel free to do as Jinkil asked, Newa shyly agreed.

At this, Benke became angry. He came to Laena to complain that she had no respect for the traditions that had sustained the Fisher Tribe for generations. If things continued this way, he said, there would be chaos.

Laena was unimpressed. She pointed out that everyone seemed to be thriving. They had ample food and shelter, they were growing stronger, and there was less bickering than there had been in the past. What did it matter if they weren't following the old traditions?

Secondly, she told Benke that since he still didn't participate actively in the group, he shouldn't care what the other people decided to do with their lives, and he should mind his own business.

He was offended by her tone; he became irritable; and then he became silent; and then he walked off on his own for a while. Finally, grudgingly, he came back and told her that she might be right. "This is a new place," he said. "It does require new ways. I see that now."

By this time, Laena was actually beginning to enjoy her role as an advisor. The trick, she saw, was not to tell people what to do, but to help them think about their problems in a new way. "If you see what new ways are needed here," she said to Benke, "does that mean you see a need for new ways in yourself?"

This time, he didn't take offense. From her tone, he could tell that she wasn't being critical or hostile. She genuinely wanted to help him.

"Perhaps you're right," he said in a low voice. He was sitting with her outside her tent, while everyone prepared for the evening meal, and the camp fire hissed and crackled close by. "I've always been a wanderer; you know that. I've always felt happiest when I was on my own, free to be myself, with no one else to answer to. But now, if I understand you, I might be able to feel free even while I am among your people, here."

"That's how I would like you to feel," said Laena. "You know, I, too, have been a wanderer, and I, too, have found it hard to surrender myself to the rules and rituals of a tribe. I don't want anyone to feel there are things they have to be and do, just because it's always been that way."

He stared at her with a new look on his face which she hadn't seen before. It was openness, she realized, and hope. She had finally broken through the walls that he'd built around himself. "Thank you, Laena," he said. "And—I apologize, if it took me a while to understand. I hope, in future, I can be a better member of your people."

Laena wondered if she should leave it at that. After all, he already had food for thought. But then she remembered urging people to climb that extra slope on the mountainside. It was never a bad thing to encourage them to push themselves a little bit harder.

"You know," she said, choosing her words carefully, "this is a difficult time for Perri. She's trying to satisfy her own needs for freedom now. Perhaps you should talk to her, Benke."

He pulled back. He looked disturbed by what she had said. "Perri is still Jinkil's wife—"

Laena shook her head. "Jinkil wants nothing to do with

her anymore. And anyway, Benke, all I'm suggesting is that you should talk to her.''

He looked deeply uneasy. "For years, ever since my own wife died, I have turned away—''

"You just told me you want to stop turning away from people,'' she pointed out. She patted his shoulder again. "Talk to her, Benke. That's all I ask.''

He nodded dumbly and backed away.

That night, Laena lay with Joq in their tent while the sun went down and Henik slept quietly beside them. Joq held her close, and she felt the heat of his body and the pleasure of his hands stroking her skin. She had missed these special, private times with him, while they had been crossing the mountains. It was good to nestle against him with her eyes closed and concentrate just on feeling him and smelling him and touching him, without thinking about anything else at all.

They made love quietly and furtively, so as not to wake the baby. Joq took her side-by-side, with one hand on her breast and the other touching her where he penetrated her. She reached down and pressed his fingers harder against her, and she circled her other arm around his neck, pulling his lips against hers. She drew her knees up high and crossed her ankles behind him, getting him to thrust deeper, so she could feel that she possessed him totally while he possessed her. The pleasure was intense, all the more because there had been so few opportunities for it. She gave little cries that were muffled by his kisses; and then she felt him stiffen as he approached his own climax.

Quickly, she disengaged from him. She reached down and held him in her hand while his body shook in little spasms and his seed fell warm and wet across her fingers. It saddened her not to have this happen with him inside her; but for the past year, ever since Henik was born, they had agreed that this way was best, for the time being, at least.

Then they lay quietly together. This was the best time, Laena thought to herself: to feel fulfilled, and to feel cared for, at peace with the whole world.

"Are you happy, Joq?'' she whispered to him.

He seemed sleepy. He had been out hunting with Orban

for most of the day, and it had tired him. "At this moment, I'm very happy," he told her.

That was good; that was what she'd wanted to hear. And yet, it still wasn't enough. "Is this what you want?" she whispered to him. "This valley, these people, this life."

Now he paused for a moment, thinking about what she'd asked him. He was always thoughtful when she gave him a big question to deal with. She could almost hear his mind taking it to pieces, examining each part, before he was willing to give an answer.

"At first," he said, "back at the village, all I knew was that there had to be a change. And you were offering a way for it to happen. You were my wife, you had proved that you had a special talent to foresee things, and I was glad to leave the village with you. I wished there could have been more of us; but that was my only regret."

"And then?" she prompted him.

"Then, I began to realize how big our challenge really was. But I saw that you might still be able to meet it, and overcome it."

"With your help," she said. "You don't know how much I relied on you, Joq."

He gave a little shrug. "Perhaps. Anyway, we had to struggle across the mountains, and for a while, it seemed that we would be lucky just to hang on to our lives. That was all I was thinking about, then: how to survive."

"And now?" she asked softly.

"Now, it seems we're finally safe. So I've been wondering what will become of us here. Is this really where we are destined to be? It surprises me, somehow. It seems— strange."

Laena let out her breath in a sigh. She was glad, in a way, to hear him say it. She didn't want him to be discontent; but at the same time, it would have been awkward for her if he had been entirely happy. "Tell me what troubles you," she said.

"I'm not entirely sure. I miss the hut we used to have. I miss eating fish; and there don't seem to be any in the streams here. I miss having wood to burn, and trees to use for making spears, or carvings, or all the other things we had in the tribe." He shook his head. "But these are just little things. I don't know why I feel discontent. Somehow there just isn't *enough* for us here.''

''Yes,'' she said, feeling it deeply. ''You're right. I think, Joq, that this is a resting place for us; but it isn't a home.''

He shifted uneasily. ''We could build a bigger tent—''

She laughed. ''No. No, a bigger tent isn't the answer. You know, I've been thinking about this myself. I'm going to have to tell everyone soon. We will have to move on.''

He was silent for a long time. ''Are you sure? Is there no other way?''

''Now that I've talked to you about it, I find myself feeling sure.''

''I see,'' he said finally.

''Will you support my decision?'' Instinctively, her hands tightened around him.

''Of course.'' The words came out with no hesitation. ''But I wonder how the others will react.''

''So do I.'' She nestled against him. ''But you shouldn't worry about that. If I am the leader, I must be the one who confronts that problem.''

The next day, she spent some time sitting alone thinking about what had to be done. It wasn't easy to face the idea of having to pick up again and move on, and she knew that if she found it difficult herself, it would be doubly difficult for everyone else.

Her people trusted her. They admired her. They believed in her. But would they be loyal enough to follow her out of this valley? She honestly didn't know.

Well, she would have to find out. Spring was turning into summer; there wasn't much time to spare. It would have to be tonight, she decided. Tonight, after everyone had eaten. That was when she would tell them what she had decided to do.

It was a small fire, shedding only a dim flickering light on the faces of the people hunched around it. But the meat was fresh and everyone seemed cheerful, happy to be there, thankful for their good fortune.

Laena watched and listened, and she said hardly anything while she ate. She fed tiny scraps of meat to Henik, sometimes chewing them first, to help him eat them. She sat close to Joq and even though he, too, was silent, she felt his presence as a constant reassurance. *He knows,* she thought to herself. *He understands that it has to be tonight. And he has promised to support me.*

Orban was flirting with Fayna, and they were laughing. Jinkil was talking about a mountain lion he had tracked and stalked all day, and planning to lie in wait for it outside its lair. Newa was listening with an expression of quiet interest, which Jinkil couldn't fail to notice. Benke, meanwhile, was sitting in the circle, actually joining in the conversation instead of making aloof, cynical comments. Hesitantly, he offered Perri one of the choicest pieces of meat, from an animal that he had killed himself that day. She paused for a second, looking surprised; and then, with a decisive motion, she accepted.

She felt pleased to see that they had been willing to listen to her, and try to change their lives instead of just staying in their old roles and complaining about them. At the same time, she felt a growing tension, because she knew she was going to ask them to consider a much bigger change than anything they had contemplated so far.

When everyone had finished eating, she stood up. Her people turned to her, realizing that she wanted to talk to them all. Conversation died. They looked at her expectantly as she stood there in the night.

"We have started making ourselves a home here in this valley," she said. "Ten days have passed. And we are doing well."

There was a happy murmur of agreement.

"When we found this place, it seemed like a paradise compared with what we had been through."

Again, they agreed with her.

"Of course," she went on, "we felt we had no other choice. It seemed there was nowhere else for us to go."

There was silence now. They were waiting to find out what she was leading up to.

"It's time to think clearly," she said, giving her voice a slight edge. Everyone was pleasantly well fed, and they had all been warmed by the fire. She needed to stir them a little from their complacency. "There are some questions that must be answered," she went on. "Is this land really big enough for us? Will it really support us? Will it last us for the rest of our lives, and our children's lives?''

Now people were frowning. Why was she talking like this? It was unsettling. ''There are animals here,'' said Jinkil. ''More animals than we can eat. Why should we worry?''

''You have to go further to hunt them now, than when we arrived ten days ago,'' Laena pointed out.

Jinkil gestured dismissively. ''That's because they know we're here now, so they hide from us. That's all.''

''Or maybe you've killed all the ones close by,'' said Laena. ''Are there really so many more, in the valley? And where will new ones come from, to replace the ones you kill? This isn't like the old hunting grounds near the village, where herds passed through on their migrations. It's very difficult to get into this valley. Probably the only easy way is at the southern end.''

Benke cleared his throat. ''There does seem to be a pass there,'' he said.

''Is it any easier than the one we came in over?'' Laena asked him.

''Only a little.''

She nodded. ''That was what I thought. You see, I'm worried that this valley here is a little like the valley of the tent people. We could eat up all the game, just as they did. It would take us longer, because this place is bigger, but in the end—'' She shrugged and fell silent.

Orban was shifting uneasily. ''Laena-mother, may I speak?''

''Yes, Orban.''

''It's just a matter of not taking too much. If we make sure we leave a few of the animals to breed and have cubs, there'll always be enough game. After all, there are only ten of us here to feed.''

Laena nodded slowly. ''But if we stay here, Orban, after a while there will be more than ten of us. You may even decide to have cubs yourself.''

There was a murmur of laughter around the fire. Orban grinned self-consciously. He glanced at Fayna. She covered her mouth and giggled.

''All right,'' said Laena. ''You see what I am talking about. Maybe there is enough game here to support us, but we can't be sure, and we certainly don't know what will happen if our numbers grow. In any case, this isn't the only thing that bothers me.''

She paused for a moment. Everyone had been drawn into the seriousness of the conversation, despite themselves. They waited expectantly.

''This place felt warm and good to us after the freezing weather in the mountains,'' she went on. ''But it isn't as warm as our old village would have been at this time of year. I think that's because we're still quite high up. Think what this means: the winters will be colder than we're used to. And they may last longer. You can see how much snow there was, from the number of lakes and ponds. And there's so little wood here, we'll have trouble finding enough fuel to keep ourselves warm.''

''But you said yourself, we have nowhere else to go!'' It was Perri speaking. ''If this is all there is, we simply *have* to make do.''

''I said we *thought* we had no other choice,'' said Laena. ''In fact, as Benke says, there is another pass at the end of the valley. We could explore that pass. We could try to travel further south.''

Now there were cries of dismay. She watched her people, and she waited. They respected her, and they trusted her, and they cared for her deeply. But she was asking them to contemplate something which was almost unthinkable.

Orban was so agitated, he jumped up again to face her. ''Laena-mother,'' he cried out, ''you told us that this was your vision. That's what brought us here. Your *vision*!'' He spread his hands, embracing the valley. ''How can we even think of leaving it now?''

''Orban,'' she said with a sad smile, ''I didn't tell anyone this before, because I knew we needed to rest. But, I tell you now: this land is not the land which I saw in my vision.''

Orban slowly sank back down beside the fire. Everyone looked shaken.

''The place I saw,'' Laena went on, ''was rich green—far greener than this—with the sun high in the sky. There were trees. The soil was thick and soft. And it was so warm, a person barely needed clothes to wear.'' She saw it again, in her mind's eye, as clearly as ever. And she saw the man and woman waving to her, beckoning to her. Her parents— or so she believed. Were they still waiting, somewhere, after all these years? She really wasn't sure. All she knew, with her deepest faith, was that the green and sunny place did exist.

"My destiny," she said, "is to find that special place. This valley was given to us so that we could replenish our strength. But I'm not sure how long we can really survive here. A single winter might be too much for us. And so, my people, I must move on, while the summer still makes the journey possible. I hope that you'll join me. But naturally, I leave it to each of you to make your own decision."

She turned to Newa, who had been holding Henik. She stooped and picked up her child. Then she turned to Joq. "We should go to our tent, Husband, to let my people talk about this among themselves."

Chapter 46

The next morning, they came to tell her what they had decided. Almost all of them wanted her to stay, and they begged her to reconsider.

Orban argued with her. Newa openly wept. Fayna said she had lost so much already in the Fisher village she couldn't bear to lose this new home as well. Benke looked unhappy, and said nothing. Jinkil was angry; he said they should stay in the valley for a year at least, take advantage of everything that it had to offer, and then maybe think about moving.

But Perri spoke up quietly and said that she had thought about everything Laena said, and she had decided it was right to move on, even though another trip through the mountains would be an awful ordeal.

And then Orban said that if Laena was really determined to go, he couldn't stay behind. She had saved him from the flood, and she had led him here through dangers that he'd thought would kill them all. She had earned his trust and loyalty, and he would follow her anywhere.

Benke broke his silence. He said he was willing at least to take a look at the pass at the south end of the valley. Privately, Laena suspected he was just feeling the tug of his old wanderlust; but it made no difference what his real motive was. As soon as he made his decision, the situation turned against the people who wanted to stay behind.

There were only three of them: Jinkil, Newa, and Fayna. Fayna wanted to learn some hunting skills, but she agreed that she couldn't hope to master them overnight. Newa, meanwhile, was a quiet, shy person who had no interest in learning to use a spear. Consequently, at least in the near future, the two of them would depend completely on Jinkil's hunting skills. If he injured himself, or fell sick, they would be unable to sustain themselves here in the valley, just as Laena and Moru had once felt unable to survive without Gorag.

And so, during the time between breakfast and noon, Laena won them all to her side.

She could see, though, that the ones who had been forced to come still resented the decision. And she saw that it would be fatal to let these resentments fester. Jinkil said that if he was going to go on this journey, he wanted a full week to plan and prepare for it. Laena hated to lose even one more day, but she gave him what he asked. Newa said that since she was the weakest person in the group, she should be allowed to carry a lighter pack, and always be roped between two other people when climbing the steep slopes. Laena disliked the idea of promising special favors, but in this case, she agreed. Fayna insisted that everyone should be allowed to vote whether the group should turn back, if they hadn't found a new home after four weeks of trekking through the mountains. Laena agreed to this, too; but secretly, she knew in her heart that she could never turn back. She couldn't imagine what would happen if her people voted against her at that time. The idea scared her, and she wished that Fayna had never mentioned it.

The next few days were spent smoking the fresh meat, repairing their clothes, stitching new boots that would be more practical for the snowy slopes, and making a new, longer rope. This last task was taken on by Joq, who skillfully joined and braided antelope hide to create something that was suppler, lighter, but stronger than the old one.

In the evenings, everyone talked together about the lessons they had learned from the first part of the journey, and the mistakes that they wanted not to repeat. Despite Laena's impatience, she had to admit that this was valuable for all of them—with the possible exception of Orban, who found it impossible to sit still for long. In the end he went off with Benke on a two-day excursion to survey the land to the south and find the most promising path. But she had to admit that this, too, was valuable.

So the days passed, more quickly than Laena had expected.

On the last night, she saw the need for a ceremony. She had never liked rituals, because they were rigid and unbending, and they stopped people from being the way they wanted to be. But she was aware of the power they could have, and she was willing to do almost anything that would increase the chances of her journey being a success.

First they feasted, gorging themselves on all the meat that was left over after they had filled their packs. They ate till their bellies were round; and then they ate still more, knowing that it might be weeks before they had a chance to eat that way again.

"Now," Laena said when everyone was done. "There are some matters to attend to. Some of them are easy. Some of them are hard. I would like to take the hard ones first."

She paused, looking around the circle for everyone's approval. They murmured their consent.

"All right," she said, steeling herself for what had to be done. She was not sure how her people would take it; but it was necessary, nonetheless. "I've spoken privately with some of you, in the last few days," she went on. "But now the matter isn't really private anymore, it's time to settle it in plain sight. We can have no secrets or bad feelings when we're trekking together through the mountains. Our lives will depend on us trusting each other, absolutely and totally." She gave them all a severe look, then turned to Perri. "Have you thought long and hard about your marriage to Jinkil?"

Perri was visibly shocked. Among the Fisher Tribe, such a thing would never have been mentioned so openly, so directly, in front of everyone.

But then Perri drew herself up, finding the strength inside herself, as Laena had known she would. "I have thought about it," she said.

"Good. Do you want to leave your marriage behind, just as you have left behind your home in the Fisher valley?"

Perri clenched her fists. "I do," she said. The words were a whisper; but they were spoken with conviction.

Laena nodded gravely. She turned to Jinkil. "Do you feel the same way?" she asked. "Do you wish to leave your marriage behind?"

Jinkil was staring at Perri with an expression that was hard to read. There was pain on his face, and resentment.

She, in turn, refused to look at him. Silently, she was crying; but she didn't make a sound.

"Jinkil," Laena prompted him gently. "I must know how you feel. We cannot decide anything till you and Perri are in complete agreement."

He turned suddenly. His pain had turned to anger. "All right, it's done," he said, making a sweeping motion with his arm.

There was a little sigh of dismay from the people gathered around. Laena waited for them to quieten themselves. "It's always sad when something dies," she said softly. "But now there is the hope of new life, which comes from moving on and leaving the old things behind us." She turned to Perri. "You are free now. I have said it, and it is so." She turned to Jinkil. "You, too, are free. We have all witnessed this. You both agreed freely. You have no complaint against each other now. You can start anew."

Perri wiped her eyes. Gradually, she composed herself. "Thank you, Laena," she said.

Jinkil still looked angry. "I don't know," he growled, "that this is how—"

"Jinkil!" She sharpened her voice. "You are the strongest of us all."

The words were like a slap. They made him pause.

"Show us your strength," she went on more gently. "Be strong enough to set an example, so we can admire you for it."

He blinked, slowly grasping what she was saying.

"Take Perri's hand," Laena told him.

Jinkil turned and looked at her. He shifted uneasily.

"Perri, take Jinkil's hand."

Slowly, reluctantly, they touched hands. As they did, something seemed to soften in Jinkil. His shoulders slumped a little. His anger faded.

"You are both free now," Laena said gently. She turned to the others who had gathered around. "Let's praise them for their courage. They have done what has never been done before."

There was some applause—uneasy, at first, but then louder.

Finally, Laena held up her hands. She turned to Fayna. "Now," she said, "there is the matter of you and Orban."

Fayna looked as if she had been expecting this. She glanced at Orban, who didn't meet her eyes. She looked back at Laena. "I think—I think we aren't ready yet," she said. Her cheeks reddened as she spoke.

Laena nodded. "That was all I needed to know. If the time comes when you and Orban decide you want to pledge yourselves to each other, then you will do so in front of us all. But that's up to you, to decide freely on your own."

Laena smiled. "The next part," she said, "is the easy part."

She could feel the sense of relief in the people gathered around. They hadn't enjoyed what she had just done. But still she was sure it was right. She had seen, too often, the trouble that came from people refusing to face the truth, and blaming each other for unhappiness and arguments that came from living a lie. There would be no lies here—at least, not while she was their leader.

She told each of them to join hands with the others around the fire. "All of us," she said, "are from the Fisher Tribe. Even though I was raised elsewhere, I myself have long since pledged myself a member of the tribe."

People nodded solemnly. Many of them still missed their relatives or friends. Many of them found comfort in the bond that still tied them emotionally with their origins.

But she needed them to feel a new bond. "We will make a new pledge," she said quietly. "It won't erase our old pledge. We will still be Fishers, but we must be something else as well, since we have left the valley where the Fishers live, and we know we will never return."

She turned to Joq, seated beside her. She had not discussed this with him, or with anyone else in the group. It wasn't something that could be decided by mutual agreement. It had to come from her, as the leader.

"Joq," she said, "repeat after me. I am a free person."

"I am a free person." He said it without hesitation, looking directly back at her.

"Freely, I have left my home," she went on.

"Freely, I have left my home," he echoed her.

"I am an orphan now. I am a child of the ice and snow."

She saw him wondering why she was asking him to say this. But he trusted her absolutely; and so he repeated what she said.

"Freely, I pledge myself to my comrades here," she went on. "We are all children of the ice now, in search of a new land to call our own."

He said the words. As he reached the end, she saw that he understood, and he approved.

She reached down to a leather cup full of water. She had gone up into the foothills of the mountains earlier, and she had gathered some ice. Fragments of it still floated in the cup. She took one of them, raised it, and touched it to Joq's forehead. "Now," she said, "you are one of our people."

The ceremony was simple; but she could feel the effect it had on the people watching. It gave them a sense of shared purpose, and they clapped their hands when it was done.

"All right," Laena said, "who wants to be next?"

"Me." Orban stood up quickly. He came to Laena and kneeled before her. "If you please, Laena-mother," he added shyly.

She did it for him just as she had done it for Joq. Then she did it for each of the others in turn—even Jinkil, who looked gruffly embarrassed kneeling before her, but made no objection, all the same.

She turned to the children and spoke the words for each of them, even though they were too young to understand or speak in return. Lastly, she told Joq to do it for her. "I, more than anyone, am a child of the ice and snow," she said. "I am your leader and your guide; but I am one of you, as well. We all care for each other as equals."

So Joq said the words, and she repeated them. And then he anointed her forehead with the last fragment of ice that was still left floating in the water.

She stood up then and picked up her spear. "Come," she said, moving a little way away from the fire.

Her people followed her.

She thrust the spear down into the ground, and clutched its shaft with her right hand. "Join your hands with mine on this shaft."

Quickly, everyone gathered around. There was just enough room for all of them to reach in and hold the spear. Their bodies pressed close together, shoulder to shoulder.

"We will care for one another," said Laena.

"We will care for one another!" they shouted.

"We will keep each other safe from harm," she said.

"We will keep each other safe from harm!"

She dropped her hand away from the spear. "And if we are strong," she finished in a softer voice, "the children of the ice will be orphans no longer. We will find a new home."

Chapter 47

At first, the journey was easy enough. They had learned how to pace themselves, how to move together, how to tackle each new slope, and how to find a secure footing among loose stones or icy rock.

The terrain was relatively easy. They found a river and followed it between grassy banks that were barely dusted with snow. There were signs of animals, and Jinkil managed to stalk and kill a white fox.

Then, on the third day, they crested a ridge and saw that they had reached another high point in their journey— not nearly as high as the pass where Laena had found the two climbers frozen under the ice, but still high enough to give a view of the way ahead. And the way did not look good.

"Remember the reasons we are on this journey," Laena told her people as they sat atop a stony ridge, eating their rations.

"I still believe in the journey," said Perri. "But when I see what lies in front of us now, I can't help wondering where the journey will end."

The others nodded silently. Ahead of them, to the right, was a huge vista of ice—a gently curving dome that seemed as big as an entire continent, stretching all the way to the horizon, gleaming in the sun. Extending from it like the twisting roots of a tree, glaciers snaked down into the surrounding valleys. The dome of ice had claimed the land; it was holding it in an inhuman grip.

Meanwhile, to the left, they found a huge range of mountains, higher than anything they had seen before. The mountains marched south in an impenetrable wall.

The only way ahead lay between the dome of ice and the high peaks. There was a clear strip of land here, snaking away toward the south. But it was strangely colorless, a swath of gray, with long, dep furrows in it, making it look as if it had been raked by the claws of some huge beast. Nothing grew upon it; it was totally barren.

"You pledged yourselves," Laena reminded them. "Four weeks, remember?"

"Yes," said Jinkil. "But at the end of four weeks, we'll have eaten all our food. If we don't find game before then, it'll be too late to turn back. We'll be done for."

"Then let's give ourselves two weeks," said Laena. "We can't tell, from here, what that land is really like. The only way is to go and see."

Jinkil gave a curt nod. "All right," he said, and started forward.

Another river led them toward the featureless gray swath. The river was cloaked with a shell of ice in many places, but the ice was thin and easily broken, so there was no shortage of water to drink. Food, though, was another matter.

Orban killed a rabbit with a lucky throw of his spear. They seized on it as a good omen, but found that it was just skin and bones, giving each of them only a tiny scrap of meat. That night, their mood was even grimmer than before, and Laena found herself pulling back from her people, feeling confused and betrayed. She had tried to do so much for them, coping with their problems, lending them encouragement, and bringing them together. Why couldn't they trust her and devote themselves to her in return? It seemed cruelly unfair.

Even Joq showed less of his loyalty than she was used to. He was silent when the others complained about the lack of game or the barrenness of the land. He never said anything against Laena; but at the same time, she felt the lack of his support.

When they finally reached the gray strip of land, it was even worse than she had feared. It looked as if the entire surface of the earth had been scraped away, leaving a furrowed mass of loose stone, gravel, and sand. When the wind blew, gray dust rose in twisting streamers that stung and scoured the travelers' cheeks and lashed into their eyes.

A wide river flowed down the center of the great ribbon

of gray, and Laena led her people toward it, hoping to find shelter on its banks. Some stunted trees grew here, and some grass was bravely clinging to life amid the loose stone. But the wind still blew fiercely, and the land was still bleak and bare.

"Maybe there are fish in the river," Laena said, although she had a sinking feeling that it would not be so.

Jinkil took his fishing spear and went and sat by the water. After a while, he just shook his head. "It's hardly like a river at all," he said. "More like a mountain stream. Just water and stones. Nothing green. Nothing alive." He stared back along it, shielding his eyes from the glare of the ice that lay to the east. "Seems like it's running off the glacier in the distance there."

Joq was looking around, trying to get a better sense of this strange, inhospitable place. "Think for a moment," he said. "Maybe the weather here has changed, the same way it was changing in our lands to the north. Maybe it's getting warmer, so the glaciers are melting. That's where this river comes from."

"And that's why this land is so bare," Laena said with sudden understanding. "It must have been covered by the glacier. The great ice-river scoured the land; and now it's retreating."

Jinkil moved impatiently. "None of this helps us any."

"But of course it does." She stared at him, then at the rest of her people. Their faces were uncomprehending. "If we walk far enough, we'll go beyond this stretch which was ruined by the ice. We'll reach the point where the bottom of the glacier used to be. The land will be green and fertile there, fed by all the water that has trickled down."

Jinkil was silent for a long moment. "Maybe," he said finally. His tone was grudging, but at least he sounded as if he was willing to try.

"This is our seventh day," said Fayna. "We have seven more. If we find nothing to eat in that time—"

"We will find something," Laena said. "I'm sure of it."

Following the ribbon of gray, Laena felt as if she were stepping across land that was so new, it had not had time yet to become a proper part of the earth. The scattered blades of grass looked pale, almost yellow, as the sun shone through them. The skimpy trees were barely holding on to life. Still, there were enough of the trees to yield wood for a fire each night. And when her people camped, the gravel was loose enough for them to scoop a hollow in it so they could huddle together under their skin tent for protection against the wind.

During the days, though, the wind was relentless. They rubbed fat over their faces, and they closed the cuffs of their sleeves and leggings by threading thongs through them and drawing them tight. But still the dust got under their clothes, chafing their skin.

And still, there was nothing to eat.

Seven days later, they sat around a flickering fire that could barely cling to life against the wind, and they shared their rations. There was a full moon shining down from a crisp, clear sky, and the vista of ice to the east was gleaming in the moonlight, stretching away like a giant frozen ocean. No one looked at it; they had grown weary of the sight during the past week, just as they had grown weary of everything else on the monotonous trail.

"I still believe," Laena said as they finished eating, "when we get to the end of the dead land—"

"I say we turn back." It was Jinkil who spoke cruelly, bluntly, without any apology. "We've got just enough rations to take us back to the valley. Who's for it?"

Laena stared at him in dismay. Then, in a flash, her dismay turned to fury. She jumped up. "How dare you!" she shouted.

Everyone stopped where they sat and stared at her. Never before on the journey had she shouted at them. Even Jinkil seemed disconcerted.

"You interrupt me, you speak against me, you show no courtesy, no gratitude—how *dare* you, Jinkil!"

He shifted uneasily. "No disrespect," he muttered. "I just—"

"Where is your faith?" She turned and glared at everyone in the group. "Where is it? Do you forget so soon? Have I ever led you astray? Have I *ever*?"

There was just a reluctant silence now.

"You promised me four weeks. Four! And then you broke your word, even though I have never, ever broken mine.

Well, you can turn around and go back if you wish. But you will go without me. And you will never see the land that I know lies waiting for us all.''

She sat down. Beside her, Joq placed his hand on her arm, but she shook it aside. He had been hardly any better than the others, she told herself. She had pleaded with them and cajoled them—but no more. If she had to go on alone, with just Henik, somehow she would do it.

''We do owe you a debt, Laena.'' It was Orban speaking.

''I just worry—'' Newa began.

''You always worry,'' Laena snapped at her. ''You worry like an old woman.''

''Laena, be reasonable,'' said Fayna. ''We know we can live in the valley we left behind—for a while, at least, and maybe for years. We know nothing about the way ahead.''

Laena clenched her fist and beat it against her chest. ''I *do* know,'' she said. ''I know there is a new land waiting for us just as surely as I knew there would be a flood that destroyed our village. Fayna, you might not be alive if it wasn't for my talent. And the man you love would certainly be dead.''

''What Laena says is true,'' said Orban. ''She's never led us astray.''

''This is true,'' said Joq. He turned to Laena. ''I apologize, as your husband. This land has been so bleak, so bare—I lost a little of the faith that I should have had.''

''Thank you,'' Laena said softly.

''All right,'' Jinkil said. He could see the way the mood of the group was swinging now. ''We go on. For a while, at least.''

''Yes,'' said Laena. ''We go on, until we reach the end of our journey.''

Another week later when she could feel the tension growing around her again, and she could sense the fear in her people—they finally came to the end of the bleak, gray corridor. A huge lake lay before them in a bowl-shaped valley. The lake was empty, as the river had been; but there were tracks by the shore. Rabbits, voles, water rats—a profusion of small rodents, hard to find, hard to spear, but food, nonetheless.

''I told you!'' Laena cried that night as they ate the first few animals that they had managed to kill. "I told you we would prevail!"

And now, of course, they were embarrassed and guilty for having doubted her. They gave her the best of the game, they muttered their apologies, and once more they pledged their faith in her.

They stayed by the lake for four days, replenishing their supplies of food. It was arduous work for the hunters, and Laena shared it with them, rooting through the tall grass, digging down into rabbit warrens, always searching for any sign of quick, furtive movement, with a spear at the ready.

As soon as they had accumulated enough meat, she decreed that it was time to move on. The lake marked a low point in the landscape. From here, another river led them back up into the mountains.

This time, there was no gray gravel and dust. This time, the snow closed in.

Laena had thought they had been tested before. This, though, was something different. They followed the river higher, and still higher, and the slopes were treacherous with snow and ice. Their pace slowed as it became a matter of searching for every foothold, testing it, moving onto it with exaggerated care, then searching again for a safe place to shift their weight.

Several times, they talked of turning back to the lake they had left and trying to find an easier path. But it seemed as if no easier path could exist. The peaks on either side were always higher than the mountains ahead. And always they were moving south or southeast, following the direction that Laena still believed, even now, was their destiny.

After two weeks, they finally reached a pass that led through to a slow descent. They were getting desperate for food again, but they found another river, and it led them into a lower valley where they picked up the tracks of a black bear. They couldn't imagine why it had come here and abandoned the lower slopes; but they went after it, and two days later they found it and killed it. It was weak from hunger, which made it easy prey. Laena, Joq, Orban, Benke, and Jinkil surrounded it and took turns wearing it down, jabbing at it with their spears while the women pelted it with rocks. Eventually, Jinkil killed it with a deep thrust to its neck.

There was nothing to use for firewood, so they chewed the meat raw. They didn't care; it quelled their hunger, and it gave them some hope for the journey that still lay ahead. To Laena, of course, the bear was a sign: further proof that they were still on the path.

So the journey went on. For several days there were snow showers, and they made hardly any progress at all. Sometimes they managed to trek down low enough to find small valleys where there were some pine trees, some bushes, and some animals that they could hunt and kill. In places like these, they rested for days at a time, eating their fill, smoking the rest of the meat, and gaining new courage to continue on. There was no question anymore that they had to continue, because they had come so far, no one could endure the thought of going back. Nor could they ever rest where they were: the lands they were in were cruel and bleak even in the summer. To stay in them till winter came would be suicide.

Weeks passed; and more weeks. The journey became something that no one talked about, and yet it was something that no one could forget, even for a moment. Their lives were not just centered around the journey; their lives *were* the journey. Even at night, they saw the landscape in their dreams, stretching endlessly before them.

Eventually, they found themselves in a descending series of mountain passes. They had long since given up hoping for anything, or expecting anything. If the land sloped down, they would follow it, so long as it led them to the south. But they wouldn't let themselves think that it might actually lead them out of the endless wilderness. Too often, in the past, they had been disappointed. They were too weary to hope anymore. They were driven only by grim persistence.

Ultimately, they reached a place where there were two paths that they could take. One led alongside a river, but the river was tumbling toward them, and the path led to a series of ascending valleys, back into the snow. The other path diverged slightly to the east. There was no water that way, just some remnants of ice on the higher slopes. But in the far, far distance, it almost looked as if there was a hint of green.

Again, they wouldn't let themselves hope for it. They wouldn't even talk about it. And yet, that was the path they decided to take. Summer was growing old, and fall was on its way; and if they didn't find a path out of the mountains, they knew they would not have many more months to live.

Chapter 48

Battered and beaten, ravaged by hunger, they struggled across a long, rocky plateau. Beyond it, they could actually see rolling hills and blue water shining in the sun. But the vision was like a mirage, forever seeming to recede in front of them.

They no longer talked to each other. Talking was an effort that cost energy, and they had no energy left to spare. They no longer argued over the decisions that should have been made, or the paths that should have been taken. There was no energy even to think about that. All that mattered was to place one foot, and then the other, stumbling onward, always onward, because the only possible hope lay in reaching their goal.

A while later—Laena could no longer judge the passage of time—they reached the edge of the plateau. It terminated abruptly in a vertical drop, a sharp dividing line between the endless mountains and the green vista that stretched away from them, like a vision of heaven, tantalizingly close, yet hopelessly out of reach.

They stared at the landscape ahead. They saw dense green grass, groves of trees, and a wide lake that shone in the sunlight. It looked so perfect, so welcoming, they could hardly believe what they saw.

Laena reached out as if she imagined she could feel the grass and the water.

"Yes, it's real," said Jinkil. His eyes narrowed as he surveyed the vista, and his frostbitten lips pulled back from his teeth.

Laena was hardly aware of him. She was still staring, still overwhelmed with the beauty of it all. Here, at last, after so many months and years, *this* was what she had dreamed of. *This* was the land she had come so far to find.

She reached for Joq's hand and gripped it tightly. "It's the place of my visions," she said. "This time, it truly is."

"But there's no way down," said Joq.

For a moment, Laena closed her eyes, half imagining that she might somehow see the path revealed to her inside her head. Then she realized that she was slumping against Joq, overwhelmed by her own weariness. Angrily, she shook herself awake.

"The cliff is taller than the length of our rope," Joq said. He peered over the edge, then looked to the left and to the right. In both directions, the cliff seemed higher than at the point where they stood. "Maybe if we walk far enough, we'll come to—"

"No." It was Perri, standing with her fists clenched, staring down at the expanse of green. "The rope has to be long enough." She started untying it from her waist.

"But it isn't," Joq said patiently. He frowned, and Laena saw him trying to concentrate, trying to hold on to the remnants of his own rationality in the face of the awful weariness that threatened to suck him down.

"I say it *is* long enough." Perri shrugged off her backpack. With a quick, casual motion, she tossed it over the edge.

Everyone stared as the pack curved through the air, turning as it fell. There was a slope at the foot of the cliff, where it curved out to meet the grassy soil of the valley. Perri's pack hit the slope with a faint puff of dust and rolled down, finally coming to rest on the grass at the bottom.

"Stupid!" Jinkil turned on his former wife. He was clenching his fists, hunching his shoulders. "You stupid—"

"We'll have to go down there now," she said. She didn't back away; she just stared at him dully.

Benke moved up beside her. "Perri," he said, "this is no time—"

"Keep away!" said Jinkil. His fingers curled into a fist.

"You're talking like a fool," said Benke.

"Shut up, you!" Jinkil stepped forward. No one was able to think clearly anymore, Laena realized. They were all as crazy with tiredness and deprivation as she was, and the sight of the land below was so tantalizing, it created a wild frustration that could make anyone want to lash out in anger. "Stop," she said weakly. "Jinkil—"

He ignored her. He growled at Benke and raised his fist.

"No!" Perri threw herself forward. She brought up her hands and started slapping at Jinkil, grabbing at him, tugging at him.

Exhausted as she was, Laena knew she had to act. She seized her spear and took a step forward. "*Stop!*" This time she screamed the word. "Jinkil, when you threaten one of us, you threaten all of us!"

He turned and stared at her, and found her spear less than an arm's length from his face. He froze in surprise. Then he seized the point of her spear in his gloved hands and tried to wrench it away from her.

The flint tore his mitten and sliced his skin. He yelped with surprise, shook off his mitten, and stared at the fresh line of blood.

"I warned you!" Laena cried. She suddenly found herself near tears. Why were they doing this? What was going wrong? She tossed the spear down and seized Jinkil's wrist. "Let me see the wound. Let me clean it."

Her concern sobered him far more than her anger had done. Frowning, he shook himself out of her grip. "It doesn't matter. It's nothing." He thrust his hand under his armpit and stood in silence, blinking, turning away from them all.

Meanwhile, the babies had started crying. Fayna was holding Henik, while Newa had Urami. Both of the children seemed to have picked up the mood around them, and were responding to it. "Hush," said Fayna, trying to quieten Henik. She glanced at Orban, leaning on his spear beside her. Then she turned to Laena. "If I may speak—"

"Yes! Speak!" Jinkil's rage seemed to have disappeared—for the moment, at least. Laena was overcome with weariness again. She sat down abruptly on the ground, feeling too tired to stand.

Fayna had long since stopped talking about the valley they had left behind. Once it was clear that the only way was forward, she had been resourceful, strong, and shrewd in her efforts to find the best path and maintain some unity in the group. "Perri's pack didn't break open when it fell," Fayna said, gesturing over the edge of the cliff.

"That's true," said Joq. "But we're not made of leather. If you think we can just jump down there—"

"No." She stared directly at him. "I just mean that it's hard to judge the distance, because of the way the land slopes out below. We may not be quite as high as we seem."

"Perhaps we could lower ourselves as far as possible down the rope," said Orban, "then let go and drop the rest of the way, and roll down the slope—"

"The children," Laena said, pressing her fingers to her forehead. "You have forgotten the *children*."

There was a long, grim silence.

Once again, Laena realized, it was up to her. They could sit here arguing, till sooner or later someone did something desperate, or stupid, or dangerous. Or, she could make a decision and tell them the way it would be.

"All right," she said, "this is what must be done." She was tired of making the decisions, solving the problems, and leading her people, She was so very, very tired. "Joq and Orban will go down the rope. Perhaps Fayna is right; they can drop from the end of it. Once they're down there, I will wrap Urami in several layers of furs. We'll lower her on the end of the rope. Then, we'll swing her away from the cliff and let her go. Joq and Orban will catch her in the skin tent, stretching it tight between them."

She saw the others looking at her doubtfully. Was she really talking about tossing a one-year-old baby as if it were a bundle of old clothes?

"Orban and Joq will throw the rope back up to us," she went on calmly, insistently. "Then we'll do the same thing with Henik. Then the rest of us will go down the rope, with Jinkil coming last. And then we will all be in that warm green land down there, and we will never have to face a crisis like this ever again, and our ordeal will be over."

There was a silence. It was very, very quiet on the edge of the plateau. No birds sang up here, and the air was still.

"It's too dangerous," Benke said at last. "The children could easily get hurt—"

Laena suddenly felt her patience snap. "There's no other way!" she shouted. "We have no food. We have no water." She slapped her hand on the rock beside her. "Do you think

I don't care about my child, Benke? I love him! But I won't sacrifice my vision and my life for him. Would you sacrifice yours?''

Again, there was a silence. People looked at each other uneasily.

"This is the dream I've pursued for years," Laena cried out. "I will *not* be denied it."

Benke shifted uneasily. "Maybe you're right."

"Yes," said Laena. "I am right."

Joq started going from one person to the next, untying them from the rope. It was badly worn in places, where it had chafed across sharp rock. He ran it through his hands, eyeing it doubtfully. It was clear why Laena had suggested that Jinkil should be the last one down; he was the heaviest. The rope might not take his weight.

Joq looked down at the ground. "There's nothing to tie it to," he said. "And since Jinkil has cut himself, I doubt he can lower people by hand."

"Tie the end of the rope around a large stone," Laena said wearily. "Then wedge the stone in that crevice there." She pointed to a crack in the rocky ground that was almost a hand's breadth wide.

"Good idea," said Joq. "That should work."

Yes, Laena thought to herself. It would work.

Joq wedged the stone as she'd suggested. "Who goes first?" he said, looking at Orban. "You or me?"

"Orban goes first," Laena said. If she was going to risk the life of Henik, she wasn't going to take any unnecessary chances with Joq.

"Be careful," Fayna said. She seized Orban and hugged him tightly.

"Throw your pack down first," said Joq. "You don't want to carry more weight than necessary."

Orban nodded. He freed himself from Fayna and tossed his pack over the side. Then, quickly, he went to the edge of the cliff, swung his legs over, and started lowering himself down the rope hand-over-hand.

Laena went to the edge and watched him. His arms were shaking with the effort. He moved lower, and lower—and he reached the end of the rope without realizing it. Suddenly he was groping for something that wasn't there. With a cry of surprise, he fell free.

He waved his arms wildly as he fell, as if he imagined he could somehow find something to hold on to. Then he hit the ground where it sloped out, and he rolled, kicking up dust. Everyone stared down at him in horror. "Orban!" Fayna screamed.

For a long, awful moment, he lay without moving. Then, slowly, he got up. He seemed to be checking himself for broken bones. He turned around, staggered, but manage to keep his balance. He looked up and waved to them.

Their emotions reversed themselves in a moment. They saw him down there, alive and whole. It was possible, after all. They started waving back to him, and cheering.

Laena turned to Joq. "Now you," she said.

He quickly embraced her. Then he went to the rope. He swung himself over the side as Orban had done.

"Careful!" Laena called. She watched him, feeling a sudden sinking premonition. He wasn't as strong as Orban. He would fall. She would lose him. It would be her fault. Everything was her fault; throughout the whole journey, it had always been her fault. She found herself clenching her fists, clenching her jaw, struggling to hold back a wave of emotion that made her want to fling herself forward, as if she could help him by throwing herself over the edge.

But then Joq was at the end of the rope, letting go, falling free. He drew his arms and legs up, and tucked his head forward. Then he hit the ground and rolled down the slope as Orban had done. And then, finally, he came to rest.

He stood up. He was unhurt, shouting up to her, waving both his arms.

Laena shook her head. Evidently, her premonitions meant nothing. Evidently, she was so weary she couldn't tell anymore where the dangers were. "I'm going down now," she said.

"But you told us we should lower the children," said Fayna.

"I know. I want to be down there with my husband. I want to hold the skin tent with him, when you drop Henik down to us. Do you see?"

Fayna eyed her doubtfully. "Laena, are you sure—"

"Yes, I'm sure." She felt foolishly bereft, up here at the top of the cliff, with Joq down at the bottom. For months they had been constantly side by side, helping each other, watching each other, warning each other of every little danger. "I have to be with him," she muttered, half to herself.

"Your pack," someone said. "Drop your pack first."

She wasn't even sure who said it. She didn't care. She shrugged off the pack and tossed it over the side. Then she sat on the edge of the cliff where the rope had been secured. She flexed her hands and took a firm grip on it. She paused for a moment, staring out at the vista of paradise. It was truly the way she had foreseen it. It truly was.

"Laena?" The voice came from behind her. "Are you all right?"

"Yes." She realized she had been drifting. She was so very tired. But she couldn't afford to be tired. She was the leader; they depended on her; she couldn't show signs of weakness. She seized hold of the rope and clenched her hands tightly till her frostbitten fingers made her wince with pain. She slid over the edge of the cliff, and she started down.

Her weight, dangling from her hands, made her shoulders feel as if they were being pulled out of their sockets. She gave a little cry as she felt the rope slipping between her palms. She had to stop herself. She squeezed harder, harder—and there was another wrench to her shoulders as she regained her grip on the rope. She hung there for a moment, gasping for breath, with her whole body trembling.

"Bring your feet up." It was Joq's voice, calling to her from below. "Stand away from the cliff."

Clumsily, she tried to do as he said. Her foot slipped, then found a hold.

She started down again. Her hands were hurting so much, she felt like screaming. Her arms were shaking. She felt herself losing the very last of her strength. She had to hold on, she told herself. She had to. For the sake of her people, for the sake of her vision, and for the sake of her husband and her child.

But her hands were cramping. They would no longer obey her. The rope was slipping again, she was falling backward, and the rope was no longer in her grasp. She caught a terrified glimpse of the world turning around her, Joq staring up at her, reaching up as if he wanted to catch her.

Then she slammed into the ground with a fierce, stunning jolt. She felt herself rolling. She cried out. The slope was strewn with rocks. She tried to pull up her arms to protect her face, but she was turning, rolling through the dust. And then, suddenly, she hit her head; and the sunlight turned into night.

Chapter 49

Laena found herself squinting up at the sun. She was lying on her back, she realized. On stony ground. Joq was bending over her. "Are you all right?" His face was wide-eyed and desperate. "Laena—"

"Yes, Joq." She fumbled and found his hand. "Yes, I'm all right. Just tired. Very tired."

She closed her eyes again, because she could no longer hold them open.

Sometimes she almost woke up. She felt herself being carried by many hands, and she glimpsed faces staring down at her. Someone was telling her that her child was safe. Of course, she thought; of course he's all right. And she slipped back into the darkness.

Then she was lying in her furs on soft grass, and Joq was pressing something to her lips. Meat, she realized. Fresh, warm meat. She felt her mouth watering. She bit into the meat, and she chewed it. But it was such an effort. She ate two mouthfuls, and sleep claimed her again.

The third time, she woke suddenly and sleep fell away from her in an instant. She felt alert. Her body was weak, so weak that she could barely move. Her head ached, and there was a tender spot on her forehead. Her limbs were bruised. And she was ravenously hungry.

She managed to lever herself up on one elbow. It was a tremendous effort. It made her feel faint.

Cautiously, she looked around. Her people were asleep around her. The remains of a fire were smoldering. The carcass of a deer had been hung on a rack improvised from four spears. The sun was low in the sky, and there was dew on the grass. The whole night had passed, she realized. It was early morning now. Everyone had come down from the cliff. They were all in the warm, green land together. They had arrived here, and they were all right.

She saw Joq asleep beside her, and little Henik near him. Fresh meat was lying on a slab of bark, near her right hand. Joq had left it for her, she realized, in case she woke. Dear Joq. She felt herself crying with gratitude and relief.

She reached for the meat and started gorging herself on it. She tried not to make a sound; this seemed such a special moment, such a private, singular time, she didn't want to wake anyone.

She finished eating. Now she was overwhelmed with thirst. She struggled up onto her knees, moving cautiously, checking herself for broken bones. She remembered long ago, when she had fallen from the mammoth. She had been lucky then, and she was lucky now, not to have hurt herself. How long could she go on being lucky? She had to take better care of herself. She had to take fewer risks. Her people were depending on her. Her vision—

But this *was* her vision. She no longer had to hope for it and plan for it and guard herself against any danger, for fear she might not live to find the place she yearned for. This was the place; she was here, and it was hers.

She managed to stand up. For a moment she swayed, feeling very light-headed. Then she walked shakily across the grass. There was a stream close by, but she was tantalized by the sight of the lake that lay beyond it. It seemed to call to her, and she found herself staggering in that direction, even though it was further away.

Her foot caught against something, and she stumbled. She turned and gave a cry of surprise as she saw a deer getting up onto its feet from where it had been sleeping in the tall grass. She had literally tripped over it, she realized. For a moment it stood perfectly still, confronting her as if it had never seen a person before. Then it twitched its tail; and then it wandered away.

"They have no fear." The voice came from her left.

Laena turned. She saw Joq walking toward her. He had been woken by her startled cry.

"The animals here have never seen humans before," he said. "They've never learned to fear us."

She opened her arms to him, fell against him, and hugged him with pure, deep pleasure.

"Are you all right?" he asked after a moment. "You hit your head when you fell. Then you seemed to come around, but you kept passing out again. You were talking in your sleep—something about a white panther. Everyone was afraid that the blow had made you lose your mind."

"I spoke of a white panther?" She looked at him in puzzlement.

"Yes. I heard you myself."

"How strange." She touched her forehead, as if she could somehow find the memory of the dream. "How strange that I don't remember it."

And yet, she thought, it might not be so strange after all. There was no need to remember the dreams and visions of the panther anymore. No need to be haunted by them.

"I'm thirsty," she said, looking up at Joq. "I have to drink. I was walking to the lake—"

"I'll carry you," he said.

Before she could protest, he stooped and lifted her. He was still weak from the trek himself, and he was barely able to hold her. But somehow he managed to get her to the edge of the water.

She kneeled there, cupped her hands, and drank. He watched her in silence, waiting patiently.

"You know," she said when she had drunk her fill, "it really is the way I saw it." She squinted up at him. "I suppose I've said that already. But do you understand how it can be, to see something in your mind before you ever see it with your eyes? It's so mysterious."

He shook his head. "There are a lot of things I don't understand, Laena. I'm just happy that your vision spoke truly."

She walked with him back to their camp, leaning on him for support. "So this is our home," she said. "This time, it truly is. Look—to the south there—the land just goes on and on. There are no more mountains. Nothing!"

Then she turned back to the people—her people—sleeping on the ground. "Is everyone else all right?" she asked. She gestured to the line of cliffs that lay at the edge of the plateau they had toiled across. "Did everyone get down safely?"

He nodded. "Even Newa. She said she simply isn't afraid of heights anymore."

"We're all stronger," said Laena. "Or we will be, once we have rested." She shook her head. "But there are only ten of us. So very few." She cast around, frowning. "You know, Joq, there was one thing about my vision that I never mentioned to you."

"What was that?"

Even now, it was hard for her to talk about it. Really, it was the most personal thing of all. "I dreamed I saw my parents here," she said. "They were on the shore of the lake. Yes, that lake over there. That's why I had to go to it just now. I almost thought, somehow—" She trailed off, shading her eyes, gazing at the water.

"We've seen no sign of any people," said Joq. "And I doubt that the animals would be so tame if there had been humans here before us. I think we're the first, Laena. The first to make that great journey over the mountains."

"Really?" Suddenly the loss of her parents wasn't such a burden after all. She looked up into his face. "You think that no one else ever did it?" She found herself smiling. "Does that mean no other leader was ever so bold, or so obstinate, or so foolish, as I am?"

He smiled back at her. "That, I'm sure of."

She turned and stared again at the lake. "It's strange, though, that I dreamed that my parents were here. Strange that everything else came true, except for that."

"Maybe they're watching over us," he said, "just as the spirit of Faltor's great-great-grandfather used to watch over the Fisher Tribe."

She tilted her head back, squinting into the dark blue zenith, as if she might sense something, or someone, in that featureless void. "You know," she said, "if they can see me now—I like to think they would be proud of me."

Epilogue

This, then, is the story of Laena and her people, who came to the great continent of North America when no human being had ever been there before.

Laena settled in that pleasant place beside the lake. She had traveled far enough for one lifetime, and she saw no reason to risk losing the peace and beauty that she had attained with such effort. Her people stayed with her, united by the hardships they had shared and the comradeship they had discovered in one another. Fayna and Orban coupled, and they had many children. Jinkil took Newa as his new wife, and they, too, multiplied. Benke and Perri never married, for they decided it was a ritual which they didn't need. But she bore him a child, nonetheless; and so the generations continued on.

Twenty years passed.

Laena was lying on a chair that her son Henik had built for her, under a screen of branches and fronds that had been laid across a wooden frame. It was midsummer, which was her favorite time. The sun was high in the sky—so high she still found herself marveling at it, even though it looked no different from her dream of so many years ago.

But *why* should the sun change the way it moved, just because she had journeyed south? She remembered long ago, when she had first met Joq, and they had talked about all the mysteries in the world around them. Even now, there was still so much they didn't know, and probably never would know. Laena had long since resigned herself to that. She was happy to stay here and enjoy the land she had found, while other people picked up the burden of adventure, traveling beyond the next hilltop just for the pleasure of finding out what was there.

Henik certainly seemed to enjoy that pleasure. He and Urami had already led a party on a two-month journey south. They had come back telling of vast hot places filled with sand, where rocks were red and there were leafless trees whose trunks were green, covered with spines. It sounded impossible, but Laena had seen so many strange things in her life, there was nothing she wouldn't believe. Her mind was still open, even though she had put to rest her wanderlust.

She heard sounds from the direction of the village—her village, built by her people. Joq was there, helping some people who were putting up a new home. All the homes were built the same way—in the style of the tents that Laena had seen in the valley of the Ghost River. The deaths of the savages who had lived there were still on her conscience, even now. She had never killed a person before or since. She had adopted their style of tent as a tribute to them, so that a little piece of their heritage would be passed on from one generation to the next.

She heard a shout from the direction of the lake. Henik and Urami were down there, building something new—a shell of wood and reeds that they claimed would take their weight and carry them across the water. Well, she could see it might be possible, and she'd told them she was all in favor of the idea, as long as she didn't have to ride in it herself.

She shaded her eyes and saw them waving to her. Maybe they had finished what they were building and wanted her to come and look at it. She pulled herself forward in her chair.

Time seemed to cease around her.

There they were, silhouetted against the bright blue lake, waving to her, beckoning to her. She felt dizzy. A circle had suddenly been completed; a circle that she hadn't even known was still incomplete, for the past twenty years.

The Henik she saw was her son, not her father. And Urami was her adopted daughter, not her mother. She slumped back into her chair, feeling overwhelmed. All these years, and she had never known; had never truly understood her vision until now.

And now she saw the true, inner meaning of it. There was no magic land where her parents had gone when they died. That had just been her wishful, childish interpretation of the dream. Her parents had perished, and she would never see them again; she had no doubt of that.

At the same time, in a sense, they were not gone. She had been a part of them once, and she was still alive. That meant that in her, a part of them still lived. And now there was her son, repeating the cycle of life, carrying the pattern on, just as Urami was carrying on the life-essence of Faltor.

She wished she could somehow look into the future and see the next generation, and the one after that, and all the others that would follow, rippling outward like waves seeking a shore. Would they ever fill this seemingly endless land that she had discovered? Would they remember her as the woman who had had the courage and the faith to journey here, and would they remember Faltor as the wise chieftain who had helped to make it possible?

"Mother, come *here*!" It was Henik's voice, and he was sounding exasperated. Well, she could understand that. He was still young and impatient, and here she was sitting in her chair, dreaming about a future she would never live to see.

She stood up. "I'm coming, Henik," she called. She should try to live more in the present, and enjoy her son while she could. She had a suspicion that before too long, he might uproot himself permanently and go in search of some land that he could truly call his own.

Laena stepped out into the sun. Her bare feet slid between cool blades of grass. She hesitated, struck by the sudden notion that if she turned her head, she just might see a white panther lying there, watching her with its enigmatic eyes.

But when she looked around, there was nothing but the land and the sky.

Laena's World:
The Factual Background

Fourteen thousand years ago, our planet was undergoing a violent transition. The last of the ice ages was ending, and global warming was occurring on a massive scale. Huge glaciers were melting, feeding the oceans, raising them by as much as three hundred feet. Inevitably, these upheavals had a severe impact on people in low-lying coastal areas who were struggling to survive.

At that time, the regions we now think of as Siberia and Alaska were linked by what has been called a "land bridge"—actually a small subcontinent that is today the floor of the Bering and Chukchi Seas. It was literally possible to walk from Russia, across this land, into North America, though the arctic climate would have made the journey daunting, to say the least.

This vanished land, which scientists now call Beringia, was a cold, dry, treeless plain. But archeological evidence shows that it was populated by animals such as mammoth—and by human tribes.

The tribes had almost certainly moved into Beringia from the Siberian mainland. Once there, they would have lived as they always lived, hunting game, feasting in times of plenty, and storing food against the months of winter scarcity. There was little incentive for them to leave Beringia, after they had made it their home. Returning to Siberia would have meant battling tribes who had already claimed that territory. Moving on toward the east or the south would have faced them with rugged terrain sheathed in ice. And so, they dwelled in Beringia perhaps for hundreds of years.

But it was a fragile home. It remained dry and habitable

while most of the world's water was locked in huge glaciers. But as the glaciers started to melt, Beringia was gradually swamped by the sea.

What happened to the people whose land was taken from them? Some of them, we have excellent reason to believe, picked up and moved on into North America. The entire American continent was empty of human life fourteen thousand years ago; there is no archeological evidence of any human settlements before then.

The journey was much longer and far more difficult than the journey that European settlers made across America thousands of years later. The Beringians had no horses and wagons; they were forced to proceed on foot. That meant they could not possibly carry enough supplies to sustain them throughout their trek. They faced starvation, thirst, and death from exposure, in conditions that were unbelievably harsh. The land that had recently been laid bare by the retreating ice was strewn with stone, gravel, and lifeless glacial pools. Bitter winds flowed down from the great domes of ice that still remained, and kicked up dust storms in the barren valleys below.

The conditions were so harsh and the distances were so great, the journey barely seems possible. On the other hand, the Beringians had already adapted themselves to a cold climate, and we can easily see that if they moved only nine or ten miles per day, they would still manage to travel three thousand miles in the course of a year.

Once they ventured beyond the ice, they found a new world packed with wild life—much of which they seem to have hunted to extinction. There were mammoth, horses, camels (akin to the surviving llamas of South America), giant ground sloths, in addition to species such as bears, mountain lions, buffalo, and bison which still survive today.

Conservation was not a concept that had much meaning fourteen thousand years ago. The hunters killed their prey by the easiest means available, such as driving them over a cliff or into a swamp, where far more animals were likely to be killed than could be eaten. The supply of animals must have seemed endless; when they were depleted in one area, the human tribes simply moved on, leaving the land empty behind them. As a result, there seems to have been a human population explosion that swept across the entire continent in just eight hundred years, according to some estimates. And then, when there was no more land and no new game left to hunt, there was an equally abrupt population crash.

But that is a story beyond the scope of this book. If we turn our attention back to the crucial moment in prehistory when the land of North America still lay undiscovered, and the Beringians were feeling the cruel impact of climactic change, we see that there must have been a time when someone was sufficiently desperate, or blessed with sufficient vision, to attempt the journey south, regardless of the hostile terrain. That person—probably leading a small group of adventurers—would have been the first human being to walk into North America.

In fictionalized terms, this book tells her story.

By the year 2000, 2 out of 3 Americans could be illiterate.

It's true.

Today, 75 million adults...about one American in three, can't read adequately. And by the year 2000, U.S. News & World Report envisions an America with a literacy rate of only 30%.

Before that America comes to be, you can stop it...by joining the fight against illiteracy today.

Call the Coalition for Literacy at toll-free **1-800-228-8813** and volunteer.

Volunteer Against Illiteracy.
The only degree you need is a degree of caring.